SPECIAL MESSAGE TO READERS

KU-289-771

THE ULVERSCROFT FOUNDATION
(registered UK charity number 264873)

was established in 1972 to provide funds for research, diagnosis and treatment of eye diseases. Examples of major projects funded by the Ulverscroft Foundation are:-

- The Children's Eye Unit at Moorfields Eye Hospital, London
- The Ulverscroft Children's Eye Unit at Great Ormond Street Hospital for Sick Children
- Funding research into eye diseases and treatment at the Department of Ophthalmology, University of Leicester
- The Ulverscroft Vision Research Group, Institute of Child Health
- Twin operating theatres at the Western Ophthalmic Hospital, London
- The Chair of Ophthalmology at the Royal Australian College of Ophthalmologists

You can help further the work of the Foundation by making a donation or leaving a legacy. Every contribution is gratefully received. If you would like to help support the Foundation or require further information, please contact:

THE ULVERSCROFT FOUNDATION
The Green, Bradgate Road, Anstey
Leicester LE7 7FU, England
Tel: (0116) 236 4325

website: www.foundation.ulverscroft.com

Fionnuala Kearney lives in Ascot with her husband. They have two grown-up daughters (both with deliberately monosyllabic names). One of seven children, Fionnuala likes to write about the nuances and subtle layers of human relationships, peeling them away to see what's really going on beneath.

You can discover more about the author at www.fionnualakearney.com

THE DAY I LOST YOU

Contentedly sipping a cup of tea at home after a fun-filled afternoon at a Christmas fair, Jess receives the most terrible news a mother can get: her daughter Anna has been reported missing after an avalanche while on a ski trip. Though she's heartbroken, Jess knows she must be strong for Anna's five-year-old daughter Rose, who is now her responsibility. As she waits for more news, Jess starts to uncover details about Anna's other life — unearthing a secret that alters their whole world irrevocably . . .

FIONNUALA KEARNEY

THE DAY
I LOST YOU

Complete and Unabridged

CHARNWOOD
Leicester

First published in Great Britain in 2016 by
Harper
an imprint of
HarperCollins*Publishers*
London

First Charnwood Edition
published 2017
by arrangement with
HarperCollins*Publishers*
London

The moral right of the author has been asserted

A catalogue record for this book is available from the British Library.

ISBN 978–1–4448–3249–5

Published by
F. A. Thorpe (Publishing)
Anstey, Leicestershire

Set by Words & Graphics Ltd.
Anstey, Leicestershire
Printed and bound in Great Britain by
T. J. International Ltd., Padstow, Cornwall

This book is printed on acid-free paper

*For the strongest women I know —
my daughters, Kate and Jane, and my
mother, Mary.*

PART ONE

Prologue

There are always before and after moments. Profound instants when, one second, life is a clear, high-pixel image and the next, it's grainy, less focused.

The day it happened, the seventh of December 2014, had been a normal day — nothing unusual about it. A band of low Arctic pressure produced the sort of cold that froze my fingers through gloves and numbed my toes through sheepskin-lined boots. The winter sky — a perfect, crisp blue — was marred only by wispy white plane trails latticing through it.

Theo and I were on the Irish coffee stall at the Christmas fair all afternoon — the most dreadful baristas, unable to produce a straight line of cream along the top of the coffee and a little too liberal with the alcohol. It was the season of goodwill. Fairy lights flashed: home-made crackers with loo-roll centres were snapped; high-pitched carols were sung; crumbling, puff-pastry mince pies were trodden into the polished parquet floor of the school hall, and the heady scent of festive cinnamon and cloves filled the air.

I remember it being a fun-filled afternoon.

When I got home, I flicked the kettle on and turned the thermostat up. I sat a while, my hands wrapped around a cup of black tea, staring into the garden in the fading light, my feet tucked up underneath me. Much as I loved her, days without Rose were precious. I had so little time to myself that merely sitting, *being*, just the act of doing nothing was a joy. Right up until the moment the doorbell rang, it's the 'ordinary-ness' of that day that I recall.

When the door pinged, I still didn't stir — not until I heard Doug's voice through the letterbox. Then I leapt from my seat.

'Jess. It's Doug. Can you open the door?'

I made my way to the hall, heard him moving about in the porch; foot to foot. *Doug has not come to my door for a very long time.*

From my jacket pocket, my mobile phone trilled. Seeing his number, I realized he would have heard it ring too.

'Open the door, Jess. It's important.'

I answered the phone and hung up immediately.

'What do you want?' I spoke through the four solid panels.

'I need to speak to you. Please.' His voice seemed to break on the last word and I opened the latch.

Doug, my ex-husband, the man whom I apparently 'strangled with my love' was standing there, shivering.

'Can I come in?'

I looked over his shoulder, expecting to see Carol, his wife, there.

'What do you want, Doug?' I repeated.

'Can I come in?' he asked again.

And that was the moment. I made the mistake of looking in his eyes; the cobalt-blue eyes that

Anna, our only child, had inherited from him. One generation later, Rose has those same eyes too. That was the split moment — between what was, and what would be. His next words tapped a slow, rhythmic beat in my head; each one etching itself on my brain like a permanent tattoo. And something happens when the body is forced to hear unwanted tidings; life-changing, cruel words. Adrenaline charges to the extremities, willing the frame to stay standing, despite the urge to fold; willing the heart to keep beating, despite the urge to snap into hundreds of tiny fragments.

My knees buckled at right angles — my entire body felled. An instant sweat oozed from my pores, seeping through to my fingertips. Fear choked me, as I fell into Doug's arms, as his familiar scent washed over me. And, in an instant, the world, as I knew it, was different.

1

Jess

Ten Weeks Later — Friday, 13 February 2015

I wake to the taste of salt on my lips. My eyes take a moment to adjust to the early morning light; my mind takes a little longer to realize that I've been crying in my sleep. With a glance at the neon clock by my bedside, my damp lashes blink. It's useless — I won't fall asleep again.

My limbs stiff, I climb slowly out of bed before crossing the landing to check the room opposite. She's there, fast asleep. I resist the urge to touch her, to rest the back of my fingers on her forehead. It's a habit; a throwback, I think, to when she had pleurisy as a baby and we failed to spot the temperature early.

Her breathing is soft, regular and rhythmic as a slow beat on a metronome, her chest rising and falling under the duvet. She turns onto her stomach, faces away from me, one hand stretched in a curve above her head, the other falling over the side of the bed. I take her arm and tuck it in beside her.

Next along the landing is Anna's room. I grab a pillow from her bed and, clutching it tight to me, take the stairs down slowly. Soon, the coffee machine clucks, promising my morning nectar.

I fill Rose's lunch box. It's the last day of school before the half-term break and something tells me she'll wake early, excited at the fact that today means no lessons, lots of playtime fun, not to mention the holiday . . . School closes early, so it's just a snack; just one slice of bread, lightly buttered and sliced in two, a piece of ham inside. Crusts removed. She hates crusts. A satsuma — the easy-peeling sort — and a bottle of water.

I stop my hands moving; wonder, if I turn the television on, will it halt the onset of what I just feel in my bones is a bad day. Before I know it, my hand is on a nearby photo frame. I don't even look at it, instead raise my arm and hurl it across the room. It takes on a Frisbee-like flight, landing, where I must have hoped it would, on a sofa three metres away. I walk from the kitchen to the other side of the room that stretches across the back of my narrow house. There should be a dining table here. Instead, there's a leather arm-chair and a frayed, unloved, tatty two-seater that Anna and I rescued from a skip with great inten-tions of reupholstering it. Slumping down into it, I run the palm of my hand over its ancient fabric, feel its bobbly surface. I reach for the tossed frame, clutch it to my chest, before releasing it to my lap — image facing down.

I pick up the phone and dial a familiar number. 'Tell me not to smash the photos. Remind me I would really regret it.'

'Jess, it's six a.m.'

'I'm sorry. Tell me. Please.'

'O-kay . . .' Leah clears her throat and I imag-ine her sitting up in bed, Gus grunting an objection

8

beside her. 'Leave the photos alone, do not break anything; you will regret it.'

'Right.' I clutch the silver frame tighter. I don't need to look. It was taken on a camping holiday in France the summer Anna was fourteen, the summer she discovered boys.

Leah tries hard to stifle a yawn. 'I would've called you in another hour.'

'I know.'

'Happy Birthday, big sis. You going to be okay?'

I giggle, a small ironic sound. 'Sure I will. I'm sorry for waking you. Apologize to Gus. See you later.'

I hang up the phone, stroke the back of the picture frame. Today is my forty-eighth birthday. It is also her twenty-fifth birthday. Twenty-five years ago, she shot into this world with the speed of a firing gun. But for a midwife with advanced catching skills, she would have flown off the bed, hanging by the cord that still joined us.

'Happy Birthday, baby.' I talk aloud, but there's no one there.

'Nanny?' I turn quickly. Rose is walking towards me, her arms outstretched. She seems to move in slow motion and I remember to take it in; to commit this image of her sloping towards me to memory, her curls all awry and bouncing as she moves. I bend down to her as she reaches me and pull her up to my chest. She puts her arms around my neck, her fingers lacing through my own twisting locks. And I'm cast back to when she was a toddler and she had barely any hair yet. What she did have was downy-fine and

9

corkscrew. She would find mine and pull it, gently unravelling the coil, fascinated by the spiral twists. I was captivated. She was not my child, but through the twists and turns of shared DNA, we had the same twisting, turning hair.

And now, here I am, my fingers laced through her mane, massaging her head in a way I know she loves.

'I had a bad dream,' she says, gripping me tighter.

Me too. I dreamt that your mummy had left us. Every night I dream your mummy has left us. Then I wake up and smell her pillow and tell myself it was just a dream.

'Don't worry, love.' I kiss her hair. 'It was just a dream.'

'Who were you talking to?'

'Nobody, I was just talking to myself.'

'Daddy says people talk to themselves when they get old.' She pulls away and peers directly into my eyes. 'Are you old today, Nanny?' Her mouth smiles, yet it's her eyes, lined by long curving lashes, that seem to laugh. The wonder of that almost makes me gasp.

I tickle her under her arms. 'Cheeky,' I say. 'Not that old. C'mon, let's get you showered before breakfast.' She squeals and runs up the stairs ahead of me, shouting that she has a card for me. At just five years old, she has no memory that today is her mother's birthday too and, all in all, perhaps that's a good thing.

★ ★ ★

10

At the school gate, I'm joined by Leah, who sidles up beside me. After I've held onto the child for an irrational length of time, I let go, and together we wave Rose into school.

Before she gets to the door, she runs back to me and whispers, 'Love you, Nanny'

'To the stars and beyond.' I blow her a kiss and she catches it in one hand, then tosses it back to me and I tap my heart. It's a thing we have; something we started when I first dropped her at 'big' school. It's something Anna and I used to do when she was little too.

She darts off, her friend Amy linking her arm at the door to their classroom.

It feels strange for me not to join her, but having managed to wrangle a rare day off by swapping shifts with Trish, the other teaching assistant for Year Six, I'm not hanging around in case someone changes their mind. My break for the half-term starts now. From the yard, Finn, Theo's son, gives me a small wave. He's tall for his age, his head hovering above his classmates, and I can tell he's wondering why I'm still on this side of the gate.

'You checking up on me?' I ask my sister, as my fingers curl a return wave to Finn and I walk back to my car.

'Yep.' Leah isn't known for subtlety.

'I'm all right.'

She shakes her head. 'Don't be ridiculous, none of us are all right. Here . . . ' She hands me a small package and a card and I put them straight into my bag. 'I know you won't celebrate your birthday . . . her birthday,' she says. 'But

11

nor should we forget the day.' She reaches for me and gives me a squeeze. It's not a hug. Leah doesn't do proper hugs. I take advantage anyway and close my eyes briefly.

'Sean is picking her up straight from school, right?' she says.

I nod. He came around last night to collect her bag after she'd gone to bed.

'It's only for ten days. She'll have a wonderful time with her daddy and it's good that his parents are on hand to help.'

I pull away. The thought of Sean, Rose's father, playing Daddy with her on holiday in some all-inclusive resort in the Canaries doesn't fill me with the joy everyone seems to expect. He doesn't even really know her; doesn't know that she likes mini-yogurts after dinner; doesn't know that she wakes up three nights a week calling for her mummy; doesn't know that she likes to choose her own clothes every day; doesn't know that she needs cuddles at night to help her sleep. He knows none of this.

'He doesn't even know her.' I say it aloud.

'He's trying. Even before Anna died — '

My head snaps around. 'Don't.'

'I'm just trying to point out that you and Anna together were a force of nature. Let him be her father, Jess. Rose is going to need him too.'

I wrap my arms around myself,

'Let's go for breakfast,' she says.

'No.' I will her to stop talking, wonder why she's not already on her way to work.

'I'm sorry' She knows what she's done. 'I shouldn't have said that.'

'You shouldn't.' No one. No one is allowed to say that Anna is dead. No one. I don't care if it's denial. I don't care if the chances of her being alive are nonexistent. I have no body to bury.

Leah reaches out, wraps her arms around my neck. 'I'm sorry,' she repeats. 'Today of all days, that was insensitive.'

'I miss her so much,' I whisper softly, then bite my bottom lip so hard that I taste metal.

'I know,' she says, her squeeze lingering, her grip unusually tight on my sleeve. 'I'm here. I love you.'

I don't tell her that it's not enough.

'Breakfast?' she repeats.

'What in Christ's name am I going to do?' I ask on the way back to our cars.

Leah shrugs. 'Just keep breathing in and out.'

'That's it? That's your advice?'

'You don't — '

'I don't what? Tell me, Leah. What is it I'm not doing? You have no bloody clue.'

I walk away yelling behind me, 'I don't want breakfast. If you hurry you can catch the nine ten to Waterloo.'

'Jess, stop. Wait.'

I'm already in the car, strapping myself in. She doesn't get it. She has never had children, and it has left her remote, detached from real life. As the engine revs into life and her form disappears in the rear-view mirror, I justify leaving her there in my head, even though I know I shouldn't have. I curse myself. She's doing her best. We all are, but Leah doesn't know what unconditional love is. Leah doesn't know how the pain of a

13

missing child takes over and has a heartbeat of its own.

I drive the short journey from the school to home, and when I get there try to busy myself with housework. On the way upstairs, I pass by a pile of Anna's shoes in the hall. They're stacked on top of one another. There are heels and flats all lumped in together — a knee-length suede, high-heeled boot embraces a brown brogue. I don't touch them. I'm afraid if I touch them, even move them to her room, that she won't come home. So, I leave them there. I try to forget all the times I shouted at her to remove her pile of crap from the front door. That's what I called them, these things of Anna's — a pile of crap.

In Rose's room, I hoover the floor, which is covered in glitter from the birthday card she made. I strip her bed, find a few pieces of Lego in the sheets, and toss them into a large box underneath. Her scent lingers on the bedding and, as I make my way downstairs to the washing machine, past Anna's mound of shoes, I inhale it.

Downstairs, my phone vibrates a message from Theo. A firm friend since we worked together over ten years ago, he's someone I know I can trust with my mood today.

'Happy Birthday' seems all wrong. Costa at 12? X

I read his text and consider saying no. Theo's probably just on an hour's break from the surgery, and I should probably be more mindful of my state affecting another. But the thought of

14

a long and lonely birthday stretching before me stops me doing the right thing.

★   ★   ★

It's exactly midday and he is there first, two coffees already in front of him, sitting in the booth to the rear of the café, our usual perch for putting the world to rights. The scent of crushed, bitter coffee beans fills the air. It pokes a memory of the day Anna went missing, the day of the Christmas fair.

'Before I sit down,' I say. 'One thing . . . '

Theo's eyebrows stretch.

'I don't want to talk about my birthday.'

The stretch reaches further, creasing his forehead.

'Theo?' I refuse to sit down until he agrees.

'Okay' He pushes a coffee to the opposite side of the table from him and I slide into the booth. 'So,' he says. 'How're you coping with the fact that today is Anna's birthday?'

My eyes close slowly.

'What?' he says. 'You told me not to mention your birthday. You never said anything about not mentioning hers.'

I pretend he hasn't spoken, take a sip of the coffee, make a face, then swap it. 'Sugar,' is all I say.

I want to talk but can't. I want to cry, but only seem to be able to do it in my sleep. An empty but easy silence falls between us. It's like that with us sometimes. We've been friends for such a long time that the quiet doesn't scare us. Theo rubs his nose with the back of his hand.

'It's no easier,' I finally speak. 'I swear. Some days — it's everything I can do to breathe.' I'm reminded when I hear these words aloud how badly I behaved to Leah. 'That line about time healing isn't true,' I tell Theo. 'All lies. Time doesn't heal.'

'It will. Days like today will always be the worst.'

My head shakes. 'Today's bad. Yesterday was worse — the apprehension . . . It's like physical pain and it's all over, every muscle, every nerve ending in my body.' I grip the handle on the coffee mug so tightly that my knuckles whiten. 'Before . . . birthdays, sharing the day together, it was such a special thing, as if she always knew that *she* was the best birthday present I ever got.'

He sips his coffee, his silence letting me know he gets it, then deftly changes the subject.

'Are you doing anything tonight?'

'Dinner at Leah's. Gus is cooking,' I tell him. 'But I'll see how I feel. I'm not sure I'll go.'

'You look like you could do with a hug.'

My eyes dart around our local Costa. 'No thanks, you're all right. Granted you're separated, but you've probably got half a dozen patients in here and you're still a married man.'

'Hmmm,' he says.

'What does 'Hmmm' mean?'

'Nothing. We're here to talk about you. You want something to eat? You should eat. You're all skin and bone.'

I refuse food. 'How's Finn doing?' I have found it hard since Harriet walked out on their

16

marriage to understand how she also walked away from their eleven-year-old son.

'He seems all right. This is the first half-term where he gets parents sharing him. It'll be strange. You spend more time with him during school hours than I do.' His smile is half questioning, but it's not something I'm prepared to get into — not today. Finn is not himself in school, seems attention seeking; but then again, that's probably only to be expected.

'Right. I should get back.' He taps his hands, palms down, on the edge of the table, then stands. 'You want that hug?' His eyes, the same colour as the casual khaki-coloured trousers he wears today, rest on mine.

We embrace. He holds me tight. I catch a whiff of his aftershave, and all I can think of is Anna. I close my eyes, pretend that this moment of closeness is with her; pretend that it's her scent — a floral, sweet one rather than a musky one — that I'm inhaling. I have to stop myself clinging to him.

'This time last year, remember the night?' he whispers.

I do remember. A crowd of us went out to celebrate my birthday and I ended up dancing on the table. It was a night for Sean to have Rose, and Anna had called to collect me in a cab after being out with her own friends. 'Taxi for drunk mother!' she had called into the pub.

'It's good to think of fun times,' he says.

Theo seems to know the exact picture I have flooding through my brain. He rests his hand on the top of my back and, for a brief second, I

17

think he's going to say something profound, something that might make a difference — some insight into how I'm going to handle this all-consuming, exhausting, loss. Instead he says, 'It's shit, Jess. Nothing I say will make it better, but I will keep on trying.'

His remark's not profound but, somehow, it helps.

★ ★ ★

It's ten forty. I'm lying in bed on the night of my forty-eighth birthday. My mother has left two answerphone messages for me, neither of which I have felt able to respond to. My ex-husband sent me a text telling me he is thinking of me. My only sister is mad at me for walking away from her this morning and cancelling dinner tonight. My beloved granddaughter is in another country with her father and his parents. My friend's marriage is over and, though he still wants to help me, I'm not sure anyone can. It's Anna I want to hear from.

I snap a Valium from a pack Theo prescribed. Tonight, I need to sleep.

I'm floating on an airbed on a calm sea, rising and falling with the gentle ebb of the dark blue ocean — the colour of her eyes . . . I recognize the beach from a holiday we'd taken years ago — Doug, me and Anna. She's there, on the sand, and she's waving to me. I'm so thrilled to see her that I slide from the airbed, begin to swim back to shore. All the while, she's laughing and waving, calling to me, 'Mama! I'm here!'

18

And as I swim as fast as my limbs will allow, I'm crying, thinking, 'She's not missing, after all. Look! There she is, you can see her.'

I stop swimming, tread water for a moment, am frustrated as I don't seem to be nearing her. 'Mama!' she continues to call. 'Over here!' And then I see it, a huge sea of white behind her. It's moving quickly and I'm confused. How can a white wave be coming for her? I'm the one in the sea. When it swallows her whole, I feel myself sinking underwater. As I fall, I tell myself she's still alive, but I know . . . I know she would never have left Rose.

I wake, groggy. My face is wet.

I cannot cry, but every night I seem to swallow the sea and the salt water escapes through my eyes.

2

Anna

Raw Honey Blogspot 02/09/2013

I love to sing! Anyone who knows me knows it; whether I'm white-wired into my phone on a Tube full of strangers looking at me oddly, or doing my thing from the back row of the choir. I'm the one in the karaoke bar who doesn't need to look at a screen to know the words. I'm the one driving along singing at the top of my voice to the radio. I still use the hairbrush as a mic in the mirror. I know. Sad, but true.

My darling daughter (DD) has definitely inherited this need to sing from me. That and long legs. She's just exhausted me for the last forty minutes; insisting on wearing every hat in my collection (over forty last count) while she sashayed around my bedroom on those legs, singing to Katy Perry's 'Roar'. We did the chorus together and she does a good tiger roar, DD; seems to 'get' the story of the song; seems to want to tell the world that even at four years old, she's not going to take any shit from anyone. I love that in her.

Afterwards, we have quiet time. Ten minutes with her in her bed and a book of her choice, where I read fairy tales with hopelessly happy endings that I dare to believe in too. And when she wraps those tiny arms around my neck and whispers 'Goodnight, Mummy,' my heart melts.

Mama is right. There's nothing quite like it. That love that you get from a child; where they look to you for everything, to fill their every need. It's brilliant. It fills me up. Her laugh, her smile, her giggle, her sunny nature. I am quite biased but she's quite perfect.

And she's like her dad: that enquiring mind, those inquisitive eyes, though they're the same colour as mine, they pucker at the edges just like his. Those eyes were the first thing I ever noticed about Him. That first look, that first day we were introduced, He seemed to stare right into me. I felt exposed, vulnerable. Then He smiled and let me know that whatever it was that He'd seen, there in my soul, that it was beautiful; that I was beautiful and that He could see it.

Comment: Crash-bambam
I've just had my first baby and know exactly what you mean about a mother's love. There's times I feel totally overwhelmed by it all!
Reply: Honey-girl
Just try to slow everything down and enjoy. It gets easier, I promise!
Comment: Idiotlove
Where'd you meet him, the soul-searcher guy? Know any more like him?! I'm such an idiot in love (note blog name) and have never, ever, felt a connection like that. That thing where you feel someone instantly *knows* you? You're really lucky.
Reply: Honey-girl
We're not together any more, but He was special . . .

3

Theo

Theo Pope could recall the exact moment he knew his marriage was over. It was the night that Leah had phoned him with the news that Anna and a friend of hers were missing after an avalanche and two people from the ski party had already been confirmed dead. Harriet, his wife of twelve years, had been beside him, folding linen. Shock had registered on her face and she had made the right noises at the news, sympathetic sounds for Jess and her family. The pillowcases were folded into four, their creases pressed down with her palm; all the while, one eye had lingered on her BlackBerry. Theo had thought it odd; remote and detached from the unfolding tragedy.

Johnny Mathis was singing about a child being born on the television. The Christmas tree lights that Theo had been fixing on his lap had fallen to the floor, some twinkling as expected, some stubbornly refusing. He had gone to Jess's immediately, and when he got back after seeing her and her ex, Doug — both devastated beyond words, both readying to drive through the night to the tiny village in the Queyras area of the French Alps — he had heard Harriet on her phone. She was in the den at the back of the house, oblivious to the fact that he'd come

22

home. He heard her whispered tone, her soft giggle. He imagined her on the other side of the door that he rested his forehead on. She would be sitting back, cross-legged, on the leather sofa. The phone would be in her left hand and she would be playing with her hair with her right; her forefinger rolling some strands of straight auburn hair, round and round itself.

He had opened the oak-panelled door that Harriet had insisted on having two years earlier — a refurbishment plan in their home that he now knew was papering over the cracks. He hadn't gone in, just stood there under the lintel, and she had looked up, her face frozen.

'Enough,' he had said. 'No more of this. Go. Go be with him. I'm tired of all the subterfuge.'

And she had. Two days later. Two weeks before Christmas. She had gone. To be with him.

★ ★ ★

Ten weeks later, with February pelting biblical rain against the surgery windows, he gathered the papers he had been reading from his desk and slid them into his briefcase. The first patient of the Saturday morning surgery was due any moment, and he just had time to sit in his desk chair when a knock sounded on the door.

'Come in,' he said.

Jess's head peered around. 'No, I'm not the scheduled Sarah Talbot. Sorry — I persuaded Sam in reception to let me in first. Perks of being an ex-employee. I'll be quick, promise.'

He beckoned her in, stood and kissed both her cheeks.

'You're soaked,' he said.

'Just from the car to the building, it's fine.' She sighed aloud. 'I won't beat around the bush,' she said. 'I need more of those tablets you gave me when . . . you know. I can't sleep. And please, don't lecture me on how addictive they might be. I have bad dreams, Theo. The snow comes to get her and then the sea comes to get me and — '

'Slow down. Sit down, Jess.' He pointed to the chair next to his desk.

She sat. 'I was going to say something yesterday but . . .'

He nodded as he pulled her records up on his screen. 'Jess, I'll give you a scrip for seven days. That's it. Make an appointment, come in and see me properly. If you don't want it to be me, see Jane instead?'

Jess nodded. 'I will.'

Theo looked at his friend: her eyes dark and tired; her hair, which yesterday had been tamed into a thick ponytail, a mass of unkempt wet waves today. He remembered she had refused food. 'Are you even eating?' he asked.

'When I feed Rose. I eat. Really' She pointed at her wrist. 'Mrs Talbot's waiting. You'll be late for everyone this morning.'

'Yeah, well you knew that would happen when you sneaked in.' He printed the prescription and handed it to her. 'Come over tonight. Rose is away so you won't eat at all. Come and have some dinner. I forgot to tell you that I finally got some help at home — we have an au pair and

24

she can cook! Her name is Bea.' He grinned.

'Be?' she asked.

'Bea, spelt BEA, short for Beatrice. Swedish. Blonde. Gorgeous.'

Jess frowned.

'I'm kidding. She's a Spanish brunette who makes a mean chicken casserole,' he said.

'Sorry.' She folded the prescription and put it in her coat pocket. 'I'm supposed to be at Leah's. I bailed last night and Gus is determined to cook me a birthday meal.' Her expression showed she'd rather miss it a second time. 'I'm just not up for being nice to anyone. Not Leah and Gus, not you and Finn. The phone rings, I jump. I'm a wreck.'

As if on cue, Theo's desk phone trilled.

'That'll be because Mrs Talbot's getting irate.' Jess leapt up. 'I'd better go. Thanks, Theo.'

And then she was gone.

The rest of the morning was so busy, he scarcely had time to breathe. Though he only covered one in four Saturday morning surgeries, lately he had come to almost resent them, feeling that he should be doing fatherly things with his son at the weekend. Finn was probably glued to his laptop, when he should be doing something with him. Something fun. Instead, a morning filled with children and their typical school holiday colds had made his own sinuses tighten.

His eyes rested on the calendar on his desk. A present from Finn years ago, it was a wooden block where each date was displayed on a card. Above it, to the right, was a smaller card for the month and beside that, to the left, another card

25

displaying the whole of the current year. He placed the correct date in the front. Saturday, 14 February 2015. A quick calculation told him it was ten weeks since his wife had left. Ten weeks since Anna went missing. Seventy days during which both he and Jess were beginning to learn how to navigate new lives.

Harriet was now living in a flat close to her office in London, able to walk to the law firm where she'd worked for the last five years. Harriet was now making love to another man in another bed in another bedroom in that flat. Theo tried not to think about it, but when he did, that was the indelible image he saw. Her making love to someone else. Someone else hearing the way she would sigh quietly, then louder and louder until she finally let out a tiny whimper. He wondered if he hated Roland, her lover; if he hated Harriet, or if a tiny part of him was jealous of her freedom. Then he remembered Finn. Finn was now the most important thing, and with his mother only visiting his life these days, Finn was proving to be a challenge.

Theo pressed the bridge of his nose with his thumb and forefinger, then lifted a gilt-framed photograph from his desk. One of the three of them skiing — but rather than think of his broken family unit, Anna came to mind. Where was she now? His stomach clenched as it always did when he thought of her. He couldn't help but picture her entombed in frozen snow. He said a silent prayer he remembered from childhood; he prayed to faceless saints whose names he had long forgotten. During the early days, after the accident, he had prayed that Anna had seen that same documentary on television as him; the one that told you to spit at the snow's surface to see which way was up or down. It would show the way out. She hadn't come out, so his prayer, over time, had changed to one where he pleaded to the Gods to ensure that she hadn't felt a thing.

Anna. It was a moment before he realized he had said her name aloud.

He opened the drawer to his left, reached in and searched with his fingertips until he felt them rest on the envelope at the back. Lifting it out, he sat back in his chair, his right forefinger circling his name in her handwriting. It was striking and bold, like her, and slightly slanted to the left. The 'o' on the end had a little tail, like a comma, sticking out the top. Theo. Panic rose in his throat and he pushed the letter back inside the drawer, for another day. Some other day.

His patient rota finished, he'd had enough. Wrapping up against the outside elements, he lifted the briefcase. Checking inside one more time, he made sure he had the papers he needed to sign. Harriet had been efficient, her training managing to summarize their legal separation in a mere four pages.

Outside, a thin layer of ice had already formed on the windscreen. He shivered in his thick overcoat, opened his car door and slid his bag across to the passenger seat. Slipping his hands into fur-lined gloves, he gripped the icy steering wheel, started the engine and whacked the heat up high.

A five-minute drive had him parked in his driveway. The house, the home, that Harriet and he had created was a modern, detached, four-bedroom 'executive villa', so called by the builder who had built it a decade earlier. It was one of ten sitting in a small, gated community. It was, according to Finn, or more specifically his classmates, 'posh'.

The herringbone driveway that his car now sat on had been a later addition. The time he and Harriet had spent poring over catalogues, matching the shade of the block to the bricks of the house — ensuring it had been just perfect — all seemed such a ridiculous waste now. Looking through the living-room window, he saw the curtains weren't drawn. Harriet had always insisted they were, hating to be on view to anyone in the street. Neither he nor Finn cared and the thought made him smile. The curtains, perfectly held back by their matching tiebacks, probably hadn't been closed since she left. In contrast, a few minutes earlier when he had driven through the street Jess lived in, her drapes had been drawn tight. A hint of a light escaping through a tiny gap at the top was the only sign she was at home.

He wondered if behind those drawn curtains she had been crying, having been unable to since the accident. It was as though, if she cried again, she would have to face the worst. Without tears, there was hope . . . As he turned the lock in the door, heard the sound of Finn's laughter from the den, he realized the plain truth was that he would have sacrificed his marriage any day, rather than lose his child.

Bea's casserole was perfect. She was out at the cinema with her newly acquired boyfriend, so Theo and Finn ate alone at the kitchen table. His son was quiet, the laughter he had heard earlier spent during *The Simpsons* episode on television.

'Did you go to The Wall today?' Theo asked.

'You know I did,' Finn replied without looking up from his food.

The Wall, the local climbing club, was Finn's only outlet for physical activity. It had taken a while to find a sport he was interested in. He hated football, found rugby too rough, thought tennis was 'a lot of running around after a tiny ball'. Both Harriet and Theo had been relieved and thrilled when climbing was the one thing Finn had stuck at and seemed to love; the one thing that took him away from the solitude of playing Minecraft on his laptop and reading what Harriet had called his 'nerdy computer books'. Theo worried. His son was quiet and liked his own company a bit too much for a boy his age.

'How was it?'

'Okay.'

'You're not very talkative.'

Finn shrugged.

'Did your mum call you earlier?'

'Yep.'

'What do you think?' Theo sat back in his chair and stared; willed his son to look at him.

'I think I'd prefer not to.'

Theo sighed. 'I know it's tough, Finn, but your mum wants to see you.'

'She always comes here. Why do I have to go there?'

'She'd like you to, just for one night?'

'Will he be there?' Finn finally raised his eyes and Theo held his gaze.

'No, of course not. No, he won't.' He looked away.

'Are you sure?'

'I'm sure.' Theo stood and began to clear away the plates. Minutes later he had already sent the text to his wife.

Finn worried about coming to you. Wants to know that Roland won't be there.

His phone pinged an almost immediate reply.

Theo, if you want to know if R will be there, just ask?! And no — he won't. Just me and Finn. All night.

He didn't bother replying, just followed his son's slow-moving body as he walked away. Another time Theo would have called him back to help clear the table. Another time, he would have asked him to adopt a less surly manner. But, he concluded, these were new and trying times.

4

Jess

I think, maybe, I'm losing my mind. Earlier today, I had another conversation with Anna while I was in the shower and she was sitting on the loo. She stayed a while and we talked about what we'd do to cover school holidays over Easter and the summer with Rose. There was no mention of a ski holiday with her work colleagues. In these pretend conversations with my daughter, the word 'skiing' is banned.

Now, I'm in the 'perennial plant' section at Hardacres, my local garden centre. My basket is laden with bulbs and seeds for the greenhouse and allotment at the back of my garden. Just beyond the anemone bulbs to my left, two women are talking about the article that appeared in this week's local paper; the one that took three inches of column space to let everyone else know there is still no news. I am rooted to the earth just like the iris in the pot I have in my hand. Whoever these women are, they have no clue how cruel it is for me to stand here, to endure their words; they aren't to know that my grip on reality is a little fragile today.

'But there's no body, that's the horror.' Woman number one.

'That's the worst, the very worst.' Second voice.

31

Number one again. 'Is there nothing new? Nothing at all? I mean, snow melts, doesn't it?'

Snow melts, doesn't it? A question I ask myself daily.

Number two. 'You'd think they'd have found her by now.'

You'd think.

'I read somewhere that there's still two bodies missing.'

I will myself to move. There are still two people missing. Anna Powers and Lawrence Taylor, both twenty-five.

'I don't know how that poor mother is still standing.'

Me neither.

I place the iris pot back with the others, lay the basket to one side and walk through one of the many tills without as much as a nasturtium seed on my being.

★ ★ ★

Leah has decreed that I need a puppy. That's what she does, my sister. She doesn't ask — she just does. I can't disguise the panic I feel when I see the tiny creature craning around my legs in her kitchen. Leah ignores my reticence.

'You didn't open the box yesterday, did you?' she asks.

I shake my head, embarrassed that I actually forgot to open my sister's gift. The pug has a pee at my ankle.

'It had the papers in it. The papers for Pug here. She's a thoroughbred.'

'You mean she's a pedigree.'

'That. See, you're a perfect dog owner already.'

I frown. 'I don't want a dog.'

'Too late. You're having her.'

'Jesus, Leah . . . ' I slump into a nearby chair. It's uncomfortable, all angular and pointy — like the kitchen, which is an *hommage* to black granite and stainless steel. Leah's home is so contemporary, it's almost futuristic — no hint of a tatty sofa here. We're in a large open-plan space that spans the width of the back of her and Gus's home. It's zoned. Leah is a 'zoner'. To my far left is the kitchen; in the middle is the huge refectory dining table and Leah and I are in the 'chillax' area. One day I'll find a way to tell her that there is nothing either relaxing or chilling about these chairs.

'I know you mean well,' I say. 'But the last thing I need in my life is something that pees and shits everywhere.'

'You need something that needs you. She needs you.'

I'm aghast. Genuinely. I cannot believe that my only sister thinks that the hole I have in my life can be plugged by a pug. A dog for a daughter. I can't even speak.

She hands me a glass of wine. 'You need someone or something to give all that unconditional love you're always harping on about, because you sure as hell don't give any to me.'

'I have it all reserved for Rose.'

Leah makes a face. 'Save a little for Pug.'

'I'm not taking the dog,' I say as it lines itself

33

up alongside my ankle again. I resist the urge to kick her gently with my foot.

Leah scoops down and picks Pug up in her hands, dumps her on my lap. A little bit of pee dribbles onto my light denim jeans. 'Her papers are in your name. It's done. Sue me.'

Two huge brown eyes look up at me from above a flat black nose. Her brow looks knitted with lines. I pick her up to throw her right back at Leah and Pug licks my hand.

'She likes you.' Leah sits opposite me, sips her own glass of wine. 'She needs you.'

'She needs someone that'll clean up after her.'

'She chose you. From some sort of spiritual doggie place, she came and found you.'

Despite myself, I smile, stroke the dog's back. 'She looks like she's frowning, or she's about to cry.'

'She is, she's perfect for you.'

I laugh. 'You'll have to take her whenever I'm away.'

'You never go anywhere.'

'That could change.' In my pretend world, Anna, Rose and I are going to see some of the warmer, snow-free parts of the world together.

'It could. Gus and I will have Pug when you go away if you take Pug home tonight.'

I have no room in my life, pretend or otherwise, for a dog. But I still find myself nodding, thinking Rose will love her. 'Okay,' I tell her, and Pug seals the deal with a small, runny shit on my lap.

Gus has prepared the most fabulous birthday meal twenty-four hours later than originally planned. I apologize for cancelling the night before as I sit down, wearing a pair of Leah's clean jeans, to a sharing platter of melted cheese and artisan bread dipped in sweet balsamic to start. An ex-chef, Gus now runs a successful recruitment consultancy for the catering industry from an office upstairs.

'So,' Gus says. 'We're going up to Windermere to see your parents tomorrow. Why don't you come?'

'Can't,' I dip a piece of garlic bread in the cheesy remnants. 'I have a dog to mind. She's too young to drive to the Lake District. She gets car-sick.'

'You're coming.' Leah's eyebrows are arched and her head is shaking. 'Mum is insisting. You're ignoring her calls. Please come. Life won't be worth living if I arrive without you.'

'Can't. The drive's too much for Pug.'

'I collected Pug from a breeder in Portsmouth for you. She was fine all the way back in the car. Perfectly happy.'

'You did? Portsmouth? When?'

'I took your birthday off. Fully intended taking you with me for the day but you fucked off and left me at the school gate. So, I drove there on my own.'

Shit. My face winces an apology. 'How long are you staying up there for?'

'Leave at seven thirty tomorrow morning, four hours twenty up, lunch and a quick walk, then same back. Gus is driving. Portsmouth and back was enough to knacker me. Pug will love it.'

I nod, know when I'm beaten, begin to steel

myself immediately for my mother's food and sympathy, for my father's fragile stares.

'You have to let them care, Jess.' Leah reads my mind. 'They're grieving too,' she adds.

Gus is searing the steaks on a hot plate. He turns them over, making zigzag patterns on the flesh. To his right, he stirs a pot of home-made mushroom sauce. Even the sizzle and scent of such lovely food don't whet my appetite but I will, for his sake, force myself to eat. Pug is asleep at my feet.

'How's Theo doing?' Leah is mashing potatoes with what looks like a half-pound of butter. Fine for her because she won't eat them. Not so good for my already screaming arteries.

'He's okay, busy . . . Finn starts secondary school in September. Can you believe that?'

'Yes, but how is he? Theo. How is he doing?'

I know a loaded question when I hear one and turn to look at my sister.

'Why?' I arch my eyebrows at her and at the plate of food that Gus has just presented me with. It has the most enormous doorstep of a steak and a mountain of creamy, oozing, buttery mash. There is a serving dish laden with carrots, squash and swede, a celebration of orange vegetables, in the centre of the table.

'Enjoy, birthday girl!' he beams.

I smile my thanks.

'Why, Leah?' I repeat. 'You know something I don't?' I slice through the steak with the serrated knife.

'You know what chambers are like. The place is rife with rumours.'

There are times I forget that Leah, as a senior practice manager for a firm of barristers, moves in the same circles as Harriet. I feel immediate colour rush to my cheeks.

'Ahh,' she says, seeing my discomfort, 'so it's not rumour then?'

I sigh loudly. 'What have you heard?'

'That Harriet's shagging her boss, Roland. That that's why she left Theo.'

I frown, try to chew my food so I won't have to confirm or deny anything. Leah's delicate kick in my shins reminds me I won't get away with that.

'Ouch, do *not* kick me.'

'Speak. Now.' She points the sharp end of her knife at me.

'Ladies, ladies . . . ' Gus shakes his head. 'Eat up!' He looks in my direction. 'Jess, you need to eat, you're fading away. And Leah, stop gossiping.'

'Yes, Leah. Stop gossiping.' I play with the steak on my plate. 'Thank you for this, Gus. I'm sorry again that I cancelled last night.'

Gus places his fork on his plate and squeezes my forearm with his hand. 'Forget about it. I've told you — no harm done and you're here now.' My hand gives his a reassuring tap. He releases me and lifts his wine glass, tilts it in my direction and smiles. His silent toast to me is all that is needed.

'Harriet?' Leah persists as Gus turns his head fully to glare at her.

'I have no idea if Harriet is shagging anyone,' I reply.

37

'If it's true, I suppose that means they're over?'

'Let's hope not.' As I speak the words aloud, I'm not sure I mean them. In the many years I've known Theo, Harriet has always been pleasant, always been polite, but she tolerates more than likes me. I've sat at her dinner table; we spent, last Christmas together, all of us: me, Anna and Rose. She constantly says the 'right thing' to me, but more often than not it has a ring of insincerity to it — except maybe after Anna's accident. She did write me a lovely letter then. My face flushes guiltily as I tell myself off for thinking badly of her, and at the same time hand Pug her first illicit mouthful of steak.

★ ★ ★

It's 11.50 p.m. and I've texted Theo's mobile to let him know I'm standing outside his front door. Moments later he opens it, rubs sleep from his eyes.

'Jess? It's late . . . Bloody hell, is that a dog in your hand?'

'It's ten to twelve. Happy Valentine's Day and yes, I'm carrying a dog. Say hi to Pug. Apparently I need a recipient for all my unconditional love.'

'Valentine's Day . . . Really?' He scratches his head above his right ear, just along the line where his hair changes from black to grey, stifles a yawn. 'And there are always conditions in love,' he says.

'When did you become such a cynic?' I shiver. 'Aren't you going to ask me in?'

38

He holds the door open for me to pass under his arm. 'Go through. I'll put the kettle on,' he says.

I cross Harriet's threshold close to midnight. As I'm doing it, I know I wouldn't be if she were still here.

'I'm sorry for getting you up.' I look around the huge kitchen as we listen to the beginning hum of the kettle. 'Have you changed something in here? It looks different.'

'Just a coat of paint. I did it last week.'

'Looks good.' I can imagine him, up a stepladder every evening, the news channel on full blast on the television, trying hard to keep busy. 'There's something I want to say'

He's dangling a couple of tea bags in two mugs, one in each hand. 'Hmmm?' he says.

'I was at Leah's earlier, finally got around to eating the birthday dinner Gus planned — anyway, she asked me about you and I realized that I've been too immersed in my own life to . . . ' Pug is pacing Theo's quarry tiles, picks a spot in the corner near the Aga and squats. I'm there immediately with some kitchen paper from a roll on the worktop. 'Sorry.'

He hands me a cup of strong, black tea, just the way I like it.

'Where was I? Oh, I was trying to say I don't think I've been here for you.'

'Jess, you had Anna to deal with. Have Anna to deal with. Harriet and I — '

I shake my head. 'It's not a competition. Friends help each other. I haven't been around for you. That's all I wanted to say, so, I'll finish

39

this cup of tea and be on my way with Pug.'

I stare at him over the rim of the mug. We have an unusual friendship; have done since that day he first came to the surgery as a visiting locum and drove into the back of my car. The memory of a much less self-assured, younger Theo comes to mind. A memory of him being on duty in A&E the night a teenage Anna drank too much and needed her stomach pumped; a memory of a colleague's drunken laughter over our 'friendship' one Christmas. But that's what it was and always has been: a deep, loving friendship. He's what I would have in a girlfriend, except he's a guy. I'm what he would have in a guy-friend, what he has with his real guy-friends. It's simple, uncomplicated, and works for us.

And right now he looks tired. Dark shadows circle his green eyes, both of which follow the only sound in the room — Pug padding across the tiled floor, sniffing out new territory. Theo takes a seat at the circular kitchen table, kicks out a chair opposite him. 'Sit. You're here now, take your time. Let's talk.'

I plonk myself down on the chair, one eye on the roaming dog. 'You must miss her.' It's a statement more than a question and he shrugs.

'I miss the woman I thought I knew,' he says. 'I miss her being around; having someone to share things with. I miss her being here for Finn.'

'Doug left me when Anna was the same age. It's tough for them. All they want is their mum and dad together.'

'I knew the relationship had changed, but I thought it was just a phase and that we'd get

40

back on track with time. I never thought . . .' He hesitates. 'I suppose whatever I thought about her leaving me, I never thought she'd walk away from Finn. Yet it's the best thing she could have done for him — leave him here in his home, at his school, with his father. Out of the whole scenario, that's both the best and shittiest thing she's done.' He laces his hands behind his neck. 'Anyway . . .'

I bite my tongue. I haven't been able to understand her being able to leave Finn either, but the facts are it happens, and no one — not a soul — questioned Doug leaving Anna in the same manner. If I'm honest, part of me admires Harriet's strength to do it, and another part of me is beyond angry that she could willingly walk away from her child when I've probably had mine stolen from me.

'I'm going to see my parents tomorrow.' I change the subject, glancing at my watch. 'Today, later this morning.'

'You're ready to see them?' he asks, acknowledging the fact that I've managed to avoid visiting for more than ten weeks.

'Leah and Gus are going for the day tomorrow. It's a lot to do in one day, but they've talked me into going. They're right. Mum is constantly phoning, tries her best, and she already has her hands full looking after Dad.' I stop to draw breath. 'Look, I just really wanted to say thank you for being there for me and to let you know I'm here for you too.'

'Don't worry about me. You have enough on your mind.'

My eyes rest on old school drawings pinned to the notice board next to the fridge. Frayed and yellowing, Finn's earliest artwork, they're years old and they make me think of Rose and how much I've missed her. Since Anna's accident, I have had Rose to look after pretty much full time, apart from the days that Sean has had her for odd weekends. Having her fill my life helps me avoid thinking. Thinking about Anna, wondering where she is; wondering if I will ever have the closure of burying her; wondering if someday she'll phone me from a bar in Brazil and explain that she's alive and kicking — that becoming a mother at nineteen was just too much for her and that she just had to get away.

'I should go,' I say. 'It's late, sorry for the midnight call.' I bend down and pick Pug up. Theo stands and we walk to the door together. 'Just tell me one thing.' I narrow my eyes under the hallway light. 'Are you all right?'

He laughs. 'I'm not sure what's brought this on, but I'm fine. Really.'

'Your wife of twelve years left you. I remember the hole that leaves. I'm sorry it took me a while to say that.' I attempt a weak smile, kiss his cheek. 'I choose to believe that Anna's alive and it keeps my lungs working. You have to find your way forward too.'

Theo says nothing, just nods and hugs me before I leave.

As soon as I get home, enter my own kitchen, the first thing I see is the red light of the answer machine. I place Pug on the tatty sofa at the far end of the room, go back to the car and retrieve

42

all the puppy paraphernalia that Leah had also bought. There's a bed-like thing; I set it up in the warmest part of the room and transfer the dog to the centre of it. I press the red light and hear Doug's low voice.

'Jess, it's me. It's Saturday night. Can you give me a call when you get back, doesn't matter what time it is?'

My stomach churns as I dial his number.

'It's me.'

'Hi, I tried your mobile earlier but your phone kept ringing out.'

'I was at Leah's — it's an awful signal there.' My mobile service provider seems to be the only one with no mast in earshot of Leah's.

'Anyway — '

Pug starts to howl.

'Is that a dog?' Doug asks.

'It is. Say hi to Pug.'

'Right.'

'Leah's idea, not mine.' Pug's sound rises to a steep crescendo. 'It's late, Doug.'

'Yes. I — '

'Oh, for crying out loud, Doug, spit it out,' I say, instantly thinking of Anna. I had spent a whole month after the accident hoping she was spitting her way to safety. Some Discovery Channel thing I'd seen once upon a time . . .

'They've found a body,' he replies. 'It's the boy, Lawrence.'

I say nothing. I can't. His first words have made my stomach contract. His second sentence fills me with instant relief, then pain, and then Gus's wonderful food threatens to reappear.

43

Words will not form. Sounds will not sound.

'Jess?'

'I'm here.' I force the syllables together.

'I thought you should know. I was going to go over to France again but, I don't know, Carol says there's not much point, not if they're sure.'

She's right.

'It's so late. Maybe too late to digest this. Call me tomorrow?' he says.

I look at the clock. It is tomorrow. 'Do you sleep, Doug?' Words I hadn't expected to say, form themselves of their own accord.

'Not really. Not well. Not any more,' he replies.

'Me neither. Thanks for letting me know. I'll call you later.'

Just as I hang up the phone, Pug howls again. She crosses the room to my feet and I'd swear she's crying.

Two hours later, the dog is still baying. I am sitting at my kitchen table with my head in my hands, cursing Leah. Anna and I seem to have a glass of vodka together, and as I pop another pill, I consider, just for a brief second, crushing one into Pug's milk.

At 3.16, Pug is Valium-free and silent. I am talking to myself, aware in the blackness of the night that Anna is not really here and I am tonight, apart from this dog, very much alone.

5

Anna

Raw Honey Blogspot 10/10/2012

Once, Death thought he had me. I was there, firmly in his crosshairs. To this day, I think he came for me and just missed out. He's probably still swearing, muttering to himself, 'Nearly had her, that Anna Powers.' I was ten when it happened, in town one Saturday afternoon with my best friend (BF) C and her mum, who had stopped to talk to someone about ten metres behind us.

I heard the sound before I saw it; knew without looking that it was out of control. When I turned, there was a small car, an odd shade of mustard yellow, heading straight for us. I remember my eyes closed as I waited, just knowing it was going to hit me. In reality it can only have been a split second between the hearing, the seeing, and the breeze on my face as it skimmed right by me. I felt it, I really did. If it had been a movie moment, it would have been slowed right down for effect.

A forty-two-year-old man with an unknown heart condition died behind the wheel. If he hadn't managed to steer a route through the crowd, it doesn't bear thinking about what might have happened. There were mothers and fathers and prams and babies and shopkeepers and there was BF. And there was me.

'*Carpe diem.*' My dad taught me that expression afterwards. *Carpe diem*. He used to repeat it a lot. 'We have only today,' Mama still says. 'We should dance, learn, love and sing.'

I still can't stand the colour yellow — in clothes, flowers, anything — but I do really try to live in the moment. And I still think Death was probably quite pissed off at missing me that day.

Comment: Heartsandkisses152
You were lucky and what a gift it is to grow up with the ideal of living in the moment. I think the world would be a better place if we could all do it, all the time.
Reply: Honey-girl
You're right!
Comment: BlahBlahBlah1985
Carpe every single fucking *diem!*
Reply: Honey-girl
I like that ☺

6

Theo

He was up hours before anyone else, had mopped the kitchen floor and made a picnic of sorts before there was a sound from Finn's bedroom. Bea was, as always at the weekends, sleeping in. The food he had prepared was wrapped in foil and packed in a picnic box he'd found in the garage. A tall flask of coffee completed his efforts.

When Finn appeared, his laptop in his hand, Theo was standing on his head in the furthest corner of the kitchen.

'Morning, son.'

'You are so weird,' Finn said through a stretched yawn. He removed a bowl from a cupboard and shook a box of cornflakes at it, poured half a pint of milk over it and went to take a place on the sofa in the den watching television. 'Why do you even do that?' he asked, glancing back over his shoulder.

'Helps me think. Sometimes when things feel a bit upside down, it's good to look at them this way'

'Yeah, right.'

'Don't get too comfortable. We're going out.' Theo lowered his legs and tucked them to his chest before rolling onto his knees.

Finn groaned. 'It's Sunday.'

47

'So it is. Lots of people are up and going to church. Lots of people are up walking their dogs. We're going to the beach.'

His son rolled his eyes, then peered at him over the top of his raised bowl. 'The beach. In February.'

'Yes.'

'Why? It's freezing.'

'Because we can. Now shift your butt up to the shower. We should go soon.'

'I really don't want to go to the beach, Dad.'

'No, Finn, you *think* you don't want to go to the beach. I can promise you when you get there, you'll want to be there.'

'You don't need to do this, you know.' Finn spoke with a mouthful of cornflakes.

'Don't speak when you're eating.'

'This father-son crap.'

'Finn!'

'Really, Dad? You say 'crap' all the time . . . I don't get this sudden . . . this sudden need to spend time together.'

Theo swallowed hard. 'My wanting to spend time with you is hardly sudden. We always spend Sundays together. We used to —— '

'We used to do lots of things together when Mum was here, yes.' Finn had walked away.

'And what, we should stop that because she's not?' Theo stood at the door to the den and tried hard to keep his voice from rising.

'Yes,' his son nodded, and opened up his laptop to his world of Minecraft. 'We should.'

Theo left the room, walked slowly upstairs to his bedroom. He pulled the bedclothes up,

48

picked yesterday's jeans off a nearby tub chair and hung them in the wardrobe. Next to them, a jumper of Harriet's hung on a hanger. He tugged it towards him, lowered his face and inhaled her scent. It wasn't perfume, but the body lotion she wore, and it lingered in all her clothes. Coconut and spiced orange. He dropped the sleeve and grabbed his coat from another hanger. Downstairs he took a hat and gloves from the coat rack near the hall door. 'I'll be back in a bit,' he called into Finn and closed the front door behind him.

In between his and the next-door neighbour's house was a path. Just wide enough for two people, it led into public woodland. Theo breathed in, blew his breath out in circles. It was cold. A thin dusting of icing-sugar-like frost lay on the ground. The only sounds around on a quiet Sunday morning were those of his heart beating and his shoe soles crunching underfoot. He shoved his gloved hands deep inside his pockets and quickened his pace. This area of green, the walking space, the rural feel of it, in what was otherwise a suburban area, only a few miles from Guildford town centre, was why he and Harriet had settled here. He pulled his phone from his pocket, removed one glove and, without thinking about it, jabbed his wife's number with his thumb.

'Theo, everything okay?'

He did love her voice; it was one of the first things he had fallen in love with. She was softly spoken, her expression gentle, a voice that wrapped you up in a blanket. It was something he had seen her use powerfully when in work, lulling her opposition into a false sense of security.

He put his glove back on, stopped walking, and held the phone to his ear.

'Everything's fine,' he said.

'You sound out of breath.'

'Just out for a walk. Look, I called because . . . I have these papers.' Theo looked skywards towards the slate-grey cloud cover through the canopy of trees. 'I know you're not coming back, Harriet. I think I just want to hear you say it.'

There was a silence which made Theo wonder if she was alone.

'I'm not planning on coming back, Theo.'

His eyes blinked closed. He lowered his neck into his coat, shivered. 'Right.'

'I'm sorry.'

'Me too. I didn't fight for you.' He listened to the sound of clothes rustling, imagined her getting out of bed, moving to another room in her new flat. 'Separation documents. That's what they are. They're not divorce papers and I need to know if I should be moving on with my life. I'm in limbo. We're in limbo here.'

'It's a separation, like we agreed.'

'I know, but it's not really, is it? You're not coming back. It's the first stage in the process.'

'Are you all right, Theo?' Harriet's voice was edged with concern.

'I will be,' he replied honestly. 'I just wish . . . '

'No, no you don't.' She sighed loudly. 'It's hard, but you don't wish — you don't wish this was different. You don't wish I was coming back. We are broken.'

The wind was high. He wiped his left eye, which had begun to water, with the back of his hand.

'It's the truth, Theo,' she continued.

Theo bent down on his hunkers, clutched his knees with his free hand. The words of her last sentence entered his brain, rolled around like a spin cycle in a washing machine. Faced with them, he couldn't deny them. 'Would you mind coming and taking the rest of your clothes?' he asked. 'That body lotion of yours hangs around.'

She was silent.

'Harriet?' He stood up again, stretched tall. 'You there?'

'I'm here. I'm sorry, I could take them when I pick Finn up Friday?'

'No. Don't do that. Finn going to yours for the first time with a boot full of your clothes wouldn't be a good idea.'

'You're right. Sorry.'

Theo turned back towards the house. 'Stop apologizing, Harriet. If we really are both to move on, we have to find the best way forward for him. I'm not sure we've figured that out yet.'

'No, but it'll come. We have to stick together where he's concerned.'

He nodded to a dog walker coming towards him.

'Are you in the woods?' Harriet asked.

'Yeah.'

'I miss them.'

Theo laughed. 'I'm trying not to resent that remark.'

'I miss you too. Of course I do. I'm not in love with you any more, Theo, but I will always love you.'

51

He felt sure he'd heard that line before — some movie or television drama; perhaps a song.

'I miss my son. I miss seeing Finn.' Harriet's voice faltered. 'Every day I have to convince myself that leaving him with you was the right thing if I had to go.'

'I think . . .' Theo ignored her underlying question. The last thing he needed was for her to fight him for Finn. 'I think I just needed to know you're sure. Because you need to be, Harriet. Once these papers go back, once I put them in the post . . .'

'I'm sure. I struggle with it, but I'm sure.'

Theo reached the path, stood aside to let the figure he could see coming in his direction pass.

'Okay, then.' With those two words, he felt his wife slip away; he felt her slip into the arms of another man he barely knew. He felt himself loosen his grip and let go. 'We'll see you Friday, Harriet. Take care of yourself.'

Theo hung up the phone and stood still, the person on the pathway now only twenty feet from him.

'I thought you'd be in here,' Finn said.

'And what if I hadn't been? Did you tell Bea where you'd gone?'

They both walked towards the house.

'Of course I did. Besides, I knew you'd be in here. This is where you always sulk.'

Theo faced his son. 'I do *not* sulk.'

'You do. A little bit. The beach is a good idea on one condition.'

Theo raised his eyebrows, not much in the

mood for more conditions being placed on his life. 'And what's that?' he asked anyway.

'We ditch the ham sandwiches and have fish and chips instead.' Finn shivered on cue. 'It's too cold for sandwiches.'

'We'll take them and have them in the car on the way down or back. We'll have fish and chips when we're there.'

Finn smiled. 'I'm ready to go. Are you?'

★ ★ ★

An hour and a half later, they were both sitting on the highest dune at the furthest end of the stretch of strand at West Wittering. The light was dull, the sun trying to break through the abundant clouds above them. An Atlantic wind whipped around them but Theo didn't care. The chips were hot, the fish was fresh and crispy, and his son was huddled next to him, munching.

'You can just see the Isle of Wight, see the outline?' Theo pointed and Finn nodded. 'Do you remember the time we all camped there one summer? Your mum got drunk as a skunk!'

Finn nodded again.

'I know you miss her. You're bound to miss her. I . . . I just want you to know that I know.'

Theo noticed the chips couldn't go into his son's mouth quickly enough, as if Finn didn't trust himself to reply. He pulled the blanket he had brought around Finn's shoulders. 'Thank you,' he said. 'Thanks for doing this today.' More nodding. 'I used to come here a lot as a boy, before my father died.' He followed his son's gaze, looked out to the grey surf.

'Why do people have to die, Dad?'

It was such an unexpected remark that Theo said nothing, allowed the question to linger.

'Anna's dead, isn't she?' Finn added.

Theo thought some more before replying. 'More than likely, but until a body is found . . .'

'No one could survive seventy days buried under snow, not even if they were in a hole of some sort.' Finn had counted the days.

'The human instinct is to survive against all odds.' Theo picked up a chip and placed it in his mouth. It was already cool.

'You're a doctor. What do you think?'

When Finn stared up at him from his huddled stance, Theo saw fear and confusion and remembered what it was like to be young and afraid. He felt bad for not recognizing that two epic events had happened within such a close space of time. Harriet is his mother. And she had left him. Anna had been his beloved babysitter for years. And she was probably dead.

He hugged his son close. 'I think we don't know until we know. We have to have hope.' Theo felt Finn's body hold back tears. He held him as tight as he could without making him want to pull away. In the distance, the Isle of Wight had disappeared into black clouds. 'However awful things might seem, we have to have hope.'

Finn's lower lip trembled. 'Did you like her, Dad? Anna?' His voice caught on her name.

'Of course.' Theo angled himself to try and catch his son's expression. 'What a strange thing to say. Now . . . ' He loosened his grip on his son and gathered the rubbish into the plastic bag he had brought. 'You put this lot into that bin over there, then I'll race you to the car.'

Finn grabbed his arm. 'Dad?'

'Yes?'

'Mum . . . She's not coming back, is she? Like, never.'

Theo drew the cold air through his nose slowly, and exhaled it even slower. 'No, Finn. I don't think she is.'

'See, I do hope. I keep hoping that Mum will come home. I keep hoping that Anna's alive but . . . '

Theo paused before speaking again. 'I know you do.' He took one of his hands and squeezed it hard. 'But we're here. Alive and kicking. And your mum may be living somewhere else now, but she loves you very much and you can see as much of her as you want, any time. Any place. We will both make sure of that.'

Theo let the statement rest with his son for a few minutes, then turned and play-punched him. 'So, what about that race?'

As Finn walked towards the bin ten feet away, Theo sprinted down the dune. 'But you have to give me a head start!' he yelled back through the wind as he slowed down and backed himself slowly up the beach. When he saw Finn running towards him, his hands waving dramatically, he turned around and ran again. The wind lashed his cheeks, made his eyes water. *It is good to be alive*, he thought, as he filled his grateful lungs with the sea air and ran, aware of his son's laughter just over his shoulder, gaining on him, getting ready to overtake. He slowed and watched Finn pass. His son seemed to be running in slow motion, his limbs all angled, his hair, salt sprayed and stuck to his head, his head glancing back occasionally, his arms pumping like train pistons. *'Did you like her, Dad? Anna?'*

At the car, Theo panted loudly, leaned his body forward, his hands on his waist. 'Not easy to run with all these layers,' he protested.

'You're just old,' Finn grinned.

'I'm forty-five!' Theo panted the words as he opened the car.

Inside, Finn rubbed his face warm with the palms of his hands. 'That was good, Dad,' he said. 'But next time let's wait for some better weather.'

'Nah.' Theo reversed the car away from the café, down towards the barriers that allowed paying visitors entrance to the beach to park. 'The crowds come with the sun. We practically had the whole place to ourselves.'

Finn unravelled his white earphones for the journey home. 'It was good, Dad,' he repeated. 'Some father-son-together crap.'

Theo frowned at his son's language, but decided against a rebuke which, wired into his phone, Finn wouldn't have heard anyway. He eased the car through the narrow barrier as Finn drummed his fingers to the music already pulsing in his ears and ignored the question repeating in his own.

'Did you like her, Dad? Anna?'

7

Jess

When we reach Windermere, I try not to react when I see my mother's hair.

'Darling,' she says, 'you came. I'm so glad you came. Your dad will be thrilled to see you. Oh, thank you,' she says as she hugs me tight. I breathe in her scent, relax in her arms, close my eyes and ignore the fact that she has gone from being an ash blonde to a piccalilli yellow. She pats her head, as if she knows what I'm thinking. 'I haven't been able to get out, dear, found this colour in a cupboard, thought I'd better try and get rid of the greys before you arrived.'

Great. It's my fault she's yellow.

'And who's this?' She looks down to the other end of the lead I'm holding.

'Pug.'

'Is that it?'

'Yes.'

'Is Pug a boy or girl?'

'Girl.'

Mum sighs with relief. 'Good, they piss less. I have enough trouble dealing with your father.'

Leah laughs out loud, comes in for Mum's second hug of the day. 'How is he, Mum?'

'Leah, love. Good to see you too. Go on

57

through, he's in the back, looking forward to seeing you all. Hi Gus. I have lunch ready. Hope you're all starving.'

Leah's eyes roll at me as Gus embraces my mother too. She points to my mother's hair behind her back and mouths the words 'What the hell?' at me, then leads the way with Gus, who hits his head on one of her empty hanging baskets. Mum pulls me back.

'Have you heard from Rose?' she asks, her expression grave.

'Just a text from Sean to say they've got there safely.'

'Oh.' She looks disappointed on my behalf, then strokes my hair. 'How are you?'

Straight away I don't resent the question that I normally rail against. Instead, I feel some strange primal comfort. The touch of a mother. 'Not so good.' I shrug. 'Yesterday was hard.'

She squeezes my hand, caresses the edge of my little finger. I miss my mother's touch. And I miss touching my daughter . . .

Dad is sitting in his usual perch, staring out over the lake from the back of the house. There's a huge expanse of windows that they both put in in the Seventies, way before they were trendy, and the view from this part of the house is spectacular. Today there are too many sailing boats to count. Some glide across the shimmering water like a knife through butter. Others, not quite catching the wind, move more slowly. Dad's eyes seem fixed on a small, slow one near the edge of the lake, close to the end of the back garden.

Leah and Gus are already with him. She has her hands wrapped around one of his, is chatting animatedly to him with Gus beside her, prompting stories with witty asides. Dad responds to neither of them but he keeps his eyes fixed on Leah's face. She's good at this, pretending that nothing is wrong; pretending that the contracted body of the man in the chair is still Dad, though both of us mourn in private. Both of us hate how the stroke has affected him; how much that tiny part of him that died in his brain, the most minuscule area of shaded capillaries on a CT scan, has really altered him. I lean in and kiss his cheek. I haven't told him yet. Mum has asked me not to, certain that if he knew — if he had any understanding of what's happened to Anna — it would kill him. He'd keel over and die. Anna is his only grandchild.

I focus on the shelf next to us. It's white melamine; one of a row of three put up by Dad years ago. I remember Mum fussing when he used the drill to put the brackets in the wall, sure he'd puncture a gas pipe or electrocute himself. The shelves are still in place, perfectly stable and horizontal, while my dad sits curved in a chair. I reach out and touch a Dinky car, one of the many he has collected over the years. It's not in a box like most of the others on display. It is from the *Thunderbirds* range, Lady Penelope's pink car. Anna used to love it and it's one of the ones he allowed her to play with when she was little.

Mum is pottering, hovering. It's making me antsy. At seventy-two, she's ten years younger than Dad and moves at a speed that belies her age. I have no idea how she cares for my father the way she does: her energy is boundless; her love for him so huge that nothing is too much.

'Can I help, Mum?' I call out after her as she heads to the kitchen to bring another foil-covered vegetable dish to the table.

'No, love. Talk to your dad. He's been so looking forward to seeing you.'

Leah looks at me. Neither of us asks the obvious question. Neither of us would, but how can she know what Dad is thinking when he rarely speaks nowadays?

He moves in the chair. Pug has taken up residence by his feet, lying on the green carpet that must be thirty years old and looks like AstroTurf. Dad's blanket, a loose lilac-coloured, stitched crochet one I recognize from my childhood, slips forward. I catch it and pull it up on his knees. I notice his fringe is long enough to push to one side and he's wearing odd socks. Mum is by my side with a bowl of roast potatoes in her hand. 'Talk to him! Honestly! He's not daft, you know.'

I shift in my chair. It's easy to pretend my father is not a shadow of his former self when I don't visit. It's less easy to start a conversation with him right now. I take his hand. 'How are you, Dad?' I ask. 'How are you really?' I make my eyes move from the plaid shirt he wears to his eyes. Gus, always a little uncomfortable with the changes in Dad, leaves Leah and me to it and follows Mum, insisting on helping her in the kitchen.

Dad's face angles a little towards me. Today

his speech is not good. He makes sounds, struggles with the formation of words, but I know what he's saying. 'The girl.'

I lean in to him, rest my head on his shoulder. 'Yes, Dad, I'm the girl.'

Leah laughs and sticks her tongue out at me. 'Always the favourite,' she mutters before she stands and follows Gus.

Dad repeats the sounds and I catch the question in it this time. I wonder if he's asking about Rose. Or if he's asking about Anna . . .

'No, darling.' Mum is on it like a hawk on a vole. 'No, Anna's not here today'

My lips tremble, I catch my mother's eye as she shakes her head at me. 'No.' I squeeze Dad's hand. 'Not today.'

My father nods and his eyes veer back to the boats. I sit back, still holding his hand, am cast back to the many times I sat here on his knee watching the same scene. It was an idyllic childhood, both Leah and I lucky enough to grow up in this beautiful place. And Anna loves it here. Right now as I look at the green space between the house and the water, I can almost hear her laughter; see her running as her granddad chases her. He taught her so much; taking her out on the water in a tiny dinghy, so small it made my heart skip a beat when they both left shore. It was my father who taught Anna to sail. It was my father who took us all on what was Anna's first snow holiday. It was my father who taught her to ski.

I stand up, pass the table, filled with enough food to feed an army. My mother has used a white tablecloth; has place settings in her best bone-handled cutlery, linen napkins with tiny embroidered daisies. A pitcher full of home-made lemonade sits in the centre and I pray that she also has something stronger as well as I head to the loo.

In the cloakroom, an apple-scented diffuser does its job so well, I almost gag. My heartbeat is rapid and I have a sudden and overwhelming urge to leave; just open the front door and go. Anna is telling me to calm down, but I'm talking back to her telling her that I'm okay, I'll just sneak out for a bit and take Pug for a walk.

There is a gentle knock on the door and I grip the edge of the sink. 'Coming,' I say.

My mother opens the door anyway, shuts it behind her. 'Food's ready, darling. Who were you talking to?'

'Myself.'

She hugs me again. 'I do that all the time.'

'I pretend she's here. I pretend she's here and talk to her,' I whisper to her lined neck, to her soft piccalilli curls.

'I know . . . Don't knock it if it helps. C'mon.' She rubs my arms up and down with her hands. 'Let's eat, we're all famished.' She goes to leave.

'Sometimes,' I tell her, 'it feels like I'm losing my mind. I just need to see her one more time. Just once — to tell her how loved she is and if she has to go, then, I . . . ' I shake my head. Our eyes meet and my mother's fill. I smudge her tears away with my thumb.

'I talk out loud to your father all the time,' she says. 'And I imagine him talking back to me the

62

way he used to, not in the broken sentences he can manage now. I imagine him and me arguing during *Question Time*. Jess, he's here physically, but I lost a big part of him in the first stroke. We both understand loss, you and I.'

'God, Mum.' I pull her back to me. 'Am I ever going to be able to feel again?'

'You will. Because you have to. You have Rose.'

'I'm sorry I've been staying away. Everything. Anna, Dad, it's all so hard. I feel like an exhausted ninety-year-old.'

'You're still a young woman, Jess.'

I attempt a laugh. 'Not that young any more.'

'You have a life to lead. Don't waste it; don't wither on the vine. Anna would never forgive you. Your beautiful girl would hate that.' Her tears have traced thin parallel lines down her cheeks. She reaches forward, pulls some toilet paper from the roll and wipes her face.

'I can't cry,' I say. 'Not properly; not since the day I heard the news.'

She shrugs. 'I do enough of that for two,' she says, straightening out her clothes.

'I blame Dad.' I blurt it out.

The look of horror on her face says it all.

'He took us on that first snow holiday. He made her love it.'

'Oh, Jess . . . ' She takes my hand.

'I know it's wrong. I know it.'

'Is that why you don't come up?' she asks simply.

I raise my hand to my mouth, exhale loudly through spread fingers. It comes out in uneven, ragged breaths. The question doesn't need an answer so she pulls me from the room. As we walk, I focus on the love I have for my mother and the love I know Anna has for me. I close my eyes and will her home, as Mum and I walk arm in arm to the dining table, and together, all five of us eat roast beef with seven different vegetables.

★ ★ ★

Leah's quiet on the way home. Pug is asleep in the carrier by my side.

'How do you think your mum and dad were?' Gus asks.

My eyes flit to Leah's who turns around to face me. 'What did you think?' she says.

'You first.'

'Mum's going to kill herself running around after him, way before *he* goes.'

'I don't know. He seems . . . He just seems to have disappeared inside himself. He seems lost.' I pause a moment before finishing. 'I didn't like the look, of him.'

'They did tell us that things would worsen over time, the risk of tinier strokes happening regularly.'

I suppress a sigh; stare out of the window; try not to think of the man I've just left as my once vibrant, athletic father; try not to think of the once glamorous woman who takes care of his every need now having piccalilli hair.

'Do you agree we need to get Mum some help?' Leah asks.

'You tried, didn't you?' Gus says. 'Last time

you and I were here, you said it to her. She said she didn't want any strangers in the house, that it would upset your dad.'

'That was then,' Leah said. 'I think it's probably time. She can't keep doing what she's doing. Can she?' She turns around again to look at me.

'Mum will do what Mum wants. If she says no strangers, then that means no strangers.'

Leah tuts. 'She needs help,' she repeated. 'The GP has recommended him for a care package. All we have to do is put the wheels in motion and, even then, it could take time.'

'Look, you've tried. Let me talk to her?'

'Tell her we'll find someone who looks like Daniel Craig,' Leah says, removing her laptop from her bag and putting her glasses on.

I smile, despite myself. My mother has a thing for Daniel Craig, though I'm certain care workers who look like him are probably quite rare.

Gus grins at me in the rear-view mirror. Leah has snapped into work mode. There'll be no talking to her now until we arrive home. Her work is her life. I remember when Anna became pregnant with Rose, together they had cried. Leah with a rare frustration; sadness that since she had willingly decided never to have children with Gus, already a father, it brought it home that she would never have 'her own' child. Anna because she, having slept with Sean only once, found herself with an unplanned and very inconvenient pregnancy.

65

★ ★ ★

By the time Gus drops me and Pug off, my
watch says seven forty and I feel like it's much
later. I am planning a cup of tea, an hour of
recorded *Downton Abbey*, a chat with Anna and
then sleep — lots of it. With Rose away still with
Sean, I take any opportunity to sleep longer and
later. There's a pile of mail lying on the hallway
floor. I open the cupboard under the stairs and,
anything with Anna's name on it, I throw into
the black refuse sack full of her post. The only
thing bearing my name that I choose to open is a
small brown padded package with my address in
Doug's handwriting. Pug is yapping to escape
the travel carrier as I rip it open. Inside, there's
an item in a clear plastic bag, the sort I use for
Rose's school lunch. A yellow Post-it is attached.

*'You said you wanted this when we got it
back. The police sent it through this week. I
charged it but Anna has a lock on it and I
haven't been able to open it with any code
that I thought she'd use . . . Let me know
you get it okay? Doug'.*

I let Pug out and she immediately wants out in
the back garden for a wee. Opening the door, I
look at it through the plastic cover. Anna's
phone.

Just as I'm staring at it, as Pug runs back in
and I shut the back door, the front doorbell
rings. I head towards it, removing the bag,
feeling her phone in my palm. It's as if I've been

66

plugged into her once again.

When I open the door, I'm startled by the shape of a man in my porch.

'Mrs Powers?' He approaches, a shy hand outstretched. He's dark blond, with tanned skin, blue eyes and trimmed facial hair. I don't correct the title he uses for me and he retrieves his hand when he senses my reticence.

'My name's Max. I'm a friend of Anna's.'

Hearing her name aloud makes me catch my breath. Hearing him say 'I'm a friend' makes me hold it. He is saying 'I am', not 'I was'. Whoever this guy is, I decide immediately that I like him.

'Come in,' I say, kicking Pug's travel carrier to one side. 'We haven't met before, Max, have we?' I know he's not one of Anna's local friends. 'How far have you come?'

'Hertfordshire,' he says. 'And no, we've never met.'

Max. I'm racking my brain to try and remember him. 'Do you work with her?'

He stares at me a moment as I roll Anna's phone over and over in my hand.

'I did,' he says. 'We worked together.'

Past tense. 'Were you . . . were you?'

We're standing in the hallway. I point him to the back of the house, to the kitchen-diner that would fit in my parents' larder. 'Were you . . . ?' I try again. My heart thumps a rapid clip-clop beat in my ribcage. My lips are dry.

'I was on the ski-trip,' he says, meeting my eyes.

8

Anna

Raw Honey Blogspot 15/10/2014

Mama's just been *screaming* at me to 'move my shit from the front door'. It's her standard rant and I'll do it — I'll move them but can't promise the pile of shoes won't build again. I'm a messy cow. One moment Mama tells me I get it from my father, and the next she's shouting, telling me that laziness is not genetic.

She's mad! She's the best mother in the world and I adore her, *but*, she's a tough act to follow; sees things in a very black-and-white way, whereas I seem to live in grey. In my world, nothing is crystal clear and I don't believe in spending too much time figuring shit out. She'd say that if my world is muddy, it's because of choices I've made. And (tough act to follow?) she's right, of course.

But there's still something about mothers and daughters — sounds crappy happy — but it *is* a special bond. Mama and I have it and I have it with DD. It's there and nothing can ever break it. (Keep telling yourself that, Honey.)

When I was little, before Dad left, I remember Mama and Dad as if they were one, inseparable. If I have a memory, they're both there: rock pooling in France on a camping holiday, peering up at me from the audience at the nativity play. He left when I was twelve and apparently I should be damaged by that but, honestly? How bad can it have been when all I can remember is good stuff. At least, that's how I recall it, but maybe, maybe when we look back, we just make people seem better than they actually were?

Anyway, suddenly, there was just the two of us, Mama and me. Sure, she's had lovers over the years, but she never introduced any to me. She kept our home a sanctuary and I loved that. If Dad had to be gone, then I loved growing up with just her and me.

But I don't seem to have inherited her selfless gene. I don't seem to have inherited the tidy gene and I certainly have no ability to see things clearly! Perhaps I *am* more like my father (though he has always said that leaving Mama was absolutely the right thing to do for him. Crystal. Clear. *Carpe diem* and all that). What I do have is a nagging conscience. It pokes me more often than friends on Facebook but I force myself to ignore it (and then, afterwards, worry I'll go to hell in a rusty wheelbarrow).

Comment: Solarbomb
You said your dad left when you were twelve.
Were you really not angry at him?
Reply: Honey-girl
I remember being upset. I remember knowing everything would be different, but no, strangely, I don't think I was angry. I still saw a lot of him, and Mama and I, we worked well together. I missed him but . . . it was okay, I think I was meant to feel different, devastated, but I didn't. I still had a mother and father who adored me and somehow we worked it out.
Comment: Anonymous
REMOVED BY USER

9

Theo

He wasn't imagining it, the woman was flirting with him. He tried to remember her name — Jane, Janet; something beginning with a 'J'. She offered him a slim hand. Long tapered fingers with short but manicured nails grasped his in a firm handshake. 'Jacqueline,' she said. 'You'd forgotten, hadn't you?' She smiled, though Theo had to look down to Finn's height to see it. She was tiny next to his own six-four frame. But that handshake had been strong and, as she stood next to Finn, all kitted out in Lycra and cleats, there was something very self-assured about her.

'No, of course I hadn't forgotten,' he said.

'Yes, he did. He forgot.' Finn snorted. 'Dad forgets everyone's name.'

'Jacqueline,' she repeated. 'Think French. Think you have to make it sound French even though I'm not. That will give you something to hook onto if you forget again.'

'Sorry,' he said. 'I definitely won't forget again. French.' He nodded.

'And talking of hooks, let's get you set up, young man.' Jacqueline play-punched Finn. 'We're doing timed races to the top tonight.'

'I'll be in the gym.' Theo jerked his head

70

towards the next-door building.

'Great, enjoy,' Jacqueline said, before steering Finn towards the wall.

Forty minutes later he was rowing hard. He stretched his long body forward on the machine, straightened his arms, then angled them at the elbows, pulling his body weight forward. The digital monitor at eye level told him he had already rowed 3.9 kilometres, which meant just over one more to go. He closed his eyes and, as his body moved, he thought of the woman next door with his son. He thought of her small, rounded body, nothing like Harriet's, who was tall and lean and angular. He thought of the breasts he had tried to avoid looking at. He thought of the way the suspension belt had wrapped around her thighs. *Shit*. He rowed harder, ignoring the sudden image of a naked Jacqueline as it imprinted itself in his brain.

When the alarm sounded and Theo slowed down, he opened his eyes to find Eddie, his gym buddy and a friend since school, staring at him, a wide smile on his face.

'Share, now,' he said. 'I want some of whatever you were thinking about.'

Theo lifted a small towel from the front of the machine and wiped his face. 'Wasn't thinking anything in particular.' His breath came in short pants.

'Liar. You're talking to someone who knows you.'

Standing slowly, he reset the machine to start again and headed to the men's showers in Phil's Gym.

'What's up with you anyway?' Eddie asked as he followed. 'You've had a face like a slapped bum since you arrived.'

'I'm not sure, if I'm honest.' Theo was surprised at his frank reply. He looked back at Eddie. 'I have an incredible urge to go out and get completely shitfaced.'

Theo could almost hear the whirring in Eddie's brain, trying to work out if there was any way he would get away with joining him; what excuse he could give his wife.

'Stop, Ed. Jules would have you sliced and diced. Both of us have to get up for work in the morning and I have to go home with Finn.' He rested his hand on his friend's arm. 'Another time . . .'

When he stood under the pressured hot water, in the shower stall next to Eddie, he called in to him. 'Stop thinking about it,' he said, before switching the control to cold, gasping out loud with the shock.

'What if I tell her you're having a bad night and need my company?' Eddie yelled. 'The au pair, what's-her-name-again, can look after Finn?'

Theo laughed. 'I'm going home, Ed. We'll do it soon.'

He listened to Ed groan. 'Honestly, you wave it at me, like waving a lollipop at a child, then take it away. Seriously. Not. Fair.'

★ ★ ★

Theo left Eddie drying his hair, slung his gym bag over his shoulder and exited through a series of doors and corridors to the climbing centre where Finn was already waiting.

'You're late.' His son pointed to his digital watch.

'By one minute.'

'Late is late,' he said, stepping into side by Theo. Looking up at the night sky — clear and star-laden, he added, 'I don't reckon aliens are ever late.'

'Right.'

'Think about it,' Finn said. 'More than likely they're a highly evolved species. More than likely they've sorted out the annoying things in humans. Like being late.'

'Right,' Theo repeated. 'Spag bol or chicken tonight?'

'I'm not hungry.'

'Tough.' Theo pointed the remote at his four-year-old Volvo. 'Get in. Decide on the way home. You're eating supper.' Theo had seen too many young people — and not just girls — through the surgery with either the start of, or a fully developed, eating disorder. It was his natural instinct to want to make his son eat. He bit his lip. 'You really not hungry?'

Finn didn't reply.

'You understand you have to eat to give you energy to do things like your climbing . . . You need to eat the calories in order to have them to spend.'

'So you tell me all the time.'

Theo took in Finn's profile as he stared through the windscreen putting his seatbelt on.

'What *would* you like?' he asked.

'Just some tea and toast,' Finn shrugged.

'Tea and toast it is.' He was in no mood for a spat.

★ ★ ★

In his son's room, Theo picked two books up from the floor and placed them on his bedside table. The top one was a young person's guide to computer technology, his last year's fixation. The second, a thick tome on the whole question of whether we're alone in the universe. The laptop, closed on his bedside table, would, Theo knew, be open up to Minecraft, his digital obsession and something he often played with his school friends online.

Theo leaned over Finn's sleeping form, smoothed his son's fringe away from his forehead, bent down and kissed his head. He noted the determined line of his chin, even in sleep. He got that from him. Next, the colour of that forelock he had just touched. That was exactly the same shade as his mother's. He also smelled the faint hue of tobacco from it.

You will be all right, he told himself, as he imagined Finn outside some shopping mall, hanging out with boys Theo didn't recognize, pursing his lips as he pulled on a cigarette. Or, worse, having the audacity to hang out of his rear bedroom window teaching himself to inhale. *You will be able to do this.*

In bed, he lay awake for a very long time. Whatever way he tried to settle, he couldn't. On his right side, he had stared at Harriet's pile of pillows for at least an hour, until he finally tossed them onto the floor. He moved his own two pillows and himself into the centre of the bed, then got up and rearranged the whole thing as it had been. He didn't want Finn to see that; to see parts of his mother vanishing from the house, from his bed.

From his left side he thought of sex; it was three months since he'd had sex. Harriet and his sex life had been brilliant; so brilliant that even when he'd known there was something wrong, he had convinced himself it didn't matter. He sighed loudly, thumped his pillow and turned over again, stared at the narrow strip of light under the door from the landing. Beyond the door was his study, then Finn's room and, further along, Bea's room. He thought of her, twenty-three years old, almost the same age as Anna. He squeezed his eyes shut so hard that he was wide awake and any hope of sleep was gone.

His watch said 01:35 when he threw back the duvet, removed a dressing gown from a hook on the back of the door and moved silently to his study. There, he switched on the light and removed a book from one of the shelves. He settled himself into the reading chair; a recliner that Harriet had bought for him years ago. The book lay open on his lap. His reading glasses lay on top of the book. She was everywhere. The life that was; the one they had together, was everywhere — in the pillows, in the chair, all around. He should move, he thought, before dismissing the idea as a bad one for Finn's sake.

This was his son's home — he just needed to get a grip.

Downstairs, he boiled the kettle and made himself a coffee, paced the floors of every room before settling in the front living room. He stood on a dining chair and unhooked each curtain slowly, allowing each one to curl into two separate piles on the floor flanking the window. He got down and stood back. That was better. There was, he told himself, as he attempted to fold the piles into something the charity shop would accept, no point at all to them.

Next he climbed the stairs and, after retrieving a suitcase from under the bed, began to pack Harriet's clothes. He had no idea of what order she would like them in, what way she would have done it, but they had to go. If anything at all was to be gained by a sleepless night, by the conversation he'd had with her yesterday rolling over and over in his head like a worn-out loop, he had to move on from that day in December. And removing her scent from their bedroom seemed like the best start. It only served as a reminder of his failure, of their failure. He slipped her shirts from their hangers one by one, placed them in the case. He removed her jumpers, already folded, put them on top. Trousers were laid, one crease only, the way Harriet liked them. He filled the suitcase quickly, moved his clothes into the empty space, took his aftershave from the *en suite* and sprayed it all over the inside.

As quietly as he could, memories of many Christmas Eves in his head, he went to the landing and pulled down the loft stairs. From the

76

top of the stairs he removed a large holdall he and Harriet had used on their skiing holidays. He pushed the full suitcase back under the bed, made sure there was enough room for the holdall on the other side — Harriet's side. Within an hour he had removed all of his wife's clothes from the wardrobes they shared, from the drawers she used. He placed his hand on the empty hangers, moved them left to right along the hanging rail, spaced them out to try and hide the stripped reality.

At 03:12, he climbed into bed, knowing he had an early practice meeting at the surgery five hours later. He was exhausted as he pulled the duvet over himself one more time. His head throbbed; a steady pulsing beat. He swallowed two paracetamol, then fell into a restless sleep, where one moment he was skiing with Anna and a holdall full of Harriet's clothes, and the next, a nameless Frenchwoman's head was smiling at him from Harriet's pillow.

★ ★ ★

Five minutes before he needed to leave the next morning, Theo sat fully dressed on his son's desk chair. He watched as Finn rubbed the sleep from his eyes and growled like a bear as his hand swiped his phone alarm off.

'Morning, son,' Theo said.

'Dad! You scared me!' Finn sat up straight, shielding his eyes with an angled arm as Theo switched on his bedside light.

'There's been more rain overnight; looks cold

and wet out there,' Theo said, before taking a seat again. 'I have an early meeting so Bea will take you to school. Wrap up warm.'

Finn slumped back on his pillow. 'Right.'

'Finn, I'd like you to sit up, please.'

Something in his tone seemed to make Finn listen. He straightened up, his back against the wooden headboard, his slim pillow bunched behind him. 'What?' he asked.

'Just wanted a word,' Theo replied as he reached across to Finn's bedside table and lifted his laptop. Finn's eyes widened. 'What?' he repeated, not before Theo had already noticed something very close to panic in his eyes.

'I want to show you something.' Theo spoke as his fingers moved on the keyboard. He kept the laptop on his knee, turned it around to face the screen at Finn. 'See that?'

His son leaned forward. 'What is it?' he asked.

'That is something I deal with regularly. That is a smoke-damaged lung. It belongs to a thirty-three-year-old woman with lung cancer.'

Finn was so silent, Theo could hear his breathing. 'And listen, hear that? That's you breathing slightly anxiously because you don't know what to say. That's your still-healthy lung breathing in and out, doing its job.' He stood up and passed the laptop back to Finn, placed it on his long limbs stretched out under the duvet. 'And that, Finn, is your laptop. Unless you want me to take it off you, along with your phone and climbing lessons, you will agree not to smoke again. You are eleven years old. Do you understand me?'

Finn's expression was one of shock.

Theo walked towards the door. 'I know things aren't easy right now. I know you're probably feeling very confused, but you talk to me, you hear?' He turned around to a silent son hugging his laptop. 'And Finn? I mean it about the smoking.'

'I — '

'Don't.' He raised a hand. 'Don't even attempt to lie to me.'

'I was just going to point out that I am, in fact, almost twelve.'

Theo chomped on a cheek, wondered when exactly his son had become a smartass. 'Yes, and if you want to make it to your birthday, you'll chuck that packet of cigarettes in your third drawer before I get home from work this evening.'

Theo closed the door behind him; tried to ignore the image he had of Finn sticking his tongue out or doing whatever foul gesture it was that 'almost twelve'-year-olds did to their father when they were pissed off at the world. He checked his wrist and sighed. He was going to be late.

10

Jess

Watching *Downton Abbey* fades in importance as I listen to Max apologize for calling so late on a Sunday. I study him as he speaks. He's tall, with tight cut hair and brooding, heavy-lidded eyes. On the third finger of his left hand there is the faint tan line of a thick wedding band. He reminds me of someone; an old college tutor of Anna's whose name I've forgotten. As he shifts uncomfortably on our tatty sofa, I wonder what possessed Anna and me to bring it home. Even if we had ever got around to reupholstering it, as planned, it really is too big for one and too small for two.

He's taking in the room, eyes scanning left and right. They linger on a large black-and-white canvas photo of Anna and Rose that I have on the wall. Pug, delighted at new blood, is pushing a tennis ball along the floor, hoping that Max will take the hint and play with her.

'How's Anna's little girl?' Max asks.

'She's doing well. Considering. She's a happy child.'

'That's good. Does she miss her, I mean obviously . . . can you tell if she does?'

I'm surprised at his bluntness. There's something refreshingly honest about it and, rather than disarming me, I'm drawn to him.

'There's times — she asks me about Mummy being with the angels.' I raise a palm in the air. 'Not my doing. I never told her that. It was something her father told her way too soon. A couple of weeks after . . . It was much too soon . . . Anyway, she's away on holiday with him at the moment.'

I stop talking, not sure why I'm rambling about Sean's belief in the afterlife.

'I suppose you're wondering why I'm here.' Max suddenly seems nervous, pulling on his shirtsleeve every few seconds.

'You don't need a reason. You're a friend of Anna's.'

'I've always thought you must have a million questions, about that day.'

'Did you see what happened?' I watch as his Adam's apple reacts to my question.

'Yes.' He pulls himself together. 'A group of us were sitting across the valley, looking through the binoculars to see if we could spot them. They had gone up top, all of them off-piste.'

'Go on,' I urge him. He's looking at me as if he's not sure I'm ready to hear. He's probably right but I press him anyway.

'We heard it first. We hadn't heard the boom, that sound you hear when it's a controlled one. When the snow came, it was as if the whole of the mountaintop just slid downwards.'

I feel an ache in my chest that seems to have started in the centre of my heart and is sending gripping, clawing pains outwards, My hand automatically rests there. Pug is circling my left foot, looking up at me. She whimpers softly.

'I was watching her ski,' Max continues. 'She was a great skier, beautiful to watch. That day she was dressed in an all-in-one red suit.'

The one I bought for her last Christmas. I searched high and low, contacted every ski store in the land until I found the one she'd circled in a magazine. On Christmas morning, she had whooped with the delight of a two-year-old getting their first doll. That was our last Christmas together, the three of us. We —

'One minute I could see her, then snow, so much of it, and I saw her go. She tried to out-ski it, but I saw her disappear . . . '

His eyes fill quietly and immediately I envy him. I envy him the ability to cry when I'm left with this constant, searing pain in my heart. He wipes the tears away with his sleeve, looks across the room at me. I avoid his eyes and, afraid that he will judge me some sort of cruel, unfeeling woman, tell him, 'I haven't been able to cry. Not since . . . Not at all. It's bizarre really, I could cry at *Bambi* beforehand and now, now . . . ' I stand. 'It's like my tear ducts are permanently blocked.'

'I can't stop,' he says. 'I was the one who asked her to come on that holiday with us.'

'You feel guilty.'

He nods aggressively.

I want to tell him that he should, that it's not my job to assuage his guilt, and that if he had kept his mouth shut that Anna would still be here with me and Rose. Instead, I tap his shoulder reassuringly as I walk across the room to the fridge. I imagine Anna trying to out-ski it.

She would have tried. She would have tried hard because my daughter would have wanted to live. Every sinew in her body would have stretched to the max. I pour a large vodka from a bottle, hold it up in his direction. 'I'm sorry, I've forgotten my manners. Would you like a drink?'

'No, thank you.' He shakes his head, angles it. 'Is that her phone?'

I sit down, place my drink on the table beside me. 'Yes, it is. The police had it, they've just sent it to Anna's father. I can't help feeling it has been sitting in some evidence locker, ignored all this time. I actually thought she had it on her.' My voice drifts.

'I gave it to them,' he says. 'She'd asked me to look after it while she skied.' He shrugs awkwardly. 'After the accident, I gave it to them, knew they'd be trying to ping it to try and . . .' He's struggling to find a way to say 'locate her'.

I pick it up again and it's moments before I realize I'm pressing the diamanté phone cover, my fingertips forced against the ridges, leaving red, circular marks. Her phone. I've phoned it, left so many messages for her. I've made sure her account remains open, just in case somewhere, on some parallel plane, it might be possible for her to hear my voice, to know she's loved and missed.

'Why?' I ask him suddenly.

'Sorry?'

'Why did she give you her phone?'

'I don't know. Just before she left, she literally tossed it through the air at me, said, 'Look after that for me, will you?' Then she was gone. The

83

signal *was* dire out on the slopes.'

I'm unable to reply. I try to quell the pointed feeling I can sense in my jaw at the word 'gone'.

'She was always on it, constantly thumbing away. I assumed it was texting all the time. I mean, some of it was, but she told me shortly before the accident that she just used it to think into.'

I swallow some alcohol, feel the burn, then say, 'I'm not sure what you mean?'

'I'm not sure either; it's just what she said.' He shrugs, hesitates a moment. 'You know, I think one of the reasons I came here is to tell you that she was happy. On the trip? She'd been a little distracted just beforehand, probably just work stuff, but as soon as we got there, she told me it was as if the mountain air had cleared her head. She was happy.'

'She was?'

'Yes. The snow was great. On that last day, the fresh fall of powder had us all excited.' He hesitates. 'The group weren't supposed to leave for another thirty minutes and had they waited . . . I'd injured my foot the day before; the hire boots, they were biting. I didn't go with them that morning.'

'Anna's a fresh-powder fiend. She'd have been itching to get going.'

He nods and I can tell from his expression he's probably regretting the visit. What to say to the mother of the woman you possibly had feelings for; who left to go skiing with friends and never returned while you rested your leg nearby. And had she just left at the allotted time,

84

not got overexcited by fresh-powder fall, they'd probably all be in the pub next to the office, mulling over their shared Dropbox of photos, downing beers. What to say? I can't help him.

He stands. 'I should probably go. I'm glad you've got the phone. There'll be pictures.'

I look at my glass, just one mouthful gone. 'I'll drop you at the station.'

'No,' he says. 'Please. Stay. I don't want to put you out. Here, take this.' He presses a business card into my hand, one with a handwritten personal email address. 'If there's ever anything you want to ask, I don't know, anything . . . just call?'

Outside, I can hear the wind has risen. From the front room, the chimney hoots an owl-like sound. The rain, which had trickled twenty minutes earlier, now slaps against the kitchen window.

I crumple the card into my pocket. 'I'll drop you at the station. It's starting to blow a gale out there.'

He doesn't argue. Before I leave, I plug Anna's phone in to charge.

'Stay, Pug. I'll be back in a few minutes.' Pug trails behind us and I can hear her cry through the closed front door.

★ ★ ★

Vodka has a way of sliding down the throat. It's like a pleasant burning sensation as it flames its way to my hungry gut. I have waited for the phone to half-charge before entering the four-digit code that I know will open it. *Incorrect PIN*. I try her birthday, my birthday — all incorrect. I frown at it, baffled, sure that it had always been Rose's birthday.

I'm almost ready to throw it in temper when there's another ring at the front door which makes me jump. Pug jerks in her sleep but doesn't wake and I automatically look at my watch — 9:08. It's late. I pad through the hall, as quietly as possible, and peer through the peephole, then open it so quickly that I almost hit myself in the face.

'Nanny!' she cries and leaps into my arms.

Sean has no choice but to let go of her hand.

'What? Hello, gorgeous girl!' I hug her so tight, I feel and hear her gasp.

Sean remains on the porch. 'She wanted to come home,' he says simply.

Rose jumps down, takes my hand and is looking back to her father. 'Come in, Daddy. Nanny will make you a cup of tea.'

He bends down, opens his arms for a hug. 'No, love, I won't stay. We talked about this, remember? I explained that if you came home I still had to go back. Your grandma and granddad are waiting for me.'

She nods, releases my hand and goes to hug him. 'Okay,' she says.

I tell her to bring her rucksack up to her room and she obliges, practically skipping up the stairs as Sean slides her small suitcase over the threshold.

'What happened?' I ask, when I think she's out of earshot.

'She just never settled.' He shrugs. 'As soon as she got there, she was crying to come back. She was crying for Anna, crying for . . . home.'

I sigh. I have never told her Anna is dead because as far as I'm concerned she's not. I have just nodded along with her father-inspired talk of angels.

'And I guess she thinks of this as her home,' he says.

I bristle. 'This is her home, Sean. She has lived here all her life, almost all of it here with her mother.'

'And you,' he says, and I can't help but think I hear a trace of resentment.

'And me.'

'Now's not the time,' he seems to hold his breath for a moment, 'but we do need to talk about ongoing arrangements.'

My blood freezes. 'Arrangements?'

'As I said, now's not the time.' His breath hits the cold air outside in vapours.

I glance up the stairs. 'Now's perfect, Sean.'

'I'm not happy with Rose living here full time.' His hands are parked in both of his low-slung pockets. I immediately think back to Anna's accident and how I leaned on him a lot more than usual for childcare. He, in turn, leaned on his parents.

Pulling the door closed between him and the stairs, I leave a gap wide enough to see and speak through. Somehow the best words that can come out seem to find themselves spoken. 'Rose seems to be quite happy. Isn't that what matters? In the circumstances.'

'She does. I see that, but I'm her father and I need to do what's best for her in the long run.'

I have only met his mother once. A small, rotund woman who likes to eat cream éclairs is the physical image I remember. I also remember him parroting every word she said when we were together that one afternoon. I question now: are these his words or hers?

'I see,' I say. But I don't. Rose is coming downstairs behind me, jumping on each step as if to make her presence known.

'We'll talk when I get home,' Sean says. 'I'm heading back there tomorrow, want to try and get the rest of the holiday with Mum and Dad.'

I open the door wider again so that Rose can hug him goodbye and I'm reminded of the night of the news. Doug here on the same doorstep. The moment I heard about the accident, the primal reaction I had. Having said goodbye, Rose disappears into the kitchen and I stare at Sean, aware of the gushing sound of that fight-or-flight adrenalin in my veins once more.

'Rose-lives-here-with-me.' The words are punctuated, staccato.

'Na-na!' Rose runs into the hall, Pug jumping around her legs excitedly. 'We got a dog!'

'We have, darling. Why don't you take her into the kitchen to play?'

'Jess,' Sean says from my doorway. 'Anna's been gone almost three months. I'm moving to Blackpool in June and I'm taking Rose with me.'

His parents live in Lytham St Annes. I picture the scene. Grandma Éclair, a woman Anna couldn't stand, taking over from Nanny Jess.

Memories of long-gone rows I had with Anna about the father of her child surface. I am, I fear, about to be punished for never really liking him.

'Over my dead body.' I hiss the words and shut the door. With my back against the panels, I see Rose standing there, looking at me, her eyes wide and frozen in her tiny face. I hold out my arms and she runs into them. Silently, I promise her I will never let her go. Never.

11

Anna

Raw Honey Blogspot 13/06/2013

Earlier today I was stopped in the street and asked if I'd take part in a television interview where they were wondering what it's like to live and date in London. I told them, sure, I'm happy to be asked what it's like to live and date in London.

So, with no prep whatsoever, this gorgeous young interviewer called Faye waved a big mic at me and said, 'So, here we have X, who we've just met. X, tell us, what's it like living and dating in London?'

So I did. I told her. I told her and her viewing public that it's shit. That it's impossible to meet someone in London. I'm a young, healthy, heterosexual woman and any man I'm ever interested in is either gay, living with someone, deeply involved with someone or married. There are no single worthy men. I've tried dating the allegedly worthy younger men and, trust me, they're only interested in a quick fuck or they're dull. And older men are gay or married.

After she laughed nervously, she asked me if I'm interested in meeting a life-mate going forward and if I'd consider online dating?

So, with no prep whatsoever, I laughed in Faye's face and told her that I'd already tried online dating, which just confirmed for me that any interesting men are gay or married. Take Marcus, for example, I told her. We dated a few times before I found out he was already hitched. To be fair he did tell me, but, as I said, only after we went out a few times, so I said 'Goodbye Marcus'. Then Leo. Leo was definitely not sure which way he bent and I told him I'd rather not be an experiment, thanks very much. Or of course, I told the lovely Faye, there's always Tinder. I asked her if she's tried the swiping phenomenon. Tinder, I told her, has the most expressive text language. There's no foreplay; someone might just say, 'You know you want to — just tug on my bone', or how about 'Wanna sit on my face?', my most recent offering. I deliberately look into camera, tell them that dating in today's world, and let's not blame London, is a hoot. Great fun.

Faye finished up gaping at me like a salmon struggling upstream. Her cameraman, thankfully, had stopped filming way before I stopped talking.

Then I told her that monogamy is an outdated idea anyway.

When I got to work I cried like a baby.

It's been over for a very long time now and still, I miss Him. I try to avoid seeing Him at all costs because it's HARD. It is really hard.

Here are the things I just miss:

His feather touch.

His voice. (He can't sing but He has the loveliest speaking voice.)

The sex. (With Him, He only has to touch me and I almost come. He's ruined me for any other man. No one comes close. Forgive the pun, dear readers . . .)

His jokes. (They're awful; so old school, but they make me laugh.)

Those lazy bed days. (There were never enough, but when we managed to snatch one together, usually in a small hotel on the river near Marlow — well, neither of us ever wanted to leave.)

His calls. (He would call me most days; fill me in on his day, ask me about mine.)

His hugs.

His kiss.

And the things I don't miss:

The fact that I could never just 'be' with Him in public.

The fact that He has a lovely wife.

The fact that I had to lie to people I love.

The fact that we could probably *never* be together. Not really. Not in a 'Hey, babe, I'm home, I've had a tough day, let's just cuddle up on our sofa?' kind of way. We could never have that.

And, see, *that's* really what I want.

Comment: Hieroglyphic 24
What a load of tosh! I'm single, living in London, heterosexual and interesting. Want my number?
Reply: Honey-girl
Hmm. No. You're all right.
Comment: Anonymous
He's married?
Reply: Honey-girl
Afraid so . . .

12

Theo

'Charles Everard is insisting on seeing you. He's refused to let the carers in and won't accept anybody else. Will you have time to slip by and see him after morning surgery?' Sarah, Theo's PA, spoke through his open door and above the sounds of the busy waiting room opposite.

Theo looked at his watch, just as his mobile phone rang, his home number showing up on the display. He nodded agreement at Sarah, gestured to her to close the door behind her and answered his phone.

'Bea, everything okay?' It was, he realized, the first time she had ever called him, and coming so soon after his discussion with Finn, his heart was in his mouth.

'Everything good, Theo. You wish I do shop for you?' Bea's English, though certainly better than his Spanish, sometimes left him feeling like he was playing charades.

'Food,' she continued. 'You wish I get big food?'

She was offering to do the weekly food shop. He rubbed his eyes with his forefinger and thumb and sighed. The cupboards were indeed bare. He just didn't seem to have the time to do everything he always did and add in the things

Harriet used to do too. Everything food-related had been her domain. Since she had left, quick meals had been the order of the day, except on those rare occasions when he'd had time to buy fresh food, in which case Bea would always cook.

Her doing the food shopping made perfect sense. She had use of the car, the one Harriet hadn't taken to London with her. Why not? Promising that he would drop some money off to her at lunchtime, he hung up the phone, trying not to think about how even buying food looked different since Harriet left.

Thirty minutes later he was driving to seventy-year-old Charles Everard's house. Once a well-known artist, the man had lost his wife to cancer nine months earlier. Since then, he had been depressed, telling Theo that the light had gone out in his life. A recurring, chronic leg ulcer meant he had also been housebound for weeks, which didn't help.

After the third knock on the door, Mr Everard answered. 'Thanks for coming, Doc,' he said, allowing Theo to pass by him along a narrow hallway lined with stacks of old magazines.

'Bad day, Charles?' he asked.

'All bad days,' his patient muttered in between bouts of spluttering.

'That sounds rough; we'd better have a look at that chest.' Theo watched as Charles took a seat in the only free chair in his living room, the sofa obscured by books and canvases and scattered painting-related paraphernalia. The television was on; a documentary about monkeys had been muted and Theo was momentarily distracted by primates scurrying across the screen. When he turned to face Charles, the man already had his shirt rolled up, exposing his skinny frame.

'Can't seem to shift this cough.'

Theo listened through his stethoscope, heard the rattle immediately. 'Think you'll need a course of antibiotics to shift it, Charles. I have a few to start you off, but Elaine will have a prescription filled for you.'

Charles wrinkled his nose. 'Don't want no women in here.'

'Elaine is a friend and colleague, Charles. I trust her. She's the only one who can get here every day and you have to let her in to dress that leg. No more of this ignoring her. She's here to help take care of you.'

'How's your boy?' Charles asked as he rolled his shirt down his shrinking middle.

'A pain in the ass at the moment. Are you eating, Charles?'

'No appetite.'

'You have to eat. I'll talk to Elaine about getting you some meals delivered. Simple, nutritious food. You don't have to eat a lot, but you do have to eat.' He sat on the edge of his patient's chair. 'Cilla would want you to look after yourself, Charles. She'd be mad as hell with you if she could see you now.'

Rheumy, pale blue eyes looked up at him and filled with tears. 'I know,' he whispered. 'But I miss her.'

'I know you do. One day at a time, eh? And some day, you'll wake up and it won't hurt quite so much.' Theo listened to his own words, hoped they were true. 'Now, I'm going to call Elaine and tell her you'll let her in later, okay?'

Charles nodded. 'Why is your boy being a pain in the ass?'

Theo shrugged and laughed. 'Because he can. Because he's almost twelve and hormones are beginning to rage and because I'm the only one around to blame.' *And because his mother left us both to be with another man.*

A spindly, liver-spotted hand reached out to touch Theo and patted him. 'Just love him. Cilia and I never had children. In those days if you weren't blessed . . . ' He shrugged his bony shoulders. 'You just weren't blessed.'

Theo stood, reached inside his bag and handed him a tiny plastic bag with three capsules in it. 'There's enough for today here, Charles. Take one now — do you want me to get you some water?'

The old man shook his head. 'No, you get on. Thank you for coming, I know you're busy.'

'Don't get up, Charles, I'll see myself out. I'm calling Elaine from the car, right?'

Charles nodded and waved him away.

From his car, he called Elaine. He called Bea to tell him he was on the way and he called Harriet. He warned her, ahead of the weekend with Finn, that their son was a smoking pain in the ass, and told her that he felt it was probably her fault. By the time he'd reached his herring-bone driveway, the one that Harriet had wanted, she was shouting down the phone at him. After his parting words to his wife, 'Yeah well, fuck you too and the boat you sailed in on', he sat in the car and drummed his forehead against the top of the steering wheel. Bea opened the front door and it was when he saw the list in her hand that he remembered he hadn't stopped at the cashpoint.

He pressed a button to lower the window. 'Bea, I'm sorry, I completely forgot to get money. I'll be back in five minutes.' Without waiting for a reply, he backed out of the drive. A glance at the dashboard told him he was already five minutes late for afternoon surgery, which would mean almost thirty minutes late by the time he could start. An afternoon of poorly and now irate patients. He hadn't eaten since Sarah had insisted he have half of her croissant at nine a.m. He had just sworn at his wife for the first time in their thirteen-year history. *And all of that before one o'clock . . .*

* * *

From his position at the end of the bar, he stared at a small crowd of people sitting at the opposite end of the pub. They were, Theo realized, waiting for karaoke night to begin. He suddenly wanted to be home, away from people, away from poor renditions of pop songs he could rarely recall. Out of the crowd he recognized only a few, including Finn's tutor, the woman from the climbing club — the woman he'd had a pretty graphic dream about. He felt his cheeks flush as Eddie took the seat beside him. Silently, Theo picked up the pint of orange juice and lemonade and swallowed three large gulps.

97

'Now, listen,' Eddie said, after initial hellos and ordering a pint of lager. 'I realize it was meant to be just you and me tonight, but you know how Jules loves the karaoke. Which sort of means she's here.' He frowned over the rim of his glass.

Theo laughed. 'I forgot it was on and, to be absolutely honest, I'm really not in the mood, so why don't you and Jules enjoy it.'

'I'm sorry, she got a last-minute sitter for the kids and she's back there gargling her throat . . . I couldn't say no.'

Theo glanced across the room to see Jules high-five the tutor as she passed on her way towards them.

'Theo!' Jules wrapped her arms around his neck. 'How are you? Christ, it's so good to be out,' she said, without waiting for an answer. She rolled up her sleeves. 'Right, Ed, order me a soda and lime. I'll drive. He has persuaded you to stay, yes?' She looked straight at Theo.

'No, really. I'm not in the mood.'

'See that girl over there?' She pointed a finger back to the crowd and Theo knew without looking that she was pointing to the nameless dream girl. *Think French.* Jacqueline . . . That was her name.

'Uh-huh,' he replied.

'She's been asking about you. Says she knows you through Finn?'

'Mmm.' He swallowed more orange juice and wished it was lager.

'Look, will you?'

'I know who you mean. She tutors Finn at The Wall. Jacqueline.'

'Yes. She's gorgeous and lovely. She's single and she's asking about you.'

Eddie was shaking his head.

'Shut up, Ed,' his wife said.

'Didn't say a word.'

'Theo.' Jules leaned into him. 'What would be the harm in having some fun and throwing in a little female company from someone who's really nice and is interested?'

'Interested in what?' wondered Theo. If it was sex, it was out of the question. He could neither take a woman home nor be out all night. He had Finn to think of. If it was his looks, she'd discover pretty quickly that there was very little beneath the allegedly handsome outer shell. He was a soon-to-be legally-separated local GP who liked to stand on his head once a day and be a father to Finn. That was about it.

Theo drained his glass. 'Another time, Jules.' He leaned forward and kissed her cheek. 'Now go break a leg.'

She glared at Eddie. 'You could have made him stay,' she said, wagging a finger at him before she walked away, tutting.

'You couldn't.' Theo put his jacket on.

'Ignore her. Just stay anyway?'

'No, go on, be with Jules. She really wants you up there cheering her on during 'Dancing Queen'.'

'She is right, you know. You should stay.'

Theo pulled the zip up on his jacket. 'I don't doubt it.'

Eddie put a hand on his arm. 'You've not been right. Not been happy for a few months. I know it's been hard with Harriet, but . . . ' Eddie ran a hand through his head of lush, dark curls. 'Is there something else going on. Is it Jess? The Anna thing?'

Theo almost laughed. *The Anna thing.* Was that how people viewed it? A young woman of twenty-four is lost in an avalanche; her family are bereft — left in limbo — caught between the despair of the fact that she is most likely lost to them and the need to hope that she may not be. *The Anna thing.* He shook his head and pushed his hands down into his gloves.

'How *is* Jess?' Eddie asked.

'She's fine.' Probably at home right now, about to take a Valium so that she can sleep.

'Tell her I said hi when you see her. And Theo?'

Theo looked at him.

'You should think about what Jules said. You want me to lay the groundwork for you?' Eddie grinned in Jacqueline's direction.

'We're not in school.'

'Oh yes, we are!' Eddie said. 'We never leave the playground. Take it from me, a physics teacher to sixth-formers. They're all still kids but the worst kids, the *very* worst ones, are in the staff room. I'll tell her how great you are, get her number for you. You'll thank me later.'

Theo gave him a loose hug. 'We'll catch up soon. Come for dinner, you and Jules.' As he said the words, he wondered how that might look. Him and Eddie and Jules in the dining room without Harriet. No, the kitchen table. That would do — just the three of them, casual,

100

something simple — something from M&S. 'See you.' He mock-saluted his friend and left the pub through the back entrance, not wanting to catch Jacqueline's eye as he left.

In the car park, he phoned Jess. 'Put the kettle on,' he said.

'I'm watching *Mad Men*. Go away.'

'Put the kettle on. My night with Eddie has been cut short with Jules arriving for karaoke.'

'I bloody hate karaoke.'

'Are you making me a cup of tea or not?'

'Don't put the car on the drive, park on the road. I've only just got Rose to sleep.'

'Rose? I thought — '

'Long story. Sean brought her home early and she's been pretty unsettled since she got back.'

'Oh.' Theo wasn't sure why but he was disappointed.

'Right. Kettle's on,' she said. 'Be quick and be quiet.'

'Two minutes,' he said and hung up.

When the door opened, he kissed her cheek and followed her silently through the hall.

In the rear room, a kitchen-den, Jess boiled the kettle in the kitchen end and he took his jacket off. He noted the tall glass of clear liquid on the coffee table, lifted it and sniffed. Vodka. Next to her glass was a blister pack of tablets. He took a seat opposite what she called the tatty sofa. A pile of photos lay scattered on the coffee table and Don Draper's face was frozen on the television screen.

She handed him a steaming mug and sat down.

'I read in the paper they found the boy's body,' he said.

'Yes.'

'You all right? I haven't heard from you. Not since you came around mine telling me how worried you were about me.'

She smiled, a tiny curve at the edge of her mouth. 'I'm sorry. You're right. I'm a bad friend. Don't believe a word I say.'

'Are you all right?'

She raised her shoulders up and down, wordlessly.

'So,' Theo said. 'I found out that Finn's been smoking.'

The single frown line she had between her eyebrows deepened.

'He's pissed off, feeling we've let him down.'

'Have you talked to him?' She folded her legs underneath her.

Theo sighed. 'I tried but I think I talked *at* him. And I told Harriet it's all her fault.'

'It probably is,' Jess whispered, before drinking from her glass.

He said nothing for a moment then nodded towards the tablets. 'Vodka and Valium?'

'If you lecture me, I'll put *Mad Men* back on.'

'Jess, have one or the other, not both, and certainly not together.' His eyes questioned hers.

'Theo. Not tonight. Save it, please.'

'I'll save it. But you'll be sod-all use to Rose if you continue like that. Speaking of Rose, why is she back?'

Jess had started to glare at him, then softened at the mention of her granddaughter. 'She was upset, didn't settle at all. Sean thought it best to bring her home.'

He nodded.

'Then he thought it best to remind me on my front doorstep that Anna has been gone for three months; tell me that he doesn't now consider this Rose's home and that he's looking to move her up to Blackpool with him when he moves there in June.'

Theo didn't speak. His mouth opened but no words came out. With Anna missing, Rose was the one reason Jess got up in the morning. He leaned forward, reached for her hand. It felt limp and small in his. 'He won't do it. That's his parents talking.'

Theo had no idea if it was or not. He just remembered Jess saying something about Sean's parents living in Blackpool.

'If he takes her . . . ' She swallowed the rest of the vodka in one go.

'He won't.' Theo let go of her hand and sat back again, the churning in his stomach almost audible. *This was not good news. Not good news at all.*

★　★　★

At eleven p.m. he unlocked the main door with his keys and punched in the alarm code on the keypad to his left. The surgery was eerily still and quiet, lit only by the security light in the car park. The only sounds were the humming of computer terminals in the reception area and the low buzz of the aging fridge in the staff room as he passed. Theo entered his consulting room, switched his desk light on and sat down. He tossed his phone and keys on the desk and sat back, his chair swivelling him to the right. Without thinking too much, he picked his phone up and dialled speed-dial #2.

'Theo?'

'I'm sorry,' he said. 'I'm sorry about earlier.'

'It's late.'

'I know, but we never did go to sleep on a row and I didn't want to start now.'

Harriet paused and Theo listened, matching the pulse of her breathing with his own. 'I'm sorry too. Part of me knows you're right. He's playing up because I left. He's looking for attention and — '

'He just wants his parents back together.'

'Theo.' There was another, longer pause. 'That's not going to happen.'

'I wasn't asking for it to, Harriet. Don't misunderstand me. I'm just pointing out the obvious. He wants his life back the way it was.'

She sighed. 'Is he asleep?' she asked.

Theo looked around the shadows of his workspace. 'I'm not sure,' he replied honestly.

'Give him a kiss for me, will you?'

'I will.'

'I'll see you Friday and I'll talk to him this weekend. He might open up a bit. He probably needs to hear the truth from me.'

'That's a novel idea. I wouldn't mind some of that myself.' He winced, hearing the sarcasm dripping from his mouth.

'I've always been honest with you.'

'Have you?' He felt her stiffen down the phone line.

'Now, eleven at night — you call to apologize and you start another row?'

'Harriet. Were you seeing Roland for longer than you said you were?'

'No, I bloody wasn't. And I don't get where you get the right to start accusing me of lying.'

Theo closed his eyes.

'Goodnight, Theo. I'll see you and Finn on Friday.' She hung up the phone.

He leaned forward, sunk his head into his hands and felt the tears come. They were body-wracking tears, not gentle, silent ones and, when they were done, he wondered. He wondered if he'd known they were coming; if he'd felt the inevitability of them back at Jess's and come here to avoid the scene at home. He wiped his cheeks with the back of his hand, reached into his desk drawer for the tissues he kept there for patients and instantly remembered what had really brought him there. He removed the envelope and pushed it deep into his coat pocket. Whatever Anna had to say, it was probably time to read it.

13

Jess

'I don't see her places. I expected to — you know, when you hear people talking about catching sight of someone, going up to them thinking they're . . . then you see that they're really no one you know and they're looking at you funny.'

Jane nods.

'Anyway, I thought that would happen but it doesn't. I do have conversations with her, imagine she's here chatting to me. Feels safer than accosting strangers . . .'

Jane Levy gets up from behind her desk and squeezes my shoulder. 'Let me check your blood pressure,' she says, reaching for the armband. Outside her office door, I can hear some children running amok.

I feel the strap tighten around my right arm and glance at my watch on my left. 'I've left Rose in the waiting room,' I tell her. 'I really hope that's not her!'

I tell her this as code for 'please hurry up', but she takes her time anyway — checks my pulse rate, my blood pressure, looks in my eyes, takes a blood test 'just to make sure I'm not anaemic'.

At first she looks sympathetic, checks my notes when I ask for a refill on the Valium prescription. Then, almost immediately, she looks hesitant.

'I can't sleep, Jane,' I say to her. 'And when I do, I dream of Anna being swallowed by a massive white wave of snow. At the same time I swallow the sea. It's the only time I cry — when I sleep. And I need to cry.' She types something short, presses a button and I hear the printer deliver what I need.

★   ★   ★

I have never asked anything of Doug. I really haven't had much to do with him at all since he left me, unless I needed to talk about Anna. I can, in the last twelve years, count the conversations we've had on a few hands.

So, I don't want to call him now. I'm loath to call him now. In my head I play out the various possibilities. Whether I call his mobile or his home phone, there's every likelihood that Carol will answer. She'll speak in that vapid voice of hers and it'll annoy me and I'll probably end by hanging up. At least during working hours I have more chance of getting him alone.

As I tap the back of my mobile with my fingernails, I'm watching Rose out of the corner of my eye. I've chosen to sit alone at the edge of the café area, not up for company today, and the other women seem to automatically respect that. The mums here are all lovely; they're people I know mostly from school and they, like me, are watching as their kids play in this vast warehouse world of swing ropes and ball parks. It is Jack Villiers' sixth birthday — thirty-two kids are all pumped up on saccharine goods, fizzy drinks and adrenalin. The boys and girls chase each other. There's a lot of squealing.

From the edge of the bigger kids' play area, I dial Doug's number. My lungs swell with anticipation as I wait, then deflate the moment he answers.

'Jess,' he says. 'Good to hear from you. Though where are you?'

I move nearer the door to dilute the background noise, one eye still on the children.

'I'm at a kid's birthday party.'

'Ahh, the joys of only working in term-time.' In one sentence he manages to irritate me but I bite my tongue. 'Did you get the phone?' he asks.

'Yes.'

'Can you unlock it?'

'No, look, that's not why I rang. I need your help.' The words feel bigger than they are.

'Okay, let me just . . . wait a sec, can you?'

I know he's put his hand over the mic on the phone, is probably moving out of earshot of a colleague.

'What's up?' he says.

I can tell that he has left the room he was in. 'I'm not sure where to start.'

'How are you?' he interrupts any flow I may have had. 'I text but you don't reply. Are you all right?'

'I'm doing okay. Well as you, I suppose.' We may be divorced but I have never doubted Doug's love for Anna; never doubted that he is currently in the same awful limbo as me.

'How's Rose?'

'Still beautiful. She's the reason I'm calling.'

With that I hear her squeal behind me. She's running towards me, towards the rope-latticed wall at full pelt, Tim on her tail.

'Hi, Nanny,' she yells before sprinting off again.

'That was her,' I tell Doug.

'I could tell.'

I can sense he's smiling. 'You know I've never asked you for anything. Not once.'

'What is it, Jess?'

'I need some money.' Kids' voices scream from the far end of the play area.

'O-kay . . . '

I hesitate for just a second, then talk. I have no option. 'I could only ever work term-time because of Rose. If you remember when she went to school I moved jobs. When I took a lesser salary, Anna paid half the running costs of everything. The mortgage, the bills . . . ' It was probably more, in reality. Anna never seemed to be short of money.

There is an empty silence which neither of us fills.

'I went part-time to look after Rose when she went to school,' I continue. 'That was our deal, Anna and me. That was what worked, what we did. As soon as she got the job in the bank, she was meant to be saving for a deposit. I suppose they might eventually have moved out . . . '

Silence.

'I've used any savings I had to get this far — not that I had much.' I rub my forehead with my fingertips. 'I'm not making a very good job of this.'

'Go on, Jess.'

'I want to keep looking after Rose. I want to be able to do that after school and in the summer holidays. But truth is, I can't keep going and . . . '

The truth is I'm also afraid I'm going to lose her. That if her father gets his way, he'll move to Blackpool and I'll barely see her grow up. The truth is that if I think Anna being missing is killing me, try taking Rose away too. I will fold.

'I know that she has some sort of policy . . . something through work. I'll have a look through her paperwork but right now . . . '

'Without a body.' He finishes my sentence.

'I have to make a home for Rose, Doug.'

'How much do you need?'

I shake my head. 'I don't know . . . but enough to get me through the next few months?'

'Is your bank account still the same?' he asks.

'Yes.'

'I'll transfer it later on, you should have it tomorrow.'

'Thank you.'

He doesn't say how much and I don't ask.

'And try to find that paperwork. Let's just see what's what?'

'I will. Thank you.'

'Let me know you get the money okay.'

'I will.'

'Take care, Jess.'

'You too.'

I hang up the phone and see that a steaming coffee with a biscuit on the side has been placed on the table nearest me. One of the mums, I

110

recognize her but can't quite place her, salutes me. I give her a little wave of thanks and sit down.

Doug rescuing me . . . How life loves to throw up these little ironies. I allow myself a smile. When he walked away, I floundered for a while, had no idea how to plot a course through life without him. When, within months, he took up with Carol, something in me changed. If she was what he wanted; if my love was so strong it strangled him; if Anna wasn't enough reason to stay — well, I was better off without him. And until today I have never needed him since. I have never needed anyone since. I sip my coffee and the woman — I remember her now: Kelly — approaches. My heartbeat races. I don't want to talk about Anna. I will my phone to ring, something.

'Jess,' she stands a few feet away, 'I won't disturb you.'

'No, sit down, please.' I hear myself speak and have a cartoon bubble in my head saying, 'No, don't sit down. Thanks for the coffee but go away, I want to be alone.'

She sits. Her hands play with one another on her lap. 'I'm never quite sure what to say. I see you often at the school. Sam junior goes.'

I hadn't realized. Sam, the choirmaster from Anna's college, a man whom Anna and the whole of the sixth-form choir adored, has a son at my school. Looking out at the screaming brood opposite, I think he must be in Rose's class.

'He's in the year above Rose,' she says. 'Jack

— Jack Villiers, the birthday boy — his family and ours are neighbours.'

'Thank you for the coffee,' I say.

'No problem.'

Silence.

'Is there any news?'

Bubble speak for, 'Have they found Anna's body?'

I shake my head.

This is the point, the same one that happens always, where people feel awkward and I feel the need to fill the space with meaningless words. Somehow, I can't today. She stands. 'We miss her at choir.' She reaches forward and squeezes my hand. 'We all miss her,' she says. I squeeze a smile and swallow more coffee, forcing the lump in my throat south. She smiles back. It is a kind smile, one I'm grateful for, but today I can't engage any more than I have. I'm pretty much running on empty.

★ ★ ★

My nose sniffs the air outside and I peer up to the low-lying, vivid sun as I wait for Rose to strap herself in. The unrelenting rain of the last week has stopped, replaced by a weirdly unseasonal warm spell. It is as if the rain has washed the whole area clean and now the sun has arrived to help it dry. I've taken my coat off and am just strapping myself in when Rose points excitedly out the window. 'Look, Nanny! It's Finn!'

I automatically turn around and, sure enough,

112

it is Finn. He's at the door of the play centre with a group of kids that I recognize from the other Year Six. I can't tell if they're on their way in or out. By the time I'm ready to drive off, they've disappeared. 'Where'd they go?' I ask Rose.

'Back there,' she pointed behind the building.

I wonder quickly if I should call Theo and decide against it. Finn is a good boy. I don't want him in any more trouble. They're kids. What's the worst they can get up to hanging around a play centre?

I'm just pulling out of the car park when Rose starts.

'Can I watch *Frozen*, Nanny?' Rose sing-songs her question nonstop from the back of the car. 'Nanny! *Frozen!*' She is in one of her demanding moods. *Too much sugar*, I scold myself.

We have a ten-minute drive home so I tell her she can, and within seconds she's turned on the portable DVD player. She's quiet, sucking her thumb while Disney's Princess Elsa is singing to her sister Ana about the cold 'never bothering her anyway'.

And my own Anna crowds my brain. My own frozen Anna . . .

★ ★ ★

Rose is finally asleep and I'm sitting on the tatty sofa, a mug of tea in one hand and Anna's phone in the other. I can't open it — no code I know will work.

I put it by my side and stare at my garden,

convince myself that Anna's okay. And some day, very soon, she's going to let me know she's okay. She'll tell me where she is. And why she's there. And if she's coming back or not.

I pick up my own phone, send a text to her.

Come home, darling. Let me know where you are? I miss you. I miss you so much I could cry. Except I can't. Help me, Anna, please?

Her phone pings and I read just the first words from 'Mama' to her on screen. I feel the familiar ache in my jaw; open and close it to try and make it go away. I'm learning all of the time that the human body has countless surprising places it can store grief.

14

Anna

Raw Honey Blogspot 26/10/2014

I couldn't help myself. That's the plain and honest truth. Falling in love with Him was never part of my plan. I've always had an imprint on my brain of what my wedding day would look like; how me and Mama would share a bottle of champagne with my BF bridesmaid and how Dad would hover nervously downstairs, just before I descended in my lacy, ivory gown. DD would be holding Dad's hand, dressed in her mini-me outfit. Mama and DD and I would have had a team of hairdressers pulling on our insane hair, desperately teasing it into traditional wedding looks.

We'd climb into a couple of vintage cars and make our way to the church. Yes. I've always wanted a church wedding with all the trimmings. And at the top of the aisle would be a man who loved me totally, completely. I would fill his world.

This is how it would have been. I suppose it's how it still could be if I could walk away from Him for good. But I used to get dizzy walking away. I'd get dizzy questioning it. I'd pull up articles on the web about falling in love and whether or not we can help who we fall in love with. Whether it's destiny or design? Chemistry or choice?

We can't stop. We've tried. This last time we were

apart for over three years — forty-two months, to be exact. Yet the moment we got back together this month, it was like we'd never been away.

I love Him. He loves me. And people make sacrifices for love . . .

So, I choose to go through life trying hard not to resent his other life. Trying hard to convince myself that somehow, somewhere, over some bloody rainbow, there'll be a happy ending for us.

And that, folks, is how I have to roll.

Comment: *Anonymous*
I have only just stumbled on this blog and am horrified. What makes you think people want to read about your sordid affair with a married man? You claim to 'love' him. Grow up. Looks like you and your mother, a woman you say is only interested in casual lovers, are definitely related. Twisted morals, both of you. The apple doesn't fall far from the tree.

Reply: Honey-girl
Why don't you and your judgemental attitude just piss off? You don't have to read my blog, and to know anything about my mother, or details of my 'sordid affair', you must have read other posts too. I've blocked you so I don't have to read any more of your disapproving shit.

Comment: *Solarbomb*
Does the married man you're seeing have any children?

Reply: Honey-girl
I'd rather not say on here.

116

15

Theo

Once, Theo had saved a man's life. He had probably, in starting treatment for lots of patients, saved many lives, but in a 'dramatic, had-stopped-breathing way', he had saved one man's life. There was no reason that pumping life back into Aaron Hughes's heart should be the image that came to him at the meat counter in the supermarket, but that was exactly what he thought of and, for a moment or two, it rendered him speechless.

'What can I get you?' A slim, balding man peered at him over reading glasses.

'I'm . . . ' He had pumped life into a heart. 'I'm cooking dinner for friends. Haven't a clue.'

Slim Man stared, his silence meaning an array of rude questions like, 'Do I look like a chef?'

Theo smiled, because he did, he did look like a chef. 'Sorry, just some lamb cutlets. Can you do that thing . . . ?'

'French trim?'

'That's the one.'

'How many?'

'Ten, please.' Three each and a spare, or four each for him and Eddie and two for Jules. She ate like a bird.

He decided there and then to keep it really

simple. Lamb cutlets, buttery mash, carrots and French beans followed by a ready-made meringue-like pudding from the freezer.

Heading home, he was quite pleased with himself. Tonight would be the first night he had the house to himself since his son had been born. In almost twelve years, even when Harriet travelled for work, naturally Finn was there. He checked his watch. She was due to pick him up in an hour and Bea was due to leave for a weekend away with her boyfriend, Nick, in forty minutes.

The worktop was full of food when Bea and Nick appeared. Theo had no idea how to behave around Nick. Bea was twenty-three, an adult, could go out with whomever she pleased. Then again, Bea was *only* twenty-three; her parents were in another country and part of him felt he should be trying to fill some 'in loco parentis' role. In the end, there amongst the bags of food, he took her aside, explained his confusion and asked her where they were going for the weekend. She had laughed, told him he was sweet, that her parents wouldn't 'give a she-et' who she went out with, but gave him the address anyway.

He was sure as he peeled carrots that she and Nick were laughing all the way to Stratford. When the doorbell rang, he flinched. He had wondered beforehand if she would ring, or if she would use her key. It was still her house too. Legally, she could come and go. He wiped his hands on a tea towel, threw it over his shoulder and went to the front door.

She looked great. Her makeup was perfect; her long dark hair pulled up into a tight plait which fell down the centre of her back. She was dressed in a navy trouser suit, her typical work attire. The jacket was open; the shirt, a pale pink silk, was unbuttoned at the top to show just enough cleavage. His heartbeat quickened. 'Come in,' he said. In the hallway, he kissed her cheek. 'You look good.'

'Thank you. You cooking?' She was staring at the tea towel.

Theo nodded. 'Jules and Eddie are coming over. Do you want to go up? He's been in his bedroom a while. Wouldn't let me help him pack a bag, so God knows what digital paraphernalia he's taking with him.'

'I'll go up. Is that okay?' She bit her bottom lip.

'Of course. You want a drink, tea, coffee?' He knew not to offer alcohol. She never drank when she was driving.

'No,' she called back. 'Thanks but we'll get going. The traffic to London will be a bitch. Friday night and all that.'

Theo nodded as he walked back to his carrots. He couldn't help but think how extremely civilized the whole scene was. Two well-adjusted adults with their terribly agreeable split, neither of them mentioning the phone call two nights ago. Within five minutes, Harriet and Finn were both standing in the kitchen, Finn's rucksack slung over his shoulder, an expression nearing pain on his face.

'Can I talk to you a moment, Dad?'

Theo glanced at Harriet and back at Finn. 'Of course.'

119

'In here?' Finn pushed open the door to the den.

Theo wiped his hands on his tea cloth, which he dropped on the work counter, and followed their son. As he passed, he raised his eyebrows at Harriet, who took a seat at the kitchen table.

'I really don't want to go. Please don't make me go, Dad.' Finn tried to stop his bottom lip trembling.

Theo held his breath. Jess and her view of love being a thing that should only be served up unconditionally, and only ever for children, popped into his mind just as his love for his son threatened to stop him doing what he knew was the right thing for everyone. He wanted to reach out and envelop the boy. He wanted to hold him, whisper that if he didn't want to go, he didn't have to. But Harriet was never coming back. And somehow, everyone had to try to move on.

'It's hard, I know. Look, your mum's come all the way down from London. She's looking forward to seeing you. I'll make you a deal. If you really want to come home tomorrow — call me and I'll come and get you. Just give it a chance.'

Finn looked at the floor, held back tears.

'Please, Finn?'

Within a few seconds, eyes still downcast, he seemed to pull himself together. 'You'll come and get me if I want to come back?'

'Absolutely. Any time. Just try it, please. We all have to find a way to get on with this. I'm sorry. God knows your mother is sorry too, but this is how it is.'

Finn nodded slowly and Theo reached for him, pulled him to him with an arm around his neck. 'Text me, call me, whenever.'

His son pulled away, opened the door. 'Okay then,' he said, his voice resigned to the new state of family affairs. In the kitchen he grabbed a carrot from the pile Theo had peeled.

'You all right, love?' Harriet asked cautiously.

'Fine. Let's go,' Finn said.

'Right.' She rubbed her palms on her jacket. 'How many have you got coming?' Harriet eyed the pile of vegetables.

'Just two, three including me. I've done too many, haven't I?'

'They'll keep. Wrap them in a polythene bag. First drawer to the left of the oven.'

'As you're here, do you think you could show me how to cut them in that way you do them?'

Harriet grinned, took the paring knife from Theo's hand and picked up a carrot. 'You watching?'

He and Finn both nodded. Harriet cut the carrot on a slant and turned it over and cut it on the opposite slant. 'Easy,' she said, 'crazy peaked carrots.' She grabbed hold of the towel on Theo's shoulder and wiped her hands again. 'We'd better move, love,' she said.

'Right.' Finn jerked his head towards his father. 'See you.'

'Come here.' Theo took hold of Finn and wrapped him in a bear hug as Harriet stood by watching.

'Just give it a go,' he whispered to him.

'You be careful with that knife,' Finn replied,

121

and Theo smiled. Their son was already the same height as his mother, who was five foot nine without shoes. A few more years and a few more growth spurts and he and Finn would be eyeballing each other at the six foot four level.

Seconds later, they were gone and the house was empty. Theo dropped the knife and slumped onto a nearby kitchen chair. The silence was audible. He leaned forward, elbows on his knees, his hands in a prayer position and his head resting against the tips of his fingers. 'Shit,' he said aloud. 'It's quiet . . . '

★ ★ ★

'It must be hard,' Jules said as she played with the last of her lamb chops.

'I can't imagine.' Eddie made a face.

'It's the family thing, isn't it?' Jules said.

Theo put down his knife and fork, no appetite left for the food on his plate. Just as he did so, his phone vibrated on the table next to him.

Here safe. Finn.

Theo stared at the screen. 'I feel like I'm grieving and I don't know what exactly I'm mourning — the loss of her or . . . or the loss of the family unit. I miss that, Finn misses it.'

'I'm sure Harriet misses it too,' Jules offered, and a sound escaped from Eddie, one that said he doubted that very much.

'She probably does, she's told me already that she does.' Theo moved his cutlery to the centre of his plate. He looked up. 'I can't actually believe she's gone. That's the thing. I know she

122

has. I know why, but with all the ups and downs we had, I never thought she'd leave, not for someone else, I never thought . . . ' He swallowed hard. 'I thought we'd agreed that, with Finn, it wasn't an option.'

Jules grimaced. 'That sounds frigging awful, Theo. 'We'd agreed it wasn't an option.' Makes your marriage sound like a cold business arrangement.'

Theo shook his head. 'It wasn't like that.' He sighed — a long, deep sigh. 'I'm not expressing this very well, so you're right. I'll shut up.'

'You loved that woman, probably still do,' Jules muttered. 'Whatever other complications you had together, I know that. I saw that over ten years of knowing you.' She turned to her husband. 'You're very quiet all of a sudden.'

Eddie held his palms up. 'I plead the fifth.'

'Well, maybe Theo needs you to speak.'

'Theo doesn't,' Theo said. 'Who's for pudding?'

He sliced three portions of shop-bought meringue roulade onto plates and placed them on the table. Jules scratched her head and laughed. 'Harriet would have had home-made meringue and fresh raspberry coulis.'

Theo winked at her. 'Harriet's not here.'

'No shit.' She ate a mouthful and made appreciative noises and pointed her spoon at him. 'You loved her,' she repeated.

'I loved her,' Theo said, his head nodding tiny, agreeing movements.

Eddie leaned forward. 'What you need, Theo, my man, is a new diversion, preferably a good-looking one.'

'Are you ready, Theo?' Jules asked. 'Could you see yourself dating yet?'

'Ugh.' Theo put his head on the table.

'Jacqueline, the climber!' Eddie punched the air triumphantly. 'She'd be a good way to start. She definitely has the hots for you.'

'No, no and no.' Theo spoke without raising his head.

'She does like you,' Jules said. 'And I like her. She's really easy to talk to and . . . ' She shrugged. 'Ed's right. She does have the hots for you; even gave him her number to give to you. Text it to him, Ed.'

Theo's head was reeling; he could feel a headache starting to brew behind his eyeballs. His friends claimed to know him, but no one could see into his head. If they could, they'd see a maelstrom of women. Harriet, Jess, Jacqueline and Anna. Anna's face central in the vortex. Lifting his head slowly, he stood and headed towards the kettle.

'Tea? Coffee?' he said, praying his guests would leave soon.

★ ★ ★

After they had left, after they had gone and he had cleaned the entire kitchen, he sat in the den, eyes on the open letter lying on the coffee table opposite him. It had taken him a few days to convince himself to open it. He stared at it, one sheet of plain A4 paper, unlined, just Anna's handwriting present on the page — all straight and ordered, her words tilting to the right as they did. Had he been capable of origami, it would have been the right size to create a small box with a lid. A small Pandora's box, with a world of hurt inside. He sat back in the chair, afraid to touch it again, afraid if he did the paper would feel real in his hands and the content would have to be real in his head.

★ ★ ★

By midday the next day, Theo had come to the conclusion that living alone with his thoughts was capable of driving him insane and that solitary living was not for the faint-hearted. He roamed the house listening to the pipes in the central heating. He watched a movie in the middle of the day and wondered what in Christ he normally did on a Saturday that was so time-consuming. By two p.m., Jess's words from the other night, her fears about Rose, were playing on a loop in his head. He dialled her number.

When her voice prompted him to leave a message, he couldn't.

Instead he opened the earlier text from Eddie and dialled a new number.

'Jacqueline,' he said. 'It seems we have some scheming friends who think you and I should maybe meet, have a meal together . . .'

16

Jess

It's a beautiful day and I'm determined to take advantage of it. I'm trying to keep busy in the garden; trying not to dwell on the fact that Anna would normally be here with me and Rose. She would help her put her tiny wellies on, her hands helping her work the child's rake I bought for Rose earlier this year. The two of them would struggle, giggling, trying to water the seeds with the snaking garden hose. I hear laughter from near the house and shade the low-lying winter sun from my eyes with my right hand. Leah, who is spending the night with me while Gus is away on a stag night, has joined Rose outside, and Pug is barking and dancing around the two of them like a wild thing.

This south-facing rear garden, all one hundred and eighty feet of it, is my haven — come rain or shine. It's also the reason that I bought this place after Doug and I split up. Today, the sun pulses its warmth on me as I work at the tall bench outside the greenhouse. The thermometer nailed onto a window lattice tells me it's seventeen degrees — pretty respectable for late February and a welcome reprieve from the rain of late. My coiled hair is pinned up in a bun, tamed into submission, and I can feel lines of sweat on my brow and

126

across the back of my neck on my hairline.

From the corner of my eye, I watch Rose and Leah. I prepare loads of tiny seed pots, drop the carrot seeds in and place them in numbered rows in the greenhouse. Leah is suddenly by my side, handing me a glass of water. 'You nearly done?'

I nod, stop what I'm doing, rest my back against the glass, and stare up the garden. 'I spoke to Mum,' I say.

'I know.' Leah is already shaking her head. 'She told me.'

'I did try. I talked to the surgery; they have a care package all ready to go. All Mum had to do was say yes, and she won't, not yet.'

'Did she ask if the person coming would look like Daniel Craig?'

'No, but if he looks like Daniel Craig, I'll go up and give him a hand.'

'Ooh, Jess, a joke!' Leah rubs her hands together.

She's right. It's a long time since I've heard the sound of my own laughter, and yet it feels wrong, disloyal somehow. Leah sees this in me, takes my own hand and rubs it.

'Gus thinks he should have a word with her; that we're almost too close to it. What do you think?'

I shrug. 'Can't do any harm. She listens to him, thinks the sun shines from his nether regions.'

It's Leah's turn to laugh. 'I've been downwind of his nether regions and I can tell you it ain't sunshine.'

'Get him to try? We can't do anything else for Mum, we can only react and support her if something goes wrong. I'd just feel so much better if she had some help.'

My rear pocket vibrates and I take the phone out. Theo. Leah looks expectantly at me and I put the phone back. Theo, I can call back. Leah is here talking to me *now*.

★ ★ ★

Later on, with Rose in bed, Leah has already consumed three glasses of wine and I've almost matched her with two vodkas. We've eaten a very mediocre Chinese takeaway which is already repeating on me. She tells me to move upstairs, now, before we both start 'talking crap'. Always the good girl, I do as I'm told.

In Anna's room, I feel like a thief. I have never been one of those prying mothers, never had any reason to be. Anna has always been so completely trustworthy. I've been here many times since her accident — many, many times — but until now it has been to look at, to stare at, to sniff or to touch her things. Tonight is different. We need to find something and I'm consumed with guilt the moment I open the first wardrobe door. Leah has chosen to sit on the floor, her back to Anna's bed base, directing operations.

'I'm not rifling through her stuff, just wouldn't feel right,' she says, her glass by her side. 'I'll be right here, making suggestions, getting you another drink, whatever.' She looks as uncomfortable as she obviously feels, her eyes darting

128

around the room. It's her first time in here since December. I can tell she's thinking what I have many times before: *How can someone with this life, these things, someone with so many memories already and so many yet to make, just not be here?*

Anna has an accordion paper file. I know — I've seen her with it. I rummage around on the floor of the wardrobe. It's not there. But the novelty slippers of reindeer heads I bought her last Christmas are. I raise them to my nose and smile at the memory of her prancing around Theo's in them.

'They don't smell like cheese . . . still new,' I say before putting them back, lining them up neatly side by side.

There are two deep drawers in her dressing table. I leave the wardrobe, crawl across the floor to it, pull open the right drawer first and there it is, lying flat on its side. I tug it out and slide it across the floor to Leah, then sit next to her. Anna's contract of employment is the first thing we find. Leah and I skim-read it until her legal eye finds the 'death in service' clause. Anna had laughed about it at the time . . . joked about her being worth a fortune dead. The multinational bank she had only worked at for a year pays four times Anna's salary to her next of kin in the event of her death. Attached to the contract is a single page 'Life Assurance Nomination Plan'. Anna has stuck a neon green Post-it note on it saying 'wishes letter'. This we read more slowly, then I throw my head back against her mattress and close my eyes. Leah sighs loudly. I am

Anna's named next of kin. According to my daughter's wishes, she has asked that the money be allocated one hundred per cent to me in order to look after Rose, in the event of her death. I also heave a deep sigh and immediately feel guilty.

What am I doing? This was Leah's idea. No, it was Doug's idea. I do not want to know any of this.

'You need to know.' Leah reads my mind. 'You need to know what happens. You need to have all of your ducks lined up in case Sean decides to play full-time Daddy in Lytham St Annes.'

Her fingers scramble through the file. 'Right, we know you control the money; now let's find the will.'

'There's no need. I know I signed a guardianship form. I know I'm Rose's legal guardian.' My eyes are still closed. Anna. Oh, God, Anna, please come home. My stomach is churning.

'Got it.' Leah pulls some papers from the 'W' section. It's a simple three-page document which we quickly scan until we reach an attached sheet outlining guardianship. I read it once, then read it again, and then drop the paper into Leah's lap while my blood seems to freeze in slow motion — an icy feeling that starts at the tip of my toes, crawls up my legs, torso and out to my fingertips. Within moments my scalp starts to tingle. The will is signed by Anna, but the guardianship section is signed by both Anna and Sean. They are Rose's parents. In the event of one or other of their deaths, responsibility for their child's welfare passes to the other. It is only in the event of both of their deaths that I am named, and have signed my name, as chosen guardian.

Leah watches me as I process the facts. I can tell by her face that she has already concluded that this is a bit of a mess. She drains her glass. 'If Anna is dead,' she says, 'Sean can take Rose. If Anna is dead,' she adds, 'you control the money.'

I lower my head to my sister's lap. She strokes my hair as best as anyone can stroke straw curls. 'It's two more reasons to pray she's alive,' I say, as if even one is needed. 'I should show all of this to Doug.'

Leah nods.

'It's a mess, isn't it?'

'It's confused,' she agrees.

'Fucking hell.'

Leah giggles nervously. 'You don't swear.'

'I do now.' I use Anna's bed to pull myself to a standing position.

★ ★ ★

Downstairs, both Leah and I are squeezed into the tatty sofa. 'There's something else.' I take the phone out of my rear jeans pocket, pass it to her. 'I can't open it. She's put some sort of lock on.'

Leah takes Anna's phone in her hands, turns it over several times, and feels the raised diamantés, just like I did when I got it back first. I have a choking lump in my throat but Leah's must rise because she starts to cry.

'Oh,' she sobs, as she presses various date-of-birth combinations to no avail.

'Her account is still open,' I say. 'It's paid from her bank every month and the phone's fully charged. I just want to get in, see her photos, just see her — '

'I have a guy in work,' Leah says, wiping her face with the back of her hand. 'He's a nerdy guy, and a whizz with stuff like this.' She shakes herself out, seems to want to pull herself together. Instead I pull her to me, put her head on my shoulder and stroke her hair. We have swapped roles. She has smooth silky hair that I have always coveted. 'Don't cry,' I whisper.

'I need to, sorry,' she says as I bang the back of my head rhythmically on the tatty sofa. *All I know is I can't lose her. I can't lose Rose too.*

And even in my thoughts, I hate the fact that I use the word 'too'. I want to stand up and run around the room smashing things. I don't do it. I can't do it because Rose is upstairs but I let the images play. In my head, I stand and run my hand along the two glass shelves nearby. Photos, ornaments, a tiny tray with pens and pencils all smash to the floor. I walk over the glass fragments from the photo frames, lift a vase from another shelf and hurl it at the back door, smashing the window. I breathe it in, this imaginary destruction. I let it feed my veins.

'DO YOU HEAR ME, ANNA? YOU HAVE TO HELP ME! I CANNOT LOSE HER.'

Tonight, Leah, though she flinches a little when I raise my voice, just behaves as if my frightened cry is completely normal.

132

The next morning, Leah crawls into my bed early. I am already awake — have been for three hours since 04:43. I was googling the snowfall in the Alps and the whole of Queyras has had little fresh powder. All of the normal half-term holiday-makers are disappointed and the travel bloggers are telling people to steer clear of the area. Doug has left a voicemail which seemed almost hopeful at what an unexpected thaw might bring. I can't think about it. I don't even respond. I cannot be someone who prays for a thaw to find her daughter's body. I can only be someone who prays for her to come home safely.

'I just called Gus,' Leah says through a yawn. 'He's suffering . . . You'd think he'd learn, but he still thinks he can drink like a twenty-year-old.'

She huddles under the duvet next to me. 'He won't be back until lunchtime. Do you fancy doing something? It's supposed to be nice again today. Let's take Rose down to the river and maybe meet Gus at the pub there afterwards. He can buy us all a nice Sunday lunch.'

I find myself agreeing, if only for the lunch offer. Sundays are particularly awful, as they were days that were carved in stone for us as a family. Our odd but fantastic family. Me, Anna and Rose. We would always spend Sundays together, except once a month when Anna had to go into work — something to do with the IT department and a crash recovery plan.

Leah's talking and I'm wondering if I myself will ever recover. My life continues but with a large, gaping hole. As Leah giggles at something Gus told her on the phone, something stag related, all I can hear is my daughter's voice; the sound of her devilish laughter; the feel of her hand in mine just before she left; the taste of those blueberry muffins she made with muesli and fresh fruit; the image of her trying to out-ski an avalanche. Yes, Gus can sort us all out with food. Today is going to be a bad day.

★　★　★

I drink too much over lunch. I tell myself off in the mirror in the cloakroom. I may not have to drive, but I do have to look after Rose.

Back at the table, I pour a pint glass of sparkling water and listen to the hiss of the bubbles before taking a sip. Rose is cackling with laughter at whatever shapes Gus is making with his hands. He's so good with her, so patient; he always has been. Today he seems to instinctively know that I'm torn; that it's a day I want to park Rose at the table with the iPad and just keep her quiet, but I hate doing that and he knows it. I'm grateful he's quietly entertaining her with books and tricks. He's doing the Incy-Wincy spider thing I used to do with Anna, but somehow a coin has appeared in the middle of his hands. Magic. I stare at the scene and wonder if he could just conjure up her mother for me, please. Pretty please.

La, la la, la la la, la la la la la . . .

I sing the 'Incy' tune in my head, drink more water. Leah leans across, kisses Gus on the cheek

134

and he laughs, makes an 'oooh'-shape sound with his mouth, which makes Rose giggle madly. I am suddenly seized with an insane jealousy which I don't understand. I don't want a man I can reach across to and kiss. I'm happy with occasional sex. I don't want someone who will stroke my arm the way Gus is doing now to Leah. I deliberately shunned that intimacy long ago — right after Doug left — so what's wrong with me?

La, la la, la la la, la la la la la . . .

They kiss, a tender, fleeting touch of their mouths and I swallow hard. She has her own form of unconditional love; my sister loves her man with all her heart. I look across at Rose and hope for her sake that my love will always flow for her and that my heart hasn't been blackened the way it feels it has. Today is a really bad day.

17

Anna

Raw Honey Blogspot 10/08/2014

I think I should have travelled, you know, done the backpacking thing. It's something I often wonder . . . How things might have panned out had I made it across Australia, me and my BF picking fruit along the way. But I didn't want to defer my university place, and then getting pregnant during my first year changed everything (not least of which meant I chose to live at home and travel to the London campus when I needed to, rather than in digs, as I'd hoped). It sounds completely unbelievable but DD really was an accident. I have no idea, other than the obvious, how she was conceived. There was no burst condom, no missing my pill. She was just meant to be. And I was just not meant to travel the outback . . .

Mama was fantastic. She never pushed me to keep the pregnancy, nor would she have judged me if I hadn't. She just gave me the space to know that I could do whatever I chose to. I chose to have DD. He came around to it eventually; took Him a few weeks but when He saw how determined I was, He caved. And the moment I felt his hand stroke my tummy, swelling with our baby, I caved and forgave Him.

But today, I'm on holiday with Mama and DD in a small hotel on the southwest corner of Ibiza and I wish I'd had the chance to travel more. I wouldn't change a thing about having DD. She's my life. But I think I allowed my world to stay small. If things had been different, if I'd had the chance to live a few pages of *Eat, Pray, Love*, I think maybe I could have been happy anyway — a different happy, but happy. I'd have moved on from Him, eaten a lot of pasta and met a Balinese yogi. I'd have ridden a bicycle with a warm wind in my loose hair.

Pah, travel, schmavel . . .

If I'd done all that I wouldn't have DD.

And I'd probably have got dysentery.

And I'd probably have got pregnant anyway since DD's soul was heading my way whatever, her trajectory already decided. She'd have had different DNA. She'd have probably looked more like the Italian tenor I would have fallen for when I heard him sing in Rome. But she'd have had the same soul . . .

I'm out by the pool, under an umbrella, using my phone to upload this. DD is sitting ten feet from me playing in the kiddies' splash area with a little boy her own age. I've covered her in sunscreen and she seems to be loving it here. Mama's finding it a bit hot. She got too much sun yesterday and she's inside now, reading on her bed, air-con on full whack.

I've been doing a lot of soul-searching and I really think that — much as I love living with Mama, much as she makes it easy for DD and me to be there — it can't continue in the long run. What if I meet someone? What if we both wanted to move somewhere else, with or without someone new in my life?

She loves me so much. She loves us both so much. Dad told me once that he couldn't take that — it's why he left. At the time I called him a coward, but now, I get it. Mama's love — she calls it unconditional but, on the receiving end of it, it feels suffocating. And I've allowed our lives together to create a situation where DD and I have become her whole life. And that's a big bloody responsibility. When you realize you're absolutely everything to someone, that without you, their life would be empty — suddenly love feels like it comes with handcuffs, and I'm not talking furry pink ones . . .

18

Theo

There was never a good time to be haunted. Day or night. Night, Theo thought, might have brought darker shadows, more menacing shapes, but daytime was just as worrying. She troubled him; the letter had knocked him sideways. He walked to the den and sat down on the large grey leather sofa, the one he'd told Harriet to take if it ever came to halving the furniture. He had always hated it. He leaned back and flicked the television on. Football. He would watch football . . .

The score was 3-1 to Manchester City. He didn't care who won. He didn't much care for football. Reaching into his jeans pocket, he pulled out and opened a tiny blister pack of paracetamol, the telling pulse across his brow meaning a bumper headache was on its way.

He called Jess's number, only to hear it ring out again. Annoyed, he thumbed a text to her.

Tried to call you twice now.

He knew he should just go upstairs, lie down on the bed, and sleep it off.

'Shit!' He screamed the word before falling back on the sofa in a lying position. He needed to sleep. And he hoped when he did, that he would wake up and all those things that poked at the edge of his brain, making him anxious, would be nothing more than bad elements of a bad dream.

★ ★ ★

Four hours asleep in the middle of the day was not how Theo envisaged spending his first day without his son. He wasn't sure what exactly he'd had in mind, but it wasn't that. At four o'clock, he stood under the pressured hot water of the shower for a full ten minutes. He ignored his phone ringing. He ignored the sound of a message pinging, knew from experience that a shower was needed to hydrate, that drinking two litres of water would be needed before he set a foot outside the house. He groaned out loud, placed his palms on the tiles, and stretched his long arms to the max. He should cancel. He was in no mood for company.

Towelling himself dry in the bedroom, he checked his phone. One message. He clicked on Jacqueline's number.

Looking forward to later. See you at seven. ☺

He tossed the towel in the wash and walked around his bedroom, talking to himself out loud. He spoke in an animated way; used his hands a lot to gesticulate; told himself that it was only a date.

★ ★ ★

She said she liked pizza. So, it was agreed between them to keep it simple — a pizza in a local Italian. As soon as she'd suggested it, he had wanted to argue, maybe try and find a venue a bit further away, one that he hadn't frequented so often with Harriet; one where he, and probably Jacqueline too, weren't so well known. He didn't change the plan, and when the head waiter greeted him by name and an arching of his left eyebrow, Jacqueline laughed.

'Maybe we should have tried somewhere a bit further afield?'

He smiled, pulled out her chair and took a seat opposite. He honestly had no idea what to do, what to say.

'You obviously come here often,' she smiled, laid her napkin across her lap.

'I haven't been in a while.'

'Hopefully you can create some new memories.'

He nodded. She knew. Of course she knew. Everyone in the town seemed to know he was now single.

Jacqueline chatted enough for them both. She ordered a light vegetarian pizza with salad in the middle while he opted for a meat feast. He wasn't drinking so she didn't either, asking only for sparkling water.

'There,' she said when the food arrived, 'Mars and Venus on a plate. Women constantly counting calories and men just want their meat.'

'You don't look like you need to count calories,' he said.

Her cheeks flushed a light pink. 'Yes, I do, but thank you for saying so. Climbing up and down the wall fifty times a day — I need to be at or under a certain weight to have the stamina. How's Finn, by the way? I missed him at club last night.'

'He's with Harriet, his mum, for the weekend.'

She nodded, her mouth full of rocket.

'It's the first weekend actually. It all feels a little bit weird.'

Right next to their table, loud conversation made both Theo and Jacqueline stare at their neighbours. The male, a very tall man whose torso towered above Theo's, sat very still. His companion, a tiny oriental woman, was jabbing his right arm with a finger. Suddenly she stood and screamed. In the most perfect English she swore a long stream of abuse at him. Her hands waved wildly, finally landing on him, giving him a push. His bulk meant he never moved. His nature seemed to imply he was also unmoved by her tantrum.

Jacqueline's eyes widened. When the woman sat down and picked up her cutlery again, Jacqueline whispered, 'It's fun here, isn't it?'

'More Mars and Venus?' Theo asked.

She giggled. 'Not sure. She's a bit of a pocket rocket and he seems to be a gentle giant.'

'Maybe he beats her at home and this is the only place she can vent. In public.'

'Okay . . . ' She picked a piece of pizza up with her hands, studied Theo. 'That could be it, I suppose. Or maybe she's the one doing the thumping. You never know people. Do you mind if I use my hands? I can't be bothered with a knife and fork with pizza.'

'Go for it.'

142

She took a bite and chewed slowly before speaking again. 'Jules and Eddie pestered me to go out with you. Sorry. I didn't mean that the way it came out. Obviously, I'm here because I want to be here.'

The next table had started up again. Pocket Rocket stood and grabbed her handbag. 'Fuck you and your whole family,' she cried before marching out the door.

Jacqueline nodded her head towards the woman's coat, still on the back of the chair. 'She'll be cold.'

'She'll be back,' Theo said.

The man called for the bill, paid with cash and left, leaving the woman's coat behind. Within seconds she was back, picking it up and putting it on. Neither of them seemed to have any real awareness that they were in a public place.

'So, 'pestered'.' Theo smiled.

'Wrong word, sorry.'

'Right.'

'They think that you — and I'm quoting here — 'need the love of a good woman'.'

Theo didn't meet her eye. The woman sitting opposite him was everything he should have wanted. Attractive, chatty, bubbly. She had kind eyes, grass green; a careful little flick at the edges with an eye pencil giving her a feline look. She had high cheekbones — Slavic blood somewhere, he concluded. She was the perfect height; he figured she'd fit right under his arm as they walked.

'We don't have to do this,' she said. 'I know you're not separated for very long, and if I'd known this was your first weekend alone, I'd have said no to this date.'

His eyebrows arched. 'You would? Why?'

She shrugged, pushed her plate away from her, half of her food still remaining. 'Because you need time to just be you. You have to adjust to that first. And before you say anything,' she held a palm up, 'I know this is just a pizza, but even that. Just being in another woman's company. It takes time and my sense is you're not ready.'

'You talk an awful lot,' Theo said.

'Sorry,' she replied, without looking sorry at all.

'Don't apologize. It's quite refreshing. I did all the talking in my marriage.'

She looked surprised.

'Harriet's a lawyer, talks all day. Wants to be mute when she comes home — came home. So, what would Mars and Venus say about that?'

A waiter handed them both a dessert menu. 'That it's unusual,' Jacqueline said to Theo. 'No thank you,' she told the waiter. 'I'm full.'

'Nothing for me either.' Theo tapped his stomach.

He listened to her talking about her niece, a gymnast, good enough to be an Olympian some day; about her family, both of her parents living in Scotland, and her two siblings — brothers. His head bobbed in apparent appreciation.

'Coffee?' the waiter interrupted her flow. She shook her head and he followed her lead.

With the waiter out of earshot, she spoke again. 'I have coffee back at mine,' she said.

Theo hesitated, embarrassed. 'Another time . . . .'

Jacqueline placed both her palms on the table. 'When I said coffee back at mine, I really did mean coffee.'

Theo scratched his head and scrunched his flushing face. He picked up the bill and placed some notes on the tiny tray. When she started to object, he told her he had asked her out. It was his shout. He reached across the table, placed a hand over hers. 'No coffee, but I'd like to drive you home?'

'Thank you. That would be great.'

Outside the restaurant, she shivered in her coat. He offered her his arm and she looped hers through it as they walked to his car. Two cars from his, they noticed the couple from the restaurant, kissing passionately in the front of a car.

Jacqueline shook her head. 'There's nowt as queer as folk,' she said.

Theo grinned, though he felt as if his insides were coming apart at the seams. The night was young and he didn't want to be alone. He so didn't want to be alone that it alarmed him.

'Drop me home, maybe come in for a proper drink? I hate coffee.' She smiled as she faced him. 'I've got a lovely rioja open.'

He held his breath, dismissed the fact that he normally never drank after a headache, squeezed her arm and said, 'A rioja would be perfect.'

19
Jess

It's the Monday after half-term but school is out because of teacher-training day. Being a mere teaching assistant, I don't have to go in. I usually choose to anyway, but today I opt not to. Rose and I are walking; on our way to the high street to have her hair trimmed. She's holding my hand and swinging it front to back like a pendulum. The playground we pass is full of children still on holidays and Rose stops walking, looks up at me. 'Can we?' she asks. I look at my wrist. 'Five minutes. That's all.'

I hold onto her hand tightly until we get inside the gate, then I relax my grip and she's off. She runs to the swings, her eyes firmly on the prize — one free, the last one in a row of six. I follow and, when I reach her, stand behind, ready to push.

'High, Nanny,' she orders. I push her high as I dare and she squeals with delight. The sound fills me, reminds me I have parts of me that can only be replenished with laughter. I focus on it as the chains clink and gravity pulls her back to me. I focus on her happiness, imagine it filtering through my pores, nourishing my soul. I push the bad stuff from my mind, like the letter I received from Sean this morning, the one where he tells me he's seeking full custody of my granddaughter. Listening to the laughter in the playground, I can hear her laugh separately from those of the other children. Like a mother can tell the perfect, unique scent of her newborn, I can hear only Rose's joy. I focus on it now, this moment in time with her, and I can feel a smile shape my lips.

★ ★ ★

I push her curly fringe to one side of her face. Abigail, the girl who also cuts my hair, has put Rose in the chair and raised her as high as possible. I realize this is the first time I have ever brought her here. It would have been Anna before. All around us is the sound of dryers and people chattering and radio music piped through to speakers.

'I don't want short hair.' Rose speaks loudly to the mirror.

Abigail smiles.

'My hair is like Nanny's,' Rose states. She holds a hand out to me and I take it in mine. 'I want it to look like Nanny's.'

I laugh. 'I'm afraid when you're all grown up that it will and then you'll want straight hair.' Mine is, as usual, pulled into a bun, pinned into the back of my head. 'Just a trim,' I tell Abigail. 'Just so it's out of her eyes.'

Rose gives a triumphant grin and she looks so like Anna in that moment that my heart almost tears apart. Any fissures that it already has have just suddenly widened. Despite my earlier

147

confidence in the world, I wonder if I'm going to be capable of watching this child grow for another thirteen years before she will probably leave home. Will I be able to keep her and Anna separate? Will I be able to allow her to grow as the little individual that she is? Like Anna, but not Anna. They are the thoughts running through my head as Abigail leads Rose to the basin and as my phone vibrates in my hand.

I look at the number. Doug. He hasn't mentioned the money he lent me and I haven't raised it. *Oh, hell, not today, please.* I push the phone back down to the end of my bag.

Rose insists I sit beside her. 'Don't let the lady cut too much,' she says to both of us in the mirror. I'm in awe; five years old, her mother probably lost to her, yet already so sure of herself. I blow her a kiss. She catches it, tosses it back to me and I tap my heart. My phone rings again and I sigh, excuse myself, stand off to the side, tell Rose not to worry, that I'm watching.

I take a deep breath and answer the call.

'Doug,' I roll my fingers in an assuring wave to Rose.

'Jess.'

Immediately, instantly, I have that same sense flow through my body as I did when he came to my house that night seventy-eight days ago. Rose is chatting to Abigail. I catch some of her words. 'Daddy', 'school', 'Nanny', 'ballet', 'Lego'. She doesn't say 'Mummy'. Doug is talking and I'm thinking, *It'll be up to me and him now — it'll be up to Doug and me to make sure she never forgets her mummy.* I cannot leave that to Sean.

'Body' is the only real word I glean from Doug's quiet speech. He probably had to practise it, and here I am not even taking it all in: poor Doug. Rose waves and I try hard to smile back but it feels as though if I do, my face will crack. I concentrate on Doug, who is crying softly into the phone. I lean into his words, ask him to repeat some.

'Say something,' he says when he has repeated them all. His voice sounds like my face: fragile.

I can feel a pain in my jaw and search my quite extensive mental medical vocabulary for a word for it. When I used to work in the same surgery as Theo years ago, the staff would play medical word search games. Mandible. That's it. My mandible is throbbing. I can feel its beat cumulate to a crescendo until the only thing I can do is open my mouth wide. A sound competes against the salon noise and I immediately wish I could haul it back, shove it back in my mouth. Rose looks in the mirror, wide-eyed.

Abigail's hand guides me to the chair next to her. I now have my own mirror. And the sounds don't stop. I pray for them to stop. Please God. Make them stop. Rose is watching me. And, in my mirror, the horror unfolds. Anna's body has been found. My beautiful girl's body; maybe just her bones have been found in a crevice on the mountainside. I have a screaming mandible. My face is wet; months of stored-up grief finally flowing. Somehow Rose has made it down from her high chair and runs into my arms. She too is crying. With the palm of my hand, I stroke her wet, twisted hair.

Abigail has my phone in her hand. She's looking at it as if she doesn't know what to do with it. In her other hand, she still has scissors. Abigail's boss, a man named Marty, is standing beside me and Rose with a mug of tea. I shake my head, hold Rose tighter.

'I put sugar in it. Try and drink it. It's good for shock.'

I do as I'm told. I have always done as I was told. Ask my mum and dad. I have always been a good girl. Why, God, why?

It's moments before I realize I'm speaking aloud. Everyone is staring. Most are crying too. Rose raises her head and I offer her some tea. She takes a few sips and burrows into me again.

'Let me call someone for you,' Marty says, and my head bobs up and down. I'm not even sure what I'm agreeing to.

★ ★ ★

Leah is brilliant. I don't know why I don't describe her as my best friend, why I reserve that title for Theo. It's probably because she's my only sister and, as such, it's a given that we're close. Theo is my best friend apart from my sister. We're in her house. It's getting dark outside. Somehow Pug has magically appeared here and is snuggling on my lap. A white-faced Gus has carried an exhausted, sleeping Rose up to bed. I am nursing my second vodka and tonic. I only added the tonic when Leah told me I should. I am a good girl.

'Has anyone spoken to Sean?' Leah's voice is

150

so quiet it's almost still.

'Jesus, no. I mean, I don't know.'

'Shall I call him?'

I nod. My brain is shrieking thoughts inside my skull. Anna is dead. There is a body. Sean is Rose's father . . .

'She's okay,' I hear Leah say, and I know he's asked about Rose and not me. It's obvious he knows already from the brief conversation and Leah hangs up shortly after.

'He knew?' I ask.

She nods.

'Doug.' He's good like that, Doug. He will have made all of the calls so that I don't have to; has offered to go to Queyras alone so that I don't have to, but I'm going. Leah has already sorted taking some time off from chambers to look after Rose. Doug has booked our flights and tomorrow we return to the Alps, this time to identify Anna's remains, Anna's effects. She was only found after a thaw but still quite high up. I understand my baby was still mostly under snow. I refuse to allow the thoughts about her body to germinate, but some slip through the cordon just because the dreaded call came. I got the call . . .

I swirl the ice around my glass, look up and find Leah by my side. She removes it from my hand. I try to resist; there's a final gulp of vodka left. She gently replaces it with a strong coffee. 'You'll need your wits about you tomorrow.'

'Thanks for having Rose.'

'No problem. I spoke to Mum too.'

I throw my head back on the chair and shake it. 'I'm not even going to ask.'

Leah's lips form a — straight line. 'She's had to tell Dad. He's taken it very badly'

And again my phone emits a loud interrupting sound. Leah looks for me. 'Theo,' she whispers.

'Theo,' I say. 'Shit.'

She hands it to me.

'I'm at yours,' he says. 'You've not responded to texts and I need to see you. Where are you?'

'Theo —'

'You okay?'

'No.' I sob quietly into the phone. 'They found her.'

'Oh, Jess. Oh, Jess . . . Where are you, I'll come, I — '

'No, I'm with Leah and Gus. Doug and I are leaving for France in the morning. We'll talk when I get back.'

'Call me . . . if you need anything at all.' Theo falls silent as my tears continue.

'I'll call you when I'm back,' I say eventually.

I can imagine him nodding, but he says nothing else and I hang up. What can he say? What can anyone say?

I turn my phone off and throw it into the bowels of my bag. Leah stands, kisses my hair and picks up her glass, walks over to the dishwasher, sniffing loudly.

I follow her form across the room and wonder if she'll just let me go home. I really want out of here, don't want to talk any more and just want to be alone. I want to go into Anna's bedroom and spray her perfume all over me; crawl into her bed; wrap myself up in her covers; breathe in her scent as if my life depends on it — because I am

152

now that woman. I am the woman who got *that* call; the call to confirm that from here on in, every single night, my last waking thought will be about my daughter's last breath.

20

Anna

Raw Honey Blogspot 04/10/2014

On my twenty-third birthday, I got a tattoo. It sits just above my knicker-line on my hip and says 'Felix culpa'. It means 'happy fault' — or a mistake that has happy consequences. I thought it was much better than having her name on my body, and DD will forever be my happiest 'mistake'.

Of course He only got to see it last night, called it a 'tramp-stamp' and laughed. I told Him to get used to it because I intend getting more tattoos whenever the mood takes me. Then He traced the letters gently with his fingers; told me it's beautiful, that I'm beautiful, that our daughter is beautiful, and that his life is beautiful when I'm in it.

I'm going to hell because I cried in his arms. Happy, happy tears, because I felt like I was home. I let myself remember our first kiss; we talked about it, how it had frightened both of us, feeling what we felt. I let myself forget the guilt that consumed me when I went back for more.

I've never stopped loving Him. All that happened during the years apart is that I got better at managing the loss. Last night, I pushed all the bad stuff out of my mind and let Him hold me. Last night, none of the other shit mattered. Last night, I didn't punish myself for taking the latest phone call from Him; the one I knew that, if I answered it, we'd start this thing again. Last night, I didn't punish Him for making the call. Last night, we made slow gentle love and I allowed myself — He allowed himself — to believe that somehow we'd make this love work.

PART TWO

PART TWO

21

Jess

Doug's holding my hand. At least, my hand is gripping the armrest, my knuckles white, my nails almost breaking with the pressure of my grasp and Doug's hand is resting over my clawed fingers. He knows that nothing has changed with me and flying. I have always been filled with a pathological fear of the plane just dropping from the sky. Now, I realize I have more real fears to contend with. Life has a habit of tossing real reasons to be afraid; like losing Anna, who, it turns out, is the love of my life. I look at Doug's hand, veiny and lined, a scar visible just above his thumb where he ironed it years ago. I loved Doug, but losing him was something I recovered from. I'm not sure I will ever recover from losing Anna.

When we're in the air, I show him the text my mother sent me earlier today. It's like a letter, must have taken my elderly mother an age to use her arthritic thumb on her phone:

My darling girl,
You will miss her, your darling girl, every day of your life. You will have to learn how to breathe again so that your breath doesn't catch in your throat and leave you short. This you will do. I know you will. You will do it for you; you will do

159

it for us and you will do it for Rose. There's not a day goes by when I don't share your pain, my darling girl.

Mum x

He reads it, squeezes my hand again, then peers at the picture of Anna on the screen that I put there this morning. It's one of the ones Max emailed me from the ski-trip.

'Is that . . . ?'

'Yes. It's from the holiday. Max, a guy from her work, sent it to me. He came to visit me.'

'What did he want?'

'Just to talk. I think he wanted me to know she'd been happy, having a good time.'

His hand is back. It's laced with his other one in his lap.

'Did you do anything with her phone?'

'Leah knows someone who can get it unlocked.'

He nods.

Though it's a short flight, I order a drink. The hostess leans across Doug and he glances at her breasts. She smells of a heady perfume, something spicy. His gaze lingers on her a moment before his eyes return to mine.

'We should talk about arrangements,' he says.

A simple word, three syllables. 'Arrangements'. I'm imagining all the connotations; all the beautiful ways the word could be used. Attached to 'wedding', 'a night out' or 'a lover's tryst'.

'You have her will,' Doug continues. 'Did she want to be buried?'

I have the most inappropriate urge to laugh

160

out loud. *She was buried.*

'They're here, all the papers.' I tap my handbag. 'Cremated,' I add.

It's the answer he was expecting. 'Do you mind if we have a small, private service? Just family? I don't think I could face some big church thing . . . ' He hesitates. 'Everyone's grief. It's too much to bear.'

I stare at him, realise in that instant that Carol has been good for him. He is in touch with his emotions so much more; this is the man I strangled with my love. I clear my throat.

'Do you remember . . . ?' I'm not sure about this and hesitate.

'What?'

'When you left me?'

He reddens, wonders what's coming next.

'You told me my love strangled you.'

He straightens up, angles his face towards mine. 'I remember,' he says.

'I've never forgotten it. It was such a potent sentence.'

'I'm sorry.'

'I'm not asking you to apologize. All water under the bridge now but . . . I poured all of the love I had into Anna.' This, I conclude, must be neat alcohol talking.

'I was young. It was easier to walk away from something I couldn't handle,' is how he responds.

Next to me, through the cabin window, orange and white lights flicker from below. I think about the lives of the people who live in the tiny houses, in the tiny villages. Has life been kinder

161

to them? I shake my head, loathe the fact I'm feeling sorry for myself.

'You're happier with Carol, I can see that. I just never did get that word 'strangle',' I say.

'I couldn't breathe. I was young, wasn't ready to be loved like that. I'm sorry . . .'

'Don't be.' I exhale slowly. 'And yes, by the way.'

'Yes, what?'

'Yes. No fuss. Let's bury our daughter as quickly and as simply as possible.'

★   ★   ★

I can't remember when, but sometime recently, on Twitter, someone posted a link from NASA. Theo told me about it. Finn had told him. They had just released the biggest picture ever taken of the universe and, when I saw it, it made me realize just what a tiny chunk of the tiniest atom I am. It's on my mind today, that picture. I'm remembering the soft accompanying music; the way the camera zoomed into what was a microscopic spot on the photo, to reveal thousands of micro-lights — planets, stars, whatever. I'm wondering now if Anna is actually one of them; whether there is any truth in Rose's preferred idea of her mum. Is she a star? She was my star . . . Where has all that wonderful, intoxicating energy gone? Has it been swallowed up by the vast universe?

I'm thinking about NASA's galaxies because I don't want to think about my daughter's body. Doug and I are unable to be in the same room as

162

her. We are only offered the option of seeing her through a glass screen. I don't know why, but I assumed I could touch her. I've asked if I can touch her, only to be told by a kindly mortician in perfect, accented English that, no, that's not possible. Doug's hand is on mine again. He squeezes it, not a momentary comforting squeeze, but a fearful, 'we need to touch each other' one. The man with perfect English but perhaps a less than perfect tact is telling us that Anna's upper body has been almost perfectly preserved by the ice. The lower part, however, has 'suffered'.

I don't want to go there, but my thoughts race ahead rapidly, working out the different things her body might have endured. Images of her flesh rotting in the sun, animals scavenging her ankles, all make me want to throw up.

'You're all right.' Doug lets go of my hand and with his right arm holds me upright. 'You can do this. We can do this.'

He nods to the Frenchman who draws back a curtain with a short string made from tiny aluminium baubles. I stare at the string, at the way it catches the light just like the diamantés on Anna's phone, then I look downwards at the tiled floor. The morgue is silent, as a place for the dead should be. The only sound I hear is Doug's gasp as he claws his right fingers into my shoulder. I can't help it — I look up.

And there she is. Someone has pulled back the shroud-like sheet that covers her, pulled it back from her face and folded it in a neat, straight line just above her chest. The top of her right arm is

163

just visible, the tattoo she had only a few weeks ago obvious. *Carpe diem*. It screams its own special irony at me. My fingers make contact with the glass and I want to just reach out and touch her. I can't. I can't plead either. My voice has left me. No primal screams — just tears, silent tears, carving that now-familiar route down my face. She looks so beautiful. Just like normal. Her face, I can tell, has had some makeup applied. Her bright blue, sapphire eyes are closed. Her hair has been combed and I wonder who got that job, how long it took them. Was her face bruised in the fall? Dear God, how many bones did she break? If I could reach into her, if I could just bend into her, would she still smell of coconut shampoo?

Doug is nodding beside me and then suddenly the curtain closes. I want to cry out, I want to scream, NO. Please, just a few minutes, just leave me here for a few more minutes with her. I feel myself slide; can hear that smearing sound of fingers on glass as I fold onto the floor. At lower levels I smell antiseptic. How has this happened? Let me into my baby. How has my baby ended up in a sterile, white-tiled mortuary in south-east France?

Doug pulls me up and I fight him. I hit him, thump him; lash at him with my fingernails until I'm held against him so tight that I can barely breathe. I hold what's left firmly in my lungs. I don't want to breathe. I do not want to live without Anna. I don't know *how* to live without Anna. Then Rose pops into my head and I exhale in a loud burst.

We're in a tiny café in the town square. It's actually very mild and the sun's heat warms my face after the air-conditioned morgue. I have my sunglasses on. Anyone looking at Doug and me would think we're a couple holidaying, enjoying a few rays, protecting our eyes behind our large shades. He hasn't cried yet today. I look at his sepia image from behind my darkened lenses. He's staying strong for me and I'm grateful. Carol will probably hear his real grief and for the first time since I heard her name all those years ago, I'm grateful to her too. By his side on the floor sits Anna's suitcase, which we collected from the local police.

Doug takes a call, holds a hand up to excuse himself. I can tell it's Carol, followed by their children, Tom and Ethan. It's obvious by the way his voice changes, and I'm filled with the most anxious jealousy I have ever, ever felt. He still has children. Only eleven and eight; he will have them in his life for a very long time and is still able to offer that unique love. Just for a moment I hate him.

When he comes back, the *croque-monsieurs* have arrived. He nibbles the edge of his, a small string of cheese stretching from the toasted bread to his mouth. I only stare at mine. I haven't eaten properly in days, know I have to eat, so reach for it and raise it to my mouth. I look to the distance towards the chairlift, still carrying people to the slopes, all of them oblivious to the fact that our daughter died here.

165

'Can I have her things?' My eyes rest on the case and the white plastic bag from the mortuary containing her red suit.

He hesitates, which makes me look at him instead. I notice a small, fresh, long scrape on his neck, and realize I did that. I did that with my fingernails.

'Of course,' he says. 'I'd just like to have something of hers, from . . . from her last days.'

'Well, we can go through it together.'

'No, just send me something.' He shakes his head.

I nod towards a small hotel just next to us. 'We could go in there. Rent a room. Go through her case. You could choose something, and then, then you could hold me until we have to leave for the airport.'

Doug takes his glasses off, eyeballs me. I leave mine on. Then he nods, raises his food to his mouth and waves at the waiter for the bill.

Within ten minutes I'm standing in a first-floor room, overlooking the same town square view; the same vista of the chairlift and snow-capped peaks just to my right. I leave the shutters and the window open.

It's a pretty grim room, furnished simply with a shiny pine bed, wardrobe and chest of drawers and one metallic-looking bedside table. On top of that sits a lamp with an uneven fringed trim. To the right-hand side of the bed there's a tiny shower cubicle and loo behind a sliding door that no longer slides. Doug places the suitcase on top of the bed and together we slowly go through Anna's things. Both of us pick up different items.

166

Mine is a silky camisole top and I can't help thinking where in hell did she wear that in December? Doug has a polo-neck ski top. Both of us raise them to our noses to draw in her scent. He lets go of the polo-neck and his hands rest on a jumper, the palest of sky-blue colours. I recognize it as the one he gave her last Christmas.

'This,' he says, 'this is all I want.'

He quietly packs the things back in the case and I drop the camisole in. When he moves the case, he lies down on the bed and pats the empty space next to him. I climb in beside him, into his open arms, and we lie there, spooned, listening to each other's breathing, to the sounds of laughter outside.

'The receptionist,' I say. 'She thinks we're up here having a quickie.'

I can feel him smile into my hair.

'She thinks we're just another average couple, wanting a little afternoon delight,' I add.

He smooths out the back of my head. 'I'd forgotten how your hair gets up my nose.'

'I thought it was only my intense love did that.'

He angles me around to him. 'Enough. Okay? It's not funny.'

'No.' I swallow hard. 'Nothing's funny.' Tears fall again and he wipes them away with his fingertips. 'She's really dead, isn't she?' I say.

He nods, silently.

'She was just so beautiful,' I say, and he pulls me to his chest. Lying there on his Lacoste jumper, which Carol probably bought, we whisper nonstop memories of Anna. We cry. We smile. And by the time we leave for the airport, Doug with her blue jumper under his arm, we agree that, somehow, we have to fight Sean to ensure Rose stays with me.

22

Jess

I'm cold. It's as if I have the opposite of a fever. I'm shaking a lot, have a clammy sweat all over, and feel as though I will never be warm again. The heating's on full and Rose is running around half naked after her shower. I tell her to get her school uniform on quickly or she'll die of the cold and, when I realize what I've said, I burst into tears.

She approaches, wraps her tiny arms around my neck. 'Don't cry, Nanny,' she says. 'It's 'cause of Mummy, isn't it?'

I'm unable to say or do anything, so I grab the nearby towel to wrap around her.

'Finn says,' she whispers in a low voice, 'Finn says that Mummy can keep singing with the angels.'

'Finn?' My brow creases.

'Nanny, you know Finn! From your class!'

I nod my head. Of course. School. Finn. Theo's Finn.

'Remember the singers Mummy was in?'

I nod again, know she's talking about the choir Anna sometimes sang with. I'm grateful for the chat of my gorgeous girl, grateful that she's here.

'She can always sing because heaven has lots of singers,' she says. 'Finn told me — for the angels.'

169

Today is not the day to tell my granddaughter that I do not believe in heaven and angels. Today is not the day to even think that I do not believe in heaven and angels.

I'm on automatic pilot when I fill her lunch box, when I drop her off, when I kiss her goodbye and nod to my colleagues who all smile sympathetically, some of them approaching to give me a wordless hug. Helen, the head, has been brilliant, telling me to take my time. They have a supply assistant in and I've been told to take 'whatever I need'. In the playground I spot Finn, just as the bell peals.

I call his name and he turns around, walks back to me. 'You're keeping an eye on Rose. Thank you.'

He shrugs, a nonchalant movement of his shoulders that only pre-pubescent boys can give. I know, though, I know he's a sensitive soul under the bravado.

'She told me that you've said Anna's still singing.'

'I hope she is,' he says, then looks as if he's doubting his own words. 'I'm not sure she is. I sort of believe more in aliens and spaceships.' His eyes glance up towards the sky. 'But I remember her at the Christmas service singing, and Rose likes the idea.'

I bite my lower lip, reach across and give him a quick hug, which he accepts reluctantly.

'Singing,' I nod. 'You're right. It's good to remember her singing.'

I head back to the car and sit in it, unable to start the ignition. Anna's voice. I can hear it as if

170

a radio has been turned up loudly. She's singing an aria — one I can't remember the name of, but I went to hear her and the other girls from college sing it in some church years ago. Her voice fills the car and I head for home. Doug will be here in an hour. We have what we both want to be a small private funeral to plan. I haven't yet told him that I've had over fifty emails asking me for the details. It looks as if Anna will be getting a bigger send-off than any of us had planned.

'I don't care.' This is Doug's response when I tell him later about the many messages. 'We need to get this done quickly and privately.'

At first I say nothing. I agree with him, but feel we cannot ignore her friends. 'We need to acknowledge the other people who loved her,' I say quietly.

He stands up from the tatty sofa, looks out of the window onto the back garden. 'I still can't believe this is happening,' he says.

'Nor me.' I join him by the window. He puts his arm around my shoulder. 'She was the one thing we did perfectly.' He seems choked by his own words.

'She was,' I breathe deep, lean into him.

'I've already spoken to the crematorium.' He breaks away from me and blows his nose. 'We can keep that small and private. It's booked for next Monday. She arrives from France on Friday then straight to the local funeral directors.'

I nod. It's as if we're having a conversation about Anna having been away and needing collecting from the airport.

'Let's just go down the road and see if the

171

church will let us hold a memorial service there,' Doug says. 'If they can do the Monday morning, then we'll take it as a sign that this thing should be bigger than either of us wants.'

We are not churchgoers, either of us. I don't know the name of the vicar at St John's. The last time I was there was a couple of years ago for a Christmas carol service, and only then because Anna's college choir, who still came together a few times a year, were singing. But I find myself agreeing with Doug, and before I know it we're parked in his car in the car park at St John's.

'Do you know where to go?' he asks.

I look around. 'There must be a house, I — '

'There.' He points to a Victorian red-brick building tucked behind the right-hand side of the church. 'Okay, let's do this.'

I want to but my legs won't move. They feel suddenly leaden, as though I've been planted in concrete. 'I — '

'You all right?'

'I don't think . . . '

He places a hand on my arm. 'You wait here. I'll do it.'

He is gone for almost twenty minutes. Each of them, I spend trying to wriggle my toes. They move but my legs don't want to. I'm consumed by the notion that maybe I'm temporarily crippled and I laugh out loud. Of course I'm crippled. Grief has finally felled me. Filled my legs with concrete and rendered me still for ever.

I look at the church, at the bell tower on its roof. I ask the God who presides over it to please let my legs work. I tell Him that I really need my legs to move. I need to move for Rose. Rose needs me to move. I tell this God that Anna was a good person and ask Him if he's real, to welcome her, to welcome her with love and kisses and open arms and . . . By the time Doug returns to the car, I am sobbing. I cannot speak. Any word I try to form comes out a guttural sound. Snot pours from my nostrils; big, globby tears fall, and even when I think the well must be dry, more come.

Doug holds me. There, in his car, with me stretched across the handbrake into his arms, I shake uncontrollably. And he holds me, kisses my hair, says nothing; just holds me until it subsides.

'He'll do it,' Doug whispers. 'Name is John, believe it or not. John at St John's. Monday morning at ten thirty. Should take about an hour. He's told us we can have whatever music we want. I have his email.'

'We should see if we can get the old choir.' I sniff.

Doug holds me out in front of him. 'Do you want me to do this?'

I know he means, do I want him to make all of the arrangements? I know he'd like it if we could do it together, but the lead in my legs stops me. 'Can you? I mean, are you able to? I'd just want a couple of songs she loved, otherwise . . . ' I don't finish the sentence, but he understands that otherwise I'd like him to sort it all. Come next Monday, I want to pretend that we're going to a surprise party for Anna.

'I'll do it. I'll call her office too, deal with the

insurance claim, to make sure they have everything they need so that you and Rose are sorted soon.'

And I know he will. He'll do Anna proud because — despite anything that passed between him and me — he has been a wonderful father to Anna, and his eyes, red raw at their edges, tell me that his tears are not spent either.

Back at mine, we share a sandwich. Doug is copying the emails that have been sent to me over to his phone so that he knows who to contact. My iPad and his phone ping at the same time and we look at each other, surprised. On the screen, I see we have a message from the French authorities confirming the release of the body. It attaches a copy of the post-mortem report. Two documents: the first a one-page summary and the other a more lengthy report.

'We should read them,' he says, not sounding convinced.

I shake my head. I need to believe she died in the fall. I don't want to know if she struggled to breathe in some underground tomb for days. He opens the summary. Thankfully it's in French and I don't speak a word. Doug studied French at university.

'She died in the fall,' he whispers, and I let go of the breath I wasn't aware I'd been holding. I'm watching him and his expression turns from one of relief to one of instant confusion. Below his creased brow, his eyes look directly at me. 'Who was Anna seeing?' he asks. There is almost an accusation in the question.

'What?'

'A boyfriend?'

'I don't know. No one, why?' I cannot fathom why he'd ask such a stupid question at this moment in time. 'Maybe the Max guy, but I don't think so . . . ' I watch Doug's face pale and feel the blood drain from my own.

He looks up from the screen. 'She was nine weeks pregnant.'

★ ★ ★

I've opened the vodka again and we're sharing the tumbler I poured. Doug put some ice in it and took the first slug. I'm not letting go of the glass. The clock on the oven flashes neon yellow, warning me I have an hour and a half before I need to collect Rose from school. I allow myself two mouthfuls in quick succession, let it slide down. I will it to turn left and cut through my heart. Just slice right through it. At least it would account for the pain I feel — as if someone has formed a fist around it and is squeezing it with the tightest of grips.

Anna started work at the bank a year ago. Since then, to my knowledge, she has had no boyfriends. If she was seeing someone, if she was sleeping with someone, she would have told me. There is Max, but they were just friends. 'Anna would have told me,' I say this aloud to a distraught Doug. 'She just would have told me if there was someone.'

He shrugs. 'A one-night stand?'

'Or a mistake. There might be a mistake in the report.'

'Jess, these people don't make mistakes like this.'

'Are you sure?' I'm now pacing the length and breadth of the kitchen-diner, the width of my house. Twenty-two steps each way. 'Maybe your French?' I stop walking.

He shakes his head. 'She was pregnant. Again.'

I hear it then, a trace of resentment, anger even, but don't react. Doug and I have not spent this much time together since we were married, and I think we probably both need to process this in our own way.

'I need to get Rose soon.' Code for: leave now, please. Thank you for your help but now I need to be alone.

'And I need to get home.' Code for: I want Carol to hold me now. Thanks for today, but I need the woman I love to help me with this.

We look at each other, both of us desperate.

'I'll call you. We need to talk about Sean, his letter, what we do . . . we never did.' Doug sighs.

'Leah has it. She has someone in work looking at our options.' I decide not to relay that she has already told me that the word 'father' trumps 'grandparent' in any court, and our chances of keeping Rose are slim. I've been pretending Leah never said it at all, and I have no intention of repeating it. Not today.

He nods, leans over and kisses my cheek. 'I'll call you,' he repeats, and then he is gone.

★   ★   ★

I see Theo at the school and he waves, comes over to me as I get out of the car.

176

'You not in work?' I ask.

'I am, just having a very late lunch. I'm in for evening surgery.' He takes hold of my shoulders. 'Was it as awful as I imagine? Stupid question, of course it was. I'm sorry, Jess. Come here.' He pulls me into a hug.

'You wanted to talk to me before, before I left for France. What was it?' I pull away from him. The low sun is shining in my eyes and I raise my right hand to shield them from the glare. He looks great; a new suit and shoes, and something like a designer stubble on the end of his chin. That's it — he just looks different. All scrubbed up and shiny. A quick thought that he's seeing someone circles my brain. 'You look really well.' I reach up and touch his face. 'I like this look.' We are here, Theo and I, having this moment in the school car park — me telling him I like his new look, when all I want to do is scream, 'Anna was pregnant!' I'm like a bird on a nearby branch, watching the scene below unfold — two friends having a nice moment together.

Theo blushes lightly, unconsciously raises his hand to his face.

'Come over later,' I say. 'Let's have a takeaway.'

'Good idea. I do need to talk to you. What time?'

'When Rose is in bed. After eight?'

'Right, see you then.'

He turns away and I watch him retreat to his car. Normally we would stand here together if we meet at the school gate, but today is different. *That* thought returns and my breath catches a

177

little when I realize what he might want to say to me. I wonder if he's sleeping with someone; how long it's been going on and whether I know her. I wonder who Anna was sleeping with, how long it was going on and whether I know him. My stomach contracts with all of it, and it takes everything I have not to throw up on the grass verge at the school gate.

I hear Rose call my name and paint a smile on my face. Whatever happens, Rose is now my reason for breathing in and out.

23

Jess

Ginger has a way of getting up my nose. Theo texted earlier to say he'd bring the takeaway, took my order and now he's here, unloading enough food from a large brown paper bag to feed an army.

'I just asked for a savoury rice.' I help him unload, my head shaking at the waste. Pug yaps around our feet, sensing food scraps.

'I thought if you saw more food, it might tempt you to eat,' Theo says.

I keep quiet the fact that the scent of ginger is already putting me off.

Within minutes, we're settled with our laptop suppers, him in the tatty sofa and me in the armchair.

'Jane is being made a partner at the practice,' he says.

'Oh.' I know Theo has had his eye on that ball for some time.

'Yep, Marsha took me in and told me how important I am to them, how the patients love me, how vital I am, yet somehow Jane is the one being offered a partnership. Bottom line is she has the money to buy in and they know it.'

We're having one of those conversations that Theo and I have where one of us does all the talking. I let him get on with it, content to listen and nod for now, until he eventually asks me how I'm doing.

'My parents are coming down here at the weekend.' I ignore the question he's actually asked.

'They are?'

'I haven't had the chance to tell you yet, but we're having a memorial service on Monday. Down the road in St John's.' I place my plate on the coffee table in front of me.

Theo just stares at the floor, as if he doesn't believe I'm telling him we're holding a service for Anna. I don't believe it either.

'So yes, Mum and Dad are here from Sunday until Tuesday.'

'Do you need any help? I can — '

'We'll be fine. Thanks. Look, Theo, nice as this is when we play happy married people with a takeaway, what's up? You didn't seem yourself at the school earlier.'

He puts his cutlery down, stops eating, and wipes his mouth with a paper napkin. 'I suppose I just know I'm talking about anything but the obvious. France, Anna . . . I don't know whether to ask you how it was, or pretend you didn't have to do it at all.'

'She was pregnant!' I blurt it out. 'Nine weeks. I had no idea; didn't even know she was seeing someone. It could be that bloke Max she works with — *worked* with . . . ' My hand goes to my chest. 'It could be anyone. I don't know. If it was Sean, I'm probably in deeper shit than I thought.'

He is silent, but I can almost see his brain working behind his eyes.

'Jess.' He clears his throat.

I have noodles tripping from my mouth. 'Theo?' The word sounds like 'Fee-ooh'. 'What?'

'There's something I've wanted to talk to you about,' he says, before breathing deep. 'You know Anna was my patient.'

'Jesus, you knew.' I let the noodles escape onto the plate. 'Of course you did — '

'Jess, let me talk.'

I catch his eye, tilt my head in annoyance. He has been talking all bloody evening. He knew Anna was pregnant. I clamp my mouth shut.

'She was my patient and so anything we talked about is confidential. She came to me . . . '

Patient confidentiality. He's hiding behind not telling me things because he swore some oath twenty years ago. His mouth is still moving and I stop the image of me slapping his face becoming reality when I hear the word 'termination'.

'What?' I say. 'Rewind?'

'She had booked a termination for her return. And look, before you go getting all pissed off, Anna was entitled to her own choices and expectant that I'd never discuss them.' He almost whispers his next words. 'Confidentiality continues after death.'

A termination. 'Why tell me now?' I shake my head.

'Because I *can* tell you now and because of Sean . . . '

I unfold my legs from underneath myself, lean forward in the chair. 'What has Sean got to do

181

with anything? Was it his? Was the baby Sean's?'

Theo reaches across from the tatty sofa and takes my hand. 'Stop talking, Jess, and please listen. Anna gave me a letter when she started working in the bank.'

My thoughts are jumbled. I think of all the times that they spent together. They were friends. We were all friends. Theo and I are friends . . . The times she worked at the surgery during school holidays, or later when she interned there for a whole summer while at university. There was the choir thing, some regular charity choral event that Theo organized; she babysat for Finn right up until she left for France. She and Harriet were close, too. Memories of our last Christmas together in their home flood my brain. Theo is still talking, my hand still resting in his.

'When she started her job, the bank were sorting health and life insurance for her and she said it had got her thinking. She said if anything ever happened to her,' he hesitates, 'if anything ever happened to her, she felt you should know the truth.'

My open mouth is gaping.

'I told her that anything we had ever discussed was confidential and that I'd be bound by oath never to speak about it — unless someone, somehow, was in danger.' He shrugs. I watch his broad shoulders move up, then down. 'She wrote the letter, only to be opened if . . . if . . . It gave me her permission to speak.'

I take my hand back, begin to rock back and forth on the chair. 'What are you talking about?'

182

He stands and I'm forced to look up at him as he paces. He stops, looks out towards the garden to the black night, and seems to be wishing he wasn't here. 'Anna was involved with someone on and off for a few years. She never told you.'

'Who? Involved with who?' My hands grip my head.

'I'd have known. What are you saying?'

'I only knew she'd been seeing someone years ago. She told me that much when she worked in the surgery the last summer she was in uni. By then it was over, but she just needed someone to tell; blurted it out one day after work . . . '

'I don't believe this.' My hands clasp my hair, pulling it at the roots.

'Recently, they'd started seeing each other again.'

'I don't fucking believe this. None of this makes sense. And I thought *we* were friends.' I stand, take his plate from where he left it. He hasn't finished his food but I'm taking it anyway.

'We are friends. It's because we're friends that I'm here.'

'Friends don't lie to each other.' I stack his plate on top of mine and am about to sit down again when he tries to take my hand.

'I never lied.'

I pull away. 'You did! When she went to see you last. You said it was about travel sickness or something . . . I don't remember! Something like that, I remember asking you around the time of the accident. And this other shit? She was 'seeing someone'. What the hell does that mean? Why wouldn't she just tell *me?*'

'Jess. Stop.'

That's twice now. Twice I've been told to stop talking. 'I can't do this. This is my house. I think you should go now.' I grab the plates and march back to the dishwasher. 'Did you hear me? Go!'

It's too much: too much to take in. Anna was pregnant again. Anna was going to have a termination. My head shakes. And I knew nothing. She told me everything, yet I knew nothing. How is that even possible?

Theo follows me, stands a few feet away. 'The guy she was seeing, the father, he was married. That's why she never told you.'

I drop the plate. It smashes all over the floor. He moves.

'Leave it!' I yell.

Both of us stare at the scattered pieces on the tiled floor. Bean sprouts, noodles, sweet and sour sauce. Pug is there in an instant and I yell at her too, before leaning on the sink.

Concrete again. It fills my legs. The words 'father' and 'married' are rolling around my head. *Anna would not do that. No. Anna would not do that.*

'When she last came to see me, just before France, she was heartbroken.' Theo is still talking. 'She had just told him she was pregnant. He'd reacted angrily and she knew it was over.'

I hold my hand up, hold my stomach with the other.

Theo moves towards me.

'No!' I cry.

He stills. 'She told me that day that she didn't want to bring a second child of his into the world

184

knowing how he felt . . . '

The nausea is coming in waves now. I breathe in between. 'A *second* child of *his?* My God. Sean isn't Rose's father?'

Theo shakes his head and my knees buckle.

He catches me but fails to pull me up; instead we both end up on the floor amongst the food and the shattered plate. I see for the first time that he hasn't changed out of that lovely new suit. Now there's orange sauce all over the knees.

'Your suit,' I sob. *Anna wouldn't do that.*

He pulls me to him and I'm enveloped by him. His arms circle around me and I disappear in his bulk. I fight him at first. I can't breathe, but his grip is so firm I give in to being held because I need it. I need him to hold me and tell me everything. He pulls me gently away from the debris, sliding me and him along the floor, sits with his back against the fridge, doesn't let go. Pug settles at his feet, her eyes like dark brown marbles, watching us warily.

'Did she tell you who?' I look up at him, my voice almost hoarse.

He shakes his head, his eyes closed.

'Why you? Why couldn't she talk to me? I don't get it.'

His grip tightens and he's stroking my hair and I can't bear it, it's so calming, so soothing. Something in me is screaming but I'm also hypnotized. 'Anna.' I speak her name. *She wouldn't do that.*

His hand keeps moving as he repeats what he knows: Anna had been seeing a married man when Rose was conceived. He is, according to her, Rose's father. They had an on-off relationship for a couple of years, more off than on, before Anna finally finished it. The relationship had only started up again last October.

None of it makes any sense. Enveloped by Theo, I'm cast back in time to when Rose was born. Anna wasn't seeing anyone. Sean was around but as Rose's dad. He and Anna had been together only briefly. Jesus . . . Sean . . . My hand forms a soft fist and I hit Theo's chest rhythmically as tears fall. *Anna wouldn't do that.*

Yet here we are, Theo and me, sitting in Chinese left-overs on my kitchen floor. She had told him about an affair. He has a letter.

'This letter.' I force myself to stop crying. 'Does it say anything else? It — '

'It just allows me to talk to you, to tell you what I know.' I feel his head shake. 'I only know Sean's not Rose's dad and that Anna was pregnant again. That's it. Jess, I could have had that letter for ever, unopened. She gave it to me to cover me talking to anyone, to release me from my oath — that's all. Maybe she'd have told me more over time. Maybe she'd have told *you* more over time. Actually, I think she would have . . . '

The tears fall again and for ages, we sit there, huddled in the strangest of poses — him covered in sweet and sour, rubbing my head, and me enclosed, foetal-like, in his arms.

I pull away, just enough to look up at him. His eyes are closed again.

'Theo.' I am sobbing.

186

They open. His lashes are damp too. With his free hand he smudges away my tears with his thumb, leans his head down to me and kisses my cheeks.

A tiny turn; the smallest of angles of his mouth. That's all it takes and we're kissing. A gentle touching of mouths, nothing else, but our lips meet and . . . cement again. This time locking his lips with mine.

We had a moment once. A long time ago. He walked me home after a Christmas party when I worked with him at the surgery. I was single. He wasn't. We shared a drunken kiss at the end of my driveway. We've never spoken of it since, not once, so it never happened.

But sitting here amongst the bean sprouts, as my heart is hanging onto bits of itself, as I fear it's going to remain a shredded mess for ever, as the words *Anna wouldn't do that* repeat over and over again in my head, it's that moment I recall, before something close to reality kicks in.

'No, no, Theo. No.' My voice catches as I move away from him, stand up. 'You are my friend. I don't have many friends.'

He struggles to stand, slips on the sauce again and finally faces me. He tries to touch my cheek, but I turn away.

'I'm sorry.' I shake my head. 'It's the shock — this whole thing.' I reach for his hand. 'I've lost Anna, the dearest person in the world to me. Sean is fighting me for Rose. I don't want to lose you too.'

He sighs, accepts the madness of the moment. 'At least let me help you keep Rose. You can prove Sean's not the father.'

'DNA?'

He nods.

'How do I get him to take the test?'

'Try asking him. Tell him you've found something in Anna's papers. If necessary, I can confirm what I knew, now I have that letter.' He reaches for and squeezes my hand.

I kiss his cheek. 'Back to cheeks. Let's forget that . . . Please.' I walk back to the sink.

'Okay. I suppose we're good at that,' Theo says, and follows me. He pulls a handkerchief from his top pocket and soaks it under the sink, dabs it on his orange knees. It will never work. His suit and my perfect image of my only child. Both ruined.

★ ★ ★

I wake with a start. Sweat runs in streams between my breasts. Tiny crusts of salt glue my eyelashes together. The clock says 03:04 a.m. The house is still, silent. The only sound I can hear is my own heartbeat.

None of it makes sense, and when something makes no sense, jars you awake in the middle of the night, it's usually because there's something missing. My weary brain lists the facts as I huddle under the duvet, suddenly cold, despite perspiring.

The letter. A letter only ever to be opened in the event of her death. Why would Anna give Theo permission to speak about an affair, about the fact that someone else had fathered Rose,

188

without actually ever saying who?

I reach for my phone and send him an immediate text.

The letter. I want to see it. J x

24

Jess

Doug has told Leah about the pregnancy. He shouldn't have. That was mine to do and only after I'd had time to process it myself. I have needed to try and get Anna's pregnancy — and the news that I know nothing about my own daughter — straight in my own head. Leah has called and I've texted back, asking for some time, just a bit of time. When I think I'm ready, I call her. 'You're up.' I look at the neon numbers on the oven.

'Just about to jump in the shower. You okay?'

'No.' Suddenly, my heart-rate quickens and I begin to sweat. I'm not ready to say any of this out loud. 'Leah, sorry, I shouldn't have called, sorry.'

'Jess — '

'Leah, just pretend I never called. I'll be fine. Talk later, okay?'

I hang up the phone, stand staring out at the garden. I'm still in my pyjamas and my naked feet are frozen on the tiled floor of the kitchen. I hug my arms, look around the room, wonder why I don't actually have a proper dining table in here. Why the tatty sofa and a worse armchair? I should get rid of them. I open the back door and am pulling the small sofa into the garden when I hear my front door open. I blow my hair from

190

my face and look up to see Leah.

She heads straight to the kettle and fills it. 'What has that poor sofa ever done to you?' she asks.

'I need to get rid of it.' I've managed to pull it to the back door but am trying to figure out how it can be so small yet still look as if it's not going to fit through. Leah approaches, pulls the sofa away from me towards its original space.

'No!' I tug it back again.

'What the hell, Jess? What's going on?'

I slump into the chair, with my right thumb and forefinger begin to pull at a loose piece of material. 'Anna and I were meant to upholster this.'

'I'll help you.' Leah squeezes into the space beside me.

'It's such a stupid size. It's too big for one and too small for two.'

'That's why you bought it.' She points to the television on the furthest wall and then to my breakfast bar. 'Up here is where Rose can do her homework while you make dinner, and over there, she can watch telly. This sofa is big enough for you and her to sit and watch something together. It's perfect.'

'It was for either Anna or me to sit with Rose in.' I nod.

'This is the chill-out zone and next door is the sort of grown-up room.'

'I don't do zones. They're your thing. I think I need a dining room.'

'You don't. You need a nice cup of tea.' She stands up, heads back to the boiled kettle.

'You need to get to work.'

'You need to let me help you.'

'I'm sorry.' I hug my arms tight, and walk to one of the two seats at the small bar that divides the room. 'I really shouldn't have called you.'

'Yes, yes you should. You need me, you call me. That's what we do.'

'No.' I shake my head. 'It's not what we do.' I catch Leah's eye, note her stretched, arched eyebrows. 'It's not what we do,' I repeat. I have never been one to 'call people', and if I did, it wouldn't have necessarily been Leah.

I feel her hand over mine; look down at the worktop that mine is clutching the edge of, as if it's the only thing that's grounding me.

'It's what we do now, Jess,' she whispers.

'Theo came around.' I lift the cup of tea she has placed in front of me, glance at the clock, aware that Rose will surface any minute. 'He knew that Anna was pregnant.'

She sips from her cup, gives a slow, acknowledging nod. 'I suppose it makes sense. He was her GP.'

'She had booked a termination.'

'Oh . . . '

'She told Theo she'd been seeing a married man.' I watch Leah's face react. Her eyes scrunch; her mouth opens as if to say something, and then she seems to think about it, stop herself. What she can't stop is herself frowning.

'Who?' she asks.

'He doesn't know, but she had been seeing him for a long time, on and off since she went to uni.'

'What?' Leah puts her cup down, stares at me. 'Say that again?'

'You heard me.'

'Jesus ... ' She takes the seat at my side, gulps. 'Jesus,' she says again.

'So, I thought I'd have a dining table in here.'

'Right.'

'I thought I'd just put the tatty sofa in the garden and make room for a dining table.'

'You don't need a dining table,' Leah says. 'You do need a break, though. The universe should give you a bit of a fucking break.'

My eyes look to the ceiling, towards the sounds upstairs. 'She's up,' I say. 'I'll just go and get her.'

Minutes later, I'm back downstairs, a sleepy Rose in my arms. 'Guess who's come to see us even though it's only breakfast time?'

She puts her arms out to Leah and my sister lifts her into her own, enfolds her, and sits down with her on her lap on the tatty sofa, which she has moved back to its original position. Rose bends like an 'S' shape into her, sucks her thumb.

'See?' Leah says. 'It's perfect.' She swallows hard and seems to be inhaling the scent of Rose's hair. '*She's* perfect,' she adds.

'Yes.' I nod. 'Yes, she is.'

★   ★   ★

Leah is back two days later, Saturday, helping me in Anna's room. She has offered to have Mum and Dad at hers, but it's best they're here.

193

Dad could not navigate her stairs; all glass and shiny and nothing for him to hang onto. She has even offered to change her dining room into a downstairs bedroom. I look at her and love her. She is a beautiful being, my sister.

But we're here, in Anna's bedroom, about to strip her linen from her bed.

'You don't have to do this,' Leah repeats.

Rose is next door in her room. I can hear the puppet voices of the DVD she's watching.

'I do have to do this sometime. So, let's do it now.' I lift the duvet from the top of the bed, snap open the poppers at the end and start to remove it. Leah pulls the other side until I can lift the cover into my hands. I raise it to my nose, tell myself that it still has her scent but, months later, all it really has is a thin film of dust, and I sneeze. It drops to the floor and we continue until there is a small pile of linen.

'There,' I say aloud, proud of myself. I have managed one thing I really didn't want to do today.

'Alan, the guy in work who I gave the phone to,' Leah says. 'He's been out for a few days but he texted me to say he's got it unlocked. I'll have it on Tuesday.'

Today is Saturday. I'm about to ask her why not Monday, when I realize what day Monday is. She won't be in work. She will be in the church with me and a hundred others.

'And the letter to Sean . . . ' She picks up the crisp white cotton linen, Anna's spare set, that we're about to put on the bed. 'It's been sent.'

My hand rubs my stomach automatically.

When Leah spoke to a solicitor friend, their advice was to work quickly with Sean, not to allow time to pass where he would be organizing another life for Rose. I'd argued. I argued because I just didn't want him to be hurt the way I knew he would be. I've never been his biggest fan, but the timing of this sucks. This whole thing sucks, but Sean is going to get our request for DNA just before Anna's funeral. I shake my head.

Our conversation is halted by a sound coming from the doorway. Both of us look up from making the bed at the same time. Rose is almost hyperventilating ten feet away.

'What are you *doing?*' she wails.

'Rose, love.' I'm by her side in a nanosecond. 'What's the matter?' I bend down to her eye level.

'What are you doing to Mummy's bed? You have to keep it the same!' She runs from my grasp and throws herself on the bed. Leah reaches for her and Rose screams.

'Leave me alone! You can't touch Mummy's bed!'

'Okay, okay, stop screaming, Rose.' I come and sit by her on the bed, rub her back. 'Tell me what's wrong, darling.'

She doesn't move from her spread-eagled position. 'You can't change Mummy's bed. We have to keep it the same.' She is sobbing now. 'For when she comes home.'

Leah catches my eye. Her face, a young forty-three until that moment, ages before me as her features crumple. Singing angels and Anna's star status in the night sky disappear in an instant. Rose thinks Anna is coming back, and I have to choose whether to break my granddaughter's heart now or break it some other day. Seeing Rose's expression, the coward in me opts for another time.

'Darling, Grandma and Gramps are coming to stay for a few days and Anna won't mind if they borrow her bed.'

Rose squeezes her eyes shut. 'No!'

Leah reaches for her hand and holds it tight. 'Sweetheart, Gramps can't manage the stairs in my house so he has to stay here?'

Rose sits up, crying. 'Nanny, you sleep in here and they can have your bed.'

'Okay' I nod. 'Can Nanny have clean sheets?'

'No.'

'Okay, come here. Don't cry. Nanny will sleep here. Come on, up to me.' I pull her tiny frame from the bed and she clings to me like a limpet. Leah watches helplessly.

'Let's go make pizzas,' she says after a few minutes. 'Rose, you want to?'

Rose nods her head, peels herself from me and jumps into Leah's arms. I follow behind, past the pile of linen that I now know I'll have to wash, dry and put back on the bed tonight while Rose is asleep.

She is helping Leah to grate mozzarella when we hear a car pull up on the driveway. I stare anxiously towards the hall.

'You expecting anyone?' Leah is rubbing her hands on a towel, about to go to the front door.

'No, but I'll go.' My slippered feet pad across

196

the hallway, expecting it to be Theo on the other side, finally responding to my texts, Anna's letter tucked under his arm.

Tonight, I do not need to see Sean and his éclair mother on my doorstep, but the Gods, in their infinite wisdom, send them to me anyway. Rose, however, is thrilled to see her daddy, so I reluctantly invite them in.

'Poppet!' Mrs Dwyer bends down to hug Rose.

'We thought we'd come by and see you both.' She mouths the rest of her sentence to me, which looks like 'because we're in the area, you know . . . '.

I bite my tongue. They are in the area. Jesus. They are here to attend their granddaughter's mother's funeral.

'How *are* you coping, Jess?' Mrs Dwyer's head shakes so much, I can't help but wonder how it's still attached.

Sean looks uncomfortable, his hands in the pockets of a blazer-like jacket, both his thumbs protruding out of the top.

'Can I get you something?' I ask as we make our way to the front living room. Rose is still covered in flour from her efforts in the kitchen, and proceeds to invite them for home-made pizza. Thankfully, Sean mutters something about having already eaten. 'Now, listen,' Grandma Éclair whispers to me as Rose chats to Sean, 'George and I are here on Monday. We'll take Rose, keep her busy . . . '

I catch Sean, who had been looking at me, avert his eyes.

'Clara,' I call her by her correct name. 'Rose will be with us on Monday. Me and Doug, who are burying her mother.'

'Yes, well, we — '

'Jess,' Sean is standing. 'Let's talk in the kitchen?'

Clara nods at no one in particular, claps her hands and bends down to play with Rose.

He begins in the hallway. 'I think that Rose — '

'Sean. Rose is coming on Monday.'

We have made it to the kitchen, where Leah is presiding over half-made pizzas. Sean glares at her. 'Leah,' he almost growls.

He has obviously opened his post.

'As you're both here,' he glances back towards the living room, 'what in Christ's name are you playing at?' The words seethe from his mouth.

Leah looks at the floor.

'We have our reasons, Sean. I'm not doing this to hurt you,' I say.

'A DNA test?' He nears me and I feel the need to back away. 'She is *my* daughter, you hear? *My* daughter.' He jabs the air with a forefinger. 'I have loved her for nearly six years!'

'I'm sorry.'

'You're doing this because you don't want her to move away with me. You're doing it to spite me. You've never liked me. Well, tough shit. I'm her father.'

He's right. I've never really liked him, and if I could have done anything to delay him taking Rose, I'd have done it — even this, had I thought of it.

'Then you won't mind taking the test.' Leah is

198

wiping flour from the worktop with a cloth. She doesn't even look up. 'You're her father? The DNA will prove it and then you and Rose can shimmy off to Blackpool happily.'

My hand touches my chest and I stare at her. I have only Theo's version of what Anna said. What if she lied for some reason? I don't want —

'I'm not sure we'll be 'shimmying' anywhere, Leah, but come June, Rose will be moving to Lytham St Annes to live with me and my parents.'

I swallow hard.

'And another thing,' his voice calms a little. 'The reason I came over tonight. I don't want Rose there on Monday. Mum and Dad have offered to look after her. Obviously, I'll be there.'

Though there is some logic in what he says, I can't imagine keeping Rose away from Monday's service, especially after today. Leah and I have already discussed how — if I talk to Rose beforehand — Monday's service may help her to move on.

Unconsciously, I start to wring my hands together. I have never had to do battle with anyone over Rose. Anna decided what to do and, if not, Anna and I decided together. Without exception we both instinctively agreed on what was best for her. This is new and dangerous territory.

'I really want her there. She needs to be there and Anna would want her there too. I think it will help her understand what's happened.'

Finally, all the while watching me, he nods. 'Okay . . . '

'Thank you.' I almost choke on the words.

'Okay, then. Is it all right with you if I have her

on Monday night? I know it's not scheduled, but Mum and Dad are leaving Tuesday and it would be good for them to spend some time with her.' His tone has become the normal business tone he uses when we are discussing access to Rose.

My screaming instinct is to say 'No'. If she's upset, it will manifest on Monday night. She will wake crying and calling for her mummy. 'I really think she'll be better here.' My voice is a low whisper. 'It's not scheduled,' I try.

'I had hoped that — '

'Sean. I'm cremating my only child on Monday.' My voice breaks. 'You have Rose for the rest of the day after the service, but please, let me hold my grandchild that night, will you?'

He raises a hand to his face, seems to press on his right eyebrow, as if he has a headache. 'Fine,' he relents. 'But Jess, June half-term week, I'll be taking Rose with me.'

I keep very still, say nothing.

Leah's voice snaps the moment. 'Take the test, Sean. Then we'll talk about who is taking Rose where.'

★　★　★

Sunday. Mum is fussing. She has arrived early, laden with the essential ingredients for a fabulous Sunday roast but, apparently, I don't have the right things to serve dinner on. And why the hell have I not got a dining table yet? I look at her. Swapping around of beds, I can do; reorganizing my house to have a dining table in it right now, I can't.

Leah comes to the rescue and says we can have dinner at hers. We can all make our way over there now and Mum smiles, the thought of being let loose in Gus's state-of-the-art kitchen obviously a good one. Normally, I'd be insulted. Today, I don't care.

I've installed Mum and Dad in my room, which is a better idea anyway as they can use the *en suite*. I've set myself and my things up in Anna's for the next few days. Rose has already asked if she can sleep in there with me, and I've told her of course she can. Everyone is now at Leah's and Gus is fawning over the family guests, or as much as he can do considering Mum is ruling the kitchen and Dad doesn't acknowledge his presence. Rose is happy to be fussed over, though, and I left her curled up with Gus on the sofa, reading a book that she's had read to her a thousand times already. I have escaped for a walk with Pug.

My pace is as quick as she'll allow as I walk towards the town, choosing to be around lots of anonymous folk today rather than a lone walk in the woods. I find myself glancing at the men I see en route, searching for clues in their faces. Not just features like eye colour, or ears and nose shape, but the way someone might smile. If I hear a laugh, I turn around, measuring it against the sound of Rose's giggle. He's here somewhere. I can feel it in my bones. *Who is he, Anna?*

I turn a corner and see Theo standing in front of me, a bunch of Sunday newspapers under his arm.

'I thought it was you,' he says.

'Had to escape the madness for a bit.'

'Can I drop you home?'

'No thanks, I need the air.'

'Right,' he nods at nothing. 'Everything okay for — '

'Everything's sorted.' I interrupt.

'Okay.'

'Your phone not working the last couple of days?'

He blushes, tugs on his shirt collar under his fleece jacket.

'I texted you, said I'd like to read the letter.'

'I know. Though I'm not sure why. I told you it just okays me talking to you about anything she'd shared.'

'You won't mind me seeing it then.'

'Why are you so angry?'

'I'm not angry.' I tug on Pug's lead as she tries to pee at the lamppost next to me.

'You seem pretty angry, Jess. You angry at Anna, me, or that moment — the one we'll both pretend didn't happen? Again.'

My own cheeks redden. 'Don't be so bloody stupid.'

A woman walks by, tosses me a glance over her shoulder. Pug yaps at my feet, dog-speak for 'Are you okay?' Cars drive by us. Horns toot. The chitter-chatter of people talking surrounds us. More people walk past us and I'd swear they're staring. Can they see it? What do they see? Two friends talking? One of the local doctors with a woman who might be a patient?

'Step in here.' He pulls me into the doorway of

a café. It's closed but he leans his body on the door, sort of places me opposite him in the alcove. 'Well?' he asks.

'If things are awkward it's because I'm mad as hell at you. Tell me something, Theo. If Sean hadn't been threatening to take Rose away, would you ever have told me he's not her father? If this bloody letter hadn't existed, if you hadn't had *permission* to tell me, would you just have let him take her to Blackpool? I'm the closest blood relative she has and you know what she means to me.' I move out of the doorway, am uncomfortable with this proximity. 'You *know* what she means to me.'

Whatever words he has are tripping over themselves in his head because he's mute.

'You would have, wouldn't you? You would have kept quiet because of your precious code of ethics. Jesus. I was right . . . ' The thought has been torturing me these last few days. Would he, could he, have kept such a secret from me?

'I . . . ' He shakes his head. 'I took the Hippocratic Oath, Jess.'

'More like a *hypocritical* oath. Things are not awkward because we kissed, Theo, though I regret that. It was a kiss, nothing more, a heat-of-the-moment lack of judgement on my part. Things are awkward because I don't know if I can trust you.'

'You don't mean that.'

I lock eyes with him. 'Yes. Yes, I do.'

He bites his top lip. 'Your friendship means an awful lot to me.'

'Yes, just not enough.' I make to walk away.

'That's it? Jess, you're being ridiculous.'

'Anna's funeral is tomorrow. I've more important things to think about than you.' I tug on Pug's lead, leave Theo in the café doorway and, as I run across the road through stationary traffic, feel his eyes bore into my back. I'm really angry at him. I'm really angry at Anna. And I'm really angry at the world, and am questioning how I've been walking this earth for so long, not really knowing anyone I thought I knew.

25

Jess

My mother is happy. She is playing hostess in Leah's house and both Gus and Leah are happy to let her. She's managed to find matching everything — something that would have been impossible in my home. By the time I return from my walk, the table is set and their house is filled with the homely scent of a roast dinner.

'Can I do anything?' I ask when Pug is settled. She's exhausted after the walk and I'm tempted to try and curl up beside her.

'No, darling, everything is under control,' Mum says, Leah by her side rolling her eyes. I sit up on one of the stools at Leah's breakfast bar, look across the huge space between me and the ceramic hob Mum is standing at. Behind me, Rose is on the floor making a Lego house from a box Leah keeps here for her, Gus sitting by watching and handing her the bricks as she commands him. Every now and then, Rose glances in my direction, as if she senses something's off. I smile each time I catch her eye, let her know I'm here.

Dad is sitting in an armchair watching them play, seems to be taking in every movement she makes. I wonder if he watches her in awe like I do, marvelling at the miracle of her, feeling sad that he never noticed his own children in the same way. It's what I do when I watch Rose; I feel sad that life was too busy for me to notice the wonder of Anna as a small child.

'This is a celebration.' My mother's announcement, clinking two glasses to get attention, interrupts my thoughts. Gus has moved into the kitchen, is standing behind her, a bottle of champagne in his hand, an awkward, unsure, expression on his face. I've known Gus a long time and this face is a distinctly uncomfortable one. He's as unsure as I am about popping champagne today.

'I know, I know it's a little strange,' Mum says. 'But I think we should celebrate Anna. She brought all of us nothing but happiness.'

Until she died, Mum; then she brought me a truck-load of confusion.

I'm just wondering when I'll actually tell Mum about Anna when I see her gazing at me and I realize she wants permission to open the bottle. She wants me to say that it's okay sharing champagne before my daughter's funeral; that it is, in fact, an all-right thing to do. I give her a tiny smile, one I don't really mean but I have no energy to argue. She nods at Gus who looks at me. I nod at him too and then pop, he twists the cork out of the bottle like an expert. He fills five glasses and I bring one over to Dad, who takes it with his good hand and I lead him back to the kitchen end of the room. Rose glances at him but pays more attention to the house she's building.

'To Anna,' Mum says, her glass in the air. 'The most beautiful, kind and sensitive soul that we were lucky enough to have in our lives for a long time, though not long enough.'

'To Anna,' everyone echoes, even Dad, but not me. I sip the drink for Mum's sake.

'I'm cooking her favourite.' Mum puts her glass down and gets back to work. 'Roast lamb, roasted vegetables, fluffy spuds and alcoholic gravy.' Everyone laughs, except me again. Alcoholic gravy was a concoction that Anna and Mum had come up with one Christmas when Mum had nothing to thicken the gravy with. Anna assured her that if you put enough alcohol in, it would thicken itself. It didn't, but the result became a firm favourite over many Christmases to follow. For a second I think of Christmas, of her singing voice, of her absolute joy for the season. She loved the tack, the gaudy, the food, the drink; the sense of family that Christmas could bring. It will never be the same again.

I drain my glass in one go, wiggle the empty at Gus, who fills it immediately, topping up his own empty glass. I'm glad I'm not the only one finding this hard, but I'm conscious of getting home — have to drive later — but right now? Give me another mouthful of champagne to help me swallow this cursed lump in my throat.

I'm not, I realize, wanting to cry for Anna. I want to cry for me. I want to cry for the mess she's left in my head. I want to cry for Rose. In fact I want to scream and shout at Anna, but I hold off. There are other people to think about today. Rose hovers by my knees. 'Come see my house, Nanny' She pulls on me and I cross the huge space to where she's built a house that somehow looks just like Theo's. Dad is already back in the armchair surveying the scene.

'It's lovely,' I tell her.

'Look,' she makes me bend down so I can peer inside the window of the downstairs. There are three figures in one room. 'It's you, me and Mummy,' she says. I hug her, tell her again how wonderful it is and catch my father's eye. A silent, lone tear is making its way south down his cheek. I go to him, wipe it away with my thumb and bend down. 'Love you, Dad,' I whisper.

Gus is by my side with my glass.

'Thanks.'

'If you want to have a few drinks I won't have any more so that I can drop everyone back to yours.'

I pat his arm. 'No, thanks for the offer, but I need to keep my wits about me. It'll be a long day tomorrow.'

'If you change your mind?' He places an arm around my shoulder and I lean into him.

'I won't change my mind.'

★ ★ ★

By the time everyone is home and my father is settled in what is my bed, and Rose is settled in what is Anna's bed, I am agreeing with Mum over a cup of tea that it was in fact a lovely day.

'Thank you,' I say.

She waves me away with an impatient hand.

'You made a fabulous dinner. You talked so easily about her all day that it felt like she was there, with us. It was lovely, Mum.'

She moves from the armchair and squeezes in

208

beside me on the tatty sofa.

'Tomorrow won't be easy,' she says.

I nod.

'I try and imagine if it had been you or Leah, and I like to think that I would never ever let you go or say goodbye. I mean, yes, we have to have a service, but it's not a final goodbye. It's just a wave . . . A wave until she's in our thoughts again the very next day and every day after.'

I cuddle into her, like the child I am.

'Just don't say goodbye. Keep her with you always.'

My eyes close. I say a silent prayer that during those moments that I will think of Anna always, I'm not crippled with the same anxiety I feel now.

She taps my knee repeatedly. 'You are the best mother, Jess, and you'll be the best grandmother, mother, whatever to Rose. You'll be whatever she needs, of that I'm sure. And keep Anna in her life. Don't let her forget her.'

'No . . . '

'You're all right?' she asks.

'I'm all right, though I'll never be the same. I'll have to find a new me without her.' I'm about to spill to Mum but I stop short. 'She left me with a few problems.'

Mum laughs. 'This is Anna we're talking about. Pregnant at eighteen, a force of nature. I'd expect no less!' She doesn't ask, maybe because she has enough to do with Dad, but I suspect it's more because she respects my need for privacy. Yet again, I'm in awe of my mother.

'Thank you again for today and thank you for being you.'

'Jess, my love, we're all just souls trying to find our way, trying to do our best . . .'

When I know Mum and Dad are settled, I make my way up to Anna's bedroom. In the dark, I undress, put pyjamas on and crawl in beside Rose. She's snoring gently. I can make out the shape of Anna's things in the darkened room: her guitar standing in the far corner; her hair straighteners balanced on the top of the dressing table; her Pudsey teddy; her record player, a present from Doug last year for her birthday when she decided she wanted to collect vinyl; two shelves full of her collection of hats. The shapes of Anna's world. In the shadows lie the grey bits, blurry and undefined; parts of her world I wasn't privy to. I turn on my side towards Rose's sleeping form; her daughter perfectly outlined, her profile the same shape as Anna's. I reach across and run a finger down it, touch her lips.

Anna always kissed me on the lips. She did it before she left for France and, of course, I thought nothing of it. 'Bye, Mama,' she whispered in my ear before she ran out to the waiting taxi.

'It's not goodbye, my love,' I whisper back. 'Never. It's never goodbye.'

★ ★ ★

The church is packed. There are people spilling out of the double doors at the front. It looks like one of those scenes that you see on television, either when someone famous dies, or someone

210

young is tragically murdered. *She was*, I tell myself as I walk up the aisle of St John's. Doug is by my side and Rose is between us. Leah, Gus and my parents follow, with Sean and his parents right behind. *She was murdered by snow.*

My family huddle into the first pew and Sean's in the next. Doug, an only child, has some cousins, but his mother, in a nursing home near the Lakes, is too ill to travel. Beyond that, I have no idea who is here. Doug hands me an order of service and there, on the front, is the photo of Anna taken on the ski-trip which also graces my phone screen. The mountains are in the background; the sun is high in the sky. She's laughing, someone having caught her in a perfect moment. Her eyes shine, her smile beams, and my heart quickens on seeing it. Doug had emailed me through the order of service so there are no surprises. I glance up to the right of the altar, see all of Anna's college friends assembled — the people she was in a choir with for two years. Sam, their choirmaster, sees me looking, gives me a small nod of his head and I remember the kindness of his wife that day at the play centre. That coffee and biscuit . . . In the front row, I see Cara and Louise, girls who Anna has known since pre-school right through to college — good friends who right after the accident came by often and then stopped. I thought Cara, Anna's best friend, would never stop coming around, but it seems there is a time limit on hope in the very young.

And then, because I can't ignore it any more, I allow myself a glance to the right, to the centre of the aisle just in front of the altar — Anna's coffin. I gasp; Doug grips my hand and I stare at the gaudy pine box that Anna would have hated. Doug had tried to explain to me that a wicker one was out of the question and I didn't dwell on why. I find myself wondering where Carol is. She should be the one holding Doug's hand. I glance around, see her three pews behind, with her two boys — an instant reminder that Anna was their half-sister. I beckon to her to come up, but we're already tight in the first pew. She holds a hand up, nods, telling me that it's okay. It's okay that I have her husband at this moment in time. I mouth a silent 'Thank you' to her. Mum takes a look over her shoulder, smiles at Carol, then turns back. I can tell she is resolutely ignoring the coffin. My father weeps silently and it's his tears, my father's rare and frail tears, which make mine finally fall.

We stand for the first hymn. It's something everyone belts out, led by the choir, but I don't recognize it. Doug assured me, when I questioned it in the order of service, that Anna knew it, had sung it. Rose wants up in my arms and I hold her tight as she wraps her legs, spider-like, around my middle. As we sit down, she decides she wants to go back to her dad and Doug passes her back to Sean. I haven't told Doug yet. I haven't told Doug yet that Sean is not — may not be — Rose's father. I'll tell him when the DNA results are back.

All of this shit is what's whirring around my head when Anna is lying dead less than ten feet from me. I believe it but I don't. I see the coffin

212

but don't want to think of her in it. I start to look at other faces in the congregation, those that I can see in my line of sight without turning around. Max is there. He's sitting with a bunch of people whom I know, from photos Anna had, are the people she worked with. All of them look distraught; all of them have had a kick in the gut that reminds them they're not immortal just because they're young.

Doug shifts in the pew beside me and I know immediately what's coming. He is delivering Anna's eulogy. He asked me if I wanted to; asked Leah, Gus, even Sean if they wanted to speak. All of us knew we would be incapable, which has left it to my ex-husband. The man who, until now, lived in my brain as someone who told me my love strangled him. Now, he is a capable, strong father and, as I squeeze his hand, I will him to get through it — for us all to get through it.

Doug walks slowly to the pulpit. The vicar, John, angles the mic for him. Doug mutters his thanks, clears his throat and looks up. He told me he was going to try and find a spot in the church and focus on it. I hope he can. Rose has found her way back into my arms and together we listen to her papa speak.

'Anna,' he says. 'We all have wonderful memories of her. She was truly the sunniest soul. She lit up a room when she entered, lifted hearts when she sang, made you feel like you were the only person in a roomful of people.

'I'm not going to . . . I couldn't . . . ' He taps his chest a couple of times with his palm, gathers himself before continuing. 'Couldn't stay up here for long, so I'll keep this short. Anna was Jess's and my only child. To have her torn away from us in this way has left a wound that will probably never heal. Yet, with every passing day, I hear her laughter in my ear, I hear her urging me to move past this tragedy and to remember her as she was — a gorgeous, free young woman, so full of life.

'I hear her laughter in my granddaughter's giggle. I see her smile in her eyes and she will never be gone.'

There is sniffling behind me. I know my own face is awash. Leah reaches across to me and dabs it with a tissue. She and Gus are sobbing, clinging to each other. My mother is staring at Doug, willing him on, stoic as ever. My father is sitting beside her, his head hung low.

'Anna loved to sing. Thank you to the brilliant choir that she used to sing with. Thanks for being such a fun part of her life and for being here today. Anna loved to ski, and thank you to all her work colleagues who were with her that day — thank you for being here. Anna is one of four people lost to you last December. May she and Lawrence and David and Ross all rest in peace. And to Anna, thank you for being the best, the very best. It was for too short a time, but Jess and I and everyone who loved you will savour each and every memory. Thank you for Rose, who makes sure each day that you live on in more than just our hearts and minds. Rest in peace, our darling girl.'

My jaw breaks. It bursts open, and it's everything I can do not to howl. I want to run up to Doug, to hold him, to press rewind, to . . . He takes his seat next to me and the music starts as he weeps quietly. Leah stands, whispers to Gus and they leave the pew. It's just a moment later when Carol and her two boys move in beside Doug. The scene is as it should be. I look behind, my eyes thanking my sister. I don't know what I would do without her.

Cara is next to sing an aria I cannot name but was one of Anna's favourites. I have no idea how she does it either, how she makes it through. That day, back when they were both ten, Anna always said she cheated death. When the ski accident happened, it haunted me that death had finally claimed her. I stare at the flowers on top of the coffin. We have white roses . . . Someone, probably from her work, has placed a large bouquet of yellow roses. Whoever it was didn't know her well. She hated yellow . . . Rose is stuck firm to my chest, her thumb in her mouth and she removes it, whispers in my ear, 'Pretty music.'

'It is, sweetheart. It was one of your mummy's favourites.'

Her arm wraps around me and she whispers again. I have to strain into her to hear. 'I know Mummy's not coming back.'

I squeeze her.

'I just want her to.' Tears form in her small eyes.

'I know, sweetheart. We all do.'

'She's singing with the angels like Finn said, isn't she?'

'She sure is.' I whisper in her ear. The choir

215

have joined with Cara and they're in full flow. 'If you listen very carefully, you can hear her.'

She seems to strain to listen, then her damp eyes widen and her face beams. 'I do! I hear her!'

I nod, smiling. I will my lips to stop trembling, will the choir not to stop singing, will the moment to last for Rose's sake.

'There's Finn,' she says, loud enough for those around to look at where she's pointing. My eyes follow her hand. Four rows back to the left of us, Theo and Finn are sitting together. Finn gives Rose a tiny wave.

'Can I go there, Nanny?' she asks.

My instinct is to say no, but the moment, this moment, was wrapped up in what Finn had said to her, and I know that Rose just wants to go to him and tell him that she can hear her mummy singing with the angels.

'Be quick, come back, yes?'

She makes her way and I watch her all of the time. Doug looks puzzled and I tell him that it's okay.

There is more singing; there are more words from John, there is an invite to those who would like to join us in the Duck and Partridge for a celebration of Anna's life after the family-only service at the local crematorium. I catch Sean hear the word family and see him stare at the floor, his face scarred from tears, and I yearn for a time when Anna's actions might make some sense. I reach back to squeeze his hand; hope he can forgive me for what I've had to do and feel my swollen eyelids close slowly as he shakes my hand free of his.

216

26

Anna

Raw Honey Blogspot 14/11/2014

I'm speechless! This week He got me tickets to see the Royal Philharmonic Choir play 'The Glory Of Christmas' at the Royal Albert Hall, and it really was breathtaking . . . We never did dates when we were together before and this was a proper date! I spent the whole evening giggling like a schoolchild and He laughed, promised me we'd do 'date' things more often.

And it snowed on the way home! I couldn't believe it! November in London and we got a heap of snow the Alps would have been proud of. I bloody love snow! And I made snow angels in Hyde Park. We rolled tiny snowballs, tossed them at each other and laughed until our stomachs hurt. We were both soaked going home and I tried not to think about what He'd say to his wife when she asked how He'd got quite so wet.

When Mum asked me, I just told her I made snow angels. She grinned, looked out the front window where I'd left one for good measure, then she grabbed my hand and we went outside and filled her garden with them, throwing ourselves on our backs, waving our hands up and down. Between both of us the hairdrier was going for almost an hour afterwards!

Mum. A bigger kid than me sometimes . . .

Comment: Nonplussed101
Date nights? Will they work, do you think?
Reply: Honey-girl
Work? Not sure what you mean but this one was great fun! I suppose you mean ongoing and yes, I hope a few date nights here and there will work.
Comment: Solarbomb
I used to love doing snow angels with my mum too.
Reply: Honey-girl
Fun, aren't they, Solarbomb?
Comment: Nonplussed101
I meant that even on a 'date' you're still 'sneaking around' really, aren't you?
Reply: Honey-girl
Thanks Nonplussed101 #howtoputadampeneron-mynight
Comment: Nonplussed101
Agh! Didn't mean to! It's just I've been where you are. I've been the other woman and the ducking and diving isn't fun at all, even on a proper date.

27

Jess

'Sweet Jesus, did I really have to hear this from Sean? What the hell is going on? What are you doing to the poor man?' Doug has taken me aside in the pub and is incensed. I am still reeling from Anna's body going behind that curtain and disappearing. I think I have come to terms with the fact that she's gone and then a thought like that invades . . . An image of her coffin carrying her remains disappearing behind a curtain to an acoustic version of 'Sweet Child O' Mine' and the whole thing seems so surreal. So, when Doug is talking to me, all I see is a fishlike movement of his mouth and I'm struggling to understand what he's on about.

'I was having a conversation with him, asking him in a roundabout way if he and Anna were . . . you know.'

No, I don't know. My head hurts.

'Then he gets all upset and tells me that you and Leah are demanding DNA from him. Fucks-sake, Jess. Really?'

I take a very deep breath, as deep as my lungs will allow. 'Can we talk about this tomorrow?'

'Tomorrow, I'm driving my family back home.'

I wince and he immediately apologizes. 'Sorry, I'm sorry, but what the hell's going on with Sean, Jess?'

He is running one hand through his thinning hair, the other is holding a pint.

'You gave a beautiful eulogy,' I tell him. 'And you have to trust me. Today's not the day to talk about Sean. Look, I've got to get home. Mum and Dad are already back there and Clara is dropping Rose off shortly.'

'Are Barbara and Geoff leaving tomorrow?'

I nod. Doug always calls my parents by their first names. Even when we were married, they were never Mum and Dad, at least not in name — though in spirit, they probably were.

'Do you want me to pick them up, drive back in convoy?'

Doug and I met at the Lakes and he went back there to live after we split up. Though we have in the past only had rare contact, I know he keeps a quiet eye on Mum and Dad. 'Would you? Though you may not get home until late; Mum drives a bit slowly for the motorway.'

'I don't mind.'

I say goodbye to him and those people I need to, realize that Theo never came to the pub, convince myself it's for the best. I'm caught at the front door by Max, who is outside with a few colleagues smoking.

'Max.' I give him a hug. 'Thanks for coming.'

'It was a lovely service,' he says. The other people hold back, don't speak, and just nod their agreement. One moves forward, offers his hand. 'James,' he says, introducing himself. 'So sorry for your loss.'

James. James Elliot. I remember the name. He's the guy who Anna did a college internship with in the bank; he helped get her the full-time job. I take him in: his clothes, his height and body shape, the colour of his eyes, his wedding ring. He's about thirty-five, a lot older than Anna. As he shakes my hand, I spot Rose in his face and immediately tell myself I'm imagining it. Nowadays, I seem to move through life spotting Rose in every man I meet . . .

★   ★   ★

Anna, Anna, Anna. I keep saying her name over and over in my head during the short trip home. When I get there, Mum's car is safely in the drive; the lights are on in the house and I let out a sigh of relief. I worry about them. I worry about her. She shouldn't be driving the distance from the Lakes at her age. She shouldn't be looking after my dad alone, lifting him alone. Leah is right, we need to intervene and make sure she gets some help. Meanwhile, I'm grateful to Doug for taking the slowest route possible home tomorrow and watching over them.

The clock reminds me I have only ten minutes before Clara drops Rose home. Sean was still in the pub when I left; unbeknownst to him, maybe mixing with Rose's real father, or maybe not. My mind wanders back to Anna's first year at university and I try to remember the names of her tutors and friends. I rub my eyes. How do I find out? Do I really want to know? If I don't know, isn't it better for Rose and me? I can hear Leah's voice already admonishing me, telling me that Rose should know who her father is, have her father in her life. God knows, Gus had a huge battle on his hands with his first wife, who used their child as weapon when she was younger. He fought through the courts for years to get access, which is how he and Leah met. She had helped him fight to see his child, had fallen in love with him and then reluctantly agreed not to have any more, he was so determined never to have to go through anything like that again.

Here, in the darkness outside my house, on the day of my daughter's funeral, is not the time I expect to have a Eureka moment about my sister. I have always told her she hasn't a clue what unconditional love is. I've said it in anger. I've snarled it to myself under my breath when I've been pissed off at her. I've had this 'mightier than thou' attitude because she never gave birth. Suddenly, I feel sick and ashamed. She loves Gus unconditionally. She gave up her desire to have her own children when she met him, she loved him that much. And she loves his daughter, Jen. And she loves Rose . . . I pull my phone from the depths of my bag, thumb a text to her.

Leah, I don't tell you enough. I love you. You mean the world to me and if I ever, ever tell you again that you don't know what unconditional love is, shoot me. You love everyone in your life that way, including me. I'm sorry. Thank you for everything you do. I don't know how I could have got through the last few months without you. Jess xxx

I can almost hear Anna chuckling. She does love it when I admit I'm wrong. She *did* love it when I admitted I was wrong, used to take a

222

childlike delight in it. As I get out of the car, the front door opens and it's Leah. Her phone is in her hand and she opens her arms to me. I breathe her in. 'What are you doing here?'

'Just came around to give Mum a hand with Dad. I read your text and you're a soppy cow.'

'No, you're my best friend and I need you and I'm sorry. I don't always see things from your eyes.'

I get a very rare tight squeeze from her before she lets go, ushers me into the house. 'Come on. Dad's ready for bed and Mum's wafting around in her nightie.' Just before we close the door, Clara's car appears on the drive. Leah disappears and I hold open the door as Rose gets out, laden with toys. She kisses her grandma and runs into the house. My immediate reaction is to be annoyed — she has enough toys. The house is coming down with toys, and then I think of Clara and the news that she will get very soon — that Rose isn't even her granddaughter — and my heart fractures. *So many ripple effects, Anna.*

Clara doesn't come in, seems a bit standoffish, and I realize that Sean is in the back of the car, looking worse for wear. She must have picked him up from the pub, and I know that he will have said something to her; I sense that he will have told her, probably ranting about DNA in his drunken state.

'Clara,' I call after her.

She stops at the open driver's door. 'I'm so sorry for your loss, Jess,' she says, and climbs into her new Volvo. I stare at the space she left for a moment before closing the door. Shit.

My father is resplendent in what I can tell are new pyjamas, sitting on the tatty sofa, Rose already by his side. Mum is pottering in a floaty nightie. Leah is standing at the fridge with a bottle of vodka and two glasses of ice in her hands.

'I have time for one.' She jerks her head towards the kitchen end and we lean against the sink, the pair of us nursing glasses of neat, iced vodka. 'Gus is picking me up in five,' she says, glancing at her watch. 'He was so cut up by today, I think he wanted a quiet half-hour.'

'Doug is going to call by here tomorrow, convoy Mum and Dad home — though we can't let her know she's being escorted.'

'I'm back in work,' Leah says.

Of course she is. Normal hours, normal life resumes tomorrow. Not for me. I have decided to take the rest of the week off but send Rose into school, if she's up for it. Every part of my body aches. Every part of me hurts; my neck, my shoulders, and my legs, right down to my fingers. I'm exhausted and know it. Helen told me to take what time I need and I'm going to. I need this week.

'You'll be okay?'

'I will. I'm staying in bed for the day.' I take a slug of the vodka, but for some reason don't feel its power tonight and put the glass on the draining board. 'Clara was odd.' I look over at Rose. 'I think Sean said something. He was pissed.'

'Poor woman,' Leah frowns. 'You've got to feel for them.'

'What was she thinking, Leah? Anna. I ask myself over and over and over again, but what was she thinking involving Sean if he was never Rose's dad, if she really was seeing someone else for years?'

Leah puts a hand on my arm. 'We like to think we know our loved ones, but they can often do things that shock.'

The doorbell sounds.

'And that, I suppose,' she waves her phone at me, 'is that unconditional love thing. If we love someone, there's nothing they could do that could make us stop loving them. Or is there a line?'

'There's a line,' I say. 'Except with your children.'

She laughs. 'So you didn't really mean what you said in your text.'

I pull her into an embrace. 'I meant every word. With Anna, my child, the truth is no matter what she's done, no matter what she could ever have done, I would have loved her. I would have stuck by her as unconditionally as humanly possible. I know you feel that towards the people you love: me, Gus, your stepdaughter. That actually makes you a better person. I put conditions on any relationship I've ever had other than with Anna.'

She grins at my confession.

Mum has let Gus in and he's standing there watching us, red-eyed. 'Am I spoiling a moment?' he asks.

'No.' Leah and I part and she says goodbye to Mum and Dad, promises to come and see them very soon. Rose clings to my side as Leah leaves.

'Are you all right, sweetheart?' I ask.

She nods. 'Can I sleep with you again tonight, Nanny?'

'Of course you can.'

'In Mummy's bed?'

'Of course.'

My mum looks on from her standing position by the door and we both know I probably won't be getting back to my own bed anytime soon.

★　★　★

Mum made sandwiches earlier and I force a leftover corner of bread into my mouth and start to load the dishwasher as quietly as possible. She appears beside me and, like automatons, we both load the plates, her handing them to me, me stacking.

'We think we have time,' she says.

I just nod; my nodding reflex, by now, perfectly tuned. Sometimes, depending on the situation, I have even perfected a tiny accompanying smile.

'Do you mind if we go up to bed? I have a long drive tomorrow.'

I decide to wait until the morning to tell her about Doug. 'Of course not. Thank you for being here. I know it's a lot for you and Dad.'

She rinses a plate under the sink and hands it to me. 'Like we could not have been here. Like we wouldn't have been part of her send-off?' She dries her hands on a tea towel with a picture of a Christmas tree and baubles that Rose gave me.

226

'Leah and you. I couldn't help overhearing earlier. About Sean . . . '

I would always have told Mum what's unravelling with Anna, but would have chosen another day.

'It's complicated, Mum.' My sigh sounds as tired as I feel.

'Isn't it always?'

'I don't know what to do with any of it yet.'

'Maybe you should just let sleeping dogs lie . . . '

The radiator beside me crackles, bubbles of water locked in there somewhere. The television that Dad is watching sounds the peal of the ten o'clock news.

'Just bear in mind that what you think you should do might not be the best thing for Rose.'

She's probably right. If she were me, and she was in my position — that is exactly what she would do. Mum would leave it alone and be glad that the Gods might allow her to keep her grandchild.

She is staring at me, probably waiting for a response and my eyes blink slowly. One, two, three . . . eight, nine, ten. As Big Ben chimes, the thought of James Elliot's hand on mine earlier today crosses my mind again.

I give Mum a gentle nod.

28

Jess

The next morning, she knows exactly what's happening when Doug arrives, knows exactly what we had cooked up between us; but, oddly, Mum doesn't object. She gives me a look that I can tell is a mixture of relief and annoyance. Rose, who I've allowed to stay home from school until they go, hovers in the background, watching as the car is loaded up.

Before Dad is helped into the front seat by Doug, he holds me as tight as he can with the strength he possesses in one side of his body. 'Poor baby,' he whispers, and I'm not sure if he means me, or Anna or Rose. I kiss his cheek, let Doug help him inside and walk around to my mum.

'I'm going to come up and spend a few days with you, soon,' I tell her. Seeing them, particularly seeing her go this morning, has released something in me. I'm frightened. I feel like I did when I left home first, or when I got married — those big events when I left the sanctuary of my parents'. I don't want to let go of my mother. I want her to make it all go away. I really don't want them to leave.

'You're okay, Jess,' she says, then climbs into the front seat of her Micra. 'You know where we are.'

I pick Rose up and together we wave at the convoy until they're out of sight.

'Can I stay home with you, Nanny?' It starts before we're even back in the house.

'You have to go to school, darling.'

'But you're staying at home. You always come to school too.'

I have never noticed this. From Rose's point of view, I'm in school with her. The fact that I consider it a working environment is one thing, but in her head, Nanny comes to school with her.

'Nanny's not well today. You know sometimes when you're poorly?'

She nods.

'If you're poorly, you stay at home and get well, and today, Nanny is poorly.'

Nanny just wants to crawl back into bed. Any bed.

'I'm poorly too, feel?' She holds her palm up to her forehead.

'You feel fine to me.' I touch it.

Then she starts to cry.

Rose isn't a crybaby. Nor is she sick. Suddenly, the reality of having to look after, I mean be solely responsible for, this little girl's well-being — emotionally, physically, mentally — hits me in the gut. I bend down to her level and hold her. She clings like a limpet and I know there'll be no school for her today. I also know I have no idea how to deal with this. I have no clue how to comfort her, how much she really knows and really feels. If I take the route that she knows everything, really understands that her mother is

229

never coming back — the poor little scrap should be able to stay home and cling to me for as long as she needs to. On the other hand, if I do 'what's best for her', she should probably get back into school and her routine as quickly as possible.

What's best for her . . . The words roll around my mind. Leah has asked me a couple of times if I was being selfish; was I sure about what I was doing? I pour cornflakes into a bowl, ruffle Rose's hair. This isn't selfish. Yes, it's what I want, but it's hard and it's going to get harder. If I were being selfish, I'd have let her go, let her be with Sean. I'd have got some sort of life of my own back. Instead, I now have Rose to think about, Rose to put first for at least the next twelve years. She looks up at me, wide-eyed, as she munches her cereal. And those eyes tell me she's grateful — that if her mummy has to be gone, she's glad I'm here. I ignore the nagging doubt I have about starting a chain of events that means Sean may be gone from her life too.

We spend the rest of the day in front of the television, both of us wrapped up in a blanket on the tatty sofa. Pug spends most of the time on Rose's lap, apart from the moments Rose takes her out on the lead in the garden. Every time she does, I hear her squeal with laughter — she seems to find it hilarious seeing Pug wee. The sound gives me hope.

We eat the scraps that we have in. Two meals cobbled together from whatever is in the freezer. When she asks for pizza, I tell her it's fish fingers today. I'm not going out. Today is just one day I don't want to see anyone or talk to anyone. This includes Theo — maybe especially includes Theo. He has blasted my phone with so many texts that I've turned it off.

This is how we spend the day after Anna's funeral — cocooned away from the world. Rose and I have a sleep together in the afternoon and, when it comes to bedtime, I convince her to sleep in my bed. I need my own bed tonight. Mum, being Mum, has already changed the linen, and I tuck Rose in, telling her I'll be shortly behind her. She's almost asleep before I even leave.

I don't go straight downstairs. Instead, I pass through the landing to Anna's room. My palm massaging my forehead, I look around. There must be something. Maybe I missed something. It's with this thought that I begin to search. It's not just a 'lift up the blanket and peer to see what's underneath' search. It's more the forensic type. I go through every scrap of paper in her accordion file. There are no more letters — not that I was expecting any. Her life was lived in the digital world. Every loving note she ever sent was a text or an email. I have some cards in a drawer in my room from when she was young, but as soon as phones arrived on the scene . . . By nine o'clock, my stomach is growling and I have been through every single crevice in her room. There is nothing. Nothing that would hint at a man, which is strange in itself. Who has nothing, nothing at all from their lover?

I'm downstairs trawling the Internet for any information on James Elliot. He is not in Anna's lists of friends on her Facebook page, which I first stalked on the eighth of December. I had to stop — the outpouring of what I considered premature grief for her was too much back then. Her laptop, which I only used for stalking her social media, has never revealed anything meaningful, and right now it stubbornly refuses to reveal anything about James . . . other than his profile on the company website. I'm googling his name when the house phone startles me. It's Leah.

'I have the mobile.'

'Oh.' I massage my stomach and take a seat on the last step of the stairs next to the landline. 'It's open?'

'I've only turned it on to check it opens. I haven't looked at anything, knew you'd want to first.'

'Right.'

'Look,' Leah says. 'Don't go off on one when I tell you this and tell me you're fine because I know you're not. I have loads of holiday due, so I've taken the rest of the week off. Let's take Rose up to the Lakes. I've spoken to Gus, he's fine with it. You know him, he buries himself in work when things are tough and I think he probably knows you and I need to be together right now. What do you think?'

'Mum and Dad only just left.'

'I know, but we could kill two birds with one stone. I've sorted out some temporary agency help for Mum while we wait for the home-care package from the doctor's. We can bed that in and you can try and relax a bit and we can make some new memories for Rose.'

'Have you really not looked at the phone?'

'Jess, I said so. I just turned it on, then turned it off again. Steve, the guy who unlocked it, set up a new PIN code. I'm the only person who knows it, so be nice to me. Look, I can just bring it over now if you like, or we could both go up north tomorrow and I'll give it to you then.'

I make an instant decision. Despite my will to be strong, right now I probably need my family around me.

'Tomorrow. Let's go early. Let's not tell Mum. She'll just fuss. I'll go and pack a bag for me and Rose.'

'A few days' clothes, no more — we'll come back on Saturday. I'll drive, I'll be there at eight.'

'Okay, Leah?'

'Yup?'

'Don't forget the phone.'

When the call is finished, I head straight upstairs and throw some clothes of mine into a bag in the dark. In Rose's bedroom, I do the same. I have no idea what we'll be wearing. I have no urge to match her clothes the way I normally would. I just feel very relieved that for a few days I'm getting out of here.

★ ★ ★

Two a.m. I'm up again and downstairs staring out through the rear window to the back garden. Every time I have tried to lie down and sleep, I'm gripped by panic. It's the night, I tell myself, looking outside to the black, star-free sky. Dark clouds chase one another — there is rain on the way. By my feet lies an empty suitcase and a pile of clothes. They are the last things she wore. I have rubbed them against my skin, smelled them until my nose hurts. I should wash them but can't bring myself to. They'll end up being repacked in the case, the case put under her bed, until the next time the night won't let me breathe easy.

On my knees, I begin to fold them. Her black polo-neck jumper. *She lied to me.* Her dark navy jeans. *She lived a lie right here with me, right here in this room on our tatty sofa.* Underwear, a matching black bra and knickers. *Who gave her the underwear?* Her Peppa Pig dressing gown. *She must have thought she couldn't tell me. What does that say about me?* Slippers, white, sheepskin. *It says, however much I didn't know her, she didn't know me either.* Her makeup bag. *Did I suffocate her? Was that it? Did the love that I thought was unconditional strangle my daughter too?*

My hand rests on the white plastic bag. The red suit is the one thing I haven't been able to touch. I open it; release the smell of death into the room. Tears fall slowly, silently. 'You have to start to pull yourself together,' I tell myself out loud. 'She's gone. You can't ask her what you want to ask her. You can't hold her and tell her it doesn't matter.' I unravel the suit and clutch it to my chest, ignoring the rips in the legs, and I sit there rocking on my knees.

Outside the rain is falling. The wind has whipped up a gale and lightning flashes nearby.

The silver zips on the red suit seem to wink in its glow. I pull open the first pocket. Inside is a lip salve and a white hanky. It is tightly creased and, when I shake it out, I have to hold my nose.

It's large. It's a man's, definitely, and my heartbeat thumps in my ears. An image appears on my closed eyelids: a tiny triangle of white peering out of a breast pocket. A dampened white square rubbing orange sauce from a new suit. There is only one man I know who uses handkerchiefs. Oh My God.

29

Jess

The morning sun shooting early shards of sunlight through the trees makes a liar of the debris on the rear lawn. Last night's wind and rain has brought many branches down. I'd normally be out there, clearing it all into separate piles of rubbish and potential firewood, happily hacking at the latter with an axe, creating a store for winter.

I blow my coffee; accept that — since Anna died — I can't seem to focus on the future, yet I'm worried constantly about it. I can't seem to plan. Take the firewood — I have no desire to go outside and do something for next winter. I may not be here next winter. I fold the white square in my hand as small as it will go, watch it spring open again when I release it. There's a tiny stain on one corner and I scrape it with my fingernail. If it could talk, this piece of cotton would tell me what that is now lurking under my nail. It would tell me the name of its owner. Not Theo. It can't be Theo's. It might tell me where it's been in the world. It has definitely been to France and back recently, which is more than I can say for Anna. Tears threaten and I chomp my cheeks, refuse to allow them to fall. The sound of Leah's car out front makes me move, call out to Rose upstairs. I've told her she can take four things, four toys, and she has been upstairs choosing for the last ten minutes. I yell her name as I open the front door.

Leah kisses my cheek and grabs my bag in one movement.

'Rose,' I call her again, as I pick up Pug's travel basket and hand it out to Leah. The poor dog, she doesn't know whether she's coming or going ever since I got her.

Rose appears at the top of the stairs. 'I can't choose. I've packed a few things in a very small bag, Nanny.'

I look at Leah, whose eyes are also fixed on the child. Standing there at the top of the stairs, the slivers of light from the landing window on her face and hair, she looks just like Anna. It makes me gasp.

'It's fine, love,' Leah answers for me. 'That small bag is fine.' She reaches a hand up to take it from her.

'And I packed my new jeans, Nanny. You forgot them.'

Leah bursts out laughing, ruffles Rose's plaited hair.

Even I can't help smiling. 'Have you had a wee?' I ask. 'It's a long journey.'

'I know how long it is, Nanny. That's why I packed so much. And yes. I 'ready had a wee.'

'I have the DVD player in my car too, so take some along?' Leah says, grabbing my car keys from the side table and disappearing outside. Rose runs back up the stairs, only to appear a minute later with a handful of DVDs, no cases on them.

I grab them from her. 'I'm always telling you to put these back in their covers, aren't I?'

She stops on the stairs and I realize my tone was curt. Her lower lip starts to tremble. 'I was trying to be fast,' she says.

I climb up, take hold of her and carry her to the car. 'Sorry, darling. I didn't sleep well last night and I'm a bit tired,' I place her on the booster seat that Leah has just removed from my car and strap her in. 'I love you, gorgeous girl.' I tickle her nose with mine.

'I love you, gorgeous Nanny.' She grins.

'Right, let's get on the road,' Leah says. 'We'll stop somewhere for brunch on the way.' Before we leave my driveway, she fishes in the end of her bag and pulls out Anna's phone. 'Right, you have it now. I've been petrified I'd lose it or my bag would be nicked. Imagine if I told you I'd lost it?' She lets out a low whistle.

It almost burns a hole in my palm and I let it sit on my lap, resting between my legs.

'0712,' Leah says. 'I'm sorry.'

'What?'

'0712. It's the code. He asked me for a number that was specific to Anna that we'd remember but not a birth-date. It was the first thing that came into my head.'

'Oh . . .' 0712. The date of the accident. The date she died.

'Obviously, you can change it. But you need it to get in the first time.'

I nod, glad, for once, that I can't read or use a phone while I'm in a car without feeling nauseous. It has waited long enough — it can wait another few hours.

Thankfully, Rose is already occupied. The zip has been opened on her bag and she has released a menagerie of soft toys on the back seat, chatting to each of them in her furry line-up.

For a while, we're silent, Leah and I. Rose is doing enough talking for three. She's talking about Anna, wondering what star she will be tonight, telling us that she can always see the stars more clearly at Gramps's house. Granma and Gramps have a better sky. But what if she wants to look at her during the day? Where is she then?

My phone buzzes in the central console and the screen shows me it's Theo. I turn the sound off.

'Don't blame him.' Leah stares ahead at the road. Rose is talking to Mr Giraffe about her mummy. She is offering to be Mr Giraffe's mummy.

'Who shall I blame, then?' I can hear nothing but a black mood in my voice today.

'Anna was his patient.'

'I know that. I'm meant to be his friend.'

'And he knows that. He was in an impossible situation.'

'My only daughter has just died.' I whisper the words. 'Don't tell *me* about impossible situations.'

I don't tell Leah that I almost called him last night after getting his messages. He's right. We need each other; but I also need more time to lick my wounds.

Rose is now counting Eddie Stobart trucks,

looking out of the window at their names on their front grilles. If she can, she knows from previous games that she has to try and spell out the letters. 'Look, Nanny!' she cries. 'It says, A, N, A! Like Mummy.'

I strain my body around to look out of the back window and yes, there it is behind us. A N A. I don't bother explaining it's missing an 'N'. I just nod.

'Mummy's not a truck in the daytime, is she?' Her tiny face scowls.

'No, darling, she's not a truck.' I shake my head, reach back and take her hand.

'So where is she?' she persists.

'Your mummy is everywhere,' Leah interrupts. 'In everything pretty that you can see during the day. Like a rainbow, or a butterfly or a bird, or a — '

'A bunny rabbit,' Rose says.

'Yes,' Leah agrees.

'Or a doggie.'

I watch Rose look at Pug's travel basket in a new light. She slides her small fingers through the grille, touches Pug's face and smiles. Pug licks her hand and Rose turns her head to one side like she always does when she's about to take a nap.

'Or even a doggie,' I smile.

Leah sighs and I can tell, like me, she's unsure if the idea of Rose believing Pug might be her mother is a good one.

'Mum will be all right with us just arriving, won't she?' I change the subject.

'She's Mum. Of course. It is interesting,

though, that we're both headed there when things are shit.'

Something in her voice, in what she's just said, makes me ask, 'You, are you all right? I know why my life's in the shitter. Please tell me you're coming home just to be with me and your life's not in the shitter too?'

She laughs. 'I'm going home just to be with you.'

'What's wrong?'

'Nothing.'

'Don't. I'm fragile but I'm not an idiot.'

'It's nothing. Jen, Gus's daughter. She's asked to come and live with us.'

I literally suck air through my teeth, knowing it's the last thing that Leah would want. Jen can be hard work, sometimes seems to resent Leah, even though she and Gus only met long after he had parted from her mother. Leah loves her, but it's not always easy.

'What'll you do?'

'Grin and bear it. What choice do I have?'

'You could run away to Mum and Dad's with me.'

She smiles.

'We could hide out together in Windermere, have Mum cook for us while we let 'the help' we're arranging look after Dad.'

Her smile widens. 'Put that way, it's tempting to stay forever . . . But I have to be back on Saturday. Jen moves in on Sunday. It'd look awful if I wasn't there.'

I hear a soft snore coming from the back and, when I look behind, see it's Rose and not Pug.

'Why is she moving out of her mother's?'

'I don't know. I don't think Gus knows either — he'd tell me. It just seems to be they've had a falling-out and her answer is to come and live with Dad.'

'Dad and Leah,' I correct her.

'Yeah, that.' She sighs a long, deep sigh. 'Hopefully, she'll realize I'm really an evil stepmother and run home to Mummy.'

'Maleficent . . . Ma-leah-cent.' I laugh, knowing the truth will be Leah tripping over herself to make Jen feel at home.

'Go on, laugh. You won't be laughing when I'm around in yours hiding on a more local level.'

'Anytime.' I shake my head. 'Anytime. Ma-leah-cent. I think that's my new nickname for you.'

'Hah-bloody-hah.' She clicks the indicators on and pulls towards the left. 'There's a McDonald's a few miles up ahead. I need comfort food.'

'Mmm.' I need comfort food too. I need comfort, full stop.

My phone pings a text and this time I try and read it, instantly feeling sick. Theo again.

'You should call him,' Leah states.

'I'm not calling him. Not yet.'

'*What* is going on, Jess? There's more to this than meets the eye,' Leah says, her brow all creased.

'You'll ruin your Botox.' I wag a finger at her.

'Answer me,' she demands.

I shrug, am about to defend my stance.

'Jesus, Jess. You only have a few friends in life and Theo's a good one. Is this still about him

242

and Anna?' She's shaking her head and I tell her to watch the road.

'It's not just that,' I say, peering over my shoulder to check Rose is asleep.

'What then?'

'We kissed.' I can't even tell her what my head is really afraid of, what scenarios I have come up with since discovering a handkerchief.

Her head shoots out from her neck like one of those old-fashioned toys that bends into a cup and sips from it. 'You did what?'

'You heard me. It was the night he told me about the letter and Anna, and afterwards . . . Well, it happened, and since then I've just been mad as hell at him. He so should have told me before any bloody letter allowed him to. I don't care what you think.' I take a breath. 'I honestly think he'd have let Sean just take Rose away and said nothing to me, even though he knew Sean wasn't her father. Bloody ethics. Like I care about his fucking ethics.' I am surprised at my own tone of voice.

'He wouldn't have.' Leah is almost spitting. 'And you're bloody unbelievable. You're saying you're mad at him about one thing and really you're mad at him because a line got crossed.'

'I'm not.' I fold my arms. 'You don't understand. I can't trust him.'

She looks at me as though I've finally lost my mind. 'McDonald's up ahead. You'd better wake Rose. Mind you, you're enough to make me seriously lose my appetite.'

My face turns to look out through my window. When I find my voice, it's cracked. 'Don't tell me off. Help me,' I whisper to her, swallowing a lump in my throat. 'I'm lost.'

She sighs, close to tears herself, and reaches for my hand. 'We'll work it out, Jess. We'll work it out, but for Christ's sake stop seeing friends as foes and stop thinking the worst of Anna. There, I've said it. She made mistakes. Who doesn't make mistakes?' She glances back at Rose in the rear-view mirror. 'Not everyone's mistakes result in such joy.'

She pulls into the slip road for the services and I'm silent, remembering Anna's first tattoo: *Felix culpa*. As we search for a parking space, cars, trucks, and hordes of people flash by my window, all of them certain of their destination. Whereas, I am well and truly lost.

30

Jess

It's obvious as soon as we land on our parents that Dad's not well. Mum seems very bothered that we've come, and suddenly the idea of surprising her so that she doesn't fuss seems like a very bad one. By the time we get there, having stopped to eat, it's almost one thirty. Mum is still in her dressing gown: it's wide open, her nightie underneath. Her hair hasn't been brushed. There are signs of Monday's makeup still around the edges of her eyes.

I let Rose and Pug into the back garden, warning her to stay near the house where I can see her. With one eye on my dishevelled mother and one eye on my wild granddaughter, running around like a dervish with the dog, I learn that Dad has been in bed since they got back. My mother doesn't want to use the words that it was all too much for him, but it obviously was.

Ever-practical Leah has been through the fridge and is making notes on her phone.

'Right,' she says, 'you need food in. I'm going up to see Dad before I pop out to get stuff and then, Mum ... ' She fixes her eyes firmly on my mother's. 'Then, when I get back, you are going to listen to some sense. You need help here. No more, 'I can manage' shit.'

Mum's face flinches and I walk across to the back of the room and pull the sliding door open. 'Rose!' I shout. 'Up near the house, please. Stay back from the water.'

Leah has left the room by the time I watch Rose return and I hear her car start up and rev out of the driveway.

'Well . . . ' Mum says.

'She's right. And you know it. Time to stop fighting. Let some people help you. It's the same advice you've been giving me, Mum, and it's time you listened.'

She slumps into a nearby chair. 'I feel like I'm letting him down.

'I'm going to make you a cup of tea. Have you had anything to eat?'

'I ate the remains of your dad's breakfast. He's only eaten half a slice of toast today.'

'And what?' I take the chance to look out of the window as I put the kettle onto boil. Rose is just outside on the patio, playing with Pug and a tennis ball. 'You had the other half?'

She nods. 'Maybe it's good you're here. Maybe things happen for a reason and maybe I do need to get some help.'

I frown, don't let her see, but I hate that expression so much. Things happen for a reason. *Do they? So, why is my daughter dead at twenty-four? Tell me, whoever is sorting out all the reasons up there?* I look heaven-bound as I dangle a teabag over some boiling water and hand it, weak and black, to Mum.

'I'm going to pop in and see Dad. Keep an eye on Rose.'

She nods. 'Make sure he's warm. He keeps tossing the duvet off himself.'

In their bedroom, Dad has indeed thrown the duvet off the good side of his body. He's propped up on pillows and attempts a smile when he sees me.

'Dar-l — ing,' he whispers.

I kiss his cheek. He's hot, not temperature hot but hot. It has warmed up outside, so I open a window a bit.

'Mum's worried about you.'

He makes an attempt to roll his eyes.

'She loves you . . . Says you haven't really eaten the last couple of days.'

He shakes his head.

'Sleeping okay?'

'Lo-ts.'

'Rose and I have come to see you. In fact, Rose, Leah and I have come to see you. Truth is we're running away. I don't want to be at home. Too many memories at the moment and Leah is having time out before her step-daughter moves in with them. This morning, running home to Mummy and Daddy at the Lakes seemed like a good idea.' I make a face.

'Wel-cc-om-e.'

I know he means that we're always welcome. I also know the few sentences he's shared this morning, more than he's said to me for ages, exhaust him. I fluff his pillows for him, tell him to rest. The room faces the lake and I look out towards it. Rose is there, as ordered, still in place on the patio next to the house. I can't see Pug but I can hear her excited barking.

247

Standing at the window, I glance around the room. It hasn't changed in twenty years. A floral wallpaper covers one wall — my mother having invented accent walls way, way before anyone else considered the idea. The pale pink peony growing from the trellis on the paper matches the shade of the other three walls. Mum and Dad sleep in a big old bed that they bought at a local antique market. It's dark wood, bulky, with intricate carvings on it that must be a nightmare to keep clean. There's a dressing table next to the window. It's dark wood but nothing like the bed in style, with clear-cut angular lines. Nothing 'matchy-matchy' for Mum . . . Sitting on top of the dressing table is her array of makeup, an open pot of cold cream. Dad has fallen asleep and, before I leave, my fingers touch his forehead.

Leah's back, unpacking a few supplies in the kitchen, muttering something about needing to do a bigger food shop. Mum is watching Rose from the back door. I sidle up to Leah. 'I don't like the look of Dad.'

'Let me handle this.' She leaves the room and I wait to see what handling this actually means. I stand at the door with Mum, both of us quiet. I don't like this. Suddenly the home that has always been my haven, my sanctuary, seems off.

'Why don't you go and have a shower, Mum?'

She looks blankly at me. 'Yes. I should. Of course.'

Leah arrives back just as she's about to leave the room. 'Mum, I've just checked and Dad actually has a temperature. I think we should call Dr Rolls.'

248

'I took it an hour before you all arrived. He was hot but — '

Leah takes my mother's hands in hers. 'You're exhausted. Really, stop being so hard on yourself and let us deal with this. Now, I'm going to call the doctor. Is this his number here on the calendar?' She jerks her head towards the calendar hanging on the wall of the kitchen, a number scribbled in the bottom left corner. Mum nods.

'You go and have a shower, Mum,' I say. 'We'll call the surgery.'

'Nanny!' I hear Rose squeal from the back garden and run to the door. She is standing there, her leggings that I had put on her this morning soaked. 'Pug peed on me,' she says.

'Right.' I look back. Mum has left the room; Leah is on the phone.

'Now, I can wear my new jeans.'

I know immediately she's lying. Somehow she's poured water on herself, probably from a nearby bucket of rainwater. She wanted to wear them this morning and I wouldn't let her. I march her out to the bag, still sitting in the hallway, and change her into her favoured jeans, wordlessly. I haven't the energy, but it does not go unnoticed that on the one hand I am struggling with the fact that my daughter has obviously lied openly to me for years, and now Rose has done the same without even blinking. The apple, I shake my head, does not fall far from the tree.

★ ★ ★

Within a couple of hours, Dad has been diagnosed with a urine infection. Leah has already been to the chemist, got his prescription for antibiotics and given him the first dose. My mother looks like my mother again and Leah has told her that there are two carers coming later today to meet her. If she likes them, they start a job-share tomorrow. Mum hasn't argued once, just nodded, and I'm embarrassed that though we knew she needed help, neither of us realized quite how near the end of her rope she was.

Rose is looking at children's television, and it's almost four o'clock before I think of the phone. I sit on the edge of my childhood bed, remove it from my bag. Turned on, the date of Anna's accident keyed in, it comes to life immediately. I scroll through her photos first and God, there are so many of them from the holiday. My heart quickens as I see her shining face fill the screen, those brilliant white teeth that cost me a fortune when she was thirteen; her body long and lean in that bloody red suit — so full of vibrancy, so full of life. How can it be?

The charge is almost dead, so I plug it in just as the carers arrive. By the time I get there, Leah has greeted them and ushered them into the lake-view room. It's clear from the outset that she has this and I'm merely an onlooker. She leaves them chatting with Mum and beckons me into the kitchen to get drinks. Behind the door she taps her chest quickly with the palm of her hand, rolls her eyes and then looks back through a crack in the door. She grabs my hand and squeezes, forces me to peer through. 'Daniel fucking Craig,' she whispers, 'who the hell knew?' She giggles like a small child as we both look at the male carer, who does bear more than a passing resemblance to the actor. 'Just watch Mum getting her flirt on.'

I laugh, take Rose out into the back garden to give them some privacy. She asks me when we can take the boat out with Gramps. 'Soon,' I tell her. 'As soon as summer comes.'

I'm aware I don't want to be saying no to her. I'm aware I can't be explaining things to her all of the time, things that shouldn't bother children — like the fact that my dad may never take her out in a boat again. She sits on my lap on one of the steps leading down to the lake. Though we have our coats on, it's cold now, the sun having disappeared behind cloud for the day. I hold her close and her flyaway hair tickles my nose. I breathe deep and, no matter how hard I try and imagine it, can't get the slightest whiff of coconut. I get the scent of the Lakes; a fresh, crisp, pine-like scent. I press my nose into her hair further — a vague hint of oranges from the last shampoo. *This is Rose.* I tell myself. She's not Anna. She's Rose. *You have to do it all over again, Jess.*

Rose turns to me and shivers. 'Let's go inside, Nanny,' she says, climbing from my lap and offering me her hand.

'Before we do,' I frame her face with both of mine. 'You told Nanny a little lie earlier, when your clothes got wet, didn't you?'

She frowns, a strange sight on her tiny features. 'How did you know?'

'I just did. You know it's wrong to tell lies, don't you?' I'm on my feet, clutching her hand as we walk back to the house.

'Yes. But I wanted to wear my new jeans and you wouldn't let me.'

So simple. And I hear her mother's voice in it. *But I wanted to be with this married man and I knew you'd never approve.*

'You still can't tell lies to get what you want, Rose.'

'Okay, Nanny. Sorry.'

The circle of life. And round and round I go again.

31

Anna

Raw Honey Blogspot 04/09/2010

I made a birthday cake today for T, my little half-brother. He's seven years old tomorrow, and though he's her uncle, DD has just started to talk and insists he's her 'brudda'. It's so sweet.

We're at the Lakes and when the cake was in the oven, we headed out to the end of the garden, where Gramps was all set up on the deck. He was so excited, the thought of introducing another child to his love of sailing just written all over his wide grin. I was less enthusiastic, my heart thumping in my chest. We dressed DD in the hut; head-to-toe in wet gear, her tiny little life-vest wrapped around her with three strong straps. She almost leapt off the deck into the sail dinghy with him.

I tried to stop myself leaping onto the boat after her, and though they set off happily, DD tucked safely between Gramps's legs, I didn't relax until she was back at shore, in my arms again.

She loved it. Everyone fussed over her. We were all there today — Mama, her sister L (L's husband G was at work), Nanny, Gramps; all clapped wildly when she got back. DD just kept yelling 'More! More!' and pulling away from me, veering towards the dinghy. It was only 'helping' Mummy to ice T's cake that finally

253

distracted her. I suspect sailing With Gramps may become her thing. He's not up for skiing any more — has a bit of sciatica — so he tells me it'll be up to me to get her to love the slopes.

When I iced the cake, I asked Mama how I'm supposed to control the fear when I see her doing something that I know she'll enjoy but might be dangerous. Mama laughed and told me to get used to it; that DD is just like me and that I'll spend half of my life practising how to smile with my heart wedged in the back of my throat.

Something to look forward to?!

Dad brought T and his younger brother E around for a pre-birthday-let's-eat-cake time by the lake. They played with Rose in the garden, enjoying the end of the summer. We ate the cake and the grown-ups sang along with my karaoke machine. Nanny B won the prize for her worryingly drunken rendition of Whitney's 'I Will Always Love You'.

It was a brilliant day.

I'm typing this a little bit pissed myself.

And I will always love them all . . .

32

Jess

Rose and I have been baking. It has never been my forte, but it was something she loved to do with Anna and . . . I want to try. My mother, who has for the first time had help feeding and settling my father down, is sitting by the muted television in the next room, her eyes closed. Leah is seated right by her going through old photographs.

I'm happy to be in the kitchen. Rose, flour in her hair, seems content to be here with me. She's standing on a chair, has already cracked the eggs into the sugar-and-butter mix and she's now beating it with a wooden spoon. I offer to help but she's determined, her face all scrunched up in concentration. Finally, she hands it to me, sighs as if she's exhausted. 'This is the bit Mummy does,' she says. So, I take it and beat it, her standing on the chair beside me, both hands on her hips, ready to tell me when to stop. I laugh and she looks up at me. 'What's funny, Nanny?'

'You are,' I tell her, and dab a bit of the mix from the spoon onto the end of her nose.

'Hey!' she says and wipes it off with her finger before licking it.

When the cakes are in the oven and I'm cleaning the inevitable mess, she's still standing on the chair and staring in through the glass door at them. The buns are small and surprisingly they rise. 'Look at that,' I say, my arm around her.

'They look just like Mummy's,' she says proudly.

I kiss her head. 'They do, don't they?'

'Mummy would say, 'Well done, Rose! Well done, Nanny!' if she could see them.' She jumps down from the chair and heads to the window over the sink, looks outside. 'See them, Mummy?' She talks to the night sky and her tiny forefinger points back to the oven.

I cross over and scoop her up in my arms. Together we stare at the heavens. 'Which one is she?' I ask Rose.

'I'm not sure,' she says. 'Sometimes she moves around.'

I nod into her head, squeeze her. 'But she's up there somewhere,' she says, cuddling into me, then fixes her thumb firmly in her mouth.

★　★　★

By the time we are both lying down in our childhood bedroom, Rose tucked into a pull-up bed between ours, Leah and I have a list. She has made this into some sort of game, as only my sister can. She's the one who has us sticking pins on donkeys in the summer, sacks on Santa in December, charades during both seasons; and she's the only person I know who can complete a Rubik's Cube while singing Madonna's 'Like A Virgin'. Tonight, she's humouring me with a

'Who's the Daddy?' diversion. She's in my bed, both of us huddled under the duvet, which is pulled up over our heads. Leah has a pencil-thin torch stuck between her teeth.

The light shines on our list. It's a short list — three possibilities. We have both come up with two names, one in common. Her offerings are Sean and James. I think from what Theo has told me, from what Anna always believed, Sean's DNA will come back negative. I offer up James and Theo. James is the common denominator, but Leah's brow has developed new ridges since seeing Theo's name there.

He's married, I tell her; he's the one who held back telling me the truth until Anna's funeral, until her letter authorized him to speak — a letter, I remind her, that I haven't seen yet. He's the one she went to see before she died. Anna used to babysit Finn for years. Theo usually drove her home. It could have started back then. I stop talking, feel nauseous even whispering the words.

'It's not Theo.' She shakes her head. 'Integrity runs through Theo like a stick of rock.'

She climbs out of my bed and gets into her own, quiet since I raised his name. 'That's why you're not speaking to him,' she says. 'Nothing to do with a kiss, but you suspect someone you say is your best friend slept with your daughter.'

I squeeze my eyes shut.

'She had a hanky.' I turn on my side towards Leah. 'In her ski suit. A man's hanky. Theo is the only man in the world who still uses handkerchiefs.'

Her head shakes in the darkness. 'You'd better have more than a hanky before you accuse him of anything. Good friends are hard to come by.'

'You think I want it to be him?' I slump onto my pillow, remember the sweet-and-sour kiss, which forces me to think of that Christmas party kiss years ago. He ended up telling Harriet about it last summer. They were having an honesty session — a confessional — during the time they were trying to save their marriage. Harriet confessed to having feelings for another man. Theo confessed to one drunken kiss with me. Of course, now I know it happened around the same time Anna was starting a relationship with her lover. A sound like a low moan escapes me and Leah reaches her hand across the divide of Rose's pull-up bed. I clasp it. 'I can't bear the thought that it might be him.'

'I tried to say it earlier, Jess.' She holds my hand. 'You need to decide what happens if you pursue this. Theo? What if it's not him and you lose a friend? James? What if it is him and he didn't know? If Anna lied about one thing, maybe she lied about others. God knows you could rattle a hornet's nest in a man's marriage, and for what? He'd then have rights over Rose? You could risk losing her to someone you don't even know.'

'I know you're right.' I retreat into the duvet. 'Mum thinks the same. She overheard you and me talking about Sean the other day, told me to 'let sleeping dogs lie'.'

'Anna's gone. Nothing will bring her back.'

Within minutes, her hand has slipped and I'm

listening to Leah's throaty snores. I reach out and touch Rose. She shifts slightly in her sleep. I turn on my side and stare at her. It's when I look at her — when I feel that primal link to Anna — that I can find myself submerged. It's like being underwater and not being able to breathe. Anna *is* gone, and to endure her loss is enough without questioning everything I thought I knew about her.

★ ★ ★

I am dazed with sleeplessness the next day. It's early afternoon and Leah has gone for a walk with Pug on the lead and Mum is keeping an eye on Rose for me. I'm hiding away; seated at the far end of the garden in what Dad calls his 'hut'. It's a small, raised, decked area with an empty garden shed in it — empty but for Dad's rocking chair. The door has been removed, allowing a permanent view over the lake. Today, it's deathly quiet. No boats, no people, very few sounds, just the chatter of random birds above my head and in the bushes next to the shed. The water is mirror smooth, just a tiny ripple when you look for one. It reminds me of a mirror hanging in Anna's room, one of those ones with wavy sides.

I turn her phone over in my hands, then switch it on and enter the correct code. 'Just give yourself some lone time,' Leah had warned. Today's the day I tackle her messages and emails. Beside me, I have a large mug of hot chocolate.

I scan through Anna's texts, find the last

thread before the avalanche struck. It's from 'Popeye', who features heavily in her messages and, when I glance, in her emails too. I'm relieved to see the number isn't Theo's, though I had never really believed it would be. I have dismissed the hanky. *It cannot be and is not Theo*, I have told myself over and over rhythmically in my head since 04:40 this morning. I imagine Popeye to be some buffed gym freak and ignore completely the fact that Theo's surname is Pope and squirrelled away in the name 'Popeye'. *It cannot be and is not Theo.*

I wonder who it is; know that now I have his number, that all I have to do to find out is to ring it. But, before that, I need to know who and what I'm dealing with. I open the last message from Anna, realize it makes no sense on its own, so trace it back to a week or so before she travelled. My eyes rest on a capitalized text from him. I'm irrationally irritated by his nickname. I remember the old and dated cartoon character, but Rose has a favourite DVD, a non-animated story with Robin Williams playing the spinach-loving sailor. If I only disliked the idea of the man before, I *hate* the image I have of him now.

YOU ALREADY KNOW HOW I FEEL are the first words I read of his.

Anna: I was hoping you'd had a change of heart.

Him: No.

Anna: WHAT ABOUT ROSE? Don't you think I'd love her to have a sibling?

Him: I'm sorry, honey-girl, really I am. You know I can't change how I feel about this. ☹

260

I rest the phone on my lap. Honey-girl? Downturned smiley face? I feel nauseous. *Theo would never speak or write those words.* This is the married man who impregnated my daughter a second time. I don't get that either. One 'mistake', yes. Two? No. Anna was careful enough to hide a relationship from me for years. She was careful enough to never get pregnant with anyone else she had ever been with. As per normal with my daughter of late, nothing makes any sense. I finish the cooling hot chocolate before scan-reading the last week of Popeye and his honey-girl's texts. Then, I stand up, walk ten paces, and heave the drink up again into the edge of the lake. I look skywards. A little too early for the stars yet, but it's still as if she's sulking, as if she knows I'm reading her stuff.

An hour later, the light is changing. I have learned that no matter how I hoped otherwise, the truth is Anna was someone's *mistress*. I roll the word around my tongue and nothing about it fits. Nothing about the woman whose texts I'm reading feels like Anna. Shadows dance across the edge of the water and it's no longer still. A wind has appeared from the east and waves ripple across the lake like dominoes. Sailing boats have emerged, some of them yet stationary, some of them being carried along swiftly, left to right.

The phone is on the decked floor next to me while I mull some of this over. Without thinking too much, I bend down, grab it, and dial the number in her contacts before I can talk myself out of it. All I hear is an automated message

261

telling me that Popeye's phone is switched off.

I'm leaning forward on the rocking chair, the curved arch tilted to the front, my feet planted flat to ground me. My head is in my hands. I'm shivering and it takes her calling my name several times before I realize my mother is standing beside me.

'Come inside,' she orders, her voice angry, as if I were a six-year-old who had left the house midwinter with no coat on.

I can't move.

'Jess, you're freezing. You'll catch your death. Inside, now.'

I start to laugh, at first a low chuckle, then something louder that makes me break into a coughing fit. 'Death can't be caught, Mum,' I whisper. 'It just jumps up and catches you unawares when you're out skiing.'

Mum bends down to me, rubs both my arms. 'Inside, please, now. Come on.' She puts her hands on my shoulders and tugs, and I only move for fear of my elderly mother falling over. We walk slowly back up the garden. She has one arm around my shoulder and her free hand rubs mine as if she's trying to increase the blood flow. I bend into her crook, want her to rub it away, this resident ache in my heart.

'I'd take it from you if I could,' she whispers, and yet again I wonder how my mother seems to read my mind. And yet again, I wonder how I thought I could read my daughter's, and how I'd got it so, so, spectacularly wrong . . .

★ ★ ★

262

The next morning, just after Mum has gone to the shops with Rose, I've finished giving Dad some breakfast in bed and Doug drops by with his sons. They run around the back garden, their shoes squelching in the wet ground as Doug and I look on from the terrace. One of them looks so like him, but with his wife's dark brown, intense eyes. The older one is a facsimile of Carol.

'Sean called,' he says. 'The test results are back. He's definitely not Rose's father and he's taken it badly.'

Whatever sleeping giant I have kicked is now wide awake. Two clear facts emerge. Anna definitely lied and Anna, in doing so, has left a string of misery behind her. Sean, his parents, Rose — all of them; all of us — are going to have to find a way to readjust to this truth. Popeye is for now shelved.

'He's coming up to tell his parents today.' Doug keeps his voice low. 'Doesn't want to do it on the phone.'

'Jesus . . . '

'It's a mess.'

'Do you think I should — '

'No, Jess, stay away.'

'But they're not too far from here. I feel responsible.'

'Jess, you are responsible!'

I flinch.

'What I mean is you are, we are, we all are, but I tell you one thing, one person who's not responsible, who always did the right thing by Anna, is Sean, and he's the one hurting now.'

I swallow hard, regret coursing through my

263

veins. I shouldn't have started this.

'You get to keep Rose,' he whispered. 'That was what mattered. It's what has driven us and, in the long run, it's what's best for Rose, but Jesus, Jess, what are we going to tell her? She's just lost her mother and now she's going to lose her father too?'

I try to run my hand through my hair, catch my fingers in the morning-time, untamed mess. The boys have found an old tennis ball; they're throwing it in the air and Pug is leaping skywards towards it.

'It is what it is.' Doug shakes his head. 'Look, can Rose come over later today to play with the boys? They were hoping to see her before you head back.'

I nod. 'I'll drop her over.'

Doug only manages to get the excitable pair back in the car with a promise of a visit from Rose. When I return to the kitchen, robotic-like, I spoon coffee and boiling water into a mug. Pug circles my legs and I pick her up and take my drink out into the back garden. It's still early. Steam rises from the patio where the spring sun fights the overnight dew on the stones. I walk towards the edge of the water, treading over the muddy footprints that Tom and Ethan have left. Putting Pug down, she bolts from my hands and runs through the mud. Rose and I will have to wash her later.

From nowhere, a deep sigh, followed by a gut-wrenching scream escape from the depths of my belly. I hurl my mug to the water, watch it soar through the air and land with a heavy splash

264

before disappearing. Then I scream again, crying at the top of my voice. GOD. IS. A. BITCH.

I feel immediate guilt and relief. Guilt because someone, somewhere will have heard that. Relief because I needed it. Back at the house, Leah is leaning in the doorway to the garden, static as a statue. My father is up out of his sick bed, standing above her, staring out of his bedroom window, his good hand flattened against the glass. Pug runs to me and I pick her up, holding her away from my clothes. By the time I stand upright again, Dad and Leah have both vanished. I'm overcome by a coughing fit after my vocal efforts and walk slowly back to the house. I use the lead to tie Pug to the patio table until I can wash her in a few minutes.

'Morning.' Leah pads across the heated tiled floor towards me and hands me another mug of coffee as I remove my shoes.

'Morning. You came to bed late,' I say. Neither of us refers to my outburst.

She yawns. 'Lots of work shit to catch up on. Then Gus kept me on the phone for an hour.'

'Everything okay?'

'It's fine. He just hates me being away.'

I play with the handle on the cafetiere. 'Sean's tests are back. He's not the father.'

Leah plonks onto one of the chairs. 'Shit.'

'Yup.'

'Nightmare.' She chews her bottom lip.

'I'm dropping Rose over to Doug's for a bit. Sean is going to his parents' to tell them. Doug told me not to, but do you think I should go over there?'

265

'Are you mad? Stay out of it.' She spoons more sugar into her own drink. 'Don't even think about it. I will sit on you if I have to until we go home in the morning.'

'I feel guilty.'

'Find a way to live with it.' She peers at me through the steam above her mug as she sips. 'You have Rose now. Just find a way to deal with the guilt.'

'If Anna were here, I'd ask her for hints. Lessons on how to deal with guilt.'

'If Anna were here, none of this mess would be happening.'

I tie my hair up with a tieback I find in one of Mum's kitchen drawers, look out through the window to the lake. *Ain't that a fact, Honey-girl. Ain't that a fact . . . ?*

33

Jess

Rose has had such fun with Tom and Ethan that she's sleeping over at Doug's. Leah and I have opened a bottle of wine, while Mum is upstairs with Dad and Daniel Craig.

'It's wrong, I'm telling you, a woman of her age.' She grins. 'If we're not careful, you and I will come from a broken home.'

It's our last night here. Dad is much improved and Mum has taken to both the carers, especially the one Leah has nicknamed Diet Coke.

I am relaxing in an easy chair, looking out at the mirror shimmers on the lake, when Leah looks at me and announces, 'I want to work on something tonight, so I suppose I'll just let you see it.'

I crane my head to see what she has in a large refuse sack that she pulls out from behind the sofa. It reminds me of the black bag I have shoved under the stairs at home; the one in which I have put all of Anna's mail. She's not here, yet the mail keeps coming. Leah removes a square box, about thirty centimetres by thirty. It is shiny and red.

'What is it?' I'm fascinated.

'I'm going to need some stuff from you to make it work anyway, so you'll have to know sooner rather than later, I suppose,' she says without looking at me.

I'm intrigued, pull the bag towards me and look inside. There are photographs, large silver stars, a CD of *The Lion King*, a book and some of Rose's smaller toys. Leah has the box on her lap and, when she opens it, there's what looks like a pillowcase inside. I recognize it as the one from Anna's bed and make a face.

'Don't worry. It's not from Anna's room. I found another set like it on eBay, knew it was a fabric Rose would recognize. I'm using it for lining.' As she speaks, I catch sight of the inside of the lid, and there is the most beautiful blown-up picture of Anna and Rose. I gasp.

'It's for Rose's birthday, a memory box for her to remember Anna by.'

My lower lip trembles and I press it with my fingers to stop it. 'What a lovely thing . . . ' is all I can muster. I drop to the floor in front of her and pull my sister into a fierce hug. 'What a lovely thing. Thank you. She'll love it.'

'Yeah, yeah, you love me, I know. I'm the best aunt in the world, I know.' She pushes me away gently. 'Have a better look.' She nudges her head towards the bag of goodies.

I'm on my knees right by the bag but shake my head. 'I don't know that I can.'

'Go on. Do lucky dip, say, five times?'

I don't move. She's already head down, concentrating on gluing the pieces of pillowcase in place.

'When did you cut them?'

'I wasn't really working *all* of last night,' she says.

I dip my hand in the bag, move it around, pull a photograph out and take a sip from my glass before I turn it over.

'Let's see?' She bends towards it to get a better look.

It's one of Anna with Rose sitting on her knee, when she was about three. They're both focusing on making a puzzle on a table and their expressions mirror each other completely.

'Peas in a pod,' Leah says. 'Perhaps there was no Dad involved. Maybe Anna just split in two. See, that's how you move forward. Pretend Rose is a miracle of science.'

'She is anyway.' My mother's voice sounds behind us and she takes the chair next to Leah. 'Jesus, put the lid on that glue will you, we'll all be high as kites.' Daniel has left for the evening.

Leah does as she is told and Mum picks up something from the box, removes a needle and thread from it.

'Mum's idea,' Leah says. 'It's a heart made from the same fabric.'

'I'll stuff it, make it soft, and it will be scented when we spray Anna's perfume on it. And the heart was my idea but the box is Leah's.' Mum smiles across at her and Leah grins back. My own heartbeat begins to settle. This is good. It is all good, I tell myself. We are here, my family and I, remembering Anna. For the first time since December I feel like celebrating her life rather than utter despair. I feel like these women here have helped me inch forward into the new landscape that is life without Anna.

'Thank you both,' I say, and delve into the bag again. I pull out what looks like a Mars bar and Leah laughs. 'That may not last when Rose sees it, but it was Anna's favourite.'

'God, remember when she was doing her dissertation?' I smile. 'Whatever food I tried to get into her, the only staple was these. At least three of them a day. And you're right, it won't last . . .'

My hand dips in again and I retrieve a tiny, pink, well-loved teddy bear. 'Beany,' I say aloud. It was one of Anna's collection of Beanie toys, her very favourite.

'Sorry.' Leah looks at me, bites her bottom lip. 'I sort of nicked that from her room the night we were . . . remember when we were both in there?' Neither of us speaks aloud in front of my mother of the night spent looking for papers.

I stand up, nuzzle Beany to my face and walk towards the large windows overlooking the lake. It's quiet out there tonight; no wind blowing, no fox barking, nothing.

'Would you mind if I scattered her here, Mum?' It's the first time I have spoken aloud of the container I have at home in my wardrobe. Doug agreed that I should keep it until we decide where to finally scatter her ashes. I'm quite sure he'd be very happy for her to be here and I think Anna would like it. I see them glance at each other in the window reflection. 'If that's what you want, darling.'

'I think she'd like that. Here, at the house, out there on the water.' I look up at the starry sky. 'The sky is always clearer here. I think Rose would like it too.' I return to my seat, replace Beany in the bag.

'You done?' Leah asks. 'That was only a trio of lucky dips.'

'I'll wait for Rose's birthday' I drain my glass, lean forward and fill Leah's and mine again. I wave the bottle at Mum who shakes her head.

They're chatting amongst themselves about the carers. Leah is trying to convince Mum that Diet Coke man is actually Daniel Craig moonlighting. He has lots of downtime, she tells her, in between making Hollywood blockbusters, and it's his way of giving back to the community. I smile.

Having spent the afternoon on Anna's phone, I'm scrolling through my own; thirteen emails in my work inbox which, frankly, can wait. In the text messages, Theo, if nothing else, is persistent:

I'm trying to find a way to say you're being stupid without making you feel any worse. We're friends. We've been friends for more than a decade since the surgery days. We've laughed and cried over that decade. (I am a metrosexual man.) So, enough sending me to Coventry because we had a kiss. Enough being angry because I couldn't tell you about Anna. I did tell you when I could. Was I wrong to? Because I did, you will win any fight Sean brings. Yet because I did, you're not talking to me. How does that work, Jess?

Suddenly, I feel very tired. Body-tired, bone-tired. My fight reflex is weary. Theo *did* tell me when he could, which reminds me of Anna's letter. I have less and less desire to insist on seeing it and have come to the conclusion that I either trust Theo or I don't. Seeing it doesn't seem to matter so much when I am here in my mother's house, surrounded by love. I close my eyes and try hard to tap into it, to allow it to nourish me. I imagine it a turquoise colour flowing through me, sustaining me.

My thumbs poised to reply, the words seem to type themselves:

You're right. I'm sorry. When I get back from the Lakes, let's talk. Or let's not? I'm trying hard to think about moving on. I'm telling myself it doesn't matter who fathered Rose. It doesn't matter what Anna did or didn't do. I loved her. If she was here today, I WOULD STILL LOVE HER.

The phone pings an immediate reply. Leah looks across at me, mouths the word 'Theo'. I nod, read the text.

Move forward. Good plan. You need a friend? x

Always x

I check my single-word reply, certain it's what I really mean, and then I press send.

★ ★ ★

When we walk back in the door of our home, Rose climbs the stairs with Pug tucked under her arm. She's whispering softly to her as if she were a doll. I bend down to pick up the mail. There are the usual windowed envelopes addressed to Anna, which I put straight into the bag under the stairs, and also a cream-coloured envelope addressed to me. I leave it in the kitchen as Rose calls down to me: Pug has weed on her bed.

An hour later, the scolded dog is dozing on the same linen, nestling in the pile of dirty washing on the floor in front of the washing machine. She looks cosy and warm just as I have a sneezing fit. I slump down on the floor beside Pug, tug at a sodden tissue up my sleeve. I blow my nose then stroke the dog, who looks at me with one half-open eye, as if she's letting me know she's listening. 'I love you, Pug,' I whisper. 'Just don't tell anyone, okay?'

I close my eyes, pinch the bridge of my nose, and breathe as deep as my streaming nose will allow. Minutes later, when I open them again, Rose is beside me lifting the dog into her arms again. She has an old neon pink Babygro and is asking if Pug can wear it. I try to explain that dogs are not dolls and shouldn't really be dressed up. Her response is to tell me all about her friend Hayley's dog who has his own coat and she just wants to make one. She lets Pug down and pulls herself up onto a breakfast stool.

I find the scissors and hand them to her. 'Be careful. You'll need to cut the feet off and you probably won't be able to close it, I — '

'Stop worrying, Nanny.' She grins up at me as she slowly trims the feet.

'Where did you get that anyway?' My hand reaches out to touch the almost threadbare outfit.

'Mummy gave it to me for 'Lou-lou' dolly but I think it will be much better on Pug.'

'Okay' I look around to see that the poor dog has rightly scarpered.

'Is that a birthday card for me?' She spots the envelope.

'No, it's for me, I'd forgotten about it.' I don't

273

recognize the handwriting, open it, one eye on Rose with the scissors. It's a pretty card with peonies on the front and the words, 'Just a note to say . . . ' Inside, some handwritten words make my heart swell.

Jess, I hope you don't mind me calling you by your first name since we've never met. I did, however, meet your beautiful daughter, and have wanted to write ever since I heard of her death. Anna was beautiful — in both body and spirit.

We met last year during the 'Choral For Cancer' event. She befriended my own daughter, Imogen, who has beaten childhood cancer and has huge dreams of being a singer. Anna was wonderful to her, encouraging her to sing, telling her not to feel like she had to do it in public; just to do it because it made her feel good. I bitterly regret not writing to Anna afterwards the way I promised myself I would. I wanted to thank her — but life, busy as it always is, got in the way. I never did write that letter so I'm writing to you instead.

I can only try to imagine the hole in your life, but want you to know I'm praying for you and Anna's daughter, Rose, whom she spoke of all of the time and seemed to love with all her heart.

In shared sorrow and with love, Aimee Gardner

I place the card on the windowsill and return to Rose's handiwork. As I stroke her hair, taming

274

some stray bits back into her ponytail, it is the kindness of a stranger that overwhelms me.

Aimee Gardner's words about Anna slot like missing jigsaw pieces into the recent confused picture of her. The fact is that she was a kind and caring young woman. That was my daughter. Yes, she made mistakes, but they're not what I want to focus on now. I do not want to dwell any more on her affair with a married man, her abuse of Sean's trust and yes, mine too — it's not how I want to remember her. Nor will she be sainted. That cannot happen either. But she can be Anna, my kind, inspiring, funny daughter.

'You think she'll like it, Nanny?' Rose holds up the now footless pink Babygro.

'She'll love it,' I tell her. I'm not sure about Pug, but Anna, I know, is laughing loudly somewhere.

PART THREE

34

Anna

Raw Honey Blogspot 15/03/2011

We're finished. Something happened. Afterwards, I felt like a mirror was held up to my face making me see me as I am. Selfish. I've wanted to puke since.

We were caught.

It was Rose's second birthday and Mama and I had combined it with a celebration for both of our birthdays last month, so everybody and anybody we know was there.

He was milling around in the background and I'd gone upstairs to the loo. He knocked on the door and, when I opened it, He pushed through, grabbed hold of me and kissed me. I told Him not to be so fucking stupid, but was smiling as I left the room, a small part of me loving that He'd taken a risk.

Outside was a man I love and respect, standing as tall as I ever remember him, and I felt small, weak and stupid. He said nothing, just stared. Gramps *adores* me and I never, ever want him to look at me like that again.

Before he and Grandma left, he hugged me hard, whispered in my ear, 'This is beneath you, Anna.' I didn't sleep a wink last night. I feel like the horrible person I am. It's over. I've told Him. The reality check forced me to think about the fallout I always manage

279

to ignore. I couldn't face it. Love, obsession, whatever it is between us, we both agree now that we have to find a way to squash it like an ant underfoot. Kill it. Dead.

35

Theo

'We have a problem.' Harriet spoke the words from behind Finn, who shoved past her and Theo to run up the stairs to his room. She followed him into the hall, took her coat off and hung it on the coat rack.

Theo stretched his eyebrows. 'Come in. Do.'

Harriet walked into the den, parked herself in the corner of the sofa that she had always preferred. 'Have you got any wine?'

Wordlessly, Theo went to the fridge and removed a bottle, unscrewed it and poured her a glass. She never drank when she had to drive. Whatever the problem was, he held off pouring one for himself.

He handed it to her, closed the door. 'What's up?'

'Our son. Our son is what's up.' She took a gulp and then placed the glass on the coffee table before turning to face him.

'I tried to have a chat with him, like we talked about. I just wanted him to know that we both love him, that we both have his interests at heart, but he just exploded — went off on one about him never being able to trust anyone, that all grown-ups are liars.'

Theo moved from the edge of the opposite sofa into its middle, chewed on a hangnail under his thumb.

'Last night, when he was asleep, I took his laptop.'

Theo groaned. 'I'm not going to like this, am I?'

'Look, I know. I value Finn's privacy too, but I really didn't even recognize him when he let go. It was like he was possessed! This isn't just pre-teenage shit. Nor is this because he distrusts his mother.' She narrowed her eyes at Theo. 'Anyway, there wasn't anything obvious until I checked his viewing history.'

Upstairs, right above them in Finn's room, came the booming sound of loud music.

'Shit, Theo, he's eleven. I wasn't expecting this crap until at least thirteen.'

'He wasn't expecting what he has either.' Theo shrugged. 'I think the combination of you leaving and Anna dying — '

'About Anna . . . ' Harriet stood, pulled her phone from her front jeans pocket and sat again. 'Crap, I can't — '

Theo handed her his reading glasses.

'Thanks,' she said, and scrolled through her phone.

'*What* about Anna?' he asked.

Harriet came and sat on the coffee table. Two feet from him, Theo was surprised at the proximity, almost flinched.

'Look.' She angled the phone towards him. 'This is what I found. Since last October, Finn has visited this website almost daily.'

Theo removed his glasses from his wife's head. 'What is it?'

'It was Anna's blog. She ran a blog. I mean, it's not obviously hers at first, but when I

282

questioned him about it, asked why he was reading it, he went absolutely apeshit.' She shook her head. 'So I read it into the night — she was having an affair, Theo . . . '

Theo scratched the stubble on his chin, stood, and edged past her. 'I'm getting a drink. Just don't say another word.'

He removed another wine glass from the cupboard, filled it halfway, and cursed the fact that the surgery was testing a new scheme for weekend out-of-hours services. During the trial period, the GPs had to cover one weekend in every four. His weekend for a possible call-out. He took one large gulp and headed back to Harriet, ignoring the loud racket booming down the stairwell.

He sat next to her on the sofa and took her phone in his hand. 'Let me see.'

Within only two minutes he could tell it was indeed Anna. Names had been hidden or changed but it was Anna. Anna, who was fanatical about her privacy, talking about her life on a public blog.

Harriet smoothed her long hair down each side of her head with the back of both of her hands. 'He was obsessed with the site. I wanted to know why, so I spent most of last night reading it. Look, do you mind if I crash here tonight? We have a lot to talk about and I really don't feel like driving back. I'll take the sofa.'

Theo nodded. 'You have the bed. I'll — '

'No. I'll be fine here.' She kicked off her shoes and put her feet up on the coffee table. 'He has an email account.'

'Who?'

'Finn. He calls himself 'Solarbomb'.'

Theo recalled his real pride when Finn had shown him a school project on the very subject.

'I haven't had time to read it all, but he has definitely commented on some blog posts.'

'Christ.' Theo ran a hand through his hair, looked up to the ceiling. 'How would, how does he even know it exists?'

'He told me today that the last time Anna babysat here — do you remember it was when we went out to dinner at Ed and Jules's place in November?'

Theo remembered it well. He had drunk too much and Harriet had said far too little about that after the fact, the rot already well established in their decaying marriage.

'Anna took a call on her mobile, went into the kitchen to take it, and he looked at what she had been typing here on the laptop.' Harriet looked around the room. 'Right here . . . Anyway, he memorized the website and has fixated on it ever since.'

'But why . . . ?'

'That's where you come in. You have to ask. He's mad as fuck at me for invading his laptop, as he calls it.' She shook her head. 'Maybe he was a bit in love with her. It happens. Eleven-year-old boy, beautiful young woman . . . '

Theo sighed, removed his glasses and tossed them on the table. 'I'll talk to him. Maybe not tonight but — '

'I think we should both do it and I think it should be tonight.'

'Harriet, he's not going anywhere, he's — '

284

'When I said we have a problem, I meant it. He says he's going to tell Jess, and that Jess should know she's been lied to. When he was crying, he talked about Rose. He's fond of her. It's all so fucked up in his head and I think he wishes he knew none of it.'

Theo looked at the ceiling, thought of Finn upstairs, confused and angry, tried to imagine what was going on in his head.

'This is wrapped up in you, whether you like it or not.' He deliberately looked straight ahead, avoiding Harriet's eyes. 'Anna was Rose's mum and she died, left Rose. Anna, it seems, told lies. Come on, Harriet. Look at this from his point of view. It's not great when he loved you both and both of you left and lied . . . '

'Thanks for that.' She glared at him.

Theo shrugged. 'I'm not saying he's right. I'm saying I think it's what he thinks, how he feels.'

Harriet drained the glass.

'Even I see that day as a turning point. Anna died then, Harriet, everyone knew it but no one wanted to face it. I lost you too that day.' He waved away the objection that she was going to make. 'I know we were in trouble beforehand, but I lost you that day. Finn lost you and, since then, he's confused and it's up to us to help him find his way again.'

She sighed, resigned. 'You're probably right.'

Neither spoke for a minute before she said: 'Jess. He's determined to tell her and I know how you feel about Jess . . . '

'Not this again, Harriet, really?' Theo shook his head.

285

She put a hand on his knee. 'You're right about what's going on in our son's head, so no recriminations. I'm saying this out of concern for Jess. I know there's no comparison to you having a kiss with Jess way back whenever and what I've done to our family. I know that. I'm sorry I poked you in the ribs with it when we were rowing the other day on the phone.' She sat back in the chair. 'It was guilt. There's not a day goes by where I don't feel guilty, where I don't wonder if my happiness is coming at too high a price. It's shameless guilt and I'm sorry' She laid her head against his shoulder.

'I just know you'd want the best for Jess and I'm not convinced reading this stuff about Anna would be good for her right now.'

No, Theo thought. *Not right now. And probably never.* He looked down at Harriet's phone, at the image of Anna's blog, and knew what he too would be reading through the night.

'Shall we go up?' she asked.

Theo blew out the full contents of his lungs. 'If you think we should both do it, now is the time . . . '

★   ★   ★

Within a few minutes, Theo had unplugged the music in his son's bedroom.

Harriet hovered behind him, barefoot. 'We both want to talk to you,' she said.

Finn was lying down, his knees angled, his fingers laced behind his head. 'I don't want to talk to you.'

286

'Well.' Theo took a seat on the edge of the bed while Harriet stood hugging her arms. 'If you won't talk, you're going to have to listen.'

Finn reached for his earphones and placed them slowly on his head. Theo glanced at Harriet, shrugged, then swooped forward and pulled them from him, yanking them from his iPod at the same time.

'You *will* either talk or listen. Which is it to be?' he asked, coiling the white wire around his hand. Finn remained still and silent.

'Right. Listening it is. Whatever it is you think you've learned about Anna, just remember the person you loved. Remember the woman that you've been telling Rose about, the woman who sang, who looked after you, who has shared Christmas here with us. That was Anna. You've been encouraging Rose, Finn, because you're old enough to understand her loss. She's a little girl, just a little girl.' He edged himself nearer his son and Finn glared, moved away deliberately.

'None of us are simple. We're made up of so many different parts. You're always talking about aliens being more evolved. Maybe they are; maybe they've managed to remove emotion from their race — things would probably be a lot easier. Anna was all of the things I've just said and, yes, she was also more. She made choices that upset you. They upset her too, I'm sure, but she still made them. And they're part of her too, Finn.' He shook his head. 'None of us are simple.'

Harriet sniffed behind him and he turned to look at her, patted the bed beside him. She came

287

and sat close, leaned against him. 'We both love you,' Theo continued. 'Both of us are here. Both of us ready to listen to anything at all you have to say. Talk. Please, Finn.'

He saw tears gather in his son's eyes, resisted the urge to reach forward and hold him.

'Grown-ups lie,' Finn whispered.

'Some of us do,' Theo replied.

'All my life, you and Mum drumming into me not to lie. But you lied to Dad, Mum. Roland.' The last word came with spittle and Harriet flinched, gripped Theo's arm with her hidden fingers.

'She didn't actually. She never lied.' Theo shook his head. 'Your mum told me she had feelings for someone else. We tried really hard to work it out, but those feelings grew stronger and eventually . . . Your mother fell in love with someone else, but I have always known and she never lied.' He leaned forward. 'And you want to know why we tried so hard? For you, Finn. Neither of us ever wanted this for you.'

'I'm sorry, Finn.' Harriet licked her silent tears from her top lip. Theo reached into his pocket and handed her a handkerchief. 'I can't tell you how much I wish I was still at home here with you and your dad. How much easier it would have been; but it wouldn't have been fair on any of us.'

'This, Finn,' Theo said, 'is what you have. You have two parents who love you, one living in town and one living here with you. It's time to try to move on with that.'

Finn bit his bottom lip.

'And,' Theo added, 'please try not to judge Anna. You still only know parts of her. It's always the parts that we don't know, that we can't see, that finish the picture. She was someone you loved.' He looked at Harriet, then back at Finn before taking his hand. 'Someone we all loved, and you cannot take it upon yourself to tell Jess things that you think she should know. They may hurt her. They may hurt Rose. That's not up to you.'

Finn burst into tears. Theo reached for him and Harriet passed to the other side of his bed and did the same. Together the three of them clung to each other, the child sobbing, his parents controlling their tears. Theo's arm, wrapped around Finn, touched Harriet's hand. Her eyes open, she laced her fingers through his, mouthed the words, *Thank you*, at him. He blinked hard and nodded.

★ ★ ★

With Finn settled, Theo made tea, put two large mugs down on the coffee table.

Harriet placed her stockinged feet next to them.

'Make yourself at home,' Theo laughed.

She grinned. 'It feels a bit weird,' she said. 'Being back here. Feels it for me, so must be really weird for you.'

'It is a bit like old times.'

'I know.' Harriet looked around the room. 'All of our things, they're comforting, familiar.'

'Any regrets?' Theo asked.

289

She hadn't hesitated a second in her reply. 'Hurting you and Finn is awful, but I am happy . . . You?'

'Do I regret you leaving me?'

Her cheeks flushed red and he laughed. 'Relax. Actually, no, no I don't.'

'Good. Thank you for what you said up there.'

Theo stretched his long limbs, tried to rub the tightness he felt in his chest with his hand. 'It was what he needed to hear.'

'Not the full truth, though.'

'Full truth, it would appear, is overrated.'

She shook her head. 'You don't mean that.'

'I mean it doesn't matter. I know you lied — I don't know when. It doesn't matter any more.'

'You handled it brilliantly upstairs. You've always been good with Finn.' She deftly changed the subject.

'Yeah, well, if this is him at 'almost twelve', I reckon it'll come in handy.'

'Do you think Jess knows?'

He frowned. 'She knows Anna was involved with a married man. She doesn't know who, nor does she need to, just as she is coming to terms with Anna being gone.'

Theo felt his wife's nut-brown eyes bore into him. 'When are *you* going to admit you have feelings for Jess?'

He coughed loudly. 'Don't be ridiculous!'

'It's not so ridiculous, and before you go getting defensive, I'm not saying there was ever anything going on, in real life or in your mind. I just know you've always loved her as a friend and maybe, just maybe, that's changed as circumstances have.'

Theo shifted beside her. 'I'm seeing someone,' he said, not sure that he was at all. 'Not Jess. Jess is a friend.'

'Oh.' Harriet tilted her head in surprise. 'Anyone I know?'

'Jacqueline Benoit? She works at The Wall.'

'Not the tutor, the tiny one?'

Theo nodded.

'She's half your age!'

'She is thirty-four.' His expression was indignant.

'She'll want babies.' Harriet wagged a finger. 'Be careful. She'll add another ten years onto your working life.'

'Jesus, you're incorrigible.' Theo drained the end of his mug.

She smiled. 'I'm sorry, really, for everything.' She leaned forward, her hair falling each side of her face.

He pulled her back by the shoulder, so that she fell into the crook of his arm. 'Stop punishing yourself, Harriet. You and me and Finn, we'll be fine, however scary it all looks.'

Theo breathed deep, inhaled the scent of her — coconut and spiced orange — and closed his eyes.

36

Jess

John at St John's recognizes me when I take a
seat in the varnished oak pew. I'm sure I see a
tic-like nod of acknowledgement. I'm late — the
service has started, the first hymn in full flow.
Rose hasn't a clue what's going on and she's
fidgeting beside me, picking at something that
looks like a knot in the wood. Perhaps this was a
mistake. I read the Sunday order of service and
the words blur before me. This *was* a mistake.
Rose has found her way onto my lap. She's
sucking on some of her hair which I left loose
today. Its fragrant scent of citrus shampoo makes
me sneeze.

I scramble through my handbag for a tissue,
start to cough so much that Rose has to sit back
down beside me. People are starting to stare. My
fingers find the letter from the bank; the one that
was in the same postal delivery as Aimee
Gardner's card. I let my fingers rest on it, look
around the church for her, sure from the tone of
her letter that Mrs Gardner is a churchgoer, and
that she has a faith I wish I did. I find the tissues,
close the bag, blow my nose and Rose jumps up
on me again.

Doug, true to his word, has taken care of all
the paperwork with Anna's employers. The

letter, a settlement statement from them confirming the insurance payout, also confirms that I will soon have two hundred and eight thousand pounds in the bank. Last night, when I read it, I let out a small, low, out-of-tune whistle. It's a fortune to me, but I know if it's to last, if it's to be there for Rose, I'll have to be careful. My eyes shut as I try to pray. Words of hope flit across my brain. I can't quite find words of thanks. Most times, I am still angry at any God who takes my daughter from me and expects my granddaughter to make up for her loss. Not so long ago, I had them both.

I pray that I will be able to let go of the anger. I pray for Rose. I pray for Sean and his family. And, just before a coughing fit forces me to leave five minutes after arriving, I pray that I can forget the man who signed the letter in my bag was James Elliot.

Outside. I'm trying a three-point turn in the crowded car park when Rose pipes up from the back. 'Can we have one of those in the garden, Nanny?'

'I'll look in just a moment, love. Hold on.'

I've almost broken into a sweat by the time I've straightened up and can turn around. 'What love, one of what?'

'Those.' She points to a fir tree, maybe about ten feet tall. 'We could have Christmas all the time!'

I smile. Christmas all the time does sound like a lovely idea; I have no idea how to tell a child that Christmas trees in March aren't that easy to come by.

I'm going to do a proper food shop today. Feeling buoyed up, determined to shake this flu-like feeling, I've actually made a list. Rose is already in dance class, and I'm standing in the middle aisle of the supermarket knowing I have an hour to get this done.

Reading the list means glasses perched on the end of my nose, peering over them to see where I'm going; making sure I don't mow anyone down with the trolley; peering through them to see what I'm actually putting in it. My forty-eight-year-old eyes can't function nowadays without them. I'm checking the sugar content of a new cereal when someone says hello and I have to do the whole looking down and peering over manoeuvre to see who's talking to me.

'Sam, hello . . . ' I say, a little awkwardly. I don't know him well enough to give him a hug. 'Sorry, glasses . . . ' I push them up onto the top of my head.

'How are you?' he asks. 'A silly question, I know.' Something makes me look in his shopping basket as I give Anna's old choirmaster the rote reply. 'Oh, okay. Some days good, some days bad. Most are getting better.'

'I'm glad.' He sighs a troubled sigh. 'It's a very strange world we live in when our young are taken away from us.'

Something tugs at the edge of my memory, something from way back — Anna telling me that he and his wife had lost twins, stillbirths,

294

before the birth of their son years later. So, I know he knows and that helps, when people really know, when people have borne a similar grief. We're standing at the preserve section and my eyes land on Anna's favourite honey. She would pile it onto a doorstep of fresh bread and munch away.

Sam is talking but I'm not really listening. I suddenly feel like I'm naked or have lost a layer of skin in the middle of the store.

'Are you all right, Jess?' His hand is on my arm.

'Sorry of course, I'm fine. I must get on, Sam. Thank you, thanks for your kind words, and I never got to thank you on the day for the choir. You all did a beautiful job.'

My heart is thumping rapidly as I push away with the trolley. I can't catch my breath. It's as if the air supply to my lungs has been pinched. I pass through the till quickly with what I have so far, shallow-breathing all the time. Outside I gasp, gulp the air greedily, and curse this bug that will neither grip me nor leave me alone. Making my way through the shopping centre, I stop at a small café, try to steady my heart-rate. I'm carrying two bags; two bags filled with food I don't remember buying.

I order a strong tea and take a seat near the door. All around me are the smells of a normal day. As the two baristas struggle with a growing queue, as I struggle with the new 'normal', I find the scent of crushed coffee beans and baked croissants comforting. Three tables away, a mother and her son sit reading a book together.

He looks about the same age as Rose and they're reading *The Tiger Who Came to Tea*. I wonder where Anna's copy is — it was her absolute favourite book. I should read it to Rose. It's somewhere in the house, no doubt threadbare and worn like me.

I sit like this for a while, conscious of time but needing to rest, to take the passing life in; to reassure myself that life does, in fact, go on — just like all the songs sing and all the books believe. But God, it just blindsides me sometimes, this new normal. And all because of a jar of honey that has, somehow, made it into my bags.

★ ★ ★

Theo is here. He seems tired — his soft eyes have dull, greying bags underneath and he needs a haircut. He has left a briefcase in the hall, refused a drink, and seems restless, as, if he's decided he's not staying. We're both sitting on the sofa in the front room. Rose, who along with me is back in school in the morning, is fast asleep.

'I went to church today,' I tell him. 'Had to leave because people were staring at the lady with the germs.'

'You do seem to have a bit of a cold.'

'It comes and goes. See? I'm fine tonight.' I wink at him and he grins,

'How was it, church?'

'Cold.' I shudder. 'Surprisingly full, but it is Sunday. I don't know. The black hole is becoming grey. It's there, every day, ready to consume me, but I'm fighting back, trying to feel positive.'

'Atta girl.' He taps my knee and I wish he'd reach out and put his arms around me. Strangely, before the kiss, before the awkwardness, that's exactly what he would have done. I wish he would take a drink, have something in his hands. He looks as if he almost wants to sit on them.

I sit back, rest my neck on the chair. 'Where can I buy Rose a train set? She wants one for her birthday.'

He seems to relax, mirrors my slouch. 'The local toy store in town, in the high street, I've forgotten the name, but opposite the hairdresser you go to. They'll do train sets.' He looks across at me. 'Yes, they'll do train sets,' he repeats. 'Are we okay, you and me?'

The last remark is so blunt that I'm caught by surprise and find myself blushing. 'Of course,' I mutter.

'We should talk about the kiss.'

'What kiss?' I widen my eyes. 'I told you it didn't happen.'

'That's really how you want to play this?'

'I'm not playing, Theo. You're my friend. I don't want to mess that up.'

'We should talk about it, not just pretend it never happened. It happened.'

'You're my friend,' I repeat the words. 'It happened because I was upset, emotional.'

'That's why you kissed me. It's not why I kissed you.'

He reaches out and tucks some of my stray hair behind my ears. My face automatically angles to touch his hand. He leaves it there a moment before I break away.

'Sean had the DNA test.' I sit back, put some distance between us.

'And?'

'He's not Rose's father.'

His face pales, but his nod, the acknowledgement of the fact, shows relief — I'm assuming for my sake. 'So, what happens now?' he asks.

'I go and see Sean, try and apologize for ruining the guy's life. That's how he will see it right now. Leah says he still has a right to be involved in Rose's life as he's named on the birth cert. It's up to him. Part of me hopes he wants to stay around for Rose's sake, but I'll get it if not.'

'Isn't he moving anyway?'

'He is. I know he's devastated. He's been talking to Doug. He went to tell his parents this weekend. I want to go and see him when he's back tomorrow and just hope he'll understand why I did this.'

Theo nods. 'Maybe you should leave well alone. Don't go over to Sean. If he wants to, he'll come to you?'

'What is it with people?' I ask. 'I just want to know the lie of the land with him. And I *do* want to apologize. Jesus, Theo, there are times when a little confrontation isn't a bad thing.'

He flinches visibly. I've prodded an old wound; one where I have often told him he needs to be more confrontational. He told me once that, since his father died when he was young, he avoids anything looking remotely like discord.

'I want to stop seeing Rose in every local male. To stop me viewing every man as Rose's father.' *Theo is my friend.* 'Leah,' I blurt her name, deciding in the moment to blame her. Ma-leah-cent. Bad Leah. 'Leah thinks it could be you.' I laugh out loud.

Theo looks like I've muted him for life.

'Yep.' I'm nodding. 'You're married, or at least you were when Anna was alive. You're an attractive man. You would never have left Harriet. The fact is, she left you.'

Theo is staring at me, trying to gauge if I'm joking or not. 'I have her phone.' I reach to the floor for my handbag. 'Anna's phone.' I wave it at him. 'There's messages, emails. I know I can probably find out if I want to find out, I'm just not sure if I should.'

'You got the phone unlocked?' he asks.

'All her contacts, messages, emails. I've learned more about Anna since reading it for a few hours than I ever thought I knew. You think you know the people you love.'

'Of course you knew her, just not all of her. I feel the same about Harriet.'

'Theo.' Something in my tone — maybe the way I'm just saying his name and the way it catches in my throat — makes him turn around. 'I don't think anyone understands. I know everyone loves me, that people are looking out for me and Rose, but I don't think people get how *that* bit feels, that *shock factor*, except you.' I find myself clutching my breast. He moves towards me and I hold my hand up. If he comes any closer, I'll stop talking and I need to say this. 'All the years we've been friends. All those times we chatted, I thought I knew and understood Anna. I thought *we* were friends. She had her life, I never expected to know every aspect of it, but she did confide in me.' I gulp back saliva that has gathered in the back of my throat. 'I now know that I focused on what she wanted me to see, the part I'd always approve of. The successful graduate who got a job offer after an internship with a bank. The hard-working mother who was kind to anyone she met. The choirgirl, for Chrissake.'

Theo takes my hand, holds it between both of us. He has dark curling hair on the back of his right hand.

'I never knew that Anna, even for love's sake, would be capable of being with another woman's husband. I never knew that she was afraid of telling me, afraid of me judging her.' Tears slide down my cheeks, and his arms, they come. They come to me and hold me close. I lean into his chest. 'I never knew, Theo, and I'm devastated. There are no words . . . '

He tightens his grip until the tears subside and I pull away. I blow my nose into a tissue up my sleeve, breathe deep, and pull myself together.

'Yesterday, even this morning, I thought I had it all sorted in my head, how Rose and I are going to move forward, that none of it matters, but . . . then this thing looms large again. What do *you* think? Should I pursue this goddamned 'Who's the Daddy?' mystery?'

He shrugs, a heavy, deep-set movement of his shoulders. 'Up to you. I suppose you run the risk of more hurt, but there'll come a time when Rose will want to know her father.'

I reach for her phone. The diamanté catches in the ceiling lights. I scroll though her numbers and find the number for Popeye. 'Fuck it.' I shrug. 'Maybe you're right. No time like the present.' I press the number to ring it.

And right at that moment a sound comes from the hall, from Theo's briefcase. It's a musical sound I don't recognize, then I realize it's the trill of a mobile. I leap up, drop Anna's phone, see it fall in slow motion, hitting off my booted feet, and my blood runs icy cold.

37

Anna

Raw Honey Blogspot 16/03/2011

Gramps has had a stroke.
  He's in hospital.
  If he dies, I'll never forgive myself. NEVER.
  I'm frightened.
  And I'm responsible.

38

Theo

She was strong. He had never had an occasion before, for all six foot four of his frame to be thrown from a house in what seemed like one smooth movement. His briefcase, tossed out after him, landed on the ground by his feet. He cursed Jess under his breath and dug out the phone to answer.

'Theo Pope,' he said into the line, and listened. He sighed heavily as he turned away from the slammed front door and beeped his car open. 'Text me the full address and tell them I'll be there in twenty minutes.' He hated being on call; ran a hand through his hair, then gripped the steering wheel. What had just happened?

He ran through it in his head during the eight-mile journey to see a known patient. A patient who regularly thought he was having a heart attack; a patient who regularly forgot his angina pills. He sensed it would be a wasted trip but could never take the chance. He was a doctor, and Angina Man could really be having a heart attack.

They had been talking. He and Jess. She had joked about Leah thinking he could be Rose's father. She had been joking, hadn't she? He nodded to himself. Of course she was . . . Then

303

she got upset. Her devastation at Anna's double life hitting her again. It was when she waved Anna's phone and dialled some number that —

Shit. He braked hard in the middle of the road. Shit! Theo wanted to turn around, to explain, to just reassure her, to . . . He kept driving. There was a patient waiting on him three miles away.

Miles Wallace was not having a heart attack. Miles Wallace refused to take his medication and Theo was not in the mood. Having given him a stern talking-to, he drove back to Jess's. It was ten fifteen and there was the faint hue of lights on at the back of the house.

Rather than ring the bell, he knocked on the door. No reply. He pushed the bell and then rang it again. Finally, he phoned Jess's mobile, which he could hear ringing from the front of her house. He bent over at the waist, prised open the letterbox. Pug came running from the back and started barking.

'Open the door, Jess.' He could see her shadow through the narrow gap. 'Open the door, or so help me, I'll knock it down.' He stood up, kicked the door, not once but twice. He could hear her footsteps scamper along the tiles inside.

'Go away,' she growled. 'You'll *wake* Rose!'

'I'm not going anywhere.'

'You bastard! Go away!'

He kicked the door again, aware his shoe was leaving a mark with each contact. 'I am not going anywhere. You open the door now, Jess. Explain to me what it is you think I've done. I want to see the whites of your eyes when you tell me.' He put his finger on the doorbell and within seconds she had opened it.

'You fucker,' she seethed.

He had a palm on each side of the frame, leaning forward, primed for another kick. 'Well, here I am, Jess, confronting the issue, eh? So come on, tell me.' He moved his face towards hers. She instinctively backed away.

'You,' she spat the word. 'You and Anna.'

'Anna and me. Ahh yes, Anna and me, what were we?' He was in the hallway now, closed the door behind him. He reached inside his jeans pocket and pulled a phone out. 'Call it. Go on, you think you know the number. Call it.' He neared her. 'Call it!'

She flinched, walked back to the kitchen, got Anna's phone and stabbed the repeat button, held it out from her ear for effect. He walked past her into the kitchen, turned right and slumped into the tatty sofa, all the while watching her. 'Well?'

She redialled the number, this time taking the time to use the directory. Theo could hear it ringing in her ear from his side of the room. 'This?' He held up his phone. 'This is the 'on-call' phone for the surgery. It's a different number to mine, obviously; it's a communal surgery phone. Whatever doctor is on call with the out-of-hours service has it on them. I didn't get a chance to explain when I arrived that I'm on call tonight.'

Jess looked as though she had been frozen in time. Anna's phone still held aloft, she hung up and didn't move for about a minute. When she did, she walked to his side of the room, asked him to budge up and slumped next to him. It was a very tight squeeze. 'I'm sorry,' she said. 'I genuinely was showing you in case he, whoever he is, answered.' Her voice had lowered to a whisper. 'When a phone went off in your bag, what the hell was I supposed to think?'

Theo leaned back as best he could in the tight space. He closed his eyes. 'Jess.' He shook his head and pressed on his eyes with a finger and thumb. A pain pulsed behind his eyeballs. 'You were supposed to think, 'No, Theo would never do that. I know him.''

'I 'knew' Anna. You 'knew' Harriet. I'm sorry.'

'Not as sorry as me.'

'Don't say that.'

'Honestly, Jess?' He leaned forward again, almost knocking her off the seat. 'Honestly, I don't know what to say. It only came to me what you must have thought when I was driving to see my patient. I almost crashed the car.'

'I never really believed, I mean, you must — '

'No, you know what, we've known each other a long time. If you could think that even for a smidgeon of a second, then we're not the friends I thought we were. You're not the person I thought you were.'

'You almost broke down my door to give me shit?' She was on her feet in a second. 'Why? Have I not had enough shit to deal with? Maybe you could cut me a little slack — I got it wrong. It looked very wrong. I had just told you I'm seeing Rose in every bloody man's eyes. I'm *sorry*, Theo.' She waved her hands around the room.

'Sit down, Jess. It's exhausting watching you.'

She sat next to him again. 'Let's at least take this next door where we can sit in comfort.' She walked away and he heard her settle into the sofa in the front living room. He had a choice; he could tell her to shove her friendship where the sun doesn't shine, or he could go and tell her exactly what she meant to him. He followed her, took the armchair opposite her, and leaned forward on his hands. 'You,' he began, 'mean the world to me.'

'And you to me, I'm sorry.' Her lovely eyes had filled with tears and it took everything he had not to kneel in front of her and wipe them away. 'And I will never again tell you that you should be more confrontational. I prefer you exactly the way you are. That was a bit scary.'

'The man you're looking for is a whole lot more complex than me, I'm afraid. I try very hard to always do the right thing. I try very hard not to let people down. It's who I am.'

She nodded her head.

He stood up. 'Now, I'm going home.'

'Why?'

'Because, Jess, in this new spirit of confronting things, all I want to do is reach across and touch you, kiss you. To be honest, my head is messed with it. I don't know what to do with it other than tell you.'

He watched her swallow hard.

'Don't go,' she whispered.

Somewhere, in the downstairs of the house, he could hear a clock ticking. It was like a warning, telling him that this time too would pass and to walk away now while he could.

She stood up, neared him, and he could feel the heat of her. He could smell the scent of her. He could almost taste her. His mouth dried. 'I'm going home,' he repeated.

She reached a hand up and touched his face. All the scenarios unfolded in his head and none of them he would recover from. She, he knew, would walk away from this, whatever this was, whatever it ended up being the next day. Her touch was charged, sending shivers through him. The reaction in his groin was instant.

He placed a hand over hers, kissed her fingers, reached out and pulled her to him. His face in her hair, his fingers coiling around the strands. He didn't want to let go. He was afraid if he let go, this moment would never pass his way again. He was afraid if he didn't he would be changed forever. 'I can't,' he whispered.

He thought of Jacqueline. They weren't committed. They weren't exclusive. Who was he kidding? He knew Jacqueline thought they were having a 'thing', even if it hadn't been confirmed as a thing.

'Stay.' Jess's head rested on his chest. Her arms clung to his neck. She raised her face to his and he lowered his lips to hers. It was soft at first, a gentle meeting of lips. Then his hands were in her shirt and, dear God, she had such soft skin. His right hand cupped her breast. She wasn't wearing a bra. Of course she wasn't wearing a bra. He had known that hours earlier. She moaned as he touched her and the sound, like a gasp with a tiny sigh effect, made his dick feel like it would burst.

She moved against him, like a stationary dance, a slow grind. She kissed him, a teasing kiss and he pulled away. 'I — '

Then she took his hand and led him, first to the hall and then slowly upstairs. Turning left on the landing they entered her bedroom. There, he threw her on the bed and peeled every item of clothing from her. When she was naked, he marvelled at her body. He undressed slowly, standing to look at her. She never took her eyes off him. He climbed onto the bed. 'Jess,' he whispered.

'Sssh, no talking.' She put a finger to his lips and then put it in his mouth. It was a good idea, no talking. Instead, he explored her body slowly. He kissed every inch of her. She arched her back to him when he licked a certain point on her hip. She was prepared, leaned into a drawer and ripped a condom open, slid it onto him so expertly that he tried not to think about it. Tried not to think of other lovers she might have had. They didn't matter. When she begged him to enter her, he almost came immediately. It took effort, concentration, to hold back. Raised on his arms, he moved inside her, slowly, rhythmically, until the soft moan of earlier became quick, gasping cries. When they came together, he collapsed to one side of her, spent, exhausted.

They didn't speak and within minutes she was asleep. He couldn't sleep. He couldn't shake the intense feeling that this woman, his friend, Jess, held his heart in her hands and she could snap it into tiny fragments without even knowing she was capable of such a thing. Her head rested on his chest; her hair spread behind her, covering him. He was afraid to move; that if he did, the spell would be broken.

Theo waited. He waited for her to fall into a deep sleep before prising her gently from him and resting her on her bed. It was quieter than his house — the woods behind him providing a cacophony at night. He crept around the bedroom, retrieved his clothes and was about to leave when he walked back to the bed. She was sleeping soundly. She had no idea, he thought, she had no idea at all what she had just done. She might as well have reached inside his chest and grabbed his heart for her own. He stared at her in the darkness, aware that he genuinely had never felt this before, that it scared him. Aware that it could probably never happen again, that scared him more. Not wanting to risk waking her, he blew her a kiss before leaving the house more quietly than he had arrived.

★ ★ ★

It was after midnight when he got in. The grandfather clock in the hall, a present from Harriet's parents for their wedding, chimed as he turned his key in the lock. 'You,' he spoke aloud to the clock, 'are leaving this house.' He had always hated it. Now it could go to Harriet's flat. He put some bread in the toaster, shook the kettle and filled it with water. Sex always made him ravenous. Harriet had always joked that the house stank of toast any morning after they had

310

sex. While he waited, he walked to the corner and bent down, head poised, stood on his head.

And all he could see was her body. And all he could taste was her sex. And even when the smoke alarm went off because the bread had stuck in the toaster, Theo Pope smiled upside down from the corner of his kitchen. It would probably kill him, this thing with Jess, but not before he had lived and breathed every moment of it he could — preferably in slow motion.

He was just unfolding when he heard him, a small rustle in the doorway. Theo craned his head and saw Finn standing in between the kitchen and the hall.

'Hey, sorry, did the alarm wake you?' He dusted his knees and smacked his hands together.

Finn didn't move. 'I was waiting up for you.'

Theo felt heat threaten his cheeks, looked away. He pulled the dried toast from the toaster. 'You hungry?'

Finn nodded and Theo put more bread in. 'Take a seat.' He spoke with a burnt offering hanging from the corner of his mouth. He smiled through it. 'You wait for the next round. I'm starving.'

He knew he was talking, aware he didn't want Finn to ask him outright where he had been so late. He didn't. Instead, Finn seemed to be hugging himself.

'School in the morning, so let's not be long, eh?' Theo waited by the toaster.

'Dad,' Finn said, and Theo turned to see his son gasp as if he were in pain. 'Dad, I'm sorry

311

but I did something stupid. I did it before you, me and Mum talked. I did it before . . .'

Theo's stomach plummeted.

The house stank of burnt toast, but when Theo tried to close his eyes at 3.33 a.m., it wasn't sex he was thinking about.

39

Jess

I awake to the sound of birdsong, reach out in the bed, and know instantly that I'm alone. My eyes have shot open, adjusted to the early morning light as my hand strokes the empty space beside me. I find myself smiling, touching my lips with my fingertips; remembering his lips on mine, remembering his lips all over my body. Normally I wake if a pin drops and I can't believe I didn't hear him go. Sitting up I look around, listen for movement in Rose's room and check my phone for a text, but there's nothing. My eyes blink at the empty screen and the reality check makes me sigh aloud. We spent a beautiful night together, Theo and I, but this isn't the movies.

Later that morning, I'm roaming the playground at break-time with trees on my mind. Rose told me on the drive to school that she wants a Christmas tree for her birthday. According to Google, there is a nursery nearby that grows them all year round and, now that I know it might be possible to have one at all, I'm panicking in case I can't get one by Saturday.

I hide my phone, know I shouldn't really have it in the playground, and I'm pushing it deep into my coat pocket when I spot Rose at the far end of the green space, sitting alone on a bench. It's not like her, so I slowly make my way around.

'Gorgeous girl, what's up?'

'Nothing. Just playing.'

'But you're not. You're just sitting here.'

'People aren't my friend.'

'What?'

'When I said I wasn't having a big party, the others aren't my friend.'

'You wanted it small, darling.' She told me this morning, right after her request for a Christmas tree in March, that she only wanted two friends over for her birthday.

'You have as many as you want, Rose.' I stop short of saying *but don't let them bully you*.

'I want to be their friend,' she says.

My already splintered heart tears apart some more. I look around us to the place where we all learn our rules of engagement. I want to tell her, to teach her, not to give in to people, but she's five years old, almost six, and I'm exhausted. The reality of bringing a child up all over again just sometimes hits me square in the jaw — a big fat sucker punch reminding me of the fact that I obviously made mistakes first time around.

'Darling, you invite the whole class if you want to.'

'Really?' Her eyes widen and she's already on her feet. I watch her run off into the centre of a group of 'friends' from her class and calm myself watching the scene by reminding myself that life is just too bloody short.

'It's good to have you back, Mrs P'

314

I turn around and Finn is standing a few feet away, both hands in his pockets.

'It's good to be back, Finn.' I give him a pat on the elbow and make to walk away.

'Mrs P?'

'Yes, Finn?'

'I sent you an email. I — '

The peal of the bell interrupts and I clap my hands automatically. 'C'mon children,' I yell. 'An email?' I say to Finn, but he has moved away with the rush of the younger children, his head hung low.

★ ★ ★

After school, the tree has to wait in favour of making party invitations. Rose wants to drop one off to 'Daddy's' personally, and I sit in the car while she runs up the path. I hold my breath as she stops to post it through the door, but then she hesitates and smiles widely. She's looking through the window and the door opens. She runs into his arms and I think, shit. I thought he'd be at work and this looks as if I've deliberately brought Rose at a time when I thought he would be. He comes out to the car with her in his arms, an expression on his face I cannot read. He looks tired; baggage under red eyes, his skin pale and wan. He's lost weight.

I wind the window down. 'Sean, Rose just wanted to drop off the . . . the invite personally'

'So I see.'

'Daddy!' She squeezes his neck with both her arms and the joy on her face at seeing him

315

unexpectedly does not escape either of us. I look away, cannot bear it.

'Why don't you stay for tea, love?' He has lowered her to the floor and she looks in the car. 'Can I, Nanny? Can I?'

My stomach sinks. 'I — '

Sean stares.

'Of course you can,' I tell her.

'I'll drop her back in plenty of time for bed,' Sean says.

I nod. 'Sean, we should talk . . . ' My voice is no more than a whisper.

'Later, Jess.' He turns and walks up the path, holding my granddaughter by the hand; holding his daughter, to all intents and purposes, by the hand.

I call Leah from the car.

'Hello,' she answers her phone. 'This is your local lunatic asylum. My name's Leah. How can I help you?'

'That good, eh?' I refer to the arrival of Jen, her stepdaughter.

'Just fab-u-lous,' she says, sarcasm dripping from every syllable. 'Sorry I haven't called. It's been a bit mad at home.'

'Can you pop in later? Maybe on the way home. I've a lot to tell you.'

'I'm in the station already. In fact, I have something for you: kill two birds with one stone. I'll see you in ten?'

When I arrive at the house, she pulls in right behind me, and before I can even open the front door is waxing lyrical about her stepdaughter.

'Coffee?' I ask.

'If you give me coffee, I'll lie awake all night thinking about how I've suddenly got a teenage witch in my home. Gus is just trying to ignore her, hoping it will get better, doing his best head-in-the-sand impression. How do you get through it? Was Anna as bad?'

I smile. Anna was in fact a brilliant teen, never gave me a moment's trouble, apart from one stomach-pumping incident when she drank too much at sixteen.

'It'll settle down,' I tell her, hoping for her sake that it does.

She has a large white plastic bag under her arm, which she hands to me. 'For you. We can change the pattern if you want. I thought we should probably just do it.'

I have no idea what she's talking about, so peer into the bag. Inside are a staple gun, enormous scissors and a swathe of red fabric.

'It's Anna's favourite, was her favourite colour,' she corrects herself with a sigh. Tatty sofa, I realize quickly.

'I printed off all the instructions from the Internet, 'Upholstering made easy'. Easy-peasy . . .' She laughs. 'Well, it looks easy, though I'm sure it's not. I thought you and I could do it some weekend?'

'Thank you.' I hug her. 'It's a good idea.'

'Like the colour?' she asks.

'I love the colour.' I don't, but she's right. It's what Anna would have chosen, so that's good enough for me.

'You look tired,' I tell her.

'I am and you look — ' She leans forward,

317

gives me a puzzled look. 'Your cold has shifted and you look — well . . . '

My cheeks redden as her eyes bore into mine. 'Theo's not the dad.' I exhale a big breath.

'Right.' She nods. 'And you know this for certain how?'

'I just know.' I shrug what I imagine to be puce-red shoulders under my jumper. 'The phone thing and he just . . . ' I meet her eyes. 'It's not him. Look, are you and Gus busy Saturday between two and five? I need help with Rose's party. Her entire class are probably coming. She wants a Christmas tree.'

'You're babbling.' Leah laughs. 'Did you sleep with him?'

I drop my head into my hands. 'Yes,' I whisper.

'Oh my *God!*' She leaps in her seat. 'How was it? He's a bit of all right, Theo. I've always thought so myself. Shit, was it good? I bet it was!'

My head still in hiding, she doesn't wait for a reply. 'Shit! She's speechless! Go Nanny!'

I know without looking she's doing that weird 'Go whoever' dance of hers, where she does a sort of wide stirring movement with her hands. Despite myself, my face cracks into a smile and I raise my head.

'You should so go back for seconds. He's made you smile.' She too is grinning.

'I don't know. I'm not sure.'

'Do not,' she begins to say, and wags an effective finger, 'do not go there. Do not start making excuses why not, when you should be acknowledging the reasons why.'

'Why?' I ask her. 'Tell me what 'whys' there are?'

'Because he's a good man. I'm sure he's not perfect, but hey, flawed men are cute too. As long as you don't have to do the whole rescue thing. That's exhausting. Sorted, flawed men are cute.' She corrects herself. 'And I think Theo is sorted.'

'Maybe,' I say. 'We've crossed a line now, though, and I think I need him more as my friend than my lover. That's a big 'why not'.'

'He could be both, Jess. What have I been telling you lately? You need to let a little love into your life. Especially now.'

'Tell me about the teenage witch.' I sit back, the subject dropped, for now.

'Ugh! She has gone from being a sweet young girl who lived with her mother and visited us once a fortnight, sweet, *all* the time — to being a stroppy cow who screams and shouts like a two-year-old and yells at both me and Gus at every opportunity. Seriously, if I could send her back, I would.'

'How's Gus with it?'

'At his wits' end. He's never seen her like this before. You know he's such a softie, so he ends up just giving in to all her moods and demands. Honestly, I've found him in tears over it . . . ' She crosses her arms. 'He doesn't know how to deal with her, any more than her mother or I do.'

'She'll have something in her life that's making her act out. Boys, girls, school, something.'

'You're a great help.'

'Sorry. Anna was a brilliant teen. It's only after

she died she became a problem.'

Leah frowns. 'I know. It's very confusing.'

She stands suddenly. 'I'm going to go before I get too comfortable. Gus has dinner on. Hey, maybe we can start calling the sofa 'Red' rather than 'Tatty'?'

I doubt that. Anna and I had a silly naming ceremony for it that involved a bottle of prosecco, two glasses, and both of us wedged into it.

I see her to the door and she stumbles on one of Anna's shoes, which has fallen from the top of the pile. She looks down at it, then up at me. I can tell the words are forming — she wants to suggest that maybe I move them from the front door, but she doesn't actually say it. Instead, she kisses me and leaves me there, wondering the same myself.

★ ★ ★

'What is it you want, Jess?'

With Rose so tired, she volunteered herself into bed. Sean is, as usual, straight to the point.

I rub my arms. 'To apologize.'

He laughs, a sarcastic sound, and parks himself on the tatty sofa. 'For which part exactly?'

'All of it. Genuinely.' I take the chair, try to eyeball him. 'I've never been fair to you when you only ever loved Anna and Rose, when you did your very best by them.'

He looks away, studies the floor.

'I never felt you were good enough for her,

320

when the truth was she probably didn't deserve you at the time and what she did was wrong, very wrong.'

'No shit,' he whispers.

'What I did was probably wrong, too, but please, put how you feel about me aside for a moment. I was trying desperately to do what I thought was best for Rose. Before I knew, before I knew there was a chance you weren't her father, yes, I was being selfish trying to keep Rose with me, but understand why? I'd lost Anna. She was my world.'

The last sentence makes me have to clear my throat. *Hold it together.* 'As soon as I did know, I thought I had reason to fight. I thought it was the best thing for Rose. To be honest, I'm not so sure now. I — '

'Do not sit there, Jess,' his voice rises. 'Do not dare to sit there and tell me you think you've made a mistake, that maybe you shouldn't have put me and my family through this.'

'Sean. I was frightened. I am frightened. All the time. I want the best for Rose. She's all I have left of Anna. But you are her father. *To her,* you're her father. We talked today about her birthday next week and she just assumes you'll be there.' My voice is desperate. I am desperate.

His eyes are heavy with tears but he won't look at me. Instead he stands and looks out through the window at the night sky. 'Do you know who it is?'

I know he means the real father, the biological donor. 'No.'

He turns and glares at me.

'I promise you, Sean. On Rose's life, I don't know. I've been bloody well obsessing about it.' I don't tell him what little detail I do know — that he is a married man.

'So how, then . . . how did you start all this if it wasn't someone coming forward?'

On dangerous ground, I answer, carefully. 'Anna's papers; there's something in there mentioning that you weren't Rose's dad.' I bite my lip. 'With Rose, I need your help. I don't know what to do.'

He plonks himself on the sofa opposite me again. 'Yow don't know what to do?' He runs a hand through his hair and I chew my lip watching him. 'I can't just drop her, just forget about her. I love her. My parents love her . . . ' He raises his head. 'We all *love* her.'

'I know.'

'And what do we do with that? Eh? What am I supposed to do?' he asks again.

'I'm hoping you'll keep on loving her. A big ask, I know.'

He says nothing.

'And if, in order for you to keep Rose in your lives, if you have to take her to Blackpool, I won't stand in your way. I'll move north. I'll move nearby to help, to support.'

Finally, he looks directly at me.

'You can have her in Lytham St Annes,' I say, with no worldly idea where these words have come from, how they're escaping my mouth. 'Or I can move up there with her, somewhere near my parents, which isn't far from you. Either way. She *needs* you in her life.' I stand up.

'Don't you want to know?' he asks. 'You set this whole thing in motion. Don't you want to know who her father is?'

And I reply as honestly as I can. 'You're her father. I see that now.'

★ ★ ★

One email. One memory of a child in school telling me he sent me an email. One decision to look at it before I forget, just one click on the website link he sent me. That is all it takes. That is all it takes to flip my world on its side again; to make everything that was pulling itself into some new shape I could live with, now look like a big black hole again.

I'm back in Anna's bed, buried under her duvet, scrambling around for the scent of her. I get out, go to her dresser and take her perfume, spray it liberally all over the sheets and then climb back in again. I have Nouska, her teddy, with me. He smells of the real her. I nuzzle my nose into his fur. I have the ragged copy of her favourite book that I found in the bottom of one of her drawers. Memories of the sound of her chuckle at a tiger coming to tea cloud my bitter brain.

My iPad, after three hours of reading her blog, has been discarded, fallen on the floor, and I don't care. All I care about is the blog post I've just read dated 15 March 2011, the day before my father's stroke. He saw her. He saw her with *Him*. All thoughts of being able to put this man out of my head have vanished. Only hours ago I thought that life could be eased by an outdoor Christmas tree. Now, I know that my father's and even my mother's subsequent lives were mapped out the moment he saw Anna with someone she shouldn't have been with. My brain whirrs into overdrive.

'Anna,' I whisper under the bedclothes. All I can do is offer her shadowy bedroom my whispered question. 'Anna, what *did* you do . . . ?'

40

Anna

Raw Honey Blogspot 02/11/2014

We were on an 'away day' this week, one of those group events that's supposed to promote the idea of team in the workplace.

It was the most bloody awful, tedious, waste-of-time fucking day. I had to crawl through an obstacle course in the pissing rain and take part in this 'allow yourself to fall backwards' into the arms of a colleague thing (in the hope they'll catch you). I didn't do that bit — just couldn't. J, my boss, and M, my friend, thought it was too hilarious; went on about it right through lunch, on and on about me and my obvious trust issues. M hit a nerve when he told me over my manky lettuce salad that I expect people to let me down.

Since then my head hurts; wondering who in my life might have let me down, have made me distrustful, so that I couldn't let go, just cross my arms and fall back . . . And truth is, I don't think there is anyone. If I'm supposed to be damaged by Dad leaving, I'm really not. We have a good relationship and he's always been there for me. Mama, never. She's never let me down. No girlfriend has ever made me feel that way. I have always felt loved, so why would it be that I can't trust — that I'd *expect* a colleague to let me fall? Is it because they're a 'stranger'? Not in my intimate circle of family and friends?

And why have I taken up with Him again. *Why???* Are the two things related?

Answers below please . . .

Comment: Deardigger
I think you're torn. I think if you're not careful, you're going to have a life of two halves. The first where you were very obviously loved and supported. The next, where for some reason, you've shunned that love in favour of a man who can never put you first. Because that's the gist of it, Honey-girl. No matter how much you love each other, he has a wife (and possibly children) already. You have willingly pitched yourself against that. And you seem to be someone that isn't going to like either outcome. If he stays with his wife, you'll always be second best. If he leaves his wife, you'll feel guilty. Neither outcome is good, so maybe, just maybe, you've cornered yourself into a life where it's *you* and your judgement that you don't trust?
Reply: Honey-girl
Food for thought . . .
Comment: Deardigger
One other thing, Honey-girl. I'm not really sure if it's just for the purposes of this blog, but it always strikes me as a little bit odd that you refer to your lover as He/Him, almost deifying him?
Reply: Honey-girl
And yet more food for thought . . .

41

Theo

If it's a Christmas tree she wants, then a Christmas tree she shall have, thought Theo as he roamed the lines of fledgling Nordmann firs in the specialist nursery. Thanks to covering some evening shifts for Marsha and being on call over the weekend, Theo had a rare day off. He had no idea why Jess wanted the tree. She had been rambling and seemed upset when she rang him at six thirty a.m. and he had tried not to resent the call on the only morning he didn't *have* to rise at six thirty. Other than her need to travel up and down to the Lakes in one day, *again*, the only other thing he had gathered from the conversation was the fact that she needed a Christmas tree in March.

He stopped, looked at the one next to him, tugged on the label that said it would grow to twelve feet. He pointed the five-foot specimen out to the guy with a spade and within ten minutes it had been potted and brought to the till. It would grow, Theo told himself as he put it in the car. For now, it was a Christmas tree in March, one more than he thought he'd get.

He caught her coming out of the house, walking to her car.

'Wait!' he shouted.

She turned around, the expression on her face a mixture of surprise and annoyance.

'I'm in a hurry, Theo.'

'I have the day off,' he said, nearing her, running a hand through his hair. 'Why don't you let me drive? We'll get there quicker.'

'I'm perfectly capable of driving quickly,' she said, opening her door.

'You're upset. I could tell on the phone earlier. Let me take you, it'll be a long day.'

She looked at the ground, seemed to be thinking about it.

'Who's picking Rose up later?' Theo asked.

'Gus and the teenage witch.' Jess raised her head, stared at Theo's car blocking her route out. 'Right,' she clicked hers shut with the remote. 'If you're not getting out of my way, let's go. You drive. And we need to get a shimmy on.'

In his car, she sniffed the air and looked behind her to where the seats had been folded down. 'Theo, you have a Christmas tree in the back.'

'Yes, yes, I do.' He opened the boot and pulled the tree out, placed the pot outside her front door before climbing back into the driver's seat.

'You got me a Christmas tree.' She smiled, looking at it and reaching across to touch him.

'I did.'

'You got me a Christmas tree,' she repeated softly. 'Thank you . . . That pine scent, it reminds me of the day of the fair, the day — '

'No.' Theo shook his head vigorously. 'This tree smells of Christmas future, not Christmas past.'

She laughed, squeezed his arm. 'My very own Marley for the next few hours. Drive? And don't spare the horses . . . '

They didn't stop for coffee. There was no stopping at all. She was quiet the whole way up, staring into the distance, but silence was never something that scared them. It was only for the last few miles when she gave him instructions on where to go that she seemed to come to life.

'Are you going to tell me why this is so urgent,' he asked as he approached her parents' house.

She shook her head.

He pulled into the driveway and parked behind her mother's Micra.

'Shall I wait here?' Theo kept his hands on the steering wheel.

'Of course not, come in.'

Before he had locked the car, she was standing on the deck at the front door. It was thin planks of weathered wood, about six feet deep, and it spanned the whole width of the house. His eyes rested on an old worn bench sitting under a wide window next to them.

'That's the snogging seat.' Jess smiled as she rang the bell. 'That would have a few stories if it could talk.'

Theo looked around the front garden; private, hidden from the road by tall conifers and pines. He knew, from hearing Jess talk about it, that from the rear the house backed onto the lake. What an idyllic place to grow up, he thought, just as Jess's mother opened the door.

'Darling, what are you doing here? Why didn't you call?' Her hand went to her head, automatically patting stray hair back into the pinned bun she wore. 'What a lovely surprise.' She was dressed in navy trousers, a pale blue shirt and a navy cardigan, buttons open.

Jess kissed her cheek, moved past her into the hallway.

'Theo,' her mother greeted him. 'Come in. It's been a long time. To what — '

'Mum,' Jess focused on her mother. 'We're just here for a quick trip. I have to get back to Rose but I need to speak to Dad. Is he upstairs?'

'He's sitting in the back, he's feeling much better now, finished the antibiotics. I — '

She stopped talking, looked from Jess to Theo and back again. 'What's going on, Jess?'

Theo wished he knew, could only offer a tiny shrug. Jess wrapped both arms around herself. 'I need to talk to Dad, to you, I . . . ' She looked at Theo as if she was wondering for the first time if he should be there at all.

Theo, sensing this, put both his hands on her shoulders. 'Jess, you go ahead, I'll — ' He looked around him and jerked his eyes towards a door off the hallway. 'I'll wait in there?' He directed the question at her mother who nodded, opening it up to a large sitting room.

'No, Theo,' Jess began, 'you drove all the way, just — '

He hugged her to his chest, whispered in her ear. 'I'll be all right here. Go say whatever it is you need to say to your dad and I'll be here if you need me.'

In the front room Theo was seated by Barbara, offered a cup of coffee, before she hurried off

330

wringing her hands. As soon as she left, he stood from the black leather chair that he supposed, from the remote control, was Jess's father's. He almost tip-toed to the set of double doors opposite him and strained to listen. It wasn't hard. The doors had a gap between them that if he peered through he could see a slim glimpse to the rear room; to what looked like a stretched window; Jess hunched on the floor next to a chair that he could only see the back of. Her hand reached in to whomever was seated in the winged chair. Barbara stood watching, her own hand resting on the high back.

'You have to tell me, Dad, please. I know you know.'

Jess.

A muffled sound. Her father.

'I don't understand, Jess. If your dad knew anything about this, he'd have told me. Wouldn't you, darling? This is ridiculous. What in God's name, how in God's name . . . ' Barbara.

'Mum! Please? Please just let me speak to Dad.' Jess.

Theo watched as Jess seemed to lay her head against the lap of the seated man. He could no longer hear her words. There was a hushed exchange, the sound of tears he knew to be Jess's. Barbara stood back from the chair, and he stood back from the door, suddenly embarrassed by his voyeurism. Minutes later, he was seated, his hands skimming through an old edition of *Country Life*, when Barbara poked her head around the door to the hall.

'I'm sorry, Theo, I said I'd get you a drink.

331

Was it tea or coffee, black or white?'

He shook his head. 'Barbara, please, don't worry. I don't need anything.'

'Nonsense,' she said, sniffing into a tissue. 'I insist.'

'Coffee.' He smiled. 'I'd love a black coffee but first, would you mind pointing the way to the cloakroom? I didn't want to go wandering . . . '

'Of course, back down the hallway here, the first door after the stairs. Coffee will be just a minute.'

In the cloakroom, Theo was surrounded by pictures of Jess and Leah growing up. It was easy to tell they had a loving and privileged childhood. Typical shots of girls on ponies; sibling images with one or other of them sticking their tongue out. One was blown up, showing Leah at about twelve with long, sleek hair, and Jess, maybe fifteen, with her wild curls framing a winking face. A picture of Anna caught his eye. It too was a larger image. She was sitting near glass doors that overlooked a lake — probably the rear room that he hadn't yet seen properly. In profile, the image caught her perfectly, in full contemplation, as she overlooked the water. A toddler, Rose, sat on her knee, her profile a mini-replica.

Theo washed his hands and made his way to the front room again. He stood at the window overlooking the enclosed garden, looked at the bench and wondered if Jess had met anyone important in her life there. Had it been where she first kissed Doug? Theo realized that the house, though Jess hadn't lived there in a very long time, held parts of her that were unknown to him.

Barbara entered carrying a tray with two cups and a cafetiere and he immediately took it from her. 'Is it okay here on the coffee table?' he asked. Barbara nodded, closing the door gently behind her, and Theo wondered if she'd been crying.

'Is everything all right back there?' He spoke gently as Jess's mother took a seat opposite him.

She shrugged, buttoned up her cardigan and placed her hands in her lap.

'Do you need to be there?' He looked to the doors.

'No. It's fine. Now, have a coffee, do you mind being mummy?'

Theo was confused a moment, then realised what she had meant and poured two black coffees. Handing her one, she shivered and clutched the china mug with both hands, warming them.

He balanced himself on the front of the black chair.

'So,' Barbara said. 'You and Jess . . . '

He smiled.

'Are you together? Or something?' she asked.

'I'd say we're possibly 'or something',' he replied.

Barbara nodded, as if it was the answer she had expected. 'That's a shame. She needs someone.' She nodded again, looked towards the double doors behind which Jess and her father remained. 'She needs someone like you in her life. You'd be good for her. Maybe good for each other . . . '

'I'd love it to be more.' Without realising it, he

had emphasised the word 'more' making Jess's mother return her gaze to him. 'I'm just not sure she's ready,' he said.

'Jess is never ready to think of herself.' Barbara shook her head. 'She's always been the same, but now is exactly the time when she should. Think of herself, I mean.'

Theo raised his eyebrows. 'Well, I think I want to keep trying to persuade her.'

Barbara smiled and when she did Theo saw Jess in her eyes. He was just about to remark on it when the double doors opened and Jess appeared in the centre. Shards of sunlight appeared over her shoulder, landing on the floor next to where Theo was seated.

'Theo.' Jess held out a hand. 'Come and say hi to Dad. You haven't seen the view of the lake from back here, have you? It's amazing.'

With a mug of coffee in one hand he stretched his other one towards her. She squeezed it, ushered him past her, where he waited a moment, glancing back over his shoulder.

'Mum?' Jess moved towards Barbara, put an arm around her and together they joined him. 'So, what have you two been chatting about?' she asked.

He tried not to look at her, avoided her reddened eyes, streaming nose, a cluster of tissues in her free hand. 'Nothing much,' he said.

'He's fibbing,' Barbara said heading over to her husband. She bent over him, smiled and adjusted the blanket covering his legs. 'He was just telling me how fond of you he is.'

Theo blushed.

'I see.' Jess attempted a smile and knelt beside her father. 'Dad, remember Theo?'

Jess's father was indeed seated in the winged chair he had glimpsed through the gap in the doors. Her father's eyes moved from Jess's face to his and he held his good hand up to shake Theo's. 'Hello,' he whispered, giving him a nod of acknowledgement before seeking Jess's eyes again. And Theo spotted it, a blink, a something, a moment — an understanding — passed between them like an electric current.

'Right,' Barbara said, walking through a door that seemed to lead to the kitchen. 'You'll need a sandwich or something before you get back on the road.'

Jess smiled and rolled her eyes at her father.

And Theo realized that neither he nor Barbara were privy to the meaning of either moment that had just passed between the pair.

★　★　★

She didn't speak in the car until Watford Gap services. Theo, prepared to give her the silent space she needed, was lost in his own thoughts. From what he could gather some shit was about to hit some fan somewhere and not knowing what to say, he was happy to wait for her to speak first. Instead, he occasionally squeezed her knee or held her hand.

'What time do you think we'll get back?' She finally spoke, turning from her stance of staring out of the window and glancing at the dashboard clock.

'Depends if you let me stop to eat. Your mum's sandwich was lovely but it's all I've eaten today and my stomach thinks my throat's been cut.'

'I'm sorry. Of course, let's stop up ahead. Do you mind if we grab something and eat in the car?'

It wasn't what Theo had in mind, but he nodded. 'What's going on, Jess?'

She stared out of her window. 'I can't, Theo. I need to process it first.'

'Something's happened.'

She hesitated then laughed, a tinny, nervous laugh, which led to her coughing. 'Anna died, Theo. That's what happened. Since then I don't recognize my life.'

He indicated left to pull off the motorway and brought the car to a stop. 'I want to help.' He reached across and felt her brow. 'And that cold of yours is lingering. You — '

'You are helping.' She kissed him lightly on the lips. 'You *are* helping and I'm grateful. Ham and cheese okay?' She pulled away and got out of the car without waiting for a reply.

Theo watched her as she walked towards the sliding doors. Dressed in her staple of a pair of dark jeans, Converses and a jumper, even today, with her worry lines in place, she looked a lot younger than her forty-eight years. He blinked slowly — he was being selfish, he knew. Since being inside her, everything had shifted for him. It was seismic and he wasn't at all sure what to do with it. He didn't want it to stop before it had started. He didn't want Anna to spoil it from the grave. He closed his eyes and prayed to her. *Please, please just let me love her. Help me love her.*

Minutes later, Jess was back with two Costa coffees and two sandwiches. She handed him his. 'One skinny cap, laced with three sugars. An irony all of its own.'

★ ★ ★

Food-fuelled, she was talking again. They were talking again.

'You know something? I get the primal thing, the unconditional love. I've felt it more for Finn lately,' he told her. 'His mother has left and I feel the need to make it up somehow. I feel I'd do anything to make him happy.'

Jess turned around to face him from her passenger seat as much as her seatbelt would allow. 'I felt that always. When Doug left . . . Who knows, maybe that's why I've never let anyone else in? We were enough, the two of us — just Anna and me.'

Theo decided to bite the bullet. There was something in this woman that made him want to confront things rather than ignore them. He swallowed hard. 'You know about the blog,' he said.

She glanced back at him, touched her throat. 'You were listening . . . '

'Yes.' He chose not to reveal he had, at first, been glued to the gap in the doors. 'I know that Finn sent you the link. I'm sorry. He's sorry, he should never have done it.'

'How much did you hear?'

'Not much. A lot of it was muffled.'

'I'm glad Finn did what he did. Did you read any of it, the blog?

He nodded. 'Some of it.'

'She's a bloody revelation, that daughter of mine!' Her laugh was sarcastic. 'And it turns out my father knows more than he ever pretended. Decided not to tell me.'

Theo paled. That was something he didn't know. The urgent trip to the Lakes suddenly made sense.

Jess began to cry softly. Silent tears flowed from her eyes and she scrabbled in her bag for a tissue. He reached in his pocket and handed her a hanky and she looked at it and laughed and cried all at once.

'Don't cry, Jess. Why are you crying?' He sensed it was a stupid question but asked it anyway.

'I'm crying because I was a shit mother,' she said. 'I let her down. Somewhere along the line, some day, somewhere, I must have let her down.'

Theo bit his bottom lip as she shook her head, stared out of the window and blew her nose into the hanky. 'I was a shit mother and now I don't know what to do.' She sobbed in a way where her breath caught in her throat, and when she whipped her head around, looked hard at him, eyeball to eyeball, he gripped the steering wheel. 'What do I do, Theo,' she asked, 'when there's no one left unscathed and there's no one left to trust?'

42

Jess

It is Saturday, 14 March, Rose's sixth birthday, and we're in the back garden planting a Christmas tree. She is so excited, it might as well be 25 December. I just want to vomit into the hole we're digging.

'Nanny,' she says, wielding the small rake, as I use the larger spade to carve out the hole. 'I love this tree. It feels like Mummy's present for me.'

I haven't discussed the tree's provenance with her, so I just nod, force my foot to put pressure on the shovel and loosen another pile of earth. It takes every ounce of energy I have to lift the tree from its tub and place it in the ground. Together we pack the soil back in. I do it with my feet and Rose thumps it with the back of her rake.

I leave her doing that and I sit down nearby on the edge of the fading deck. I run a hand over its surface — it needs painting. My hand is shaking and I use the other one to still it. *Be still*, I tell myself. All around me, everything needs painting. It's all looking tired. Like me. *Be still . . .*

★ ★ ★

My mother is singing 'Happy Birthday' down the phone to Rose and she squeals with delight when it's finished. She is beyond excited about the party and I am beyond petrified — all those children, here in the house; so many people here in the house.

Rose runs off, Pug circling her legs, barking madly. I put one hand over my ear and try to talk to Mum.

'How're things up there?'

We have spoken a few times this week, agreed not to discuss the other day. Things are calmer, but though I've had time to think and am less emotional, I've been plunged back into uncertainty and have no idea how to plough ahead. I'm also mindful of what I said to Sean. If he takes me up on my offer regarding Rose, I may be moving much closer to my parents. I may be leaving this house that I love. I may be living another life. Theo flashes across my brain and the idea of running away from him doesn't seem a bad one either, when I hear a loud crash from the kitchen followed by a louder, 'Nanny!'

I run in the direction of the noise.

Rose is standing there with Pug in her arms. 'She made me do it, I was running away and then I knocked into the thing and it fell.'

There's a glass vase that was full of flowers in pieces on the floor. Anna bought it for me one year in Spain. She had fallen in love with it, making sure I knew how difficult it had been to carry back in her hand luggage. It had meant she had no room for booze at all and did I understand that? I loved that vase. I bend down and pick up the sodden pieces. Rose bends down to help.

'No, darling, keep back. I don't want you to get cut. Keep hold of Pug until I clear it up, will you?'

She nods, her big eyes wide and worried. 'It's just a vase, Rose, don't worry.' And it is, it's just a vase, I realize, as I get the dustpan and some kitchen roll to soak up the water. I have the memories; nothing can break them.

By two o'clock, my nerves are frayed, and that's before a single child arrives. Rose is behaving as if she has mainlined on soft drinks, even though she hasn't touched one yet. She is wired with excitement.

Theo and Finn are first to arrive. I take Finn aside. 'Don't worry. You did nothing wrong,' I whisper in his ear, aware that he has been avoiding me all week in school. I give them both jobs. Finn is blowing up the last of the balloons and Theo is putting the Rice Krispie buns that Rose and I made this morning out on plates. I'm unwrapping ten pizzas ready for the conveyor belt system in and out of the oven. When the doorbell rings, it's Leah that's first to arrive and for a brief, sick, second I worry if Rose actually gave her party invites out. *Focus ... The children will be here.*

On cue, about six children walk together up my path. Behind them, Gus follows, carrying what looks like a cheese and meat platter. I nod at him. 'For the grown-ups,' Leah says, already behind me.

Within an hour the place is mayhem and I'm counting down to going-home time. Thankfully six or seven of the children didn't arrive. I don't care why; all I know is my house has children

341

coming out of the crevices. I've told them to stay downstairs, but inevitably they're all fascinated with loos and they've been in the bathroom and in my tiny *en suite*. I send Theo to round them up.

'Jesus.' Leah is watching the proceedings. 'There are times, quite a few of them actually, where I'm really glad I didn't have kids of my own. I'm not sure I'm cut out for this stuff.'

I'm watching Gus doing card tricks with a few of them; they're engrossed in the magic of it. 'How did you *do* that?' one of them shrieks. Theo's out in the back garden on the phone, pacing up and down. Whoever he's talking to, it looks serious. When the door rings again, I see Rose stop what she's doing and stare back down the hallway. I have everything crossed for her. Outside, Sean is standing on the step, bearing an enormous package. He looks so much better than when I saw him last week; looks like he's slept, is dressed in pressed chinos and a sweater.

'Daddy!' Rose runs towards him, grabs his legs, and he bends down to her.

'Is it my beautiful girl's *sixth* birthday today?' She nods dramatically; her finger goes in her mouth as she eyes the package. 'Let's bring it up to your bedroom for now and we can open it together later when your friends have gone.' Her little face is at first disappointed and then she looks at her father and beams.

'Thank you.' I mouth the words as he climbs the stairs, resist the urge to run after him and hug him. He's here, and that's all I want for Rose today.

'He came,' Leah whispers when I get back to the kitchen.

'He did.'

'Good on him,' she nods.

'He's a good man.' I haven't told Leah the full details of my conversation with Sean, just told her that I'd apologized and asked him to come to the party. Theo is back in the room, pulls the rear door shut. 'It's nice out there when you're in the sun,' he says. 'It's warming up. Maybe we'll have a good summer.'

But I can't think that far ahead as I scan the room, hear Sean's tread on the stairs, and take the whole scene in. I can only get through today, and today I have a pain where my heart is. Today, I miss my daughter with a passion.

We do the singing of the song. All of the children join in. I hear Theo's singing voice for the first time ever and it's Anna's I miss. She should be here. She should just *be* here.

I'm washing some plates up for the pizza and Gus is suddenly beside me, a tea towel in his hand. 'Thanks,' I say, and hand them to him.

'No problem.'

Everyone is down the other end of the room or in the living room with Leah and Sean. Some, including Rose, have even made it out into the garden with Theo and Finn. At first, I stare out of the window at Theo as I speak.

'I know,' I tell him.

'Huh?' he says, a plate poised in his hand.

'I know, Gus. I know about you and Anna.' My voice cracks on the last word.

He says nothing, puts the plate down slowly,

343

and grips the edge of the work surface with both of his hands. His eye-line follows mine and lands on Rose.

'Don't do it,' he says. 'Please.'

'What time is it? Is it nearly chucking-out time?' Leah comes into the kitchen and stares longingly at the oven clock. 'You all right? You look pale?'

'Yes, fine, just this cold. Not quite time yet, I'm afraid,' I tell her. 'Just pizzas to go.' There are four already in the oven and I line up the next lot. 'Do you want to call them in, Leah? Gus, you can start slicing this lot up, cut them small.' I slide them along towards him, hand him a knife and a bunch of paper plates.

'Right,' he says.

'Kids!' Leah bellows at the top of her voice. 'Pizza! Come and get it.' Then she stands aside, her hands in the air, her face creased as the hordes descend.

Sean is eating pizza standing at my breakfast bar for two. 'I've got a tenant for the house,' he says, and my tummy leaps inside. 'So, I'll actually be moving within the next fortnight.'

I can only nod. My right hand is wiping the worktop next to him, my left is wiping my brow. I am sweating bricks and feel awful.

'I've thought about what you said,' he continues. 'I've been thinking about nothing else the last few days.' He eyeballs me as I near him. 'I love my little girl and I want to stay in her life. I think she needs me in her life.'

I drop the cloth and throw my arms around him. My eyes squeeze shut and relief floods

344

through my body. I feel his arm on my back, cautious but still returning this very unusual embrace of ours. As I open my eyes, I see Gus watching from the hall.

'Thank you,' I whisper to Sean.

'Look, what you do is up to you.' Sean faces me. 'But, what you said, what you said about you both possibly being nearer? That would be great. It would be great for my parents too. They're in shock, but they love her and always will.'

'It must, have been awful for them.' As I speak, I'm aware my hand has gone to my heart which is beating wildly.

'They'd love her nearer them but if you both stay here, that's ok too — I'll just need a bed when I come to visit Rose.'

I take his hand in mine. 'You will always be welcome in my home, Sean, wherever that might end up being.'

With the children gone, the adults plus Finn eat the remaining pizza, tuck into Leah's amazing platter and have a well-deserved drink. I stand to the side, there but separate, unable to stomach breaking bread with this man. Leah has taken Rose into the front room to give her the present and I watch from the doorway.

Rose is in awe of the memory box. She has run her tiny hands over the picture inside the lid; trembles slightly as she holds some of its contents as Leah explains what the box and each thing inside it means. Rose, the patterned, scented heart in her hand, throws her arms around Leah, tells her that it's her 'bestest present'. My own heart slows its rapid beat as I watch the scene. Pug, who has decided she's bored with proceedings, grabs hold of the Mars bar and runs away with it.

'Noooo!' Rose squeals, but she is laughing as she chases her.

Back in the kitchen, Theo is somehow driving Sean home. I don't ask how or why. Today I am going with whatever the flow dictates. Leah yawns. 'Kids are exhausting. I'm knackered.' She nuzzles into her husband's neck. 'Better get home and deal with your little darling.'

Gus looks away.

'How's that going? What's it like having your daughter actually living with you, Gus?' I can't help myself, can't resist the dig.

'She's all right,' Leah replies for him. 'It'll all settle in time, won't it, love?'

He nods. When I look at him today, I can't bear it. I think of how proud Leah was when she brought him home to meet Anna and me for the first time and of how quickly they had got married afterwards. I was so happy for her. She had taken a long time to find someone she felt she could live a lifetime with and I have — way before this moment in time — worked out that only a year after them marrying, Anna was carrying his child. I feel queasy, sick with the knowledge that could destroy what's left of my family.

Since talking to Dad, since him revealing the truth that he had seen them together, known about the affair; since promising not to do anything that will hurt Leah, my mind is racked with images of Gus and Anna together. I've had to close my eyes every time it happens because it's like an assault on my senses. It's such a physical picture. I'm imagining them making love; him telling her he loves her and then going home to Leah. As he stands to go now, avoiding my eye-line, I just feel torn and saddened by the whole ugly mess.

Rose is building a Disney-like castle in the middle of the room, Sean's present to her. 'A castle for his princess,' he said. Before he leaves, she asks him to help her to hang the silver star from Leah's memory box on top of the Christmas tree outside. Her thumb is planted in between her lips as she says a sleepy goodbye to her daddy and waves him away. Leah and Gus kiss my cheek before leaving. I try not to recoil from his touch, thank them for their help. Theo, with Finn and Sean already on the driveway, kisses my cheek too, then whispers in my ear. 'Can I come back later?'

I hesitate for just a moment. This should stop before it starts. I shouldn't get involved. And, God help me, Anna flashes before my eyes and I wonder how many times she might have had the same thought but for different reasons. And God help me because I nod. With a small jerk of my head, I tell him to come back later. As I watch the cars drift away, I'm consumed with one thought. *How am I ever going to un-know what I now know?*

When Theo arrives at nine o'clock, I ask him to hold me. We squeeze into the tatty sofa and he does just that. I don't talk; I let him fill the space between us. His arms tighten around me and

347

they are what I need tonight. Strangely, with his arms around me, I feel I can tackle anything, as though I'm finally capable of making decisions.

And I'm really going to miss him.

43

Anna

Raw Honey Blogspot 01/12/2014

Rose is not me. ROSE IS NOT ME! I tell Mama this all the time but she still seems to think we're one and the same. It pisses me off and, because of other shit going on, I've been feeling unsettled, so tonight I touched on the subject of Rose and me moving out. That perhaps I didn't *have to* save up for a deposit to buy? Maybe it might make more sense for us to rent something small nearby, just the two of us.

God we had a row.

It seems to be the week for it . . .

One like we've never had before. She lost it — ranting about giving up a job that she loved in the surgery to work part-time in a school so she could look after Rose. She did that. Although I never asked her to. I do appreciate it and I'm grateful, really, and told her so — but there'll come a time when Rose and I have to move on. I'm twenty-four years old and I think I'm ready.

She yelled at me that that was good. Good that I'm ready and hopefully I've got childcare sorted because if I thought she was running to wherever it would be that I moved to twice a day, I had another think coming. Right. Consider me told. Then she yelled at me that I never think things through — that I jump first and think later. Yep. Right again.

She didn't like it when I talked back, that I considered out loud I might have other options, even though I know I don't. She didn't like it when I told her that her 'unconditional love' felt pretty laden with fucking conditions.

Comment: Sideycrab
God, she sounds like a nightmare! I'd move on if I were you, Honey-girl.
Reply: Honey-girl
She's all right. I love her to bits and she does want what's best for me. It's just she's not always right about what's best for me.
Comment: Snoopblah16
If you're still seeing your married lover, things would be easier if you moved away. I mean it might be easier to see him, but you have a child and it sounds like she's close to your mother. At some point you have to move on but I'd be careful about upsetting your mother when she's your route to the best, and also free, childcare. Rent, bills etc — all EXPENSIVE.
Reply: Honey-girl
'Free' childcare is clipping my wings. Which makes it EXPENSIVE . . .
Comment: Anonymous
A married lover. Karma is so-o-o-o going to get you.
Reply: Honey-girl
Anonymous, if karma exists, you're right, I'm probably doomed. I willingly got into bed with a married man. No one forced me. I could tell you that we can't help who we fall in love with.

350

That's what I believe, but you sound like someone who'd argue. If it helps in your judging of me, I do worry about karma. I try to be a good person, a good mother, a good daughter, but yes, I've done bad things. Yes. My bad is BAD in the karmic view of things. If there *is* some universal weighing scales out there, I'm probably an epic fail. Or am I? Is the idea of karma just some people's way of refusing to understand and beating me with a stick?

44
Theo

Anna had collected hats. All sorts of hats, but mostly flat caps and trilbies, soft hats that would sit on top of one another and harder hats that would sit into one another. She used to laugh and tell him that when she had more space, when she had 'her own place', she'd have a hat room, all shelved out, just for hats.

He had bought her one once, for her eighteenth birthday. Harriet and he had arrived at the local pizza house where Jess was hosting a party for her, and Anna had laughed like a mule when she saw them arrive with the present, although wrapped, obviously a trilby. She had been wearing it when she saw him last. Years later, that same hat, sitting opposite him, the head underneath it telling him she needed to arrange a termination. She had been the last patient of the day and they had talked at length. Before she left, the last thing Theo had ever said to her was not to worry, that things would work out. The last thing. She had stood up, shoved her sodden tissues deep into her coat pocket and looked up from under the rim of the hat. 'Thanks, Theo. For everything.' That was the last thing that she had ever said to him.

He heard the sound of footsteps on the stairs

352

and lifted Harriet's hatbox, which had prompted the memory, from the floor up onto the bed. 'Just the holdall under the bed on the other side and this hatbox,' he told Harriet. She took hold of the box, took one look around and checked the drawers one last time.

Finn was at a friend's house, something that Theo was really hopeful about; a boy his own age from the climbing club, who was also going to the same secondary school. Harriet had been pleased too, when he'd told her. 'New friends are exactly what he needs.' She had nodded as if she had organized the event herself.

Theo crossed over to the other side of the bedroom and reached in under the bed, tugging on the black bag. 'When you're sorted, can you bring this bag back? It's handy for skiing.'

She frowned as he looked out of the window at the car on his driveway. It was the car she always drove now — Roland's, a high-spec Range Rover; not something they would ever have spent money on. He narrowed his eyes, tried to get a better glance at the driver.

'Skiing?' She sat on the bed. 'I wouldn't have thought you'd ever want to ski again.'

He sat next to her. 'An accident. It could happen anywhere.'

She nodded. 'You're always so pragmatic.'

'Don't tell me. Roland's the spontaneous sort. No matter-of-fact nonsense from Roland. Maybe you and he even fight? Is he more of a challenge, maybe offers some stimulating argumentative debate?'

'What's up?' she asked.

'This,' he said. 'This is up. It's all wrong. You here, picking up all of your clothes, and leaving with Roland in a car worth more than I earn in a year. And you and me, so bloody civilized.'

'Is it the car or the fact I'm taking all my clothes?' She pinched one of his hands playfully.

Theo didn't laugh. 'It's not the car,' he shook his head.

'If I told you now that I'd come back, go back to the way we were. What would you say?'

He thought of Jess. He thought of Finn. 'I'd say Finn would be very happy. I'd offer to help you unpack.'

She rubbed his hand where she'd pinched it with her long fingers, and kissed him on the cheek. 'Liar,' she whispered, before standing up and looking out of the window. She waved down to the man waiting in the car; a tiny wave, a smile on her lips. 'Theo, you and I both know that we're good friends. We've always been good friends and hopefully we'll stay good friends. Where does it say that this can't be civilized?'

'I'd like to go outside and punch him.'

'No, no, you wouldn't.'

'I'd take him. I've seen how high he sits in that car. Five ten at most. I'd just have to look down and jab.' She smiled.

'You're not taking this very seriously,' he said. 'And, by the way, when we were married, I wanted a wife, a lover. I had enough friends.'

Her back to the window, she bent over at the hip and placed her hands on his knees. 'We were both, Theo. Stop talking shit.'

'I miss our life together. When the clothes go,

I'll miss that bloody scented lotion of yours.' He shrugged, laid both his hands on top of hers. 'I know that this is the way forward for us, for our family, even for me; but just tonight, it's hard.'

Her hair fell in long lengths from each side of her face, almost touching their hands. He raised her chin a fraction and kissed her gently on the lips. 'I could take him,' he said.

'You could.' She laughed. 'But please don't.' She stood up. 'Is now a good or a bad time to ask how it's going with the 'climbing woman'?'

Theo made a face. 'It's not. Not any more.'

'That was short-lived. How did she take it?'

'I called her. She's fine. It's not as though we were a real item, I mean — '

'You called her? You broke up with someone on the phone?' Harriet tutted loudly.

'Do not.' Theo grabbed the black bag and passed her as he headed for the landing. 'Do not claim to be able to tell me the best way to break up with someone.'

'Ouch.' She winced.

'Jacqueline and I were only together once.'

'Too much information and that makes it worse.' She caught hold of Theo's sleeve. 'Look, a woman doesn't like being broken up with after, you know, after *one* liaison. It might make her feel used.'

Theo shrugged. 'She was fine with it. We're both grown-ups.'

'Good.' Harriet held the hatbox in both hands as she followed him down the stairs. 'Just remember that when you get outside. You're a grown-up and grown-up men don't punch or jab

355

other men, especially if they're not as tall as them and especially if they're your ex-wife's lover.'

Theo looked over his shoulder at her. 'My ex-wife's lover. Now, that's an 'ouch'.'

She grimaced.

'I'll behave,' he said, shaking his head. 'Let's get this over with.'

★ ★ ★

When she had left, he chose the furthest corner of the den and stood on his head. Minutes later Bea poked her head around the door.

'She's gone? Mrs Harriet?'

'She's gone.'

'Why do you do that to your head?' She tried to look at him upside down and laughed.

'Most of the weight is in the arms. It's relaxing.'

She shook her own head. 'Doesn't look so. See you in the morning, Theo. I'm going to bed early to read.'

He said goodnight and closed his eyes, allowed his mind to empty of all the what-ifs in his marriage. As they emptied, others flooded in, all of the what-ifs of Jess and him, like what if they were never to be together again?

Women don't like being broken up with after, you know, after one liaison. It might make her feel used.

No, Harriet, they don't. Neither do men . . .

45

Jess

The day after the party, the day after Theo held me, just held me without talking or moving for hours, I wake with a pounding headache. I feel as though I've been hit by a truck and it's backed over me again. I'm struggling. I can hear Rose, who sneaked out of bed earlier and is now in Anna's bedroom. Last night, she set up her train set in there and it takes everything I have to walk across the landing and join her. My throat feels scratchy and my limbs heavy.

'Morning, gorgeous girl.' I lean down and kiss her.

'What's wrong with your voice, Nanny?'

She's right, I sound awful. 'Just a cold,' I reply, heading back to the house phone ringing from my bedroom extension. I'm in a cold sweat and out of breath by the time I get there.

'You sound like shit,' Leah says when I pant into the phone.

'Feel like it too.'

'Go back to bed. I'll come and get Rose.'

'No, no, I'm fine.' I don't want Rose going back there today. I know it's irrational. Rose has spent her life in and out of Gus's house, but that was before I knew what I know.

'Don't be silly. I'm on my way over.'

357

She arrives within fifteen minutes. I've taken something to reduce my temperature so she doesn't panic. Leah doesn't do illness, or vomit, or any of those things that women who are mothers don't panic about. She lets herself in and hands me a takeaway coffee. 'Skinny cap,' she says. 'Where's Rose?'

'In Anna's room,' I reply; my voice is definitely going.

'Shall I call Theo? You really look awful.'

I shake my head. I looked fine about ten hours ago when he left.

She calls out to Rose, and within moments I can hear her dressing her in her room. She lets Rose choose her own clothes; they're chatting animatedly together and inside, as my chest and lungs struggle, the real ache is in my heart.

'Nanny's not well today, so you, Uncle Gus and I are going to spend the day together. And you haven't met Jen, have you? She's Gus's daughter. I think you met her before, ages ago, when you were very little, but she's lovely. You'll love her.'

Gus's daughter.

If I had the energy I'd probably scream the word 'No' repeatedly at the top of my voice.

'Can we take Pug?' Rose asks.

They've reached the end of my bed.

'Of course we'll take Pug,' Leah says. 'We'll all bring her for a long walk later, tire her out.'

Rose chuckles. 'Will I be back in time to play with my train set?'

'Yes, don't worry, Miss Disney Castle meets train set.' Leah looks over to me and grins. And there they are, two of the most important people left in the world to me, extraordinarily intertwined, neither of them knowing. Rose grips the fabric heart from the memory box in her tiny fingers. I cough viciously from the bed.

'You drink that coffee. I'll bring you some soup or something later, when we come back.'

I can't even lift my head from the pillow to shake it or nod. 'Thank you,' I croak.

She blows a kiss at me. 'Not going near you,' she says back over her shoulder. 'Don't want what you have. Blow Nanny a kiss, darling?' Rose sends me one of her special ones, where she kisses the tops of her fingertips, then blows it to me. I'm supposed to catch it in my hand, tap it into my heart and do the same back. I do it badly, end up coughing again and Leah scarpers with Rose in tow, not wanting 'what I have'.

When they've gone, I reach for my bedside drawer. I haven't succumbed to these tablets for ages but today I need to sleep. My body needs to rest. I swallow a Valium with a slug of the coffee, lay my throbbing head on the pile of pillows I've made and wait for the relief that sleep will bring.

I'm floating on an airbed on a calm sea, rising and falling with the gentle ebb of the dark blue ocean — the colour of her eyes . . . I recognize the beach from a holiday we'd taken years ago — Doug, me and Anna. She's there, on the sand, and she's waving to me. I'm so thrilled to see her that I slide from the airbed, begin to swim back to shore. All the while, she's laughing and waving, calling to me, 'Mama! I'm here!'

And as I swim as fast as my limbs will allow, I'm crying, thinking, 'She's not dead, after all. There she is. Look, you can see her.'

I stop swimming, tread water for a moment, am frustrated as I don't seem to be nearing the shore. 'Mama!' she continues to call. 'Over here!' And then I see it, a huge sea of white behind her. It's moving quickly and I'm confused. How can a white wave be coming for her? I'm the one in the sea. When it swallows her whole, I feel myself sinking underwater . . .

★　★　★

Anna is wearing her red suit. It looks ridiculous and I'm trying to tell her so, but my voice won't work. She's sitting there laughing at me; or, rather, lying there laughing at me, stretched out the full length of the sunbed. The day is scalding — the type where an egg would cook on the pavement. Sweat is dripping from me yet she seems fine, wrapped up in that snug suit that fits her so well. I wonder if she's cold. I wonder if she's dead.

I shout out to her. 'Are you dead, my love?' I cry. 'Anna, listen to me, please, I need to know.'

She looks straight at me but doesn't reply and I realize then, she can't see me. She can't hear me. 'I need to know,' my hoarse voice repeats. 'I need to know what to do.'

I wonder if I'm dreaming.

★　★　★

Rose is twenty. It's her birthday. I'm whoop-whooping out loud from the corner of my kitchen. There's a crowd of us here and it's weird because there I am whoop-whooping with the best of them, yet here I am hovering above the room, as if I'm seeing the whole thing from a different point of view. I wonder if I'm dead. Do I die just before Rose is twenty? I try and do the maths, see how long I've got left, but my fuzzy, cloudy head can't work it out. I'm quiet up here in the corner, content to watch my image down there taking part. I look younger. And my parents are there, both of them. I'm stupidly pleased that my dad, who I think is probably near the end of his days, has in fact outlived me. Then I realize how awful that is for him — how that means he has to endure a pain I know too well, to outlive a child. I want to reach down and hug them, Mum and Dad, but I can't. I'm stuck up here on the ceiling watching.

Rose looks stunning. Her wild curls have been tamed — all plaited into her head. Beside her, Leah is standing with her arm around her. She says something funny and Rose moves, embraces Leah and then Gus. His arm circles her back and, as she turns around, I recognize the dress she's wearing. I see the obvious swell in her stomach. Anna, I reach down from the ceiling and touch her. It's Anna.

★ ★ ★

Theo's beside me in the sea. I stay close to him — am afraid of the snow that I know is coming

361

towards us and the ocean behind us. I tread water, try hard to concentrate, conserve my energy. *He is quiet and I wonder if he knows, if he knows our fates are sealed, swimming here like this, together. I can almost hear his voice from another time. 'We build our own traps,' he said. We were talking about someone I knew years ago, someone who was finding it hard to leave an abusive partner. At the time I thought he was hard — she loved the man. And now, my legs underneath me moving at marathon pace to stay afloat, I see Anna wave from the shore. She looks beautiful, ethereal. 'Mama,' she yells at me. 'Look at me!' She swirls around, as if she's showing off a new dress. I hear it before I see it, the snow that will take her from me and Rose.*

'Don't look, Theo!' I tell him to turn around, to save himself. He reaches for my hand and, as Anna vanishes, the sea takes us. We've built this — this trap — by being here together; we will die here together. We are swirled around and around like a washing cycle. My lungs swell with water. I cannot breathe.

★   ★   ★

I awake. I have no idea how long I've been asleep but it's dusk. Rose is my first thought. Leah has her; Leah took her, I tell myself. I crawl out of bed, coughing all the time. My chest feels too tight. I tell myself off, take the few steps to the *en suite*. I need a pee. Anna's not here; that's because she's on some beach under an avalanche. I know

362

my thoughts are jumbled. Should ring Leah, I think. Bed. Just back to bed.

★ ★ ★

Round and round we go, Theo trying to grab my hand. I want to just yell at him and ask him what the hell he's doing in my dream anyway. Sand and pebbles beat against my skin, against my face. I remember pebble art when Anna was small. She would make pictures of things made out of pebbles stuck onto paper. If I can just reach out and grab some, we can make some pictures together. We can . . .

★ ★ ★

Leah's calling my name and I can smell a familiar scent. Theo, musky, aromatic. My eyes open and I see his face as he pulls me into a sitting position.

'C'mon, Jess. Okay, you're awake. Good.' He has a stethoscope on my chest where his hand once was.

'Theo.' I croak his name.

'Can you just hold her upright for a bit?' He's talking to Leah, who has a strange expression on her face.

I feel him tap on my back, pulsing it with two fingers. He has lovely fingers . . .

'Right.' He places me back on the pillows gently. 'I'll phone straight through to the hospital so we can bypass A&E, but we need to get her in. We'll need an X-ray to confirm but I'm fairly

363

sure it's pneumonia.'

I hear Leah question him as only she can, and I want to smile and tell them to just play nicely.

★   ★   ★

I had a bad night. I don't remember having it, but according to Theo the next day, I had a bad night.

'Leah stayed until the early hours but she has an urgent meeting this morning she had to go in for. I told her I'd stay.'

I'm not sure where I am. I'm not sure what's happened, but I am sure I don't want fuss. 'Rose?' My voice is low and croaked, my breathing laboured.

'Don't worry. I took her to school and Gus is picking her up. She knows you're not well so she'll stay there a few days.'

'No,' I try to move.

'Lie the hell back down, Jess. You're pretty ill.'

I do as I'm told only because I can't do other-wise.

'Jesus, you've been delirious for the last twenty-four hours. Let the antibiotics do their work and you have to rest. This is serious.'

I can tell that by the unusual rhythm in my chest. It hurts to breathe. Theo is shaking his head, muttering that he can't understand it. 'How?' he asks me. 'How can I leave you at midnight with a slight cough and this happen so soon?'

Beats me. You're the doctor.

'You scared me,' he says, squeezing my hand.

You were in a washing machine with me. I win.

364

He leans in to me, strokes my damp hair away from my forehead. 'You'll feel so much better in a couple of days, I promise.'

★ ★ ★

Next day, I demand to be released. I'll be fine at home. I want to go home; I need to get Rose back, I tell anyone who will listen. Leah marches into the room and orders me back to bed.

'Your X-ray has come back and you have fluid on your lung. What the hell is wrong with you? Gus, Sean and I have it covered with Rose. Just lie the fuck down, will you?'

Leah doesn't shout at me. Ever. I start to cry and have to stop really quickly for fear I'll choke.

Soon, I'm sitting up on fluffed-up pillows, behaving myself. 'Sorry,' I croak. 'Just worried about Rose.'

'Rose is fine,' she shakes her head. She's short, abrupt.

'I scared you,' I said. 'Sorry.'

'You did. And poor Theo. When he got to yours Sunday night. He was so upset. You were delirious,' she says. 'Talking a lot of crap.'

I was? Suddenly I'm afraid. A nurse comes in and shakes a tiny white paper cup at me, hands me my glass of water, asks me how I'm feeling. I swallow three tablets. I'd make it six if it meant I could get out of here quicker. Leah is staring at me and I have to look away. *Delirious.* What in God's name did I say to her that night, to Theo, to anyone who was listening to my feverish rants?

'Confused,' I tell her. 'I don't remember

365

much. I took Valium on top of pain relief. Theo and I were in a washing machine, Anna was on a beach covered in snow.' I try to shrug my shoulders but it hurts, everything hurts, and I end up having another painful coughing fit. She's by my side, helping me catch my breath, a glass of water in her hand. 'Did I say anything stupid?' I ask.

I love this woman, would do anything for her, and would do anything to avoid hurting her. I pray I haven't said something about Gus before I've even decided if I'm ever going to say something about Gus.

'Apart from calling me names?'

I frown.

'Maleficent,' she says. 'Or 'Ma-leah-cent', followed by a cackle giggle to be exact.'

She's back in her chair, and I'm relieved, crisis averted. 'Mum wanted to drive down. I told her not to dare, that we have it all under control and that you're on the mend. Call her as soon as you can?'

'I'll do it tonight.'

'And I asked Gus to bring Rose by to see you after school.'

'Good,' I whisper.

'I've got to get to work. You'll be fine. Theo said he'll drop by later too.'

She kisses my cheek and is gone. I feel sick to the core, have an empty feeling in the pit of my stomach from thinking that my feverish rants could have been responsible for ruining my sister's life. Anna could have been responsible for ruining my sister's life.

366

46

Anna

Raw Honey Blogspot 28/11/2014

Bloody hell, what do you reckon silence weighs? If you could lift it up as a real thing? Yesterday's silence weighed a tonne. He didn't speak and I found myself babbling, making excuses, but I knew. I suppose I should say I *know*. I know that somewhere, on some level, when this thing happened in that hotel room in Marlow, I *knew* what I was doing. I'd only just gone back on the pill and told Him not to bother with a condom. He'd asked me if I was sure. And it's that question — the memory of Him asking — that filled the silence between us when I told Him I was pregnant.

He went ballistic. I've never seen Him like that, and any romantic notion I ever had of us being together disappeared in that instant. It was as if in between any words He was using, what He was really saying was: *We could get away with one child. We are never going to be able to 'hide' two. And I am never really leaving my wife.*

He used other words but that's what He meant. Then He used another one I never thought I'd hear Him say. 'Termination.'

I told Him it was over.

I've now finished with the love of my life. Honey, I

tell myself, don't be so bloody dramatic. You're twenty-four. You'll fall in love again — stop thinking about Him. Honey, stop crying and telling yourself you'll never feel love like that again. If that's true, well, be bloody lucky you loved each other at all. You can move away. You can and will put Him behind you. You can and will remember Him kindly when all of this is over.

But all of it has to be over and first I have to face doing something I don't want to do. I already fantasize about this child's possibilities. It's no more than a tiny collection of cells, but what if those cells were to form the heart and brain that would cure cancer?

Fuck . . . This is my fault, because when this thing happened in that hotel room in Marlow, I knew what I was doing.

My naïve mess, and only I can sort it. And whatever happens, I'll have to live with it for a very long time.

I howled on the phone to C earlier and now she's on her way around. I have thirty minutes to pull myself together because I've never told my BF, C, about Him. I love the bones of her, but way back in the early days, when I told her I was seeing a married man, she let me know she disapproved. Then He and I had one of our regular break-ups and C did everything to encourage me and S to get together; felt that he was the best route for me to forget 'the other bloke'. All I could do at the time was hope she was right.

S and I were together only once and I just found myself in a situation that had what seemed like an easy solution. I let S believe he was going to be a father after one unfortunate coupling. An awful thing to do to anyone.

I think, if I'm honest, my latest shit-fest is no more than I deserve.

Readers, I've been thinking about friends. I have half a small handful. C, of course, ever since the time Death tried to run us over and missed, but T too. He's an unlikely mate, because he's also a good friend of Mama's. I met him for the first time when he was on duty at A&E and I had my stomach pumped — drank too many smuggled-in blue alcopops at C's sixteenth birthday party. At the time T worked the doctors' bank at the hospital and was locum at the surgery Mama worked in, so she recognized him when she arrived to pick me up. He's just a guy who since then I've instantly trusted, and over the years he sort of became my local dad: gave me summer jobs, babysitting work, and a reference for the job at the bank. J, my boss, showed it to me, and I remember wishing I really was the person that 'T described on that sheet of paper.

He's the only person I've ever told even half the truth to. I blurted it out to him one day after work because I knew I could trust him and, more importantly, because I knew he'd never judge. He's a mate and a father figure, but without the worrying about me or the criticizing bit a dad would have.

He's also my GP and God, his poor face, when I told him what I needed today. He's so good, but even his poker face goes south sometimes. He listened, and when his Kleenex ran out, he gave me his lovely crisp white hanky from his top pocket. Who carries hankies nowadays? More to the point, who looks like T (cute-and-young-for-his-age-pretty-good-looking) and carries hankies?

Thinking about friends now, I wonder if I've just followed Mama's lead? She has a lot of acquaintances but very few friends. Post-Dad, she trusted no one. Reality moment! I have indeed followed Mama's lead! I have few friends and apparently I have trust issues!

Looks like the only thing I've done of my own accord is have an affair.

I've always thought that if T wasn't married that he and Mama would . . . It doesn't matter. He is married and neither he nor Mama would contemplate such a thing. Good moral fibre, the pair of them. Unlike me. Unlike little slutty me.

47

Theo

Charlie Everard, having been blue-lighted in two nights ago, was in the same hospital, so Theo took the chance to go and see him.

'Doc!' he cried as Theo craned his head around the drawn curtain. 'You working here today?'

'No, No,' Theo said. 'All right to come in?' He hovered by the curtained entrance to his cubicle. The man nodded.

'I'm visiting a friend but I heard a whisper at work that they'd admitted you.'

'You came to see me. Over and above the call of duty, Doc! Thank you!'

Theo glanced at the intravenous drips, tried to read the notes on the end of the bed without making it obvious. 'What have they said to you, Charlie?'

Charles Everard scowled. 'I don't know what's going on. They never tell us anything. We're only patients. Fodder for their experiments.' He gave Theo a knowing nod, tapped the edge of his nose with his forefinger.

'Do you mind?' Theo lifted the notes. 'Your leg, nasty infection.' He shook his head as he read. 'Well, they're blasting you with targeted antibiotics. It's why you will have felt dizzy, why you fell. All those toxins floating around your body.'

'Don't like being in here at all, Doc, don't mind saying. Cilia was in here before she died. How long before I can go home?'

'Charlie.' Theo shot him a warning look. 'It's going to be a couple of days, but you need to rest, eat to keep your strength up, and you should be home soon.'

The old man grimaced.

'Elaine tells me you're painting again?'

The expression on his patient's face changed in an instant. It was like one of those Transformers things Finn had as a child. One thing one moment, and the next something completely different. Painting brought him happiness; converted his old frown into a joyous smile.

'It's good to see you smile, Charlie.' Theo grinned.

'It makes me happy, and I only ever make it happy,' he said, the laughter lines plumping on his face.

'Not sure what you mean?'

'I paint, it makes me happy, then I owe it some happiness, so I only paint happy. I paint happy things!'

'Okay, I get you.' But he didn't. He spent a few more pleasant minutes with him and walked away thinking there were still a few toxins floating in the old man's body yet.

★ ★ ★

He stopped at the Costa in the main foyer. Armed with a skinny cappuccino with chocolate sprinklings on top, he headed to the ward on the second floor. From just outside the room, he heard Rose's laugh. As soon as he saw Jess, he could tell her breathing was much better. Though it was late, much later than bedtime, Rose was just leaving with Leah and Gus as he arrived. Rose clutched a small fabric heart and Jess held something white in her hand. When they had left, he raised the hand, kissed it. 'What's this?' he asked, placing the coffee by her side.

'Rose brought it in for me, told me that she knows I don't want cut flowers, only like them in the garden, so she thought I should have one of her mummy's T-shirts so I can smell her.'

Her lower lip trembled and he leaned forward, kissed it still.

'Ssssh,' he whispered. 'That was a lovely idea. Of course I knew you don't like cut flowers too, which is why I brought you your favourite coffee.'

'You never knew that.' She tried to smile but coughed instead and took a sip of the hot drink. 'Thank you,' she said. 'How long before I get out of here?'

He laughed, the second time he had been asked that in twenty minutes; the second time he was lifting a clipboard of notes from the end of a bed. 'Your oxygen levels are up. The X-ray taken earlier today showed you're really responding to the antibiotics. I reckon day after tomorrow if you behave and rest.'

'I have to get back to work, Theo. I've had so much time off. Helen can only have so much

373

patience with me.' She shook her head. 'Time off when Anna . . . then the day at the Lakes and now this. She's going to have to replace me at this rate.'

He took a seat beside her. 'You have to get well. Pneumonia is no laughing matter and has a high level of recurrence if you don't allow yourself to heal now. You're going to need a couple of weeks off.'

'I can't, really.'

He sat back and shrugged. 'You're going to have to.'

'Leah can't be looking after Rose. I — '

'Gus works from home. Between them they can work it out for a week or so, let you get some rest.'

'No, no, I don't want that.' Her eyes fired up. 'There's something I should tell you, Theo. What Dad told me up at the Lakes . . . I should probably have told you as soon as I knew but I needed some time to figure out what I was going to do.'

He steeled himself, felt his arms fold in front of him, some sort of defensive, protective measure. He wasn't sure if he was protecting her from him or himself from her.

She sipped the drink, took as deep a breath as her lungs would allow.

'It's Gus.'

He feigned his best perplexed look, willed his face not to give him away. Lying, feigning, did not come naturally to him. *Tell her, tell her you know. Tell her you've known about Gus since you read Anna's letter; that Anna saw fit to*

374

*include a whole new unimaginable dilemma for
you. Tell her now. Speak now or forever hold
your peace.*

'Gus,' she repeated. 'Gus, my brother-in-law,
Gus, Leah's husband, Gus.'

He put a hand to his face, cupped his chin and
mouth.

'I know. I need you to promise me to keep this
between you and me, Theo.' Outside Jess's room,
an alarm sounded at the nurses' station. Staff
shouted orders at one another, feet hurried along
the corridor. Jess looked towards the door.
'Someone's in trouble,' she said her voice low.
'Have I been watching too much *Casualty* or is
that the crash team?'

Theo nodded. 'Your dad, how did he know?
What — '

'He saw them once, told Anna to finish it and
she did apparently, until a few months before she
went to France when the whole thing started up
again.'

'What will you do? About Gus. How do you
feel?'

She coughed into a tissue, grimaced and
flopped back on her pillows.

'Do? Haven't a clue . . . And as for how I feel.
I'm gutted. Every time I think about him and
Anna, I want to throw up. Every time I think of
him with Leah, I feel like punching his lights out.
Now you see why I don't want him picking Rose
up from school?'

'Could Sean do it?'

'Sean is working his last week of notice and
he's leaving on Friday for Blackpool.'

'Oh . . . Does Rose know yet?'

She shook her head. 'I haven't had a chance to say anything. I think he wants us to do it together.' She grasped the T-shirt, automatically raised it to her nose and inhaled. 'It's all such a mess.' In the distance, further along the corridor, another alarm sounded. 'Though there is always someone having a worse day . . . '

Theo said nothing, just sat with her, kept his hand closed over hers.

'I could pick her up, just for a few days.' As he spoke the words, he had no idea if he actually could. He was scheduled all week for afternoon surgery.

'Thanks, but no. I'll just have to give in on this one. I want everything as normal as possible for Rose. Normal for her when I'm not around is to go to Leah and Gus. The bastard.'

She closed her eyes for a few moments before saying, 'I need a holiday. I've got the insurance money agreed. Did I tell you that?'

He shook his head.

'Ha!' she croaked. 'I didn't want to think you were after me for the money. I can't call it my money. It's Rose's money, really. Anyway, I think it would be good for her and me to take Easter fortnight off, go somewhere sunny.'

'That'll be good for the lungs,' he smiled. 'Providing of course you let them heal in the meantime and you can fly.'

'I'll be a good girl,' she said sighing. 'I've had years of practice.'

They sat together, quiet, him not wanting to make her talk, her not needing to. Theo tuned

376

out the clattering sounds of the hospital, the familiar antiseptic smell.

'You and me.' Her low voice broke the silence. 'We're not a thing, are we?'

He grinned. 'Depends what you mean. Would a 'thing' be so awful?'

'I'm not sure I can do it . . . whether it's in my makeup any more. So much has happened. I don't know who I am right now.'

'Whoever you are, I like you. Now, stop talking.' He squeezed her hand.

'So you talk,' she whispered.

He sighed deeply. 'I don't know if we're 'a thing', but I know there's a lot of change around and we're all trying to find our feet. Brave new world and all that . . . I also know I spent twelve years doing all the talking in my marriage. Right now, I'd like to just be.'

She covered his hand with her free one, smiled, and together they sat until he was thrown out by the staff at nine o'clock. She called him back and as he approached she rooted in her bag for something.

'This, just so you know, is not because we're a thing.' She handed him her spare front door key. 'This,' she smiled, 'is just so you can get in tomorrow and spray my ferns.'

*　*　*

Back home, Finn was waiting. He put bread in the toaster as soon as Theo walked into the kitchen. 'I thought you might be hungry.'

Theo smiled, curled a fist and play-punched

377

his son's shoulder. 'Thanks. It's been a long day. Where's Bea?'

'Studying upstairs. She has an English exam tomorrow.' Finn picked his thumbnail, the way he did when he was nervous. 'How was Jess?'

'Stick the kettle on as well, son, would you?' Theo pulled a chair out from the table, the legs leaving a thin black line on the tiled floor. 'She's all right. Still has a bit of fluid on the lung but she'll be fine in a couple of days.'

Finn turned to the toaster, waited for his father's food to emerge. He held a knife in one hand, the butter in the other. 'I've been thinking about what you were saying this morning over breakfast.'

Theo pulled open the tie from his neck. Finn and he had talked about the blog over breakfast. Theo had asked Finn not to read any more and Finn had agreed.

'I've deleted it from my history. Promise to wipe the address from the memory bank — the one in my head, I mean.' He caught the toast as it leapt upwards, buttered it and brought it to the table with a cup of black tea.

Theo bit into it, licked the excess butter from his lips.

'And that standing-on-your-head thing that you do, Dad. I've tried to do it, can't get myself up, even against the wall.'

Theo grinned, stood, straight away. 'C'mon, I'll help. He grabbed a cushion from the dining chair next to his and laid it on the floor near the wall. 'Right. Kneel down, head forward and push yourself up a bit. I'll do the rest for you.'

Finn did as he was told and Theo caught his legs, pulled them up against the wall, and held them there.

'Y-i-kes!' Finn squealed. 'Not sure I like this.'

'Can you hold yourself there a moment?'

'Yes.'

Theo placed his head on the floor beside Finn's. In one swift movement, they were side by side, upside down. His fingers splayed right next to Finn's; he moved his hand to touch them. Finn opened his scrunched eyes.

'Okay?' Theo asked.

'Yep.'

'So, just gently shut your eyes and think of good things. Think of the good things that happened to you today. Never allow any bad stuff in. It's like a mini-meditation.'

'I have a mini-headache.'

'Ignore it.'

They stayed there, both of them, until Finn curled himself down to a kneeling position after a couple of minutes.

'Don't stand up too quickly,' Theo warned as he did the same. He went straight to the table and ate the remainder of the cold toast.

'I suppose, I still don't get why?'

'Helps me relax, helps me filter the noise out.'

Finn stood slowly.

'Do you trust me, Finn?' Theo asked his son, a memory of his own time reading the banned blog coming to mind.

Finn sat next to him. 'I think so. Yes,' he said.

'You may or may not have read about this already. Stand up a moment, come here; we need to move into the hall to do this.'

He stood in the hallway at the end of the stairs, asked Finn to stand under the doorway in the kitchen, his back to him. 'Right, I need you to fall back, in as straight a line as possible.'

'What?'

'I'm here, right behind you. I won't let you fall.'

Theo thought he could hear Finn's swallow.

'I just fall back; I can't look? I mean, how far away are you? What if I do fall?' Finn asked.

'You won't. Cross your arms over your chest and just drop back.'

Finn steadied himself on the doorway, moved back and forth a little. 'I don't think I can, Dad,' he whispered.

Theo approached, whispered in his son's ear. 'I will catch you. I will never let you fall. Trust me.'

Finn nodded, stood very still and then let go.

Theo caught him, right under his arms, his head falling against his stomach.

Finn opened his eyes. 'For a second there . . . '

'Trust . . . '

'I know.' He threw his arms around his father. 'I love you, Dad.'

'You too, son.' Theo squeezed his son hard and then thumped his back. 'C'mon. It's late. Bedtime, you have school tomorrow.'

'Dad, one more thing.' Finn stood back from Theo in the hall, made to go upstairs. 'School . . . I'm nearly twelve, nearly in secondary. Can I start walking home from school? I think I'm ready.'

Theo stared at the boy before him, the boy who would too soon have a growth spurt, then another; the boy who would, no doubt, do some foolish things over the years to come.

'You'll come straight home. Walk on the path, no dawdling?'

Finn nodded. 'Trust me,' he said, and grinned.

48

Jess

Sometimes, I wish I could forget how to remember. I wouldn't remember that Anna is dead. I wouldn't remember that Gus, and not Sean, is Rose's father. I wouldn't remember that Sean leaving has presented me with dilemmas I would never have predicted. I should go, because moving away from Gus is a good idea, but moving away from Gus means leaving Leah behind. I should leave Leah behind because I'm not certain I trust myself to watch her life unfold in front of me when she's married to a man I now consider unworthy of her.

I've tossed it round and round in my head, examined it every which way, and it always looks the same. I can read Anna's phone and iPad legacies; learn that she loved him, that he loved her; but what I can't do is place the 'Him' in Gus's body and understand it or forgive him.

I'm judging, I know. I close my eyes for fear of Anna's image with her scolding eyes turning up on the seat there beside my hospital bed and telling me that I know nothing, that I know nothing of love unless it's for her. I'm already arguing the point in my head. I loved Doug. I love Leah. I love Rose. I love Theo. My eyes open, blink rapidly several times. I'm confused

— it's all these drugs they're pumping into me. Even forgetting what we have or may have become lately, Theo is my friend. He's been my best friend and the thought of being hundreds of miles away from him, and not having him down the road, is filling me with a quiet despair I hadn't expected.

The doctors come and there's less prodding and poking. One of them has a tap of my lungs on my back. I hear rather than see him as he says, 'Clearing up nicely. How are you fixed if we let you home? Can you just take it easy for the next week or so?'

I nod so much it makes me cough, which I try hard to swallow back in case he changes his mind. He's now standing in front of me. He's older, probably early sixties. He looks as if he's the head honcho, has an air of respectability and reliability about him. The students here today, who hope to tread in his footsteps, are armed with their notebooks, and with serious expressions hang on his every word.

'What about your daughter?' he asks.

I frown, wonder how he knows about Anna and what it has to do with me going home or not.

'You'll have some help with her, will you?'

Rose. He means Rose.

'Yes, I have lots of help,' I say, wondering where it will come from.

'Okay then. Let's get you sorted out with a prescription for the rest of your antibiotics and a check-up back here next week. Finish the course,' he says, 'or we could see you back here very soon.'

'Thank you.' My heart skips at the thought of going home. And, immediately, I wish I could forget how to remember again. I wish my home wasn't a home; I wish it was just a house I could leave without feeling the tug on my heart that I do. It's where Anna spent half her life. It's where Rose came home to from the hospital. Suddenly, I'm unsure of everything, and staying here in this bed with its hospital edition waffle blanket seems a better option. Suddenly, with Leah and Theo in work, I realize I would usually call Gus, ask him to come and take me home.

Instead I wait for my discharge to be confirmed and I call a taxi.

When I get home, there is such an air of quiet in the house that it's almost palpable. I open the back door, allow some fresh air through, and fill my lungs greedily. I'm longing for a cup of my own coffee, take my time brewing one, just looking around. Yes, this house is a home. I'm not convinced that I *can* actually leave it.

I march up the stairs, only to get halfway before I have to gasp for air and sit on one of the steps. I'm pissed off; I don't have time for this healing thing. At the top, I turn right and walk into Anna's room, step over Rose's train set and several of her toys. If I didn't know better, I would think Rose was slowly moving in here. Some of her small clothes lie on Anna's bed and I pick them up for the wash. Beside her bed, sitting on top of her bedside table, is a small selection of photos scattered just under her night light. I pick one up. It's one of Rose and me taken when she was tiny. She's nestled into my arms and I look like I remember feeling: nervous, terrified at this little thing coming into our home but thrilled all the same.

Next to it is a group shot. It's a big one, about six inches by eight, taken a couple of years ago. Anna and I are monkeying around, making faces by pulling on the edge of our mouths with our forefingers. Rose is giggling, watching her mum. Leah and Gus look on smiling. Dropping it onto the bed, I leave the room and head back downstairs. Panting, I grab my keys. Pug is missing. I miss Pug. To hell with this; I slowly walk to the car, get inside, put my seatbelt on and drive to Leah's.

'I've come for my dog,' I say when he opens the door. Pug barks in the background and I walk past Gus, to the rear of the house, where she jumps up on my lower legs. I bend down to pick her up and cuddle her, my breathing still a little laboured.

'Should you be out?' he asks. 'You still don't sound so good.'

'What? You were hoping I'd be struck mute, that I'd lost my voice for good? No such luck, Gus.' I take a seat at my daughter's lover's dining table and put Pug on my lap. 'I'll have coffee, one of those ones from your posh machine, black, no sugar.'

He doesn't know where to look, heads to the coffee machine on the far side of the room. He rubs his hands on his jeans. An image of those sweaty hands on my daughter's skin invades my brain and I blink it away.

'We really loved each other,' he begins to talk,

doesn't look at me. 'I want you to know that. She was both the greatest love of my life and the greatest problem.'

I wince on Leah's behalf.

'But I love Leah too. And she had given up so much for me. When we met, you know I told her I didn't want any more children, I already had one. She readily agreed, became a stepmother to Jen. I love Leah too. Sounds so simple . . . '

'Please. You'll get no sympathy here.'

'I'm not looking for sympathy, just trying to explain how an impossible situation began.' He hands me a cup of coffee, doesn't have one himself, puts his mobile phone on the table and sits opposite me.

'I don't want to know, Gus.' My tone, still a little husky, is also very matter of fact. 'My daughter was barely an adult when you started an affair with her. What I do want to know is what you expect me to do now?'

'How did you find out?' He moves his chair. Though there's a table between us, he seems to want to distance himself further from me.

'It doesn't matter. Answer the question. How do I go on knowing what I know? That you impregnated my daughter, had a child with her while staying with your wife, my *sister*, who had already agreed not to have your children.' I bang the cup on the table; it splashes everywhere and the normally house-proud-to-the-point-of-OCD Gus doesn't even flinch. 'She had your child and you allowed Sean to become involved.'

He holds a hand up. 'Whatever else I did, I had no hand in that. I wanted no part in that.'

386

I let out a breath, slowly. 'She was pregnant again.'

His features fold.

'You asked her to have a termination.'

'Yes,' he whispers. 'And she was livid, had finished with me. I'm not sure she was ever going to forgive me for that.'

Tears slide down Gus's cheeks and I look away. I have no interest in his sadness.

'She finished it?'

'Yes. And she meant it this time. I'd pushed her too far.'

'She realized you'd never leave Leah.'

He says nothing, prods his brow with two pointed fingers.

'And why would you? Look around you, Gus. You have the 'perfect' home, the 'perfect' wife. It doesn't matter whose life you ruined on the way to 'having it all'.'

'I didn't ruin Anna's life.'

'I loved you, Gus. You were a brother to me.'

His Adam's apple moves as he swallows hard.

'Your phone.' I nod my head towards it. 'How did you do it?'

'I have two,' he whispers, 'one is for work. I keep a password and lock on it. Anna only ever used the work number to contact me.'

'Still risky.' I raise an eyebrow.

'I was careful.'

'I bet you were.' I resist the urge to rush to the other side of the table I remember Leah buying and throttling him. 'I need to know, what you'd have done.'

He shrugs, glances around the room, as if he'll

387

find the answer written on a wall somewhere.

'What would you have done had she lived?'

'I'd have gone on *loving* her!' he cries. 'I loved her. I really did. This time she meant it when she finished with me and I would have respected that. Again. We were apart for longer than we were ever together. I respected it then too.'

'And Rose?'

He hesitates a moment. 'I always got to see her grow up anyway. Anna would have let that continue. Ultimately, she didn't want to hurt Leah any more than I did, any more than I do.'

I sit there, Pug on my lap, looking to lick my face, my brother-in-law staring at me as if the next words out of my mouth are life threatening.

'Are you going to tell her?' he asks quietly.

There it is, the sixty-four-thousand-dollar question.

'If this was the movies, I'd say, 'No, Gus, I'm not, but you are.''

He leans forward on the table, puts his head in his hands, and mutters the word 'No' over and over again quietly, rhythmically. I stroke the dog's head in tandem with his words. 'What's to be gained?' He has the gaunt expression of a desperate man.

'Truth?'

'Why? Even Anna thought it was overrated.'

'Anna was honest and true until you embroiled her in your mess.' I spit the words out.

'Anna could be selfish as much as anyone else. She knew the score with me, Jess. It wasn't as if I ever lied to her.'

I close my eyes, know that there's some truth

in what he says. She wasn't handcuffed, she wasn't raped — she went willingly into the relationship.

'We were both to blame. She —'

'Don't.' I won't have him badmouth her.

'I just want you to understand, to try and explain.'

'I'm going now, Gus.' I stand up. 'I'm going to get Rose. It was you who was picking her up?'

He nods.

'No need now.'

I am halfway down the hallway when he calls to me. 'She's a wonderful child, Jess. You and Anna have done a wonderful job. There's no reason why you can't carry that on. There's no reason why anything has to change.'

I march back to him as quickly as my legs and lungs allow, face up to him. 'What sort of fucking idiot are you? Anna is dead. The moment she was swept away by that snow, *everything* changed for me. Yet you, who loved her so much, are sitting here carrying on. Life goes on, blah, blah, blah. You disgust me.'

He looks down at the table, probably to avoid my pneumonic spit. 'I disgust me too . . . and you're wrong. I meant there's no reason why anything has to change for Rose. Nothing is the same any more.'

'Yeah, well, you look fine to me.' I turn my back on him again, stomp towards the front door.

'I loved her,' he yells.

'You don't know the meaning of the word,' I shout back. And then I see her — my heart almost stops in my chest. Jen, his sixteen-year-old daughter, sitting halfway up the stairs, face blank. I stare so hard that he comes to see what I'm looking at and I can tell straight away he had no idea she was even home.

'I have to get Rose,' I say, and leave the house. In the car, I try and regulate my breathing, turn the ignition on and head towards the school to pick up Rose. Shit. Dread courses through my veins. It's one thing if it was my choice to tell or not to tell. It's another thing completely if it gets tossed cavalierly at Leah by an already angry stepdaughter.

49

Anna

Raw Honey Blogspot 07/12/2014

M has hurt his foot so won't be joining us today. It's so gorgeous out there — metres deep in places of fresh powder — and I'm itching to get going. A few of the others have bad heads after doing Jägermeister shots until the early hours and I've been running around hurrying them all up, yelling that the fresh air will cure them.

Talking to M last night just about life and stuff, I learned that he meditates! Told me he discovered it when his marriage to his childhood sweetheart ended in divorce after only a year. We had a long, long chat and he's promised to teach me some 'meditation techniques for idiots' this week. The biggest joy in life, according to M, is learning to be still; being grateful for the now; delighting in what we have rather than coveting what we think we'd like. Usually, according to M, what we think we want isn't always good for us anyway.

M's words have had a strangely calming influence and forced me, in the early hours of this morning, to face that my life for the last few years has been so many lies. My affair; my hurting another woman I love, even if she never knew; my involving S in the lie; Gramps . . . A termination; a deed where I have to convince myself a cluster of cells isn't life when I really believe it is.

I'm angry at myself for doing so much in the name of love. It was love. I still ache at the thought of not having Him in my life, but was it all worth it? M is probably right. 'What we think we want isn't always good for us.'

So, my task for today — when I'm out there amongst the beauty of those mountains, swallowing that clean air that I'm lucky enough to be enjoying — is to just stop a moment and try being still. Who knows what tomorrow will bring?

Ha! M a guru!

I have, without realizing it, been sitting ten feet away from Yoda in work! ☺

Text from Anna's phone, 7 December 2014
Mama! I tried to call you but you're not answering! It's a gorgeous day — reminds me of the first time I came skiing with Gramps and you. I couldn't believe the sky could be so blue, the pines so green, and the sun so warm, yet the air and ground frozen. I'm off out now. I'll FaceTime you when I get back. Give my Rose a squishy hug from me and I'm blowing you both a kiss. Love you both to the stars and beyond xx

50

Theo

'Theo!'

It was the end of the day; the doors had been locked and only a few of the staff remained in the surgery. He turned at the sound of his name to see Elaine at the main reception, and walked back towards her.

'I have something for you. Charlie gave it to me earlier when I was in the hospital.' Elaine tugged on the innards of her handbag and pulled out a square white envelope. 'He said you'd understand?'

Theo folded his arms. 'What is it?'

'Well, I don't know!' She rolled her eyes at Samantha, the receptionist, who was packing up for the day. 'It looks suspiciously like a card. Not your birthday, is it? Shit! Is it, Sam?'

Samantha shrugged and looked at Theo.

'It's not my birthday,' he muttered as he opened the envelope. Inside was a card that had once been plain white — the sort that craft shops sold to DIY card-makers. The white front had had a face drawn on it with yellow pencils. A combination of light, sideward sweeps and large coloured dots made for the most unusual smiley face Theo had ever seen. He laughed out loud at the two black eyes and upturned black line mouth. Inside Charles had written:

*I only paint happy! Thanks for all you do,
Doc. C.E.*

'You coming to the Duck for a quick one?'
Elaine asked.

Theo looked at his watch. It was already
almost seven. 'Just one. I'll follow you; see you
over there. Get me half a lager in?'

He texted Finn to let him know he'd be back
at seven thirty and grabbed his coat and briefcase
before heading across the road on foot to the
pub. His plan was to eat with Finn and maybe
both of them pop in and see Jess for half an hour.

The pub was heaving. As soon as he entered
he remembered why: karaoke night. Jules saw
him enter and waved with both arms as she
headed in his direction.

'What you doing here?' she asked. 'Thought
you hated — what was it you called it
— 'Eighties singsong crap?''

'I do. Just having a half with work.' He jerked
his head towards a bunch of people at the bar.

'Ed's babysitting tonight. We both went to see
Jess earlier and they said she'd left?'

He blinked quickly. 'She has?'

'Apparently,' Jules shrugged. 'Got to go, Theo,
I'm on in a minute.' She kissed his cheek and
headed into the melee that was the karaoke
crowd. There, in the middle of them, he caught
Jacqueline looking in his direction. He raised his
head, smiled, went straight up to Elaine and
whispered in her ear.

He was heading to the exit when he felt a hand
on his arm.

394

'Theo. You hate karaoke,' she said, kissing him on both cheeks.

'Jacqueline . . . '

'I hope you're not leaving on my behalf?'

'No, no, I — '

'You did tell me during our short time together that you hate karaoke. You also told me that you hate confrontation.'

Theo reddened.

'I never got to tell *you* that I hate things being unresolved.'

'Oh?' Inside, his stomach churned. He had, he thought, resolved things with her when he'd called her.

'I thought it was just too early for you, too soon after you splitting from your wife, well, that's what you told me, but . . . ' Jacqueline curled her hair around her right ear, sought direct eye contact with him. 'It's not that though, is it? If it was that, you wouldn't avoid me and this is the second time you've actively avoided me.'

His blush deepened with the memory of spotting her in the supermarket and darting between the aisles the previous week. He'd been sure that she hadn't seen him.

'I'm sorry.'

'You should be. You told me you weren't ready and I get that. So why the running away?'

Theo couldn't lie. 'I suppose I feel guilty when I see you.'

'Why? Because we slept together once? You were separated?'

Theo looked to his left to where Jules was

priming herself to burst into song. Harriet's words echoed in his head. *Look, a woman doesn't like being broken up with after, you know, after one liaison. It might make her feel used.*

He could have, he debated, told Jacqueline the truth — he had feelings for someone else and the night he had spent with her had only served to prove that. He prided himself on any words he spoke always being truthful. He also recognized that sometimes dishonesty lay in the unspoken words, like the fact that he had never told Jess he knew about Gus. He hadn't wanted to hurt her. He hadn't wanted to be responsible for delivering a bombshell that could destroy her family.

'Is there, was there someone else?' Jacqueline ran her fingertips over the top of her lips.

'I'm really sorry, Jacqueline. It was all just too soon.' He nodded sagely and she mirrored the action like she understood. He omitted the words that would have hurt.

'Just don't cross the road when you see me?' she said. He kissed her cheek, squeezed her hand. 'Thank you. I won't.' He turned to leave and she caught his sleeve.

'And Theo?'

'Yup?'

'I know you're new at this but don't break up with someone on the phone. Better to eyeball them, let them know where they stand.'

He nodded. 'Got it. Sorry.'

Within one hundred seconds, he was back in his car, practising his deep breathing, calming his rapid heartbeat. He texted Finn with instructions, saying to be ready in ten minutes; that they were going out.

* * *

When she opened the door, he held her spare key aloft. 'I was giving you enough time to answer, then I would have used this,' he said as he handed it to her. Her eyes rested on the casserole dish in his hands.

'Bea's chicken casserole. I've been telling you it's good. There's enough for four here because I'm quite sure you won't have eaten.'

She frowned. 'I'm not hungry, but come in.'

Theo kissed her cheek as he passed and Jess reached out to Finn, pulled him into an awkward embrace. 'Hi, Finn,' she said. 'Chicken casserole. Yum.' She made a circular movement with her hand on her tummy, then mimed sticking her fingers down her throat. His son smiled, any nervousness at being there disappearing fast.

'You'll love it,' Theo reassured her. 'Now sit. Rose,' he said, as soon as she came into his eye-line, 'why don't you help Finn get the plates and cutlery out?'

'Can Finn and I sit on 'tatty', Nanny?'

Jess nodded as Theo dished up one small round bowl for Rose and a large plate for Finn. They made their way to the other end of the room and ate supper from their laps, chatting in an animated way that Theo knew wasn't the norm for a six and eleven-year-old. Finn liked Rose; he felt for her; maybe he even felt some sort of 'absent mother' kinship.

'If you're going to serve that, I'd like it hot?'

Theo stopped staring at the children. 'Right. Sorry. Here you go.' He filled a small bowl and handed it to her.

'Thank you for this. I fed Rose toast an hour ago.' Jess looked at her granddaughter who was eating every morsel on her plate. 'I really need to start cooking properly again. I'm not sure I even remember how . . . '

'Well, until you remember, I'll get Bea to make double and you can freeze it.'

Jess smiled, reached across and patted his hand. 'You're a good man, Theo Pope.'

He narrowed his eyes. 'Uh-oh.'

'What?'

'I think the last person who told me I was a good man was Harriet, as she left with a suitcase to live somewhere else with someone else.'

She shrugged. 'Well, she was right, wasn't she? You are . . . '

They sat in silence as they ate. As he loaded the plates in her dishwasher, she came and stood beside him. 'I went around to Gus's earlier.'

'You left the hospital and went straight there? Jesus, Jess, I thought you heard the bit about taking it easy.'

She gripped his wrist, squeezed it so he felt her fingernails.

'Ouch,' he whispered.

'We had a row. Things were said.'

Theo shook his head.

'Jen was there. Neither of us knew it, but Jen was there and she heard the whole thing.'

'No . . . '

'Yes. So now I don't even have to worry about ever breaking my sister's heart. I know her witch of a step-daughter is going to do it for me.'

'Maybe not.'

She arched her eyebrows and he looked back towards the children. Rose was giggling as Finn attempted her Rubik's Cube.

Jess wiped her brow with a napkin. 'I don't know what to do,' she said.

'You wait,' Theo said. 'Shit has a way of spreading when the fan blows.'

'Nanny!' Rose came running. 'Look!' Rose held the solved Rubik's Cube in her hand. Jess examined it and grinned at Finn. 'Well done you,' she said. 'That's down to the wonderful classroom assistant you have. Brilliant, she is.'

'She is,' he nodded. 'Though she wouldn't know one end of a Rubik's Cube from the next.'

'Oh yes, she would.' Jess mixed it up and smiled mischievously. 'Time me, go on.'

Finn set the stopwatch on his phone. Exactly six minutes and forty-three seconds later, Jess handed it back completed to him.

Theo was impressed. Rose hugged her hip. 'I didn't know you could do that, Nanny'

She ruffled her hair. 'There's lots of things you don't know about me.'

'But Finn was faster.' Rose laughed as she ran back to the tatty sofa. Finn, not knowing what else to do, followed her, his hands pushed deep into his jeans pockets.

'He's looking more and more like you,' Jess whispered as she stared after him.

'I know.'

'And Rose, she looks just like Anna.'

Theo perched himself on the edge of a stool. 'Why didn't you call me when you left the hospital?'

'I just wanted out, was afraid they'd change their mind.'

He watched as she circled her left wrist with her right thumb and middle finger, rubbed it around and around as if she had an itch. Then she raised both her hands to her face and, through her fingers, sighed. 'It was a tough afternoon.'

Theo listened to the rhythm of her breathing. 'You should be sitting down,' he said. 'Come on.' He steered her towards the front room, seated her on the sofa. Moving her open laptop to the coffee table, he sat next to her. His eyes rested on the screen as it came alive. Jess's eyes closed as she laid her head back.

'You're leaving.' He stared at a page of property rentals near Windermere. 'You've decided to leave, haven't you?'

She opened her eyes, saw what he had seen. 'I haven't decided anything yet, Theo.'

He could tell she was deliberately keeping her voice low. 'I knew. Something about the 'good man' comment.'

'Theo — '

'Don't.' He stopped her touch, stood and excused himself.

In the tiny cloakroom, tucked under Jess's stairs, he had to bend his head to stand at the sink. Thankfully, there was no mirror. He stared at the blank wall, leaned on the sink. Ever since

. . . Ever since he wasn't sure when, he had felt this might happen. She had unravelled the truth. The truth had unravelled to her. It no longer mattered which. He had chosen never to tell her and she had found out anyway. He wondered as he stared at the matt white wall; he wondered if his reasons for not telling her had ever been altruistic. Maybe the truth was that he had known Jess might choose to move away from Gus, that Jess might choose a fresh start elsewhere. Maybe he hadn't been nobly trying to save the ripping apart of her family as much as keeping her near. He gripped the sink's edge until his thumbs whitened, chomped his cheeks until he tasted blood, and then opened the door to find Jess on the other side.

'I haven't decided anything,' she said, trying to take his hand.

'The children are both inside,' he said, tugging it back and heading towards them.

★　★　★

Neat vodka. It seemed to work for her. Theo downed a half-glass in one go and sat in the den, listening to Harriet's grandfather clock chiming eleven, followed by loud ticking. Time, it seemed had slowed down. He felt sure with each swallow that the 'tick' seemed to last forever, that the gap before the 'tock' arrived seemed longer. He closed his eyes.

The next morning, as a brass band seemed to drum a beat in the temple area of his head, Theo listened to a voicemail left at midnight.

401

'I'm sorry. The last thing I want to do is upset you and I know I have. I've been reading Anna's blog and it's made me face up to her death in a way I hadn't thought I could. It's made me realize a lot about myself that I need to look at. I wasn't expecting that — to learn more about me — as I realized I knew little about her. Anyway, I'm rambling . . .

Call me? We do need to talk.'

51

Jess

Just when my body needs to rest, I can't sleep again. Rose came to bed with me last night. I was too tired to argue and thrilled to hear her chatter again. Her chatter. It's been missing as long as Anna has and I never even noticed. She's been here. Rose has been talking but it's only when the sound of her *babble* returned that I realized it had been missing at all. It's like blood to my veins, pollen to bees, or love to the soul. I need it.

I texted Theo early and asked if he could bring her to school for me and I got a one-word reply. *Yes.*

Rose is munching on some toast I managed to make her. She has crumbs all over the bed and I honestly don't care. What I do care about this morning is breathing well enough to allow me to get into a car and find Leah. I lift the phone, call my parents' house. It's only eight thirty in the morning but Mum will be up, the breakfast table all set. Dad will be being cared for by the carers.

Mum answers after two rings.

'Is she there?' My voice mirrors my concern. I haven't been able to reach Leah on her phone all of yesterday afternoon and evening and through the night too. It has never happened before. Gus

403

isn't answering his phone either. Every nerve in my body tells me that Jen revealed all.

'You still sound awful.' My mother focuses on me and doesn't reply. 'I'm worried about you.'

'Is she there, Mother?' I fight the urge to raise my voice just as she lowers hers.

'Yes,' she whispers. 'She arrived late last night, has been on the phone for the last hour. There's a lot of swearing involved.' Mum sighs.

'I'm sorry.' I close my eyes. 'We always still run home to you.'

'To be fair, love, this time, Leah couldn't come to you.'

The doorbell rings and my eyes blink open. 'Rose's lift is here, Mum. I'll call you in a bit.'

Downstairs, my nerves are jangling. Nothing fits right. Everything feels like I'm viewing it drunk. Everything except Rose's babble. At the door, I pull her back, release a hair bobble from my wrist and tie her hair into a loose ponytail. It will have to do.

Finn, not Theo, is standing on the other side. 'Morning, Mrs P. Dad says you're to go straight back to bed, and Rose, you ready? Mrs P, do you want Bea to collect her this afternoon?'

Rose looks up at me, a confused expression on her face.

I shake my head. 'Tell your dad I'll get her. I'll be fine, and thank you.' I wave them goodbye. Theo doesn't look up from the driver's seat, as if he's looking at his phone. I will him to glimpse; forget that I look like I feel: exhausted, bedraggled. His eyes remain cast down until the back door opens and Rose climbs in. Then he throws his left arm over the back of the passenger seat, looks in the rear-view mirror and reverses out of the driveway. Not a glance. Not a peep.

From the hallway, I call Mum's again. My feet are bare, chilled on the cold tiled surface. I shiver, regret not wearing my dressing gown. Again, she picks up after two rings.

'I don't know what to say to her. I don't know if she'll even talk to me.' I dispense with any greeting to my mother.

'Give her time. She's reeling.'

'I just, I just . . . ' I chomp down on my jaw, determined not to cry.

'You have to let them work it out, Jess.'

'Do you think they can?' Part of me is hopeful and part of me is horrified by the idea. Assuming what's happened is that Jen told Leah, I've been both angry at her and relieved that the burden was taken from me. I'll never now know what I would have done with this.

'I don't know,' Mum concedes, 'I really don't know. Now look, Jess, I don't want you getting all wound up over this. You're not well.'

I rub the top of my head with my hand, massage a brewing headache. 'Mum, my daughter — ' I catch myself mid-sentence. 'Anna, had an affair with the man married to my only sister. They had a child together. Leah had given up having a child with him.' I shake my head. 'It's awful in too many ways to count and I'm angry for her.'

'Won't change a thing.'

'No,' I agree, instantly aware that Mum and I haven't talked about this, about Dad, about the

405

fact that he kept what he knew from her. 'Are you okay, Mum?' I ask. 'We haven't had a chance to talk.'

'No . . . '

'I — '

'Jess, please, don't worry about me. You concentrate on you and your job here is to not let it mar *your* memory of Anna. Don't let it spoil your love for Rose.' I have a feeling that both have probably been ruined for Leah but my instinct tells me that even now, nothing Anna did could have made my mother love her less.

'The latter's guaranteed, the former I'm working on. Today . . . ' I try to take a deep lungful of air. 'Today, I think I'll just be grateful I'm breathing better.'

'That's a good start.'

'Mum?'

'Yes, darling?'

'Send her back to me. She won't pick up my calls. I need to see her.'

'She'll be back when she's ready, Jess. You need to get better and she needs to do whatever she needs to do, wherever she needs to do it.'

I say goodbye and hang up, head straight back up the stairs to bed.

★　★　★

Sean, whatever else I have ever said about him, has proved to be a good man. To his credit, he has managed to sell his move to Blackpool as the 'best idea in the world' to Rose. He took her to his place for supper and they ate pizza amongst the boxes. And now she's full of chatter about the 'holidays' she's going to spend there. I search her eyes as she speaks; search for any tell-tale sign that I had been expecting — tears over potentially losing her daddy too. Then it hits me. In her six years she has already learned what *really* losing someone means. In her own little way she has figured out that Blackpool — it's just geography.

We're going through her memory box on her bedroom floor. Her babble includes 'Anny Leah' at least a hundred times and it feels as if there's a woodpecker tap-tap-tapping her name in my brain. I check my phone — nothing from her. And Theo has definitely gone to ground too. I cross my arms over my chest and hug myself.

'Know what, Nanny?' Rose says. Anna's eyes, Doug's eyes, just chipping away at what's left of me.

'What, darling?'

'I love this one best.' I never did get involved in contributing to this box for Rose. I never did go through photos or bits that I thought would make it even better than it already seemed. Leah didn't bother reminding me, seemed to know that it was something I just couldn't do. There are still moments, and Leah understood that. The moments, they seem to have a life of their own; they come upon me, steep themselves around me, a ghost-like beckoning, drawing me close. And I have to stop. I have to recognize them, send them on their way, and disperse them into nothing, because if I move a fraction towards them, they will swallow me whole.

Rose hands me a photo. Leah took it last summer, here in the garden. There's a rug on the grass and Anna is sprawled on her back, her sunglasses on and her hair fanned out above her. Sean is sitting next to her, his feet touching one another, his legs dropped down, and Rose is tucked into the well. Sean is laughing at something Rose said. And there in the background is me, just my face tucked into the top left-hand corner. I remember photo-bombing the shot and thinking I was hilarious. 'Why is this one your favourite?' I ask.

'It's my family,' she says with a tiny shrug. She's just short of saying 'Duh, Nanny, really?'

I hand it back to her, the shot of Sean and Anna who were not an item but were her 'parents'. The shot with her crazy grandmother in the corner. Her family.

★ ★ ★

The next day I meet Theo for lunch in Costa. I make sure I'm early; get some sandwiches in, the favoured coffees, and I'm sitting in the booth at the back when he arrives, looking harried.

'I have to be back in forty minutes,' he says, reaching down to kiss my cheek.

'That's okay, it won't take you that long to say what you have to say.'

He frowns, removes his jacket. He's in casual mode today — a pale blue sweater over navy chinos. He lifts his coffee, removes the lid and I smile. He always drinks his coffee without it, lets it cool a while and then gulps, whereas I quite like the tiny hole in the lid, the tiny sips I can take. I want it to last.

He rips open the chicken sandwich packing, tucks into the middle of the first triangle and stares at me.

'You just have to apologize,' I tell him. 'It won't take long.'

The eyes stretch as he pauses chewing.

'You just have to say 'Sorry, Jess. I didn't mean to sulk for ages over the fact that you may have decided to move away. I realize you have a lot to think through. It can't be easy for you. Let's face it, you were already floating in a sea of grief and now you have this to deal with too. And I understand, I understand you have to do what's best for Rose.''

He swallows, places the half-eaten sandwich back on the packaging. 'I don't sulk,' he says, 'but yes, all of that. I'm sorry.'

'And I, I have to say — 'Theo, you mean the world to me, have always been there for me. If you and I are a 'thing', we will work it out. I don't know how or where, but we will work it out. If you and I are not a thing, then what we did have will always be very special to me.' See?' I check my watch. 'Two minutes, that's all.'

He picks the sandwich up and I open mine. Together, we eat, all around us the buzz of people coming and going in their lives. It seems as if there is a camera speeding up those around us and we remain; we remain here, at a normal pace, silent.

I'm first to speak. 'Leah knows. Jen told her and Leah's gone to the Lakes, won't take my calls.'

His eyes widen. He struggles to find the right reply, places an elbow on the table and cups his face with his hand.

'Speechless?'

'What can I say?' He sighs a deep sigh, reaches for my hand and tugs it towards him, wraps it up in both of his. 'I'm sorry.'

For a while we sit, both of us lost in our thoughts, before he checks the time.

'I have to think about getting back.'

I nod.

He squeezes my hand. 'What do you want, Jess?'

Nerves make me laugh, a jittery, anxious sound. If I'm honest all I *want* is my daughter back. I want the life I had. The family I had. 'I'm not really sure,' I tell him.

He shrugs. 'It's not complicated. Do you want to move or do you feel you have to move? Do you want a relationship or not? What do *you* want?'

According to my daughter I'm a tough act to follow, black or white, with little grey. She does, at least, say I'm not quick to judge, but adds it to the fact that I could be controlling. She wanted to move out and I made sure she couldn't. I don't want that. I don't want to be that person.

'I want to raise Rose in a way that she has roots and wings. I think I got the roots right with Anna but I might have stunted her flight.'

'None of us is perfect.'

'No. You're a sulker . . . ' I smile.

'Okay. Maybe,' he concedes.

'I'll need help, Theo. That's the truth of it. I

410

think being nearer Sean would be good for Rose. I think being near Doug and his boys would be good for Rose. I think being at the Lakes, having that upbringing, would be good for Rose. I think being near Granma and Gramps would be good for Rose. And I think, if I can't have Leah near me, it would be good for me. I need the support network, can't do it on my own.'

'If we were a thing, you wouldn't be alone.'

'If we're a thing, geography wouldn't matter.'

He nods. 'Rose,' he says. 'Rose is your priority. Finn is mine.'

Theo is telling me his home is here with his son, that there will be no running into the sunset with me up North. I wouldn't want it any other way.

'There will be times when Sean has Rose and Finn is with Harriet. We could try it, see. If it's a thing, it'll survive, if not . . . ' I shrug, squeeze his hand.

* * *

I drive back via the M&S at the petrol station, stock up on ready-made soup and bread. At home, I throw it on the worktop and almost have a heart attack when I turn around. Leah is sitting on the tatty sofa. My heart thumps against my ribcage as I glance towards the front of the house.

'I walked over, no car,' she explains. 'A long drive back first thing this morning so I needed the air. Are you up for going out? Well enough, I mean?'

411

I nod. My keys are still in my hand.

'Let's go, there's somewhere I want to show you.'

I drive; she gives me directions to the local park. We haven't hugged; we haven't kissed. She's not talking. This is completely unfamiliar territory, yet I know to keep quiet. Let her be the one to speak.

Just inside the wrought-iron gates, there's a large pond about a hundred metres in. It's obviously where we're headed. I try to keep up with her, try to hide the fact that my lungs feel like exploding. We take a seat at the nearest bench. Anna and I used to come here to feed the ducks. I don't speak this memory aloud.

'It was here, a few years ago. I never told you at the time.'

Those words, alien to us. 'I never told you at the time.' Seven words, and I know this won't be good. Leah tells me everything.

'I was sitting here,' she says. 'I'd figured out that I would leave him if he didn't want to . . . that it was worth leaving him for.' She gazes into the distance, tears brimming in her eyes. I don't know what's coming but I'm finding it hard to keep it together. I reach towards her and she backs away. 'No. I need you to listen. I was pregnant. This was the spot I started to bleed. Right here, right here on this bench.'

I swallow the lump in my throat.

'I was on my way home to tell him, to persuade him that we could have a child together. And I lost it. Just like that.'

I hold my shallow breath.

412

'I worked it out in my head last night that it was eight months later Rose was born.'

I gasp, need air.

'He must have had a particularly virile month,' she says. Again her eyes cast towards the horizon.

I try to take her hand, but she refuses.

'You have to understand,' she says, 'I'll never forgive him. It's over between us. But, more than that, I will never forgive her. You need to know that.'

No words will come out. Some spill in my brain like, 'Please', 'In time', but they don't make it to my mouth. Nothing does.

'I'll always love you, Jess. You're my only sister, my best friend.' She shakes her head and breaks down. The sound of her guttural crying snaps my heart into pieces. 'I'll always love Rose,' she sobs, 'because I can't turn that off. I won't let her be blamed for this mess. But that's it. That's the best I can do.' She falls into my arms and I hold her tight for a very long time.

At home we eat soup. I tell her she has to eat. She tells me that I do too. She lets me know that she's moving in with a friend from work who has a spare bedroom and will stay there until she decides what to do.

'Your home,' I can't help myself saying it. I think of the excitement she felt when she and Gus had found such a gorgeous house near us. That's the thing: Leah had wanted to live near her sister. Near me and Anna. 'Your beautiful home . . . '

She shrugs. 'Turns out it's only a house. And houses get sold.'

She comes with me to collect Rose and Rose leaps into her arms. 'Anny Leah!' She has never been able to say 'Auntie' properly. Together they walk back to the car, hand in hand. Finn walks by me, his backpack slung high on his shoulder, his face angled to ground level.

'Finn?' I say. 'Walking home today?'

'Yeah, Dad agrees it's time. You coming back soon, Mrs Powers?'

'Next week,' I say, without realizing it was even in my sights. 'I need some normality.'

His head jerks towards the school. 'They're all crazies in there,' he grins. I point the remote and Leah and Rose climb in the back seat. Rose is singing a song, giving Leah explicit instructions on the chorus.

When I drop her off, Leah gets out and blows us kisses before climbing into her waiting car, already loaded with what she needs to take to another place. She does a three-point turn in five, looks at me in her rear-view mirror and drives away.

52

Anna

Raw Honey Blogspot 29/03/2015

Here's what I know, readers.

My daughter lied. My daughter died. My sister cried. Her husband lied. And I have cried. My daughter's daughter has cried.

There have been too many lies, too many tears and not many conclusions. And it's only because my daughter, 'Honey-girl' to you, is dead that there should even be a conclusion, isn't it?

It feels like there should be some nice ending. I'm not even saying a happy one, just an ending. But there's none. 'Honey-girl' — in my head, anyway — lives on. I still talk to her every day. I've even had the fights with her that I would have had if she'd lived. In my head, we storm off from each other regularly. This can only happen because I did know my daughter. Despite the pain of the last few months; despite my anguish that I had lived in the same house with a woman I felt I didn't know at all, someone who had made some selfish, selfish decisions — that is not *all* she was.

She was a brilliant mother to her only child. She was, to me, when she was alive, a brilliant daughter. And when I say brilliant, I mean just that. She dazzled, she shone, she sang. Her presence was vivid and bright and anyone who met her felt that. They are

415

the parts, the parts that I choose to remember, that I choose to focus on.

On dull days, where a grey mood will loom, and other inevitable features in her psyche surface — I will push them away. I'm not ignoring them, you understand. I know they exist. Existed. I know that now, and I can never un-know it. I can, however, choose to protect myself and her daughter from it. I can choose to file it away, for discussion with whoever brings it up on those grey, dull days, as I know they will. And I won't shy away from it. I will listen, close my eyes, breathe deep and try hard to move past it all again.

Honey-girl lied and Honey-girl died, but she also lived and I will not live my life not forgiving her.

Do not imagine this is easy, reader. Do not imagine that the gaping chasms she and her lover blew into the very fibre of my family can be forgotten, but they have to be forgiven. At least by me. I can't go on, can't learn from her life, and can't learn from the things she taught me even after she died, unless I forgive.

I cannot say the same for my sister. I hope to some day, but that's a feeling steeped in optimism, rather than bare, base facts.

This will be the last post on this blog. It may or may not ever be read because I will be closing it down today. Thank you, Honey-girl, for finally using your date of birth as a password that actually works.

So, this is all I can offer in summary, to readers who follow this blog. Finding it, reading it, has taught me things about human nature, not least my own, and for that I suppose I'm strangely grateful to my daughter, Anna.

Yes. Her name was Anna. It means Grace, or blessing. And yes. I was blessed.

Epilogue

The Lakes, 7 December 2015

The package is delivered by a brusque courier, a young man who would rather be home in the warmth than out in his van on this icy December day. It has layer upon layer of bubble wrap on it, which Rose will love popping when she gets back from school. Pug barks, circling my feet.

Within a couple of minutes the picture is revealed. I hold it in my hands. It's about thirty centimetres by sixty. I recognize the image from somewhere, but I can't quite place it at first. It's in Mum and Dad's cloakroom . . . There's a picture there of Anna and Rose, in profile, looking out at the lake. I turn the canvas left to right and back again. How did he do that?

Somehow, the artist has included me. It's triple profile, simple black lines on a yellow canvas. I chew my lip, try hard not to cry. It's here in my hands, the three generations — me, Anna and Rose. I look to the bottom of the canvas. Charles Everard. I don't know him but, in three simple black silhouettes, he has captured us all in stunning simplicity. It's beautiful.

The card, one with an image of the Madonna and child on the front, has Theo's handwriting

417

inside. Unlike that of any other doctor I've known, it's neat, legible, with a slight slant to the left:

'This artist likes to paint happy things. I hope you feel happy when you look at it. Thinking of you both today. T x'

I call him straight away. 'It's perfect,' I say when he answers. 'It made me smile this morning and I think it always will. Thank you.'

'You're welcome. I sent it by courier so you'd have it first thing, but I'm leaving shortly, I should be there by two.'

Enough time, I reason. Nothing is happening until three fifteen when Rose is home from school.

'Is Finn coming?' I ask.

'No. Harriet's coming to stay here for a couple of days. I can't take him out of school in the first term.'

I nod.

'Jess, I gotta go. She's just arrived.'

'Drive safely.'

'Will do. Love you.'

And he's gone. He's gone before I can say the words on the tip of my tongue. *I love you too, Theo.*

I make two coffees and, with my coat on, open the door on the side of the house, walk a few feet of narrow path to the small rear garden. Nothing like my own garden, now being looked after by tenants; the only familiar thing in it is Doug. I hand him the hot drink. He has run an electric lead from the small shed to where I have Theo's Christmas tree sitting in a pot just outside the rear window. It was Doug's idea; get some lights on it so that Rose can see it out here at night. I look up at the darkening sky and grimace, still trying to get used to the weather up here.

'Do you think the rain will hold off?' I ask him.

He sniffs the air. 'Doubtful,' he says, and flicks a switch inside the shed.

Immediately it's Christmas, and my smile is wide. The tree is covered in white lights. On top there is a star, edged too in tiny lights. The star alone flickers on and off. I put my cup on the windowsill and hug him. 'Thank you. Trafalgar Square in a small terraced garden in Windermere.'

He packs up a couple of things and finishes the drink before handing me the cup. 'I've got to go into work, but I'll see you later. Carol and I will do the school pick-up so we'll bring Rose straight there. You all right, then?'

I nod. There is only one thing I have to do, one thing I have to remember.

Doug doesn't come back in the house, just lets himself out through the side gate. He doesn't get to see the picture Theo sent, the one that I spend the rest of the morning staring at.

I eat lunch at Mum and Dad's. She's in one of her nervy moods, running around the place doing things that have already been done. Dad's sleeping in his chair and I pull his blanket around him and sit next to him. I glance at the clock on the living-room wall every five minutes and leap from my chair when the bell rings at ten minutes to two. Theo has to steady himself when

419

I literally jump into his arms, my feet leaving the ground, my arms as tight around his neck as the thick scarf he wears will allow.

He lifts me into the hallway and shuts the door behind me. When our lips meet, it's a chaste kiss, both of us aware of my mother standing behind me. 'There's some stew on the hob, Theo, shall I warm some up for you?'

Theo grins, removes his gloves and scarf. 'That would be lovely, Barbara, thanks.'

I watch him eat, watch the clock.

'Have you heard anything?' he asks in between warming mouthfuls.

I shake my head and he nods.

★　★　★

By three, it seems that everyone who is coming is here; the dull day has made sure we have little light left. Wrapped up in scarves, hats, gloves and wellies, we trudge our way through the back garden to the small deck at the end. Doug guides and holds Dad. Carol holds onto the kids — both of her boys and Rose. Theo is holding me and I'm holding Anna. I look back towards the house, still hoping to see Leah pull back the sliding door, but knowing she won't.

It's cold out here, everyone audibly shivering, so I don't waste time. I remove my right glove, hand it to Theo, steady myself, and turn into the right direction for the wind.

'Anna.' I speak loudly. 'You loved it here.'

I unscrew the top of the canister, which is not in fact an urn but a tall circular container. I place a hand inside, allow my fingers to form a fist around my daughter's ashes. There is no electrical charge, no plugging into her like I had hoped for, just my fingers on the fine, grainy remains of her body. My heartbeat is slow and steady, the sound echoing in my ears, reminding me of my own life force. My jaw feels clamped but I force my mouth to open. 'You loved it here,' I say again, 'and we loved you and always will, my darling girl.'

I let the powders slip through my fingers, see most fall on the water below, some whisked away by the breeze. I see her here, as my hands fill again and again. Still images of her lifetime fill my head, nothing movie-like, no movie reel; it's as if she's stopped moving and I'm forced to take my time, to look and savour each image.

Everyone comes forward to help Anna leave, and when Rose fills her tiny hand, the image I have of Anna is one where she had just given birth, shock and joy on her tired face. Finally, I raise the canister into the wind and watch the last of her be taken. I replace the lid, look down at my hand. People have started to move back to the house where Mum has some soup ready. My hand is grey, covered in Anna. I wonder which part of her I can't let go, whether it's her femur, her hand, her heart. I bend down, reaching forward, and plunge my hand into the freezing water.

Then I feel it, like a clash of her energy with mine. I squeeze my eyes, take the pain, and tell myself it's her — not just the icy water. It's Anna, the last of her clinging onto me. 'Rest, my

421

darling girl, it's time to sleep . . . ' I move my hand about and stand up. Theo takes it and squeezes it in his and together we walk back to where my dad stands, stooped, at the door watching us.

★ ★ ★

When it was done, Theo stood by the kettle waiting for it to boil. Leah hadn't come. Though she had known she wouldn't, he could see disappointment etched on Jess's face.

'You can't fix everything.' Doug was standing by his side. Theo didn't reply.

'How are you two going?' Doug asked.

Theo turned to face him, unsure how to behave. His girlfriend's ex-husband asking how it's going. 'Well.' He kept the reply deliberately short.

'I'm glad.' Doug nodded. 'All things considered, she seems happy.'

It was Theo's turn to nod.

'Way back when she came up here first, I helped her move. She had this bag, a stash of anything that came addressed to Anna. I was horrified, there were credit card bills that needed sorting; lots of stuff she couldn't deal with — basically, anything that had a window in the envelope she'd shoved in a bag under the stairs. We went through it, both of us, before she moved.'

Theo was still nodding, a slow, rhythmic movement.

'There was one thing I didn't show Jess. A tenancy agreement, just a couple of pages long.'

422

Theo felt his Adam's apple rise and fall.

'Anna was moving to a two-bedroom flat nearby . . . But you know that, don't you, Theo, since you'd signed it as guarantor for her.'

'I haven't told her,' Theo said quickly, glancing at Jess. He hadn't ever told her he'd known about Gus since Anna's letter either. There was, he had reasoned, nothing to be gained.

'I know,' Doug replied. 'Me neither. I think we both have her best interests at heart.' Both men stared at the large table where people were still eating, where Rose sat on Jess's knee.

'Was the flat just for her and Rose?'

'I would never have been involved if it hadn't been,' Theo said. 'That's what she told me.'

Doug sighed. 'I suppose we'll never really know, but you're right.' He looked to Jess. 'It's best that she knows nothing.'

'She knew Anna was thinking about moving out, she knew from the blog. I just didn't see the point in . . . ' Theo shrugged. 'In rubbing her nose in it.'

'What I don't understand,' Doug said, 'is why Anna didn't ask me for help?'

'You might have told Jess her plans. Or Jess might have found out you'd helped and blamed you.'

Jess looked across in their direction.

'Right.' Doug smiled broadly. 'She's looking over now, so smile. Big smile.'

Theo did as he was told.

'And if you ever hurt her, you'll have me to answer to.' Doug feigned a laugh, knew he was being watched. 'She loves *fiercely*, and God knows she deserves the same back.' He clapped Theo on the back. 'Remember that.'

★ ★ ★

It's a black, cloudy, night. I feel sorry for Rose, who is star-searching right beside me, her tiny hands making prints on my mother's glass.

I allow myself to think ahead to Christmas in three weeks. We will all be here, Mum fussing over everyone, feeding us until we burst. Dad loving us all from his chair. Leah too, hopefully. My heart feels as if it's in a vice when I think of her; how I miss her, miss what we had. I'm trying hard to respect the fact that she still struggles with the loss of her marriage, to respect the fact that she didn't come today. Yesterday's telephone call with her had given me a little hope that she might. She has agreed to try and somehow forgive Anna so that she and I can move forward, but if the last year has taught me anything, it is that love can be a complicated, conditional thing. I just don't know how Leah's and my love will look in the future and I hate that.

Rose's hand slips into mine. Her fingers curl around the edges and the feeling grounds me. I love that. She points with her free hand to a patch in the cloud; whoops with delight at the tiny cluster of stars. And I hear Anna, hear her voice as if she was standing right beside me.

— **I miss you, Mama.**
— **I miss you, today more than most.**

424

— I know . . .

— I heard your laugh in Rose again this morning; that deep chuckle that you used to have.

— Thank you for making sure she laughs. Give her an extra-tight hug from me today. Tell her that her mummy loves her.

— Unconditionally?

— Ha! You're funny . . . but yes. Yes . . . I love you, Mama.

— You too, to your stars and beyond.

Acknowledgements

Thank you, as always, to friends and family. To my beta readers Claire Allan, Anstey Spraggan and Jacqueline Ward, thank you for help throughout, comments on point as always! Thanks to Ger Downing and Jo Cannon for help on some research points — any mistakes are my own. Thanks too to Steph, Doody, Jan, Penny, and Ann — a wonderful focus group.

Continued thanks to my agent, Maddy (the best agent in town) Milburn and her brilliant crew, Cara, Thérèse and Sarah.

A huge shout out of thanks to everyone at HarperCollins, I'm really grateful for all you do. Thank you to Liz Dawson and Jaime Frost in publicity, the cover design team, and the sales teams in the UK and Ireland. A BIG FAT thank you to the editorial team, particularly Kim Young and Martha Ashby whose instincts and keen eyes have really helped make *The Day I Lost You* appear on the page just like I had imagined it in my head. #fabeditors

To Aidan, thanks for your love and endless supply of cups of hot green tea. And finally, to you readers, thank you, for helping to make my dreams come true.

We do hope that you have enjoyed reading this large print book.

Did you know that all of our titles are available for purchase?

We publish a wide range of high quality large print books including:
Romances, Mysteries, Classics
General Fiction
Non Fiction and Westerns

Special interest titles available in large print are:
The Little Oxford Dictionary
Music Book
Song Book
Hymn Book
Service Book

Also available from us courtesy of Oxford University Press:
Young Readers' Dictionary
(large print edition)
Young Readers' Thesaurus
(large print edition)

For further information or a free brochure, please contact us at:
Ulverscroft Large Print Books Ltd.,
The Green, Bradgate Road, Anstey,
Leicester, LE7 7FU, England.
Tel: (00 44) 0116 236 4325
Fax: (00 44) 0116 234 0205

Other titles published by Ulverscroft:

DEVASTATION ROAD

Jason Hewitt

Spring, 1945: A man wakes in a field in a country he does not know. His name is Owen. Injured and confused, he gets to his feet and starts to walk. A war he has only a vague memory of joining is in its dying days, and as he tries to get back to England he becomes caught up in the flood of refugees pouring through Europe. Among them is a teenage boy, Janek, and together they form an unlikely alliance on their way across battle-worn Germany. When they meet a troubled young woman, tempers flare and scars are revealed as Owen gathers up the shattered pieces of his life. Nothing is as he remembers, not even himself — and how can he truly return home when he hardly recalls what home is?

HAG-SEED

Margaret Atwood

Felix is at the top of his game as Artistic Director of the Makeshiweg Theatre Festival. His productions have amazed and confounded. Now he's staging a *Tempest* like no other: not only will it boost his reputation, but it will heal emotional wounds as well. Or that was the plan. Instead, after an act of unforeseen treachery, Felix is living in exile in a backwoods hovel, haunted by memories of his beloved lost daughter, Miranda — and also brewing revenge. After twelve years, his chance finally arrives in the shape of a theatre course at a nearby prison. Here, Felix and his inmate actors will put on his *Tempest* and snare the traitors who destroyed him. It's magic! But will it remake Felix as his enemies fall?

BLUEPRINTS

Barbara Delinsky

Jamie MacAfee's life is almost perfect. She loves her fiance, and adores her job as an architect on her family's home renovation TV show. Her beloved mother Caroline has built up her own confidence after a painful divorce, working as the very successful host of the show. Everything is going to plan . . . and then the lives of both women are changed overnight. When the TV network decides to replace her with Jamie as the show's host, Caroline is left feeling horribly betrayed. Then tragedy strikes, leaving Jamie guardian to her small orphaned half-brother, and fiancee to a man who doesn't want the child. *Who am I?* both women ask, as the blueprints they've built their lives around break down. It's time to find out what they really want, and where their future lies . . .

THE OUTSIDE LANDS

Hannah Kohler

Jeannie is nineteen when the world changes. The sudden accident that robs her and her brother Kip of their mother leaves them adrift, with only their father to guide them. Jeannie seeks escape in work and later marriage to a man whose social connections propel her into an unfamiliar world of wealth and politics. Ill-equipped and unprepared, she finds comfort where she can. Meanwhile, Kip's descent into a life of petty crime is halted only when he volunteers for the Marines. By 1968, the conflict in Vietnam is at its height; and with the anti-war movement raging at home, Jeannie and Kip are swept along by events larger than themselves, driven by disillusionment to commit unforgiveable acts of betrayal that will leave permanent scars.

THE CURIOUS CHARMS OF ARTHUR PEPPER

Phaedra Patrick

Arthur Pepper gets up every day at 7:30 a.m. He eats his breakfast, waters his plant, Frederica, and does not speak to anyone unless it is absolutely necessary. Until something disrupts his routine. On the first anniversary of his beloved wife Miriam's death, he finally sorts through her wardrobe and finds a glistening charm bracelet that he has never seen before. Upon examination, Arthur finds a telephone number on the underside of a gold elephant. Uncharacteristically, he picks up the phone. And so begins Arthur's quest — charm by charm, from York to Paris to India — as he seeks to uncover Miriam's secret life before they were married. Along the way, he will find hope, healing, and self-discovery in the most unexpected places.